PRAISE FOR THE ALASTAIR STONE

"The magic is believable, the characters c̲o̲m̲e̲ ̲t̲o̲ ̲l̲i̲f̲e̲, and the twists, turns and mysteries to be solved glue your eyes to the page. You will never forget these characters or their world."
—*Jacqueline Lichtenberg, Hugo-nominated author of the Sime~Gen series and* Star Trek Lives!

"Alastair Stone is like Harry Potter meets Harry Dresden with a bit of Indiana Jones!"
—*Randler, Amazon reviewer*

"Somewhat reminiscent of the Dresden Files but with its own distinct style."
—*John W. Ranken, Amazon reviewer*

"I am reminded of Jim Butcher here...Darker than most Urban Fantasy, not quite horror, but with a touch of Lovecraftian."
—*Wulfstan, Amazon Top 500 reviewer*

"An absolute delight for 'urban fantasy' fans! Smart, witty and compelling!"
—*gbc, Bookbub reviewer*

"In Alastair Stone, author R.L. King has a major winner on her hands."
—*Mark Earls, Amazon reviewer*

"Once you enter the world of Alastair Stone, you won't want to leave."
—*Awesome Indies*

"You will fall in love with this series!"
—*Amazon reviewer*

"It's getting hard to come up with something better than great to describe how good this book was."
—*Ted Camer, Amazon reviewer*

"You cannot go wrong with this series!"
—*Jim, Amazon reviewer*

"Warning—don't start reading this book if you have other things to do."
—*ARobertson, Amazon reviewer*

"Once you start, you need to get comfortable because you will stop reading all of a sudden and discover many hours have gone by."
—*John Scott, Amazon reviewer*

"R. L. King has my purchasing dollars with fun-to-read, suspenseful, character-driven stories…Damn fun reads."
—*Amazon reviewer*

"I have been hooked on this series from the first book."
—*Jim P. Ziller, Amazon reviewer*

"Awesome and exciting. Love this series."
—*Cynthia Morrison, Amazon reviewer*

"Amazing series. The characters are deep and identifiable. The magic is only a small part of what makes these books great. I can't wait for the next one!!"
—*Amazon reviewer*

ALSO BY R. L. KING

The Alastair Stone Chronicles

Happenstance and Bron

Shadowrun (published by Catalyst Game Labs)

AWAKENING

ALASTAIR STONE CHRONICLES: BOOK TWENTY-EIGHT

R. L. KING

MAGESPACE
PRESS

Awakening: Alastair Stone Chronicles Book Twenty-Eight
First Edition: December 2021
First Paperback Edition: December 2021
Magespace Press
Edited by John Helfers
Cover Art and Design by Gene Mollica Studio

ISBN: 978-1-953063-09-0

CHAPTER ONE

"**D**ID YOU HAVE THE DREAM AGAIN THIS WEEK?**"
Michael slouches against the couch cushion and ponders how he wants to answer that.

Yes, it is a couch, but no, he isn't lying on it. When he'd first started coming here, he'd been surprised to discover that wasn't the way it worked—not usually, at least—but decided it was probably best not to get your ideas about the way things worked from comic strips.

The woman sitting across from him no doubt notices his hesitation, but she doesn't say anything about it. She jots a note on the pad in her lap and waits patiently. This isn't anything new.

He studies her. She's in her early thirties, with short, dark hair, medium-brown skin, and a serious face. He'd found her by picking a name at random from the list of those who took his insurance.

Well, mostly random: her office wasn't too far from his apartment, and he'd liked her name.

Dr. Imogen Farley.

He's never known anyone named "Imogen" before, but it makes him feel…comfortable. Like she's somebody he can trust. He can't explain it, but that's all right. There are a lot of things about his life he can't explain.

She's still waiting for an answer, and he knows from experience that she'll sit there as long as she has to, her level, nonjudgmental gaze settled on him. If he doesn't say something soon, this will be a long session.

"I guess I have." The words are reluctant. Even though the dreams were the reason he'd sought out Dr. Imogen Farley in the first place, he still feels strange talking about them out loud.

She jots something else on the pad. "Was it the same as before?"

Sometimes he wishes he could see what she's writing about him. Other times, he wonders if she's writing about him at all. Maybe she's updating her grocery list, or playing tic-tac-toe with herself while pretending to be interested in what he's saying. She's very good about keeping the contents hidden, so he'll probably never know.

"Same as usual," he says.

He doesn't need to describe it again. If she *is* actually writing things about him on her legal pad, she already has pages of notes describing the odd dreams he'd been having at least a couple times a week for the past several months.

In truth, he doesn't even know why they bother him so much. That's part of why he's here—to try to figure it out. Most people, when they experience dreams where everyone around them glows with bright, vivid colors and they can make things move or start fires or even fly merely by thinking about it, would probably be overjoyed at their newfound imagination. They'd probably assume they'd watched too many superhero movies and the dreams are nothing but their subconscious's way of mining the material to spice up their drab, everyday lives with a little night-time pizzazz.

Michael has never been particularly blessed in the imagination department. At thirty-five, he can barely remember his childhood or even his secondary school years. They'd crawled by in such a dull, droning manner, every day the same as the previous one, that there didn't seem to be much point for his brain to hold on to more than a representative sample of events. Even his time at university had been nothing more than a relentless slog.

Dr. Farley looks up from her pad. "Okay, Michael," she says gently. "I'd like to try something else this week. Instead of talking about the dreams themselves, let's delve a little deeper into how they make you feel."

She has a great therapist voice: mellow, accepting, nurturing. More than once, Michael has considered asking her out, but he's never pursued it. Even if she weren't his therapist, he's sure she'd never go out with a guy like him. She's probably married, anyway, or gay. Plus, he already had a girlfriend. Sort of.

"What do you mean, how they make me feel?" He's playing dumb a little—he knows exactly what she means, but he wants to hear her say it. He always feels better when she directs their conversations.

Of course she can see right through him—that's a standard therapist superpower—but of course she pretends she can't. "You've said before that the dreams bother you. Why? They aren't frightening, are they?"

They are, but not the way she means. "They're not like a horror movie or anything, if that's what you're saying. No monsters, no blood, nobody getting hurt."

"But you feel anxiety when you experience them."

"Yes."

Nod. Jot. "As I said, I'd like to try something with you, if you're willing."

He doesn't ask what it is. He trusts her, and if she can do some-thing to make the dreams go away, he's willing to follow her down whatever path she wants to lead him on. "Let's do it."

She looks pleased. "What I'd like you to do is close your eyes for me. Take a few deep breaths, relax your muscles. You can lie down if you want."

There it is—the lying-down thing. Maybe there *is* a reason she has a couch instead of just a chair, even if it isn't one of those fancy quilted-leather lounger things from the comics. This one probably came from IKEA.

That's an odd thought. Why does thinking about IKEA suddenly spike his anxiety? He's never even been there. Jessica had wanted to go once, but the idea had made him inexplicably edgy. They'd ended up having an argument and not going.

"Michael?"

"Oh—sorry." He rearranges himself on the couch, stretching out his long legs and rolling his shoulders. "I don't think I need to lie down. Bit of a cliché, isn't it?"

She chuckles. "You do whatever makes you comfortable. I want you to be comfortable for this."

After another bout of rearranging, he ends up with his back pressed into the corner of the couch, between the cushion and the arm. He takes a couple more deep breaths and closes his eyes. "Okay. I'm ready."

"That's good." Paper rustling. "What I'd like you to do is picture the dream in your mind. Try to re-create what you see when you have it, starting at the beginning. If it helps you focus, you can describe it to me, but you don't have to."

"Okay…" He notices his heart starting to beat a little faster, so he takes more deep breaths.

"As you visualize the dream, I want you to notice when you start feeling anxious. Do you think you can do that, Michael?"

"I can try…" This is new. It's only been the past two or three sessions that they'd even begun focusing on the dream at all. Initially, he'd sought out Dr. Farley because of a general feeling of anxiety and dissatisfaction with his life. A sense that there had to be "more to it," as he'd said at their first meeting. The whole process had been a little foreign to him, and he'd been embarrassed at first, but before long he realized *everybody* in America seemed to be in therapy for something. Far from being the vague stigma it probably would have been back home, it almost seemed to be a mark of pride around here.

Americans were odd, that was certain. But when in Rome...

He tries to do what she asked. He closes his eyes, struggling to picture the dream in his mind's eye. It's harder than he expected—almost as if something is trying to block the visions. Every time he settles on an image, another thought intrudes: *I should pick up a few things at the market on the way home,* or *Jessica's going to be cross at me if I don't plan a night out soon,* or *Need to collect those books from the library tomorrow.*

"Michael, can you tell me what you're seeing?" Her voice is softer than before, slipping into his thoughts without a ripple, like one of those Olympic divers when they get it right.

He strains to focus harder, and hesitates a long time before he speaks. Not because he wants to—he'd described the dream in more general terms to her before—but because he can't seem to make his mouth work and sounds come out.

"Are you all right?"

"Yes, yes, fine." But is he? His heart is beating faster again, and suddenly he wants to leap off the couch, thank Dr. Farley for her help, and tell her this whole process is absurd and that will be quite enough of it.

"Tell me what you're seeing. Don't worry about whether it makes sense. Just say whatever comes into your head."

He pulls in a few deep breaths and shifts on the sofa. "Er..." *Just do it. It can't be that hard!* "I see...I'm walking in a town. Not this one, though. Not around here."

"Do you know where it is? Do you see any landmarks at all?"

"No. It's...dark. Evening. A lot of people out and about, window-shopping. It's a nice street—I think the town is fairly wealthy."

"Is it in England?"

"I don't think so. It's here in America, somewhere."

"You're doing very well, Michael. What else do you see?"

He swallows. Why is this so hard? It's a perfectly normal, pleasant scene, the kind he sees some version of every day. The people look normal, too: men, women, kids, going about their business of eating, drinking, walking, shopping. "I'm walking along the street."

"Do you know where you're going?"

"I don't think I'm going anywhere in particular. Just…walking."

"Okay, that's fine. You're doing great."

It always starts this way: walking along the street. The place is always the same; even though he can't pick out any specific landmarks, he knows it's the same. It feels familiar, as if he's been here many times before, even though he's sure he never has.

He never knows how long the calm part will last. He remembers always hoping in the dream that this will be the time when everything progresses normally—he'll be walking along a normal street with normal people on a normal day, and either the images will fade or switch to something else.

In front of him, a large woman walking a tiny dog suddenly lights up with a brilliant blue glow.

A million miles away, Dr. Farley must notice something, because she speaks softly: "Are you all right, Michael? Did you see something?"

"Er—" His heartbeat quickens, and tiny beads of sweat begin popping out all over his body. He swallows hard and draws his legs back in from their stretch.

"What do you see?"

"Blue," he manages to sputter out. It feels like he's trying to push the words through six feet of Jell-O.

"Blue? What's blue?"

He tries to picture it in his mind, but it keeps skating away. The blue light dances and flickers around the woman, surrounding her body in a beautiful outline. Next to her, the little dog lights up too, but its glow is weaker, and green. "She's…blue." His voice shakes.

"Michael..." She sounds like she's speaking to him from the end of a long, metal tube. "There's someone there who's blue? How is she blue? Is her skin blue?"

But he isn't listening to her anymore. All around him, other nimbuses of light are flaring around the other people—all of them. The tall man in the gray sweater is limned in deep purple. Bright, vibrant gold outlines the skipping little girl trying to drag her parents along faster. The tired-looking woman sitting with her back pressed against the side of a building flickers orange, like fire.

And they're all looking at Michael. Not in a menacing or threatening way, but more like—anticipation. As if every one of them knows something and they're all waiting for him to catch on.

"No!" He isn't even aware he's jumped up until he opens his eyes and discovers he's standing in the middle of Dr. Farley's office, every muscle tensed, fists clenched. "No! I can't do it!"

"Please sit down, Michael. It's all right."

For the first time ever, he spots an identifiable emotion breaking through her bland therapist's mask.

It's fear.

She hides it quickly, but he doesn't miss it.

In horror, he realizes he has to be the cause of it. He isn't a particularly menacing physical specimen in his neat buttoned shirt and jeans, but he's a tall man, and she's a small, slim woman, and they're alone in her office. This is the first time he's ever had that reaction.

"Oh, bloody hell, I'm so sorry." He doesn't sit back down, but he does back away from her, raising his hands in what he hopes is a placating gesture. "I'm sorry, Dr. Farley." That is the first time *that* has ever happened, and scares him more than his sudden outburst had scared her.

"It's fine, Michael. It's fine." The mask is already firmly back in place. She glances at the clock on the table next to her. "We're almost out of time, so this might be a good point to stop for tonight. Are you all right? Can I get you anything?"

His mind ticks through possibilities—*a new brain* and *a fifth of Scotch* are the first—but he only shakes his head. "No…thanks. I'll be fine." Now that he isn't thinking about the dream anymore, his heart rate and breathing have almost returned to normal.

She looks as if she isn't sure she believes him, but finally nods. "Okay. I think we made some good progress tonight. Maybe next week we can see if we can get a little further with the dreams."

"Yes…next week." He runs a hand through his hair and then turns it to a quick wave. "I'll…er…see you then. Thank you, Dr. Farley."

He already knows he'll never go back there again.

Jessica is in a bad mood when he gets back to the apartment, which isn't anything new.

"Did you stop at the store?" is the first thing she asks him. No greeting.

"Oh. Damn. No, I'm sorry, I forgot."

"How am I supposed to make dinner when you didn't get the stuff I asked for?" She lets out a loud, exaggerated sigh. "You're such a flake, Michael."

He doesn't argue with her. He rarely does, because it wouldn't do any good. Instead, he drops into a chair at the tiny kitchen table. "We could go out—get some takeaway. Or I'll go pick it up and bring it back here, if you'd rather eat in."

She rolls her eyes. "I *told* you I was on a diet. We can't all be skinny like you."

"So, what do you want, then? Should I go back to the market now?"

"Don't bother. I'm starving. I'll just put something together from what we've got. But can you *try* to remember next time? I hate always having to remind you about everything."

"Yes. I'll remember. I'm sorry. I've just—got a lot on my mind, I guess." He gets up and gets a beer—some microbrew one of his coworkers had recommended and he doesn't particularly care for—and returns to his seat. He pops it open and watches her as she moves around the kitchen, her every movement radiating annoyance.

He's been with Jessica for almost a year now, and they'd moved in together two months ago. If he was being completely honest with himself, he hadn't wanted to do it. In fact, over the past few weeks he'd begun to seriously ask himself why he was still with her in the first place. He'd met her at a mixer at the small, obscure university where he worked as a lecturer in the Anthropology department and she was an assistant professor of History. A friend had set them up. She'd liked his accent, and he'd liked her straightforward manner. They'd ditched the mixer and gone out for coffee, and two dates later they were sleeping together.

The only problem was, once they started seeing each other regularly her straightforward manner morphed from charming to domineering, which didn't mesh well with his easygoing, slacker lifestyle. The sex was good, at least—when she was in the mood, anyway. After they'd moved in together, she steadily put on weight; it didn't bother him, except now she constantly claimed to be "on a diet" and seemed to blame him for her extra pounds.

He hadn't spoken much with Dr. Farley about their relationship, but more than once as he lay next to Jessica in bed and listened to her heavy breathing, he wondered what would happen if he broke things off with her.

"Are you listening to me?" Her annoyed voice breaks into his thoughts.

He jerks his head up. "Er…sorry. What?"

She rolls her eyes at him again—she does that a lot, he's noticed—and holds up two packages of pasta. "Do you want the rigatoni or the spaghetti?"

"I don't care. You choose."

She snorts and mutters something about *can't even make up your mind about pasta,* but turns away and begins noisily opening one of the packages.

"Are you all right, Jessica? You seem…tense."

Her shoulders tighten, but when she turns back to him, her expression is thoughtful, not annoyed. "Yeah…I'm fine. Sorry. I've got some things on my mind, too. I need to talk to you about something."

Could it be possible? Is she going to break up with *him*? He feels guilty for thinking it, but it *would* make things a lot easier in a lot of ways. "Okay…let's hear it."

"Not now. After dinner."

"Why wait?"

"Just…let me tell you when I'm ready, okay? Why don't you go watch TV or something until dinner's ready?"

"Do you want me to help?" He hopes she doesn't say yes—he's rubbish at cooking, and would much rather pick something up from a restaurant.

Her only answer is a snort of derision.

Back to her old self, then. That's strangely comforting.

They mostly eat in silence, except for a couple of perfunctory attempts at conversation from each of them. Finally, they both bow to the inevitable, Jessica pulling out some papers she has to read for work and Michael scrolling aimlessly through his phone. When they finish the meal, he gathers the dishes and takes them to the kitchen, then returns to the table where she still sits. "So—what's this you wanted to talk about?"

She pushes the papers aside, but doesn't look at him. "I suppose I should just come right out and say it. It's not easy, though. I'm afraid of how you'll react."

"Go ahead." He's already braced himself for her words: *I want to break up*, or *It's not working between us*, or *It's not you, it's me*. He's already prepared his response, appropriately distressed, but gallantly accepting: *I'm sorry to hear that, love, but whatever you think is best*, or *I'll be gutted to lose you, but I won't stand in your way*, or—

"I'm pregnant, Michael."

He's actually drawn breath to begin one of his canned responses when her words catch up with him. "*What?*"

She glares at him. "What kind of response is that?"

He struggles to get himself under control, which is difficult because everything about him is reeling. All he can manage to sputter out is, "You're—"

"Pregnant. Expecting a baby. *Your* baby." She speaks slowly, as if addressing a small child.

He doesn't miss her distress, though, even though she's trying to be her usual straightforward self. "A...baby."

"I thought you'd be happy."

"I—" He has no idea what to say, which is never good because when that happens, he tends to blurt out whatever is on his mind. This is no exception. "How—?"

Her glare intensifies. "Do I have to explain the birds and the bees to you?"

"Of course not, but we were so—"

So careful. He'd always been careful, since the last thing he wants is an unexpected child. Or an expected one, for that matter. He has enough trouble managing his own life, especially after this new business with the disturbing dreams, without adding someone else's into the mix.

"Accidents happen. I was as surprised as you were, when the test came back." Her stolid façade is beginning to crumble, and glimmers of tears sprout in the corners of her eyes. "Michael...I thought you'd be happy."

"I—I am, but—"

But he isn't. In the space of a few seconds, the possibility of ending this relationship—the one he'd already convinced himself neither one of them wanted to continue—has not only crumbled around him, but now he faces a new, irrevocable tie to this woman he's suddenly sure he doesn't love.

"But what?"

She's definitely upset now. This isn't going well. Michael wishes he could rewind time, get a do-over, say something else that would buy him some breathing room. But do-overs only happen in fantasy books. Like magic, or dragons, or good fairies.

In the real world, you dealt with your screw-ups.

He forces a smile. "But nothing. I *am* happy. That's wonderful news. You just—caught me by surprise, is all."

She studies him, as if trying to figure out if he's telling the truth. Then she ventures a hesitant smile of her own. "Really? You're happy?"

"Of course I'm happy. Why wouldn't I be?" Why not, indeed? *Because I don't want kids? Because that's* why *I made it a point to be so careful? Because I don't love you?* In his mind's eye, he pictures a duck: calm on the surface, but paddling frantically to stay afloat beneath the water.

She looks at her hands. "So you don't think we should..."

"Should what?"

"You know. Don't make me say it. I know we've been careful. I know you don't want children yet."

Now the duck is paddling through a field of depth charges. As hard as it is, he knows the answer—the only right answer. He might be a slacker, but he's not a cad. He plasters on what he hopes is an encouraging smile. "Jessica, love, that decision isn't mine to make. It's yours. I'll support you, whatever you decide to do."

Her shoulders slump as she let go of some of her tension. "Really? You will?"

"Of course I will. We'll make this work." *Somehow.*

And then suddenly she's there next to him, with her arms around him. "Oh, Michael, thank you. I was so scared you were going to leave me when you found out."

He thinks about the dreams, and his speculations about their relationship before she'd made her announcement. He realizes that, deep down in his mind, he'd already been laying the mental groundwork for telling her it wasn't working out. He thinks about what his life will be going forward: Jessica getting on his nerves for her nagging, him getting on *her* nerves for his irresponsible ways, years of short sleep, nappies, parties full of screaming kids, holidays to places like Disneyland and the zoo instead of Hawaii or Cabo…

He pulls her closer. "I'd never do that, love."

"I'm so glad." She snuggles into his shoulder. "I love you, Michael."

He strokes her and hopes she doesn't notice he doesn't say it back.

He doesn't mention Jessica's pregnancy to any of his colleagues at work, but they find out anyway.

"Why didn't you *tell* us, Michael?" Darlene McCoy gushes a few days later when they pass each other in the hall.

"Er…tell you what?"

She looks at him as if she can't decide whether he's serious. "Your good *news,* of course! I heard it from Trudy, who heard it from Nicole over in the History department. Jessica's telling anybody who'll listen! Congratulations!"

"Oh. Er…thank you. It's still a bit of a shock, I guess. I didn't realize she was telling anyone yet."

She gives him a sly smile. "It's so hard to keep such wonderful news to yourself. You're going to be a *great* dad. Your life's going to change *so* much!"

"Yes. I'm…sure it is."

When he gets back to his office, a cluttered space barely larger than a coat closet, he finds an email waiting. It's from Professor George Rutledge, his department head, asking him to stop by when he gets back.

He sighs. Rutledge is all right—a distant presence who doesn't get involved in the day-to-day lives of the faculty unless he has to, but he always seems cheerful enough in the hallway. Maybe he'd heard the grapevine gossip about the baby too, and wanted to offer his congratulations.

Well, there's no way around it. He can't exactly ignore the email. He supposes he can feign excitement for a few more minutes, and then hide in his office for an hour before heading home.

Rutledge's admin looks up from her computer screen. "Oh, hello, Michael."

Good. She's not going on about the baby. "I got an email from Dr. Rutledge. He wanted to see me?"

"Oh. Yes." Something flits across her face, almost too fast to see. "He's free now, so you can go right on in."

George Rutledge always seemed to dominate any room he occupied, to the point where everyone else felt subconsciously crowded out. A distinguished-looking black man with graying temples, bulbous nose, and tiny wire-rimmed glasses, he possessed the kind of bulk that made people fear for their furniture and the pleasant manner that made them feel ashamed about it. At this moment, he's seated behind his large desk, looking through a stack of papers.

Michael clears his throat softly. "Dr. Rutledge? You wanted to see me?" He braces for the inevitable conversation. Rutledge and his wife have four children and seven grandchildren. He doesn't talk about them, but their framed photos are all over his office.

"Oh. Yes. Please sit down, Michael."

Huh. This is odd. Maybe he *doesn't* want to talk about the impending baby. Michael takes one of the guest chairs in front of the desk and waits.

Rutledge looks at his papers again and seems slightly uncomfortable, but when he speaks there is no hesitation in his voice. "Michael, there's no easy way to say this."

Michael tenses. Those had been the same words Jessica had used before she'd told him she was pregnant. An utterly absurd thought pops into his head: *Is he pregnant too? Big as he is, I'm not sure anyone would notice.* He struggles against an involuntary and utterly inappropriate laugh, and remains silent instead.

Rutledge looks almost fatherly. "I'm afraid some of our funding for the department has been cut, and we need to make some adjustments. I'm truly sorry to inform you that we won't be renewing your contract going forward."

It takes a moment for the words to sink in. Of all the things he'd thought Rutledge might say, this wasn't even on the list. Sure, he isn't even close to tenure. Sure, he'd been gently warned a time or two about snapping at a student or taking too many sick days to sleep off hangovers, or not making enough progress on his research. But everybody had things like that—didn't they?

"Er—" is all he can get out.

"I'm so sorry, Michael. I wish there was another way, but—" He spreads his hands as if to say, *well, there isn't.*

Michael is still in shock. The first thing that comes to him to say is, "But—I just found out Jessica's expecting a baby!" He doesn't say that, though. Partly because it would be disingenuous, given his feelings about *that* situation, but mostly because he knows it won't make any difference.

Instead, he says, "So…I've got until the end of the semester."

"Yes." Rutledge shuffles papers on his desk. "The University has resources to help you look for another position, so of course you should feel free to take advantage of those…"

Michael doesn't miss that his boss seems suddenly uncomfortable, and thinks he knows why: he hasn't offered to write a letter of recommendation, and apparently doesn't intend to. This has very little to do with the funding, and they both know it.

He sighs. The end of the semester is only a few weeks away, and those weeks will fly by. Definitely not enough time to secure another teaching job before the following semester starts, unless he gets lucky and finds someplace that's truly desperate. Even then, not too many universities would be desperate enough to hire a lackluster candidate like him.

He stands. "Right, then." It doesn't seem appropriate to say *thank you.*

"I really am sorry, Michael. I've enjoyed working with you."

Michael nods. It's one of those professional lies, and they both know that, too. "Take care, Dr. Rutledge."

"Talk to Ellen to work out all the details. My best to you."

He doesn't talk to Ellen. He sweeps past her on his way out, and she's savvy enough not to try stopping him.

When he gets outside, he keeps walking. The University is small, located on the outskirts of a medium-sized town nobody has ever heard of. He leaves the campus with his hands in his pockets and his head bowed, deep in thought about nothing and everything. By the time he looks up to see where he is, he's reached the center of town.

He drops onto a park bench, hands still jammed in his pockets, and thinks about his next steps. He has a few days' vacation time saved up—back in the Before Times (that is to say, two days ago) he'd been thinking about seeing if Jessica wanted to get away from it all for a little while. Now, though, he doesn't think he can even bear going home.

In a few weeks, he'll be unemployed. He has a little money put away for a rainy day, but that won't last long with a child on the way. Would Jessica want him to marry her? Probably—it made sense. If he intends to stay with her, he might as well. But would she even *want* to stay with him now? Even if he could land another teaching job, it won't be anywhere near here. The area only has one university within a couple hundred miles, and Jessica has a good job there. Tenure track. Everyone in her department loves her— students *and* fellow faculty. If she won't leave, will that mean he'll have to end up taking a job outside his field, to make ends meet? Working in a grocery store, maybe, or selling shoes?

He runs his hands through his hair, making spikes. How has his life spiraled so completely out of control in such a short time?

How has he ended up where he is?

Once again, the familiar feelings rush in. There has to be more to his life than this. Sometimes he feels it even when he isn't sleeping: the certainty that *something* more has eluded him, that he's missing some vital component of the life he was meant to have. He'd mentioned it to Dr. Farley once, and she'd gently suggested that it was probably because not much in his real life was going the way he felt like it should. That the idea there was some better, stronger, more intelligent "fantasy Michael" out there could sometimes provide comfort.

He knows she's probably right, but can't shake the thought that she isn't. Is it connected with the dreams somehow? The weird colored nimbuses around everyone on the street? The way those people all look at him, as if expecting him to figure something out?

He yanks his hands from his pockets and sighs.

This isn't getting him anywhere.

If he were wise, he'd walk back to the university, retrieve his car, and drive home. He could talk this over with Jessica when she gets home. She'll probably be annoyed at him for losing his job, but she's smart and practical. They'd figure something out.

He almost does that.

He almost stands and starts walking.

But then, as he sits there watching the traffic go by under a gray, overcast sky, another thought takes him over, so powerfully he shivers.

Home.

In his mind's eye, the little English village where he'd grown up overlays the ugly city street in front of him. He'd left more than five years ago, moving to America to get away from a general sense of malaise that had been growing even then, but now, suddenly, he knows what he needs to do. He knows it with a level of certainty that almost frightens him.

He needs to go home.

Jessica is livid when he calls her with the news.

"What do you *mean,* you've got to go to England?"

"I'm sorry, Jessica, but I do." He's still sitting on the bench, still watching the traffic go by.

"Why? Did somebody die?"

"No."

"Is somebody sick?"

"No, that's not it either. I—can't explain it. But I've got to do it. I'll only be gone a few days."

"I don't get it, Michael—you've got work. We've still got things to talk about. You can't just…run away."

"I'm not running away." But is that true? He doesn't even know. All he knows is that the urge to do it is nearly overwhelming him. It's one of the oddest feelings he's ever experienced. He'd thought he understood the meaning of "compulsion" before, but he hadn't. None of that was anything compared to what he's experiencing now.

He hears her sigh over the line. "Okay. If you must go, let me come with you. I could use a vacation. I could take a few days—"

"No." The word comes out too fast, and too sharp. "I—I need to do this on my own, Jessica. I promise—it will help me get my head together." He has no idea if it will or not. He hasn't told her about his contract not being renewed; at least he doesn't have to worry about her hearing *that* from anybody else.

"Get your head together." Her voice drips with contempt. "Is this something that shrink of yours put you up to?"

"No." He stands, unable to stay seated any longer. It's almost as if something is physically *tugging* him. "Jessica, listen—I've got to go. I'll talk to you when I get back."

"Michael—"

"I'm sorry." By the time he breaks the connection and puts the phone back in his pocket, he's already walking fast.

The certainty that he's doing the right thing grows with every hour closer his plane gets to England. By the time it touches down at Heathrow, he's sure he's done the right thing. Or at least the thing he was supposed to do, even though he has no idea *why*.

He'd slept most of the way over, which was strange in and of itself. Even the coach-class ticket had set him back more than he'd felt comfortable paying, and usually he has a lot of trouble getting his tall, long-legged frame comfortable enough in the torture-rack seat so he can manage even fitful sleep.

Not that he's gone home that often. In fact, the last time he'd made this flight was when he'd come over to America in the first place five years ago, to take the job he was about to lose in a few weeks. He'd hoped it would be the beginning of a promising new career.

Yes, and how did that *work out for you?*

As he walks through the airport toward the exit (no need to stop at the baggage carousel; he hasn't brought any luggage, which had earned him suspicious looks from several airport personnel along with an extra-thorough pat-down by a humorless TSA agent) it occurs to him that he barely remembers his time growing up in England. That seems odd to him, whenever he bothers to think about it. Jessica regularly regaled him with stories of everything from her early childhood to her carefree days in college whenever he'd listen. She had boxes and computer files full of photos from every stage of her life, plus diaries and journals ranging from childish crayon scrawls all the way up to more online files where she detailed the events of her days and how she felt about them. But whenever she asked him about his own past, all he could conjure were a few representative memories. He has no photos, no journals…barely any clear memories. He'd always written it off to being a forward-thinking sort of person who didn't like dwelling in the past, but it wasn't normal to remember so little, was it? He hadn't been brave enough yet to bring it up to Dr. Farley, since it didn't seem as urgent as the strange dreams and the general feeling he was missing something important in his life, but it had always been on his list.

And now he'd never have a chance to do it.

Sitting in the cab on the way from the airport, he checks his phone for messages. There are several texts from Jessica, spaced at irregular intervals over the course of the twelve hours he'd been at the airport or in flight:

Michael? Where are you?

Damn it, don't avoid me. We need to talk.

You didn't really already leave for England, did you?

Answer me as soon as you get this!

There's also a voicemail, which he listens to while watching the dreary, overcast London scenery roll by out the cab's window. His attention skips over most of the details, but the gist is clear: She's had enough of his bullshit, and if he doesn't get in touch with her right away and come home, she's leaving him. Now that she's going to be a mother, she can't deal with his irresponsibility any longer.

He thinks he should have felt worse about that—guiltier, anyway—and then feels guilty because he *doesn't*. If he feels anything, it's relief. Sure, he'll still have to pay child support, which he doesn't mind (assuming he can find another position), but that's a small price compared to being tied to a woman he doesn't love for the rest of his life.

To stall having to declare a destination, he'd instructed the cabdriver to take him to Victoria Station. Once he finishes reading Jessica's texts and listening to her final voicemail, he doesn't spend much time looking out the window. He has no idea why he picked Victoria; it had popped into his head when the driver asked his destination. He doesn't ask questions anymore, though. Something deep inside him is growing more and more convinced there's a method to his sudden madness, and he intends to roll with it for as long as it persists. Despite his lack of clear memories, London definitely looks familiar to him. He *has* been here before, probably many times. He finds that comforting.

At the station, his certainty falters. He's here, but now what? Should he go home? The problem is, he doesn't really have a *home* in England anymore. His parents are both dead (he knows that, but can't remember how they'd died) and he'd lived in a series of flats while he was at university, none of which had been memorable. He drifts to the food court and buys a pasty and a cup of coffee, then finds a table where he can watch the commuters and tourists streaming through the concourse.

Everybody else looks like they know exactly what they're doing and why they're here. Why doesn't he? Why *is* he even here? Sure, after the one-two punch of Jessica's pregnancy and the upcoming loss of his job, it would have made sense for him to go off by himself for a while to get himself together. That was normal. But flying all the way to the other side of the world to escape his problems? That *isn't* normal.

Or…is it?

He tightens his hand around his coffee cup as a snippet of a thought surfaces.

He'd done this before.

He'd moved from England to America to get away from something…

But…he *hadn't*. That much he does remember, why he left. He'd simply been feeling unsatisfied with his life, and decided a change would do him good. When the position at the American university had come up, he'd taken it without much thought.

But…

Damn you, stop it.

The coffee sloshes onto the table as he smacks the cup down. He can't even call Dr. Farley for an emergency consultation, since it's the middle of the night in America.

Why the hell has he done this?

A flash of blue catches the corner of his eye.

He jerks his head up, and this time he almost crushes the paper cup. His breath catches in his throat.

A young man with dreadlocks and a hooded sweater has just ambled by, close to his table.

A young man with a bright nimbus of blue light flickering around him.

He must have noticed Michael's shock, because he pauses with a narrow-eyed glance of confusion. "All right, mate?"

"Er..." Michael swallows again and deliberately disengages his fingers from the cup before he spills more coffee all over the table. "Yes. Sorry. Fine."

The man gives him a dubious side-eye and hurries past, but Michael isn't looking at him anymore.

They're *all* glowing now.

It's just like in the dream. Every single one of the hundreds of people hurrying through the Victoria Station concourse is surrounded by a bright, flickering envelope of color. Red, green, yellow, blue, purple, they outline each person and move along with them, extending anywhere from a couple inches to almost a foot from their bodies. Some are brighter, some darker, some have little black patches or edges that crackle like fire, but all of them behave the same way.

Michael takes several deep, gulping breaths, trying the technique Dr. Farley had taught him to use when his anxiety grew too strong to deal with. He closes his eyes and mentally counts to twenty, then opens them again. Surely the weird lights will be gone.

They aren't gone.

In fact, they seem stronger than ever, and now a few people are looking at him. Some show suspicion, some pity, some confusion, all fleeting as they hurry by.

Still gasping, his heart thudding now and dull heat forming at the base of his neck, Michael tears his gaze away from the crowd and looks down at his hands.

They're glowing too.

Not only are they glowing, but they glow with not one color, but *two*.

Shocked, he lets the rest of the world drop away as he stares at himself. The bright nimbus extends more than a foot from his body, with a large purple stripe closer in and another one of brilliant gold farther out.

He gasps.

What's going on?

What's wrong with me?

Is he dreaming again? Is this whole trip to England nothing but some kind of delusion, and he'll wake any minute in his bed back home, with Jessica complaining his thrashing has disturbed her sleep?

He leaps up, shoving his chair back so hard it overturns and crashes to the ground.

People really are looking at him now. Nobody stops, but they glance back over their shoulders as they go. He sees fear and compassion in their eyes. None of them look like they expect him to know anything. They all look like one might stare at a homeless man acting out some kind of mental issue in public.

Is that what I am? Mental?

Has everything—the job and Jessica's pregnancy and the dreams—finally been too much for him?

Have I finally cracked?

"Sir?"

He jerks back and spins.

Two uniformed security guards, a man and a woman, stand a few feet away, watching him with wary concern. A bright blue glow surrounds the man, and the woman has an equally bright green one. Streaks of red flicker through both of them.

"Er—" His voice shakes. He can't think of anything else to say.

"Are you all right? Do you need help?"

"Er—" *Say something, idiot!* "Er...no. I'm—I'm fine. I don't need help."

"Are you sure? You haven't been drinking, have you?"

"No. No drinking." He struggles to get his voice under control. He has to ignore these strange glows. They're all in his mind, nobody else can see them, and if he doesn't pull himself together, he'll be hauled off to a hospital somewhere. The kind with padded walls and soft handcuffs.

He blinks a couple times and tries to focus on the two guards' faces, not their glows. The woman is small and slim, with short dark hair, an attractive, pixieish face, and big, serious eyes. The man is much taller, with broad shoulders, a healthy tan, and short, dirty-blond hair.

Had they looked like that before? He could have sworn they hadn't. They'd been older when he first saw them. The woman had been Indian, and the man was black. Now they were both white. How could this be possible?

And then, to his sudden horror, he recognizes them.

Both of them.

He's seen their faces before, he's sure of it. But as hard as he pummels his brain, he can't remember where.

"What are your names?" he demands. It comes out too loud, and more hurrying people glance their way. Somebody pauses to pull out a phone and begin recording.

"Sir, we—"

"*What are your names?*" He's yelling now, his voice booming to fill the cavernous space.

Then they're next to him. The man is gripping his arms, and the woman is in front of him.

"Come on, sir," she says gently. "We'll take you somewhere you can get some help. No one's going to hurt you. Just please come along with us."

Her pleasant voice has an American accent.

He struggles, suddenly certain if he goes with these people, no one will ever see him again. He has to get home! He flings himself forward, trying to rip free of the man's grasp.

"Jason! Hold him!" The woman's green glow flares even brighter around her as she takes a step back.

Michael whips his head back and forth and pulls harder, but the man's hold is too strong. He can't get free. He tries to kick, but his flailing foot hits only air. As he jerks his neck around, he gets a quick glimpse of the male security guard's name tag.

THAYER.

Something explodes in the back of his mind.

He knows that name!

He's *sure* he does! But how can that be possible? He hasn't been to Victoria Station in years. Hell, he hasn't been to *England* in years!

Where would he ever have encountered this man, this "Thayer"?

The woman steps in front of him, looking stern but kind. "Come on, sir. It's all right. Nobody wants to hurt you, I promise."

Her tag says *THAYER* too.

"Let me go!" he screams, thrashing harder. He's now thoroughly convinced that if he doesn't get away from these two and get free *now*, something horrible will happen to him. They'll drag him down beneath the station, and—

"Help me!" the male Thayer—Jason—snaps. He tightens his grip on Michael's shoulders and hustles him down until he's kneeling on the dirty floor.

"No!" Michael barely has any idea what he's doing now. He thrashes and flings himself back and forth, anything to rip free of this man's viselike grip. Do they have drugs? Will he soon feel the pricking sting of a needle sinking into his arm, bearing him away to unconsciousness? Discordant images fly across his mind's eye; some of them he recognizes, while others are utterly unfamiliar.

Jessica's frowning face.

A massive old house next to a graveyard.

The two Thayers, but dressed in normal, casual clothes instead of security-guard uniforms.

A lecture hall, one he doesn't recognize, full of students.

A handsome young man with dark, blond-tipped hair.

George Rutledge, his eyes disapproving.

A broad-shouldered, dark-haired man in an old-fashioned suit.

His and Jessica's apartment in—now he can't remember the name of the town.

Another man in a fine suit, with brown hair, graying temples, and a knowing smile.

The last image lingers in Michael's mind as the flashes slow like a film reel winding down.

That one is important.

That man is the key to everything.

He has no idea how he knows it, but he does. He's certain of it.

He has to get a better look at the man's face, but already it's fading.

He jerks his head to the side, barely aware that he's screaming.

Who is the man?

How does he know him?

Why is he important?

What is *happening* to him?

"Al! Stop it!" The male Thayer is yelling now.

Michael stops in mid-wrench when the words sink in.

Al?

Who is Al?

Could that explain what they're doing to him? Do they have him confused with somebody else?

He isn't "Al." "Al" sounds like somebody dangerous, or at least disreputable.

He's Michael!

I'm MICHAEL, damn you!

The visions speed up again.

Lecture hall.

Looming manor house.

Dark-haired, broad-shouldered man.

Pale tower with red-domed top.

Black BMW sedan.

Kindly old man in flat cap.

Gray-and-black tabby cat with wide green eyes.

Both Thayers, now looking at him with worry in an unfamiliar living room.

Intense-looking, black-haired man with cold gray eyes.

Swirling, circular lights floating in midair, like a doorway.

Brown-haired man, smiling.

Smug.

Laughing.

He knows. This man knows.

Knows what?

Michael's head lights up with sudden agony, as if someone has driven a spike into his brain.

Something is building inside him, some kind of energy that feels like it's burning him from his core. It's hot and thrumming and intense, but not quite painful. *Should* it be painful?

What is going on? What are they doing to him?

"Al!"

The guard is yelling again, shaking him, but he barely notices. He's long since stopped noticing if there are still any other people— or even the station itself—around him any longer. All that's there is him and the guard and what's going on in his body. The building energy feels like it's taking over his entire being. It's too big to be contained inside him. It wants to be released.

It wants *out.*

"*NO!*" he screams. He can't take it anymore. If he doesn't do something with it, it's going to destroy him. Is this what it feels like to have a mental breakdown?

Am I dying?

His instincts take over, telling him what to do, and he obeys without question.

He locks eyes with the man (with Jason—with *Thayer*). Instead of trying to wrench himself free, he stops struggling, clamps his grip around the guard's arms, and holds tight. Beyond Thayer, he can see the other one (*the other Thayer*) looking at him with wide, fearful eyes.

She knows.

She knows what he's about to do.

She's lunging forward—

He releases the energy.

It all happens fast after that. Jason Thayer barely has a chance to scream before the energy is all around him, engulfing him, devouring first the blue nimbus around him, then his flesh, then his skeleton, until there's nothing left but fluttering ash and the echo of his scream in Michael's head.

Behind him—behind the spot where he *was*—the energy continues radiating outward, catching the stricken-faced woman as she dives for him. It devours her too and keeps going.

Michael is ground zero.

He doesn't want to watch, but he can't close his eyes. The blast is the same color as the light around him, purple and golden and beautiful. It devours everything in its path—not just the people, but the floor, the walls, the *air*.

It leaves behind…nothing.

Not the drizzly, overcast London day. Not the sky or the ground or the cars.

Nothing.

Michael is standing in the middle of a white, featureless space.

No floor, no walls, no ceiling.

He might as well be floating, for all the sensory input he's receiving.

The silence presses in on him in an almost physical sensation.

He screams, but no sound comes from him.

When the world changes around him and his awareness drops away, his last vision is of the brown-haired, smiling man.

Only the man isn't smiling anymore.

CHAPTER TWO

I T WAS DARK.

Pitch dark.

So unceasingly dark it almost seemed as if the walls were contracting, creeping inexorably forward until they threatened to crush everything in their path.

That was strange, because Alastair Stone's last clear memory was of being surrounded by blinding, unrelenting whiteness.

What was also strange was how disoriented he felt.

It took a moment for more memories to come back. When they did, he clenched his fists.

Aldwyn.

Bloody *Aldwyn.*

His dragon ancestor had tricked him by abducting his son and luring him to another dimension by pretending to help. Aldwyn had never wanted Ian, but he'd used him anyway, correctly guessing Stone would risk everything, agree to anything to ensure his son's safety.

But why? What did he even want?

More memories returned: the ring Aldwyn had given him. The note, telling him it would return only one of the two of them to safety so he'd have to make a choice. The white-walled prison.

None of it made sense. Why had Aldwyn wanted to imprison him?

None of that mattered now, though. All that mattered was getting out of here.

Tentatively he tried to lift his arms, and was surprised to discover they weren't restrained. He sat up slowly, mindful of the muddy, sloshing sensation in his head. He felt the way he did when he slept too long after drinking too much.

How long *had* he been sleeping, or unconscious? He didn't remember passing out. Probably more of Aldwyn's doing. He did remember snippets of strange dreams, though—dreams of living another life where he'd been a mundane.

The dreams had seemed so real…

"Ian?" His weak voice sounded croaky in the darkness. He didn't expect anyone to be there with him, but it was worth a try. "Aldwyn, can you hear me? Answer me, you bastard!"

Nothing.

Pure, unrelieved silence, except for the faint hiss of his breathing.

This wasn't good.

If he was still in the same place he'd been when Ian had faded away, and if Aldwyn had been telling the truth, he was still on another dimension. One he knew nothing about, including how to get home.

How long was Aldwyn planning to keep him here, wherever "here" even was? He couldn't have been sleeping for too long, since he didn't feel hungry and his mouth wasn't dry. Maybe the dragon had just wanted to keep him on ice long enough to do whatever he'd planned to do. Maybe he'd be coming back any time now to explain things.

Stone didn't think that was too likely, though.

He'd been avoiding the obvious next step—checking to see if his magic still worked—on purpose until now. Partly, it was to give himself a moment to clear the last of the lingering disorientation from his head and gather as many memories as he could. But the real reason—the one he didn't want to admit even to himself—was his fear that it *wouldn't* still work. If that was true, he'd have damned few options, except to wait for Aldwyn to show up again.

If he ever showed up again.

But he had to know. If it *wasn't* true, if his magic did still function, Aldwyn might be surprised to discover his descendant still had a few tricks up his sleeve. Stone had no idea if his draconic ley-line teleportation method worked across dimensions, but he was fairly sure Aldwyn didn't know he had access to it at all. The other dragons had never seemed in a big hurry to share anything with their renegade associate, or vice versa.

First, though, he had to know if it was even an option.

He raised his hand, feeling it shaking even though he couldn't see it, and concentrated.

Instantly, a bright globe of light sprang up around it, illuminating his prison.

He squinted, expecting pain as his eyes adjusted from the utter darkness to the stark white.

Except the walls weren't white.

"Bloody hell..." Stone whispered. His glowing hand dropped to his side.

He knew where he was, and it wasn't some other dimension.

What was Aldwyn playing at?

He stood carefully, pausing a moment to make sure his balance was solid, and raised his glowing hand. With a flick of his magic, the glow around it rose until it hovered near the room's low ceiling. Then he turned slowly in place.

The symbols and sigils on the room's cracked walls were familiar, because he'd spent a lot of time studying them, and photos of them. The musty smell and dust-covered floor were likewise familiar, as was the raised platform in the center. Instead of a cracked box, though, the platform now held a mattress, which was where he'd been lying. A floor-to-ceiling pile of fallen rock still blocked the doorway and the hall beyond.

"No..." he murmured. How could this be? Had Aldwyn done something to knock him out, then brought him from the other dimension to the chamber beneath his Surrey house? The same chamber where Aldwyn himself had been imprisoned for nearly two centuries?

Why would he do that? Was he trying to make some point? If he wanted to imprison Stone, wouldn't it make more sense to leave him on the other dimension?

Unless...

What if there had never *been* any other dimension? Aldwyn had proven he could hijack both teleportation portals and ley-line travel—at least when used by his own scions. That was how he'd managed to grab Ian in the first place.

Gabriel had searched for Ian, and told Stone he was on another dimension. But Aldwyn was a lot older and more experienced than Gabriel—could he have done something to spoof Ian's location?

Stone growled in the back of his throat. None of this was important right now. All that mattered at the moment was to get the hell *out* of here, and make sure Ian was all right. Everything else could wait. He could track down Gabriel, or Kolinsky, or Madame Huan—hell, he was fairly sure hijacking people and holding them prisoner was against *some* draconic agreement, so maybe he could even convince the others to finally get off their asses and do something about Aldwyn.

"Okay..." he murmured. "But first things first."

He looked down at himself. He was still wearing the tuxedo he'd been wearing at Aubrey's wedding. He'd removed the tie before he sought Aldwyn out, but everything else was still as he remembered.

He patted his inner jacket pocket. Good, his phone was still there. He might not get a signal down here, but he'd be out soon enough. He pulled it free and tapped the screen.

Nothing happened.

He frowned. Dead already? He had the newest, most high-tech phone currently available, and its battery usually lasted well over a day before he had to charge it again.

Had he been sleeping for a whole day, or even longer? He certainly didn't feel like it.

Easy enough to check: he ran his hand along his jawline, feeling for stubble.

There wasn't any. He was as clean-shaven as he'd been at the wedding.

So he *hadn't* been out for long.

He shifted to magical sight, looking for any lingering traces. If he'd only been unconscious or sleeping for a brief time, he might still pick up bits of the teleportation energy Aldwyn had used to bring him here.

His aura blazed bright purple and gold, with the narrow band of silver around the outer edge. Aside from that, he detected nothing.

But wait—

There *was* something else. Not teleportation energy, though. Whatever it was, it was faint and fading, hovering around the platform and the mattress. He had to squint to see it at all, and before he could do anything to try analyzing it, it dissipated into nothingness like so much steam.

Odd...

All right—enough stalling, and enough investigation. It was time to get out of here.

If he could.

He still didn't know if Aldwyn had done something else to the room, like warded it from the outside. The ley-line teleport wouldn't go through wards, except his own.

Or, if his dragon ancestor was watching him somehow, it would be easy for him to hijack the teleport again.

Damn it, enough, Stone told himself with annoyance. *You're stalling.*

He *was* stalling. But no more. He had to get out of here before the air went bad. He had to find out. Once again, he couldn't make decisions without all the available facts.

Okay, here goes…

He gathered the energy to him and considered his options for landing spots. If Aldwyn *was* watching him, he might be keeping an eye on his usual places: the Surrey house, the London house, the Encantada house, Caventhorne. But if he went somewhere else without his phone, it might be difficult for him to find a way to contact anyone. Nobody had pay phones anymore, and convincing a stranger to lend you their mobile long enough to make a call rarely worked.

Stop dithering, you muppet. Bugger Aldwyn and whatever the hell he was trying to do! If the dragon wanted to hijack Stone, great. At least then he'd get a chance to tell his ancestor exactly what he thought of this whole mess.

He was going home, and Aldwyn could pound sand if he didn't like it.

He closed his eyes, visualized the pattern, sent out a prayer to the Universe that this would go the way he wanted it to, and released the energy.

Before he even looked, he knew it had worked. It had done *something*, anyway. The musty odor of the underground chamber was gone, replaced by something familiar but ever so subtly off.

He opened his eyes and let his breath out in a long *whoosh* of relief when he spotted familiar, wood-paneled walls. He was standing in the upstairs study at the Encantada house. He was home, and Aldwyn hadn't hijacked him.

Maybe Aldwyn didn't even know he'd got free.

Hang on, though...

He'd been so relieved to be free of the prison that he hadn't taken time to do more than verify where he was. But now, on second look, the place *did* look different.

Not much different—the big desk and the leather couch were still there, and the floor-to-ceiling bookshelf on the wall still held stacks of books. But his laptop wasn't on his desk anymore, the blinds were closed, and everything was covered in a healthy layer of dust. The room smelled like it hadn't been aired in a while, which was strange since he'd only been here a short time ago. It was where he'd found Aldwyn's card, under the desk where Raider had knocked it.

That was part of the problem. Where was Raider? The cat had an almost preternatural sense of knowing when he was here, even when he popped in magically instead of coming through the door like a normal person.

"Raider?" That didn't always work, since cats were independent beings and often prided themselves on ignoring any attempt to summon them, but it couldn't hurt.

Nothing. No distant *thump* of a feline form jumping off a high perch, or pitter-pat of paws on the wooden floor.

That didn't worry Stone, though. There was an easy, sure-fire way to lure Raider out of wherever he was hiding, and suddenly that was important to him. He needed his furry sounding board to help him work through what was going on, and then he would call Ian and make sure he was all right.

As he headed downstairs, the feeling struck him once again that something was off about the house. There was a lot of dust, for one thing. He'd never been the world's best housekeeper (and he'd never got around to hiring one, either, despite his frequent thoughts that he should) but he did run a dust cloth over the place every now and then.

He reached the kitchen. The sleek, ultramodern space looked as unused as ever, which didn't surprise him. Verity had managed to teach him a few simple cooking techniques, but he still preferred the convenience of picking something up from some local restaurant.

Still, he was sure he'd left a stack of mail on the breakfast bar, and it was gone now. Verity had a key—had she come over and tidied up? That didn't seem possible—she wasn't much more a fan of housework than he was, so she was unlikely to have come down here to clean his place. *And if she had, she'd have dusted, right?*

Something was definitely weird.

"Raider?" he called again, louder this time, and opened the cabinet where he kept a supply of the upscale canned food that was the cat's regular diet when he wasn't schmoozing leftovers from Stone's takeaway meals.

Except there wasn't any cat food there.

The cabinet was empty except for a few stacked plates.

"What the *hell?*" Stone muttered aloud. He *knew* there should be food in the cabinet—he'd just picked up a dozen cans a couple days before the wedding. Even if Verity had come by to feed Raider, she wouldn't have gone through that many cans in a couple of days. The cat was a glutton, but not *that* much of one.

Suspicious and unsettled now, he hurried to the refrigerator and flung it open. When he'd left, it had contained several bottles of Guinness, a few random condiments, and the leftovers from the

Chinese food he'd brought home from the Dragon Garden two days before the wedding.

The condiments were still there. The Guinness and Chinese food were gone, replaced by several bottles of a microbrew he'd never heard of.

Also, still no sign of Raider. He should definitely have heard Stone rummaging around in the kitchen by now and come down to investigate.

Overcome with sudden weariness, he closed the refrigerator. Whatever was going on, he was beginning to suspect he wouldn't figure it out on his own. The landline phone was still on the counter where it usually was, so he summoned the handset with magic and dropped onto one of the breakfast-bar stools.

Time to call Ian.

But then he realized he didn't remember Ian's number.

He rarely called his son these days. They usually communicated by text, and even on the rare occasions when they spoke on the phone, the number was safely stored in Stone's mobile phone's memory where he could reach Ian with the tap of a contact button.

The perils of living in the twenty-first century, he supposed, but right now it frustrated him more than amusing him. How could he not know his own son's phone number?

He *did* know Verity's, though, and she'd have Ian's. With a shaking finger, he tapped in her number and listened while it rang, hoping she'd pick up and it wouldn't go to voicemail.

It rang twice, and then, "Hey, Ian—are you at the house?"

Stone blinked. Ian? Why would she think Ian was calling? "Er— Verity?"

Dead silence.

He tried again, in case somehow she hadn't heard him. "Verity? Are you there?"

A gasp.

What was going *on*? He was about to say something else when she spoke. Her voice was soft, tentative, almost as if afraid he'd hang up if she spoke too loudly. "…Alastair?"

"Yes, it's me." He didn't entirely succeed in keeping the annoyance out of his tone. Had the whole world gone mad?

But then it clicked. Of course she'd be surprised. No doubt, if Aldwyn had kept his word and sent Ian back safely, she'd know at least something about what had happened. She wouldn't know about Aldwyn because Ian hadn't known about Aldwyn, but she might know about the white prison room. Ian would likely have found her and told her everything he knew. "Verity—I've got to talk to you. I'm back, but something's gone strange and I'm hoping you can help me make sense of it."

Again with long silence. "You're…back. It's really you."

Now he was getting seriously annoyed. "Verity, what's got into you? Yes, I'm back. I don't know if Ian had a chance to tell you what happened, but I'm fine. I'm at the Encantada house. Why do you sound like you've seen a bloody ghost?"

"How did you get away?"

He narrowed his eyes. "Er—it wasn't difficult, once I woke up. What's going on? What did Ian tell you?"

He heard a couple of slow deep breaths before she spoke. "Alastair…we need to talk. Right away."

Her reaction was entirely at odds with the facts as he was aware of them. The Verity he knew would have been upset about the whole business with Ian's abduction—hell, she *had* been upset when she'd left to take Jason home the day of Aubrey's wedding. She'd have been worried that he'd apparently been held prisoner. But this didn't sound like 'upset'. This sounded like 'utterly shell-shocked.'

"Is Ian all right?" he demanded. "Did he get back safely?"

"Ian's fine." Her voice still held an odd edge.

He slumped in relief. Aldwyn had kept his word about that, at least.

"I'm serious," Verity was saying. "We need to talk. You said you're in Encantada?"

"Yes. Where are you?"

"Right now, I'm in New York. But I can come to you. Give me a couple of minutes."

What the *hell?* "Wait—you're in New York, and you're coming in a couple of *minutes?*" That wasn't possible—even if she was sitting on top of a portal, she'd still have to drive up from Sunnyvale, which would take at least twenty minutes in optimal traffic.

"It's...a long story. I guess you haven't been back to the house very long." Another pause, and when she spoke again, there was a different edge to her voice. Suspicion. "Wait."

"What?"

"Please don't take this wrong—if you really are Alastair, you'll get it when I explain things to you. But I need you to tell me something so I know it's really you."

"*What?*" He made no attempt to hide the annoyance now. "Verity, this is absurd. Why wouldn't it be me?"

"Please. Just—humor me, okay? It's starting to sound like there's a lot of stuff you don't know. But I need to know you're...you."

"Is someone pretending to be me?" Was *that* the reason Aldwyn had imprisoned him? To steal his identity and masquerade as him? But why would he want to do that?

"Not that I know of." Another sigh. "Please, just—tell me something only you and I would know."

Part of him didn't want to play along with this ridiculous charade, but it was becoming clearer that if he wanted her to give him answers, he'd need to. "Fine," he said wearily. He paused to think, and the answer came to him almost instantly. "Unless you think my evil mastermind grandmother is trying to pass herself off as me, whoever it is likely won't know what I did to Acantha in Windermere."

There was a long exhalation on the other end. "Thank God," she said, now in obvious relief. "Alastair…oh, God, it's good to hear your voice."

Stone gripped the phone so hard his hand shook. "Verity, what is going *on?* We talked a day or two ago. Why are you sounding like I've been gone for years?"

Long silence. "Let me come to you. I'll be there in a few minutes. Just…wait for me, okay?"

Before he could ask more of the dozens of questions bubbling in his head, she broke the connection.

Stone let the phone drop to the counter and plowed both hands through his hair. He had hoped Verity would shed some light on his confusion, but instead, she'd only made it worse.

He couldn't focus on anything, so instead he wandered the house while he waited for her to arrive. What he saw confused him even further. Raider's litterbox was no longer in the downstairs bathroom. His bed was neatly made, the clothes he'd tossed across it when he changed into his tuxedo before the wedding hung in the armoire. A stylish, plum-colored silk shirt that wasn't his lay draped over one of the chair arms. Dust was everywhere. The bathroom was clean and silent, the towel he'd left hanging over the shower door gone. Upstairs in the attic, his workroom was neatly arranged but even dustier than the rest of the house. Everywhere he went, he got the definite impression he was moving through a space that had not been used in a long time.

Deep within him, a slow feeling of dread began to mount.

"Alastair?"

The voice came from downstairs as he opened the attic door and headed down the narrow staircase toward the third floor.

"Where are you?"

He hurried the rest of the way down, confused. How had she got here so fast? She had a key to the house, so getting in wouldn't have been a problem, but he hadn't been wandering around long enough for her to drive from Sunnyvale. "Verity?"

She was at the foot of the stairs, looking up at him. Her eyes were huge, her mouth hanging slightly open.

"Alastair..." she whispered. And then, before he could get a good look at her, she was rushing forward, flinging her arms around him in a hug so fierce and crushing he winced.

"Verity..." The hug felt good, but the confusion didn't. He gently pushed on her shoulders. "What is going *on?*"

Before she could answer, he got his second shock.

When she'd said goodbye to him at Aubrey's wedding, she'd been wearing a black cocktail dress and heels, with her short, dark hair in a sleek bob—quite different from her usual, casual style of ripped jeans and leather jackets. Now, though, something about her had changed.

A *lot* of things about her had changed. Everything about her look, from her understated designer jeans to her deep-green blazer to her longer, swept-back hairstyle and expert makeup, looked...different. Older. She looked like a successful young executive with just enough of an offbeat streak to keep her from appearing too conventional.

She still looked like Verity, but a more confident, settled version of Verity. Despite her obvious shock, she held Stone's gaze with a steady one of her own.

"I...don't even know what to say," she whispered. "I don't know where to start."

"Let's start with why you're acting so bloody strange," he snapped. "I mean, if Ian told you what happened I can see why you were worried, but this is taking things a bit far. We last saw each other, what, a day or two ago?"

Something changed in her expression. "Oh, God. You really don't know."

"Know *what?*" He was almost shouting now, making no effort to hide his mounting exasperation. "Verity, what's going *on?*"

Her face held a gentle stillness as she reached out to take his hand in both of hers. She looked like a doctor about to deliver devastating news to a grieving family. "Alastair…it hasn't been a day or two. You've been missing for…a little over three years."

CHAPTER THREE

S TONE DIDN'T KNOW HOW LONG he stood there gaping at her before he decided he must have misheard her. "Come on, Verity, I'm not in the mood for pranks. What's really going on?"

Her face didn't change, and she was still holding his hand. "It's not a prank. You've been gone for—" Her eyes went fuzzy for a few seconds as she thought about it. "—three years and almost two months."

He pulled his hand back as if the rest of his body didn't recognize that it was his. It dropped to his side. He almost protested again until his brain filled in what little detail he had: Raider's absence, the missing litterbox, the dust around the house...

"But..." he began, and then stopped. His mind didn't seem to want to give him the right words. "How...can that be possible?" He thought about the underground chamber beneath the Surrey house, and once again his interior voice offered its opinion: *Aldwyn was down there for close to two hundred years. How is it impossible for you to have been there for three?*

But Aldwyn's a dragon!

He's also a master mage...and you're immortal...

"Alastair?"

He jerked his head up. She was still looking at him, intense but sympathetic. And why was she calling him "Alastair" now? Two days ago—*three years ago!*—she'd almost always called him "Doc."

"I—" He shook his head. "This is…I don't know what to say. How…?"

"I don't know," she said gently. "I was hoping you could fill that in." She nodded toward the sitting room. "Come on—let's sit down." Her breath hitched, and her voice shook. "I…don't know what to say either. I thought—we all thought—we'd never see you again."

He didn't move to follow. Sudden thoughts flooded his mind, too fast for him to make sense of them. So many questions, so many things he didn't know. He grasped at one: "But—if I've been gone for three years—what about the house?" It sounded absurd. Out of all the things he could possibly be worried about, *that* was the first one that came to mind?

"Come on. Please. Sit down." Verity was still trying to encourage him into the sitting room. "I know you've got a lot of questions, and I'll try to answer them the best I can, but…"

"But what?" He started moving, but slowly, as if afraid his body wouldn't obey him. His feet felt like blocks of concrete. He let her lead him to the sofa, where he slumped down.

She took the chair opposite him. "Well…before we get too far, I should call some people. They're going to want to know."

It occurred to him that she sounded every bit as shellshocked as he felt, which he supposed made sense. "Ian…"

"Ian, yeah. And Jason and Amber…Eddie and Ward…"

"Aubrey." A jolt of terror so strong it was almost physically painful struck him. "Gods, Verity, is Aubrey—"

"Aubrey's fine," she assured him quickly. "He's…kind of semi-retired now, with Susan, but he's doing great. We can talk about that later too." She let out a long breath and stared at her hands in her lap. "So many things to catch you up on." She brought her gaze up again. "Before I answer anything else, though…where *were* you? What happened? Where have you been all this time?"

A brief wave of impatient resentment hit Stone. He didn't want to talk about what he already *knew*. He wanted to find out what had happened in his absence.

Three *years!*

It sounded unbelievable—but then, a lot of things connected with him would sound unbelievable to most people. A lot could have changed in three years, and even though Verity had assured him Aubrey was all right, he still had a lot of other people in his life. She hadn't even answered his question about the house. If he'd been away that long, how did he still own it? Surely the world must think he was dead by now.

Aldwyn was going to pay for this, that was certain.

But right now, Verity had to be as confused as he was, and he owed her at least *some* explanation. "I…can't tell you much because I don't know. What did Ian tell you about what happened?"

When she answered, it was with an immediacy that made him think she still went over this stuff a lot more often than she wanted to admit. She paused to gather her thoughts and spoke as if viewing something in her mind's eye. "He came back after the wedding, looking pretty spooked and worried. He said somebody had abducted him and stuck him in a white room. He said whoever it was, they were trying to get to you."

Stone nodded wearily. "That much is true."

"He said whoever did it left you some kind of note, and that you thought you knew who it was, but then after you read it, you said you'd been wrong."

"Yes." He'd lied to Ian because Aldwyn's note had warned him about revealing anything. He wondered if that was still true—but given how easily Aldwyn had got hold of Ian, he didn't plan to test it.

Not until he tracked the dragon down, anyway.

"So, you know who did this?" She was staring hard at him now.

"I'm…not sure anymore." He hated to start off this new conversation with a lie, but he couldn't risk putting anyone in danger until he had more facts. Instead, he forged ahead, trying to distract her. "Whoever it was, though, they obviously used Ian as a way to get to me, because they knew I would seek him out."

"He was pissed when he got back. He said you lied to him—something about a ring that you said would bring you both back. You told him to put it on and grab your hand, but only he returned." She narrowed her eyes. "He thought you did it on purpose, to save him. Did you?"

"Of course I did." He answered without hesitation. "I knew the ring would only return one of us. Did he think I'd leave him there?"

She didn't answer that. "We've been looking for you. All of us have."

"All…who?"

"Me, Ian, Eddie and Ward, Gabriel…even Jason and Amber, in case there was some mundane way to track you. But none of us found anything. Not even Gabriel."

He noticed instantly that there were a couple of names missing from her list. "Did Gabriel go to Kolinsky? Madame Huan?"

Verity lowered her gaze to her lap. "Nobody's seen Madame Huan for a long time. She was one of the first ones I thought of, after you disappeared. I went to her shop to try to talk to her, but her assistant said she hasn't been back for ages. She said she was in China somewhere, and might not even be coming back at all." She looked up at him again. "Does she have anything to do with this?"

How do I even answer that? Madame Huan was a dragon, so in an abstract sense she *did* have some small connection. He knew how she felt about Aldwyn, though, assuming she hadn't lied to him. "No. She's not connected with it. I know that much. What about Kolinsky? Did Gabriel contact him?"

"I don't know. He didn't say. I couldn't—I didn't even know where he was. Jason said he'd been outside his shop once, a lot of years ago when he went with you, but he couldn't remember exactly where it was. Gabriel said he'd look into it, but never came back with anything." She shifted in her seat and glared at him. "You still didn't answer my question, though. Where *were* you all this time? Were you in that white room Ian talked about? Were you unconscious? Held prisoner somewhere?" She looked him over. "If you were a prisoner, you'd surely have known time passed, but how could you have been asleep for three years and still look exactly the same as I remember you? Hell, you're still wearing the same *clothes* you disappeared in."

Stone looked down at the tuxedo he'd forgotten he was still wearing. He ran his hands down the lapels; the fabric still felt as crisp and fresh as it had the day he'd left the Surrey house. "I...don't know exactly. I think I must have been asleep—in some kind of magical suspended animation. When I woke up, I was in that room under the Surrey house. Remember, the one we found in the catacombs?"

Her eyes widened. "You're...kidding."

"Trust me, Verity, the last thing I have any desire to do right now is kid."

"You've been under there the whole time? For three *years*?" She didn't look like she believed it. "But...we tried tracking spells. Even Gabriel did, both here and in England, and nothing ever turned up. How can that be? I don't know anybody with that kind of magic. Do you?"

"I...do," he said carefully. "And I've got no idea how long I was there. When I woke up earlier today, I felt like I'd been asleep for maybe a day at the most." He stroked his jaw. "I didn't feel hungry, I didn't need a shave...believe me, Verity, I haven't got any idea what happened. I need to do some investigation. But first, I've got so many questions for you, I don't even know where to start." The whole thing felt suddenly overwhelming. How was he going to catch up on three years of lost time? He wasn't even sure he could think of all the right questions.

"Okay." Clearly, she'd figured out that he wasn't going to say anything else about his own ordeal before he got some answers. "I'll do my best. But…please let me get in touch with the others first. It's not fair to let them go on thinking you're still missing…or worse."

"Worse…" He stared at her. "Do people think I'm dead?" He gestured around in sudden agitation. "What about the house? What about the University? How did—"

She raised both hands in a placating gesture. "Calm down. It's okay. We—the people who know you best—didn't think you were dead. Not just because of what Ian told us, but because…well, by now we're pretty convinced it's not that easy to kill you these days. And as for everybody else…we'll explain it. But nobody thinks you're dead. Can you settle for that for now, until I get everybody together so we can do this all at once?"

He didn't want to—he wanted her to answer all his questions *now*—but that was neither practical nor kind. "Okay," he said wearily. "Okay. I'll do my best. But you've got to answer two questions for me. Then I'll hold on to the rest."

She looked skeptical. "What are they?"

He didn't want to ask them, but he had to know. "What happened to Raider?"

To his surprise, a smile lit up her face. "He's fine. Doing great. I kind of semi-adopted him, and I've got another cat now too. He's living in my place in San Francisco. I'm sure he'll be happy to get back to his real home again."

Stone was surprised at the relief that flooded him. Odd what shock did to one's priorities. "I'm so glad to hear that."

"What's the other question?"

He swallowed hard. This one was even harder than the last one. "Has anyone—well—died while I was away?"

Her smile grew kind. "No, not that I'm aware of. Everybody's fine, at least in our little group."

"Okay." He stared at his hands again, feeling like he should do something—say something—but his mind and body refused to co-operate. Finally, he managed, "Go ahead, I guess. Call them." Another memory surfaced. "But—wait a moment. I do have one other question."

Verity had already pulled her phone from her bag. "What?"

"How did you get here so fast? You said you were in New York—what were you doing there, by the way?"

"Ah. Right. It's definitely going to take a while to get you caught up. A lot of things have happened since you disappeared. I was in New York because I've been doing a lot of work with some of the people in Bron's family. Remember Bron?"

"Of course." He narrowed his eyes. "What kind of work?"

She flashed the kind smile again. "I promise—we'll answer all your questions. But I need to make these calls. Tell you what—in answer to your other question about how I got here so fast, why don't you go downstairs to the library. I'm guessing you haven't been down there yet since you got back?"

What was she on about? "Er…no. Hadn't made it down there yet."

"Go check it out."

"…All right. But—"

"Just go look, then come back up. You'll see." She shifted her gaze down to her phone screen, clearly indicating she wasn't going to answer anything else until she finished.

Stone rose heavily to his feet. When was the world going to stop feeling like he'd wandered into some kind of funhouse? This was definitely *not* fun.

Three *years*.

A lot of things have happened since you disappeared, she'd said.

He briefly considered going back upstairs and trying to go back to sleep. Maybe when he woke up, the world would make more sense.

But he didn't do that, because even now, in his current confused state, his innate curiosity was stronger than his disorientation. He glanced at Verity, who appeared to be waiting for him to leave before she made her first call, and trudged out of the room to the stairs leading to his basement library.

It should have been dark down there, but as he descended the stairs he spotted a faint light flickering in the half-closed doorway. He approached it with care. Was someone doing a ritual down here? Were those candles? "Hello?" he called.

No answer.

He crept forward and pushed the door the rest of the way open. "Bloody *hell...*" he murmured.

Most of the space looked the same as he'd left it: the large inlaid circle on the floor, the overflowing bookshelves, the big desk and comfortable leather sofa.

But the glowing, multicolored disc that floated on the far side of the room had most certainly *not* been there before.

Even at his most absent-minded, he would have noticed a portal in his basement.

He stopped in the doorway, gripping the frame and unable to tear his gaze from the shifting pastel colors.

If he hadn't truly believed it before, he did now.

This wasn't a dream, and Verity hadn't lied to him.

He *had* been away for a long time, and in his absence, someone had built a teleportation portal in his home. The one he'd been in the process of building himself when a ritual had destroyed his efforts.

He approached it, shifting to magical sight to examine it more closely. It looked no different from the ones he was already intimately familiar with in the Surrey house crypt, Caventhorne, and the London house.

Who had built a portal in his basement? And why?

"You see it now?" came a soft voice from the doorway. "How I got here so fast?"

He dragged his gaze away from the swirling colors to find Verity standing in the doorway, still sporting her kindly, understanding smile.

"You've...built a portal in my basement."

She chuckled. "Not me. Not *that* much has changed—I'm still no good at that kind of magic."

"Then...who?"

"It was kind of a group effort. Gabriel, Ian—he's gotten to be a real whiz at portal science—Eddie and Ward..."

Stone staggered back a step, shifting back and forth between Verity and the portal. "But...why? There's already a portal in Sunnyvale." Another frisson of dread shot through him. "It's still there, isn't it?"

"The portal's still there, yeah. But we all figured it would be...easier to move around if we had a private one here, and this seemed like the best place to do it." Her brow furrowed. "You...don't mind, do you? I know you don't need to use one anymore, but..."

Being angry about his friends constructing a portal at his house was the last thing on Stone's mind, which was currently reeling. He took several deep breaths, recognizing that if he didn't get himself under control soon, he'd be doing a lot of reeling today.

"I—" He needed a diversion, so he indicated the phone in her hand. "Did you make the calls? Are they coming?"

"Yeah. Most of them should be coming through any time now—Eddie and Ward, and Ian. Jason and Amber will get here when they can, since they can't use the portal. I didn't tell anybody you were back yet—just that I had something important I needed to talk about." She grinned. "I think this one's worth one of your reveals, don't you?"

Stone barely heard her because another thought had just hit him, staggering him back again. He suspected that would be happening a lot today. "Gods...I just realized—"

"What?"

"Jason and Amber. Their child—"

She smiled. "Yeah. Their little girl's three now. I'll let them tell you the rest."

"So...I missed..." Somewhere deep within him, his anger at Aldwyn began to bubble again. He drove it down with effort. This wasn't the time.

But he's taken so much from me...

"Yeah," she said gently. "Everything went fine, though...partly thanks to you. They'll always be grateful to you for what you did when Amber had her accident." She pointed at the portal. "Anyway, if you want to have your big 'ta-da!' moment, you'd better get out of here before people start showing up."

Normally, Stone would have relished the chance to surprise his friends. But now, as the shocks kept raining down on him like blows in a boxing match, he could barely compel himself to move.

Verity gently took his arm. "Come on. Let's go upstairs. Are you sure you're not hungry? I don't think there's any food here, but we could get something delivered. Probably should anyway, if everybody's going to be here."

"You...do whatever you think is best," he said in a dull tone. "I'm sorry—this is all...a bit overwhelming, suddenly."

She stopped and pulled him into a hug. "I know...God, I can't even imagine how it must be for you. But I'm just so glad you're back. We never stopped trying to find you, but after all this time I don't think any of us thought we were ever going to see you again."

"I'm sorry..." he said again. He returned the hug, but then pulled back. "Come on. Let's go."

R. L. KING

CHAPTER FOUR

THEY STARTED ARRIVING FAST AFTER THAT. Stone waited on the second floor, where he could hear what was going on downstairs but no one could see him.

Eddie and Ward showed up first. "What's this about, Verity?" Eddie asked, the confusion obvious in his voice. "Is somethin' wrong?"

"Let's wait for Ian to get here. I'd like to wait for Jason and Amber too, but they can't make it for at least an hour, and I don't think I can last that long."

"*Is* something wrong, then?" came Ward's soft, even voice.

"No, nothing's wrong, I promise. Have a seat in the living room. I know it's late for you, but I ordered some pizzas and drinks."

Stone, from his hiding place, glanced at the clock in the hall. It was nearly five, which meant it would be the middle of the night in England.

"Hey, Verity, what's up?"

Ian.

Stone's whole body tensed, then relaxed, at the sound of his son's voice. Verity hadn't been lying to him—Ian was fine. He sounded as confused as Eddie had, but well. Thank the gods Aldwyn had kept his word about *that*, at least.

"Okay," Verity said after she'd got them all seated. "Sorry to take all of you away from whatever you were doing—"

"Fast asleep for a change," Eddie muttered. "But that's all right."

"This will be worth waking up for, trust me."

"Come on, V—what's going on? You're acting weird." That was Ian. Stone still couldn't see them where they were seated, but the voices carried well enough so he could follow the conversation with ease. Even though, by his reckoning, he'd heard them all a day or two ago, they still warmed him.

His friends, and his son, had never given up on him. They'd dropped everything and come running when Verity called.

There was a pause, and Stone could almost picture Verity gathering herself, trying to figure out how she wanted to word what she had to say.

"I have some good news," she finally said. "Some *really* good news."

"What is it?" Ian asked. "I could use some good news."

"Somebody…called me today. Somebody I hadn't heard from in a long time."

"Who?" Ward asked.

"Did Madame Huan finally get in touch with you?" Eddie. "Did somebody find out something about where Stone might be?"

"Not Madame Huan. But…you could say that." Stone didn't miss the fond amusement in her tone.

"Wait—somebody might know where Dad is?" Ian's voice was sharp and full of excitement. "Who was it?"

Stone couldn't draw out the suspense anymore, and that was probably the best cue he was likely to get. He descended the stairs and stopped in the sitting-room doorway. "That would be me," he said softly. "Hello, everyone."

Normally, he would have been delighted at the sea of gaping faces and wide-open eyes staring at him from their various spots around the room. Except for Verity, who was smiling, they looked like a gallery of gasping guppies. Nobody said a word.

"Come on—nothing to say? I'm disappointed. I would have expected some kind of cheeky quip from you, at least, Eddie. You're slipping."

"Uh—" Ward began.

Eddie opened his mouth, then closed it again.

Ian was the first to find his voice. "...Dad?" he whispered.

Stone inclined his head. "Hello, Ian. It's good to see you—even though it feels like I just saw you a day or two ago."

Ian shot a sharp glance at Verity, and then he was on his feet, rushing to engulf Stone in a crushing hug. So hard, in fact, that it hurt. Unlike Verity, Ian had significant upper-body strength, and he was using all of it.

"Oi—I'm glad to see you too, but don't break my ribs!"

Ian broke the hug and glared at him. "I should kick your ass," he growled, but his eyes glittered and his voice shook. "What the hell was that stunt you pulled with the ring?"

The tension held for a few seconds, during which Stone thought his son might do just that.

Verity broke it by stepping in. "Come on, you two. You can fight later if you want. Maybe we can sell tickets."

Eddie had stood too; his eyes were still wide, his face as pale as if he'd just seen a ghost. "Stone...mate...gods *damn* it's good to see you!" He hurried over and gripped Stone in a bro-hug, clapping him on the back several times as if trying to verify it was really him and he was really there. "We thought..."

"I know." Stone was surprised that *his* voice shook too. It was beginning to sink in that he truly *had* been gone for three years instead of a day or two, and also how his friends must be feeling to see him again when they'd finally begun to accept that they might not. "It's good to see you too, Eddie. All of you. I'm glad to be back."

Then they were all talking at once, mostly with versions of *where have you been?* and *how did you get back?* and *what have you been doing all this time?*

Stone raised his hands to stop them. "Listen—I know you're all burning with curiosity, but I don't really want to tell this story multiple times. Verity's told me Jason and Amber will be here at some point soon. Suppose you answer some of *my* questions first, because I've got a lot of them, and I'll tell you my story when they get here. Or at least as much of it as I *can* tell."

None of them looked happy about it, but they grumbled and agreed, settling back to their seats.

Stone looked them over. None of them were taking their eyes off him, almost as if they expected him to fade away if they let him out of their sight.

Eddie and Ward looked mostly as he remembered them, which made sense, since they were older and three years' change wouldn't be as obvious with them. Eddie had his hair cut a bit shorter and hadn't shaved, but he sported his familiar West Ham jersey and baggy cargo pants, while Ward wore a neat button-down shirt and corduroy trousers and didn't look like he'd been roused from a sound sleep. Aside from possibly a touch more gray in their hair, they were the same old friends Stone remembered.

Ian had changed the most. He'd be close to twenty-five now, Stone realized. He was obviously still keeping up his rigorous workouts, but he'd filled out the last of his teenage slimness to a more mature, powerful frame. His hair was a little longer, worn stylishly swept back from his face, intricate full sleeve tattoos covered both his arms, and artful stubble framed his sharp jawline. Most obvious of all to Stone, though, there was a new seriousness to him—a new calm that had replaced the carefree hedonist he'd been three years ago. Stone wondered how much of that was because of him.

I've missed three more years of my son's life because of you, Aldwyn. You're going to pay for that.

The pizza delivery person broke the tension by ringing the doorbell. Verity hurried off, and a few moments later returned with three large pizzas and several frosty bottles of soda and beer. "Sit down," she told Stone, waving him to the place of honor in his favorite chair. "Just...ask us what you want, and let us be happy that you're here."

When they began opening the boxes, Stone realized he *was* hungry. He grabbed a pizza slice and a bottle of beer and tried to corral his madly spinning thoughts.

"Sorry it's not Guinness," Verity said. "The pizza place downtown doesn't have it."

"That's the least of my concerns right now." He scanned the group and latched onto a question. "Tell me what's happened, from your side. Starting at the day of the wedding."

They all looked at each other, almost as if trying to decide who would tell the story. Finally, Ian set his slice down and began. "As soon as I put that ring on and touched the stone, I appeared exactly where I'd been trying to go before, at the Surrey place. It was like nothing had changed...except you weren't there. I realized what you'd done to me the second I started to fade out and you didn't." He glared. "Why did you do it, Dad?"

"You know the answer to that."

"You shouldn't have."

"Why not? You're my son. And I thought I'd have a better chance of figuring out how to get away from that place than you would."

"How did that work out for you?"

Verity started to say something, but didn't.

Stone shook his head. "Ian, I'm not going to argue with you about it. What's done is done. What happened after that?"

Ian held the glare for long enough to establish that the subject would come up again later, then dropped it. "As soon as I was sure you weren't with me, I texted Gabriel and went to find Verity."

"By that point, Aubrey and Susan had already left, so we didn't have to tell them right away," Verity said. "Once Ian told me what happened, we got everybody together—Ian, Eddie, Ward, and eventually Gabriel—and tried to figure out what might have happened."

"Didn't get far wit' that, though," Eddie grumbled. "Ian didn't 'ave anything for us to go on. 'E didn't know who took 'im, where 'e was, or anythin'."

"You know, don't you, Dad?" Ian demanded. "You know who it was. When I gave you that note, you acted like you already knew who it was from."

"I was wrong, though," Stone said, mindful once again of Aldwyn's admonition. To change the subject, he said, "What did you do then?"

"We did a tracking ritual," Verity said. "We figured with Gabriel's power and Ian's blood, we could find you."

"But you didn't."

Ian shook his head. "Gabriel said he told you I was on another dimension, but he couldn't trace which one." The glare returned. "And he said something else, too, after I told him what happened."

"What's that?"

"That he didn't give you that ring."

Oh, bugger. Stone had forgotten about that. He didn't blame himself much for it, though—he had so many things running through his mind that it was a wonder he remembered his own name at the moment. "No. He didn't."

"He said he didn't know anything about it. So who *did* give it to you?"

Damn. Here it was. They were all looking at him now, serious and curious.

"I...can't tell you that."

"*What?*" Verity's glare joined Ian's. "What do you mean, you can't tell us? You know, don't you? *Somebody* had to give it to you."

Suddenly, what little hunger Stone had felt deserted him. He dropped his half-eaten slice of pizza back to his plate and bowed his head. "I'm sorry, but I can't tell you."

"Why *not?*" Ian demanded. "Why is it such a secret?"

"It's...a long story." He hated to speak so abruptly to his son this soon after their reunion, but it couldn't be helped. "I'm sorry, Ian, but I can't and that's all there is to it. Do you want to hear the rest of the story?"

"I do," Ward said.

Stone shot him a grateful glance. "So, After Gabriel and I did our tracking ritual, I went looking for someone who could help me."

"And you found someone?" Eddie asked. "Who?"

"I can't say." A sudden idea occurred to him. He turned back to face Ian. "Did you talk to Gabriel about this at all?"

"Yeah, of course. He told me about the ritual—that he thought I was being held on another dimension, but something was blocking him from figuring out exactly where."

"He didn't say anything about anyone else who might know?"

Ian shook his head. "He said because I'm your son and he and I have a relationship, you two would have been the best ones to try it."

"Are you talking about Kolinsky, or Madame Huan?" Verity asked. "Did one of them give you that ring? Or Mr. Harrison?"

"Who's Mr. Harrison?" Ian narrowed his eyes.

"A friend," Stone said, distracted. "You don't know him—and no, I'm not talking about any of them. Harrison hasn't turned up again, has he?" he asked Verity.

"Haven't heard a word from him since before you disappeared."

That didn't surprise him. Even if Harrison had tracked down the Calanarians who'd been trying to create a portal to Earth, and re-established the link between the Nexus and the Obsidian, he wouldn't necessarily have sought out Stone unless he had a reason to—and would have been even less likely to look for Verity.

"So, wait," Verity said. "You didn't get the ring from Harrison, Kolinsky, Madame Huan, or Gabriel? Do you know *other* powerful mages you haven't told us about?"

They just wouldn't let this go, would they? He bowed his head. "Verity, please. There are reasons I can't tell you. Ian, I suggest you ask Gabriel about it."

"He knows?"

"He doesn't know everything, but he might be able to lead you in the right direction, if he'll tell you anything at all. Not that it will matter, honestly. You don't know the people involved." Stone hated this. He'd barely been back for a couple of hours, and already he was being evasive again, pushing his friends away when he needed them the most. One more thing Aldwyn would have to answer for. "Please—keep going. Tell me what happened on your end, and then I'll answer your questions once Jason and Amber get here."

All four of them exchanged glances, and he could tell they were all frustrated with him.

Ward broke the tension. "I think we should do what he asks. I for one am glad to have him back, and this whole situation has got to be stressful for him, too. Perhaps he needs a bit of time to…decompress…before we start peppering him with questions."

Stone gave him another grateful look. "Thank you, Ward. That's exactly what I need. Come on, you lot—I imagine a lot of things have changed in three years. Tell me about them." He swallowed. "Tell me about the bits of your lives I've missed."

They looked like they might protest, but that last bit put things in perspective for them. They looked at each other again and settled back into their seats.

"I don't even know where to start," Verity said.

"I'll start." Eddie took a long pull from his beer and indicated himself and Ward. "Not much 'as changed wit' Ward and me. Without all the magical shenanigans you kept gettin' up to, Stone, we went back to doin' what we do best—bein' magical boffins, lookin' after Caventhorne, and gettin' used to the new world."

"New world...Oh, bloody hell, I almost forgot. The Change." Stone had been so focused on his own problems, he'd completely forgotten that he and Verity had finally discovered the source of the odd astral changes that had been sweeping across the world, affecting people with magical backgrounds who hadn't inherited the Talent. He focused on Eddie and Ward. "Did they ever figure out how to counteract it?"

It wasn't they who spoke, though, but Verity. "There is no counteracting it. It's reality now. And I wouldn't say that too loudly outside here. A lot of the Changelings would take offense."

Stone had so many questions. He bowed his head in frustration, jamming his hands into his hair. He felt as if he were trying to corral all the heads of a hydra, and every time he got hold of one, a dozen more writhed away from him.

"No," he said firmly. "Don't tell me about that yet. There'll be time enough for me to discover all the things that have happened in the world at large during my absence. To keep my sanity, let's stick with what's happened to you lot specifically." He swept his gaze around the group. "Unless any of them turned up among our little group."

"One," Verity said softly. "But let's hold off on that."

Stone almost asked her why, but decided not to. He wasn't going anywhere—he had time to find out. He gave his hair a final swipe and wondered if anything remained in his liquor cabinet. He was definitely going to need something stronger than beer before this night was over. "Okay. One at a time." He pointed at Verity. "You first. I'm...still getting used to how different you look."

She smiled. "Is that good or bad?"

"You look…brilliant. More…mature. Settled. Like you're ready to take on the world."

"I guess I kind of have, in a way."

"Still working with Scuro, and Hezzie?"

"Yes to both. Our shop's doing well…" She looked around the group again. "Really well. So well we've…expanded."

"Expanded? That's good news, right?"

"It is. But…Alastair…A Passage to India is gone. Marta met someone—another mundane from a magical family—and decided to go back home to England. They're married now."

Stone stared at her. "Bloody hell…" He remembered the portal keeper had mentioned the possibility of returning home, but he never thought she'd actually *do* it.

"Yeah." She spoke gently, but then smiled. "She's doing great. They did some traveling, and then they opened up a little pub in the Leeds area. I've been there once—it's nice. They're both happy."

Stone stared at his hands. So many times, he'd planned to stop in and chat with Marta on his way to use the portal, but then he'd learned the ley-line method and mostly stopped using it, and now she'd moved on. His guilt faded, though, as he remembered what else Verity had said. "Wait…you've expanded, you said?"

"Yeah. Somebody had to take over the space, since we couldn't just let the portal be in a mundane business. So Hezzie and I opened a branch shop down in Sunnyvale. We've hired some more employees, and made some changes so the portal's accessible to mages at all hours without needing to go through the shop." She smiled at Ian. "Ian and Gabriel set up a separate dedicated portal between the two, so we can travel back and forth. Ian's gotten to be quite a whiz with portal stuff."

"Is that right?" Stone looked at his son with new respect. Dedicated portals between two locations were both easier and less expensive to construct than standard portals, and were safer to dismantle if necessary, but they still took a lot of care and knowledge.

Ian shrugged. "What can I say? I've always been good at math, and when Gabriel started teaching me, it just sort of...clicked."

"That's brilliant. So, Verity, between that and the portal here, you've got more travel options now."

Her smile turned to a wry grin. "More than you know. I've been working a lot more with Bron's family, and they've got private portals all over the country. They kind of made me an honorary family member after I helped them out with some things, so I have access to most of them now."

Stone shook his head in wonder. "I'm impressed." It was more than that, though. Verity's entire demeanor had changed along with her updated style of dress. Even though, by his reckoning, it had only been a couple of days since he'd seen her last, in the space of that time she'd developed a confidence and poise he'd never noticed in her before. She'd always been confident, but now it was a lot more obvious.

See what getting out from under your shadow for three years has done for her, came a sudden, bittersweet thought, but he quickly banished it. Whatever had happened had obviously been good for her, and that was all that mattered.

"So," he continued, "you're still working with Hezzie, and you said before you're still healing for Scuro. And now you're working with Bron's family too. How do you have any time to sleep?" He kept his voice light, but it was a serious question.

"It's hard sometimes, but that's okay. I'm happy. That's not even all I'm doing. I'm also still working with Jason when he needs a magical touch for his cases, and..." She glanced at Eddie.

Stone didn't miss the look. "And what?"

"Well...remember before, when I was all hot and bothered about trying to organize the mages?"

"Yes..."

"Well…that's sort of happening now."

"What?" Stone sat up straighter, shifting his gaze between her, Eddie, and Ward.

"Not like I was trying to do before," she said hastily. "No council telling us what to do or anything like that. No magical law enforcement—not formally, at least. But there is sort of a…central organization now. Or a few of them."

"What?" Stone hated to repeat himself, but her words had shocked him. How the hell had they got themselves organized in three years? Herding a roomful of cats with ADD would be easier than trying to organize mages. "Why? Did something happen?"

"The Changelings," Ward said. He spoke with his usual calm. "They're here to stay now, and there are quite a number of them."

"And a lot of them don't like us very much," Verity added. "The ones who know about us, anyway."

"Why not?"

She shrugged. "Because, aside from other Changelings, we're the only ones who can see them, and we have the power to mess with them. You said you didn't want to talk too much about them yet, and that probably makes sense. It will really be better if we show you anyway."

"That's fine." Stone waved it off. "But tell me about these…mage organizations."

"Don't get yer pants in a bunch, Stone," Eddie said. "Like Verity said before, they're not any kind of governin' body, and it's not like anybody has to register or anythin' like that. They're more…advisory."

"Advisory?"

"Yeah, and they provide assistance to mages if they want it, that kind of thing."

Stone narrowed his eyes. "Are they working with the mundanes? Verity, you mentioned law enforcement?"

Verity shook her head. "Not formally. I mean, a few of us do—like I work with Leo Blum sometimes, like you used to. But it's all very under-the-table. Don't worry—we mages are still keeping our secrets, and everybody likes it that way."

"Think of it more like what was goin' on at Caventhorne before you stepped out," Eddie said. "Central clearin' 'ouse for magical information, gettin' help wit' magical problems, that sort of thing. And a little bit o' keepin' mages in line, but nothin' formal."

Stone wasn't sure how he felt about all that, but this wasn't the time to get into it. "Okay..."

"Oh, one other thing," Eddie said. "They do testin'."

"Testing?"

"You know, to determine magical ability. Mundanes who know about magic can bring their kids in to get tested, to find out if they have the Talent. If they do, the organizations can 'elp 'em get trainin' if they want it."

Stone made a noncommittal noise.

"They also test for levels of magical ability," Ward said. "We're still working on it, but we're trying to put a classification system in place, to help gauge relative power levels."

"You're involved in this?" Stone glanced at them in surprise.

"Not directly," Eddie said. "But in the UK it does go through Caventhorne, so we get the reports and they listen to our suggestions."

"What about in the US?"

"There are a couple of branches," Verity said. "One in New York, and one in Los Angeles."

Stone let his breath out. "Bloody hell. Things *have* changed. I'd never have thought three years would make such a difference." An irrational thought poked its way in: *I go away, and everything changes.* But that was ridiculous, and fairly conceited. He had a lot of power, yes, but he'd mostly kept to himself with regard to magical society as a whole. Most of the more powerful mages did.

"Yeah, the whole Changeling business really tipped things over the edge. We'll talk later about that."

"Fair enough." Stone cast about for another topic, and remembered something else Verity had told him. "Ian, I want to know what's going on with you, too, but before you tell me, I need to know something else. How am I not dead?"

"What do you mean?" Verity tilted her head.

Ian got it, though, and grinned. "Oh. Right. You can mostly thank Gabriel and me for that."

"How so?"

"I knew you weren't dead. Whoever took me, they went to a lot of trouble to do it so they could grab you, so I was sure they didn't just want to kill you. And Verity told me about how hard you are to kill—I'm really curious about that, by the way, and no, I didn't tell Gabriel—so that made me even more sure."

"Yes, and…?"

"Well…we figured if you weren't dead but nobody knew where you were, people would start thinking something was up if you didn't make a few appearances."

Stone was beginning to get it. "Wait… you've been… *impersonating* me?"

"Yep. Mostly Gabriel, and not very often. I've been taking care of keeping all your bills paid, maintaining the properties, taxes, all that mundane kind of stuff. Fortunately you've got enough money to keep everything going pretty much forever, so finances weren't a problem. Gabriel used illusions to impersonate you to the University. As far as they know, you're on an extended research trip-slash-sabbatical to travel around the world exploring occult stuff. He connects with them every few months so they know you're still alive. You're…kind of in limbo as far as your employment situation goes. They haven't fired you, but you're in some kind of inactive status. It's the best we could do, since we couldn't exactly show up and teach your classes."

"Bloody hell…" Stone murmured.

"Yeah, you owe those two big," Eddie said. "We 'elped keep up the pretense, but they did most of the work."

"It wasn't all out of love," Ian said with an arch smile. "If you disappear and the world thinks you're dead, I'm the prime suspect, and the rest of these guys are right up there at the top of the list. We didn't think you wanted a bunch of cops tromping through your properties."

"No…I did not." The words came out sounding distracted, which wasn't surprising. "I…don't believe all this."

"Trust me—I'm glad you're back and we can hand this all back to you."

Stone let his breath out in a long, slow exhalation, then shook his head. "Sorry—I'm still trying to get my mind around how much I'm going to need to catch up on. I'm still feeling like I went to sleep for a day or so, but…obviously that's not the case. There's not just what's going on with all of you, but what's happening in the world…current events…history…"

"There's time for that," Verity said gently. "Take it easy. There's no reason you have to make an appearance to the world yet. You don't even have to tell the University you're back until you're ready. And you've got all of us to lean on."

"Yeah," Ian said. "But I still think you know who's responsible for this."

Stone was spared answering by a knock at the door.

Verity popped up. "That will be Jason." She hurried out, and a moment later returned.

Stone had already grown used to being stared at in frank shock, so this time wasn't any different. Jason and Amber stopped in the doorway, mouths hanging open in astonishment.

"…Al?" Jason ventured, almost as if expecting him to fade away like a ghost.

"Hello, Jason. Amber. It's good to see you. Apparently I've been gone a while."

"Holy...*shit*. Al." Jason strode over and gripped him in a hug almost as hard as Ian's. "It's really you." He pulled back and glared at Verity. "Why didn't you tell me?"

She shot him an impish grin. "I figured it would have more impact this way."

Jason barely paid her any attention and immediately focused back on Stone. "But—how—? What—?" He still looked like someone had punched him in the stomach.

"Eloquent as always," Stone said dryly.

"Sit down, you two," Verity said. "There's pizza left, and more beers and soda."

Everybody shifted around to make room for the pair of stunned newcomers, and Stone took a moment to look them over. Jason was obviously still hitting the gym; his dusty-blond hair was a little shorter now and he'd grown a short, neat beard. Amber, despite giving birth three years ago, still maintained her athletic frame. She, too, had a shorter hairstyle. Neither of them looked any older, and, unlike Verity, their styles of dress hadn't changed appreciably.

"Tell us what happened," Jason said. "We've all been looking for you for three years. Where have you been?"

Quickly, Stone caught them up with the same information he'd told the others. "But enough about me. I want to know about *you*. I'm so sorry I missed the birth of your daughter. I've got three birthday and Christmas presents to catch up with, don't I? Tell me about her. What did you name her? Where is she now?"

"She's home with a sitter," Amber said. "But...Alastair, there's something else we need to tell you."

Stone tensed. "She's all right, isn't she? There wasn't any lingering difficulty from—"

She raised her hands. "No, no. Nothing like that. She's fine. She's perfect. But..."

"She's not alone," Jason said with a grin.

"What?"

"She has a little brother," Amber said.

Stone slumped back in his seat, feeling like he'd just had the wind knocked out of him. Again. "You've—got another one?"

"It's been three years," Jason said. "So yeah, two." He pulled out his phone, fiddled with it, and offered it to Stone. "That's our son, Jaden Carl Thayer. He just turned a year old a couple months ago."

Stone took the phone with a shaking hand. The image showed a blond toddler with blue eyes, standing unsteadily while holding on to the edge of a table. He held a stuffed cat in his other hand, and wore a tiny Thayer Investigations polo shirt.

"Bloody...hell..." he whispered. He hadn't even got his mind around his old friend having *one* child, and now he had two. He made another mental tick on his list of things he'd have words with Aldwyn about. The list was getting long.

Jason took the phone back. "So...that's our son." He swiped the screen and handed it over. "And...this is our daughter."

Stone's hand shook even more. This time, the image was of a little girl with medium-brown hair, grinning at the camera. She wore sweatpants and a T-shirt with a smiling dinosaur on it, and faced the photographer with the confident gaze of a child who'd never known anything but love. He thought back—not so long ago, by his reckoning—to when he'd used his magic to heal this child's injuries while she was still in the womb following Amber's car accident near Truckee. And now, here she was, alive and well and already three years old.

A twinge of regret surprised him. He'd never made any secret that he wasn't fond of small children, and his jokes about not changing diapers hadn't actually been jokes. But this was different. This child likely wouldn't be here without him, which forged a certain connection between them. "What's her name?" he asked, still staring at the photo.

Jason and Amber exchanged glances. "Her name's Alice. Alice Harte Thayer," Jason said softly.

"And yes, because you're too polite to ask, we named her after you," Amber added with a smile. "It was my idea, actually, since she wouldn't be here without you. I would have insisted even if Jase wasn't onboard with it. But fortunately he thought it was a great idea."

Stone felt as if someone had just hit him with a baseball bat. He looked down at the little girl's bright-eyed, smiling face, then back at his two friends. "You…"

"Yeah." Jason's voice was rough. "Yeah, we did. Not even gonna make a joke about it, and don't you either, okay?"

"I…wouldn't dream of it." He swallowed and handed the phone over. "I…don't know what to say. I'm honored."

"But he still won't change diapers," Verity said with a grin.

"That…is true. But I *am* honored."

Amber mirrored Verity's grin. "Don't worry—nobody's expecting you to."

"Ah, so I'm good enough to save their lives, but not good enough to change their nappies?" He swept his hand across his forehead in a mock (or possibly not so mock) gesture of relief. "But seriously, they're beautiful, you two. I'm just sorry I missed so much of their lives. I take it the agency's still doing well?"

"Really well," Jason said. "We've moved to a bigger office and hired a couple more employees."

"Brilliant. I assume Gina is still working for you…?"

"Oh, yeah. Our favorite catgirl's still around."

"She's not the receptionist anymore, though," Amber said. "Jason promoted her to doing records and research full-time, and she loves it."

"When she's not busy organizing the Changelings," Verity said.

"Wait, what?" Stone shifted his attention from Jason and Amber to her. "Did you say organizing the—"

"Yep. That's something it's probably better to show you than tell you about, but she's big in the Changeling community around here now."

"Community? I take it there are a lot more of them now."

"Oh, yeah. Like I told you before, a lot's changed while you've been away. There are quite a few of them, and most of them have gravitated toward some of the larger cities. There are whole neighborhoods now that are mostly Changeling."

"Not that we mundanes would notice," Jason said. "Though it's not hard for even us to tell something's different about the areas where they congregate."

"Wait," Stone said as he remembered something Verity had mentioned before. "You said before there was one in our little group."

This time, all of them exchanged glances. But it was Jason who spoke. "Yeah."

"Well...don't keep me in suspense. Who is it?"

He tapped his phone. "Jaden."

"*What?*" Stone thought he'd misheard. "Your son?"

"Yeah," Verity said. "I was the one who noticed. When they invited me to meet him at the hospital, naturally I took a look with magical sight so I could tell them what color his aura was."

"So...they can be *born* that way? I thought it was like a virus—something that has to be caught."

"That's the way it was at first," Eddie said. "But we've learned a lot more about it now. Parents with magical blood can pass it on to their kids if they were exposed, even if they don't get it themselves."

Stone shifted to magical sight and scanned the group. All their auras looked the same as he remembered, with no sign of any Changeling overlays. "So...you two never got it, but your child did. But only one?"

"Yeah." Amber sipped her beer and snagged another slice of cold pizza. "We got them checked out. Alice is one-eighth shifter, which doesn't mean much. She's a little stronger and tougher than the average kid, and her sense of smell is a lot better, which can be really frustrating for a little kid, but she's not a Changeling."

"Probably because I'm the one with the magical heritage," Jason said. "Since I'm a guy and it passes through the female line in our family, Jaden got the magic blood but not the talent."

Stone found it amusing to listen to Jason, who'd always been the most stubbornly mundane of their group, talking about magical heritage like an expert. "So...what's your son's gift? Did he get some bearish quality that isn't related to being a shifter?"

Verity chuckled. "That would have made sense, wouldn't it? But no."

"He's...kind of a wolf," Amber said.

"What do you mean, *kind of* a wolf? Like a shifter wolf?"

"Not exactly," Jason said. "I mean, I gotta take V's word for it because I can't see it, but from what she tells me, he's...something between a dog and a wolf. It's hard for me to get my mind around it, but Amber says she can smell it too."

"Also, he's not like a shifter because he doesn't shift," Amber said. "He's all wolf, all the time."

Stone frowned, remembering the young homeless boy he and Verity had encountered at the abandoned house in Minnesota. He'd been a wolf too, using his Changeling abilities to protect his mundane family from threats. "That's one thing I don't quite understand yet about the Changelings. From what I remember, their Change is somehow connected to their personality. Is that no longer true?"

"No, it's still true," Verity said. "Almost all of the ones I've heard of fit—like Gina, who's crazy curious and became a cat, or somebody who likes to collect stuff becoming a goblin or some kind of bird."

"But what about babies, then? Was your son a wolf from birth, or did it manifest later?"

Amber grinned. "Nah, he came out furry. Well, Verity wasn't there at the actual birth, but she saw him when he was a couple hours old, and she spotted it then."

"That's fascinating. So...it's possible that Changeling children can give us some sort of insight into their personalities practically from birth? I don't suppose he's old enough to test that hypothesis."

"That's our Al." Jason mirrored his wife's grin. "He thinks babies are just lumps of clay until they're old enough to go to college."

"Oi, I'm not *that* bad. But you're telling me a one-year-old has enough of a personality that you can tell he fits with being a wolf Changeling?"

"He has a lot of personality," Amber said. "You should hear him cry. It does kind of sound like a howl."

"That's...quite all right. I'll take your word for it."

Verity laughed. "Don't count on that paper yet, Alastair. But seriously, there probably *is* room for study. Some of what I've been hearing from Caventhorne suggests that the small percentage of Changelings who *don't* do well with the Change are the ones whose manifestation *doesn't* fit their personality."

"Like Michele Berry."

"Who?" They were all looking at him in confusion.

"Oh. Right. It's been three years for you. My student, who committed suicide because she couldn't cope with being a supernatural seductress."

That sobered everyone quickly. "Yeah..." Verity said, bowing her head. "It's getting better, though. There are systems in place now among the Changeling community to help them deal with it. Most of them have changed now, but every now and then a pocket of people who weren't exposed turns up. And of course new ones are always being born."

Stone slumped back in his chair. Suddenly, he felt a deep exhaustion that had nothing to do with his three-year sleep. "This is all…overwhelming. So much has changed…"

"Yeah," Verity said. "For us, too. But we'll get through this. We can help you get caught up on what you've missed."

"And you can tell us about who was responsible for this," Ian said firmly. "Because I've got a few things I want to say to them."

Apparently, there was no chance his son was going to let this go. "I do too," he said carefully. "But first, I need to be sure I'm right. I've got to check on a few things."

"Why can't you just tell us what you know?" Jason asked. "It's pretty obvious you've got some strong suspicions about who's behind it."

"I…do," he admitted. "I'll tell you that much. But what I *can't* tell you is anything else. Not yet, anyway. This is…complicated."

"Are we doing this again?" Ian frowned. "Dad, even before you disappeared, you've been keeping stuff from us. Don't you trust us?"

And just like that, the honeymoon was over. Stone scanned the faces around the table. All of them were looking at him with the same serious expressions. They were his friends, his inner circle— the people he trusted more than almost anyone else in the world. If it were up to him, he'd spill everything he knew to them, right here at the table.

But it wasn't up to him. He still didn't know what Aldwyn's plans were, or why he'd done what he did—but he *did* know that the dragon had implied dire consequences, at least to Ian, if he told anyone about what had happened to him. He wouldn't risk that, not until he'd had a chance to find Aldwyn and have some choice words with him.

He did his best to look sincere, which wasn't difficult because in this case he *was* being sincere. "Listen," he said softly, directing his words to each of them in turn. "I *do* trust you. All of you. I'd trust any of you with my life in a second. Hell, Ian, you've been looking after my affairs, keeping people from thinking I'm dead, and I owe you an enormous debt for that." He looked at his hands and sighed. "But…there are things going on here that you don't know. Reasons why I can't tell you everything." He raised his gaze. "I hope all of *you* will trust *me* enough to accept that—at least for now. At least until I've done a bit more investigation. Because the truth is, I *do* know who's done this to me. But I don't know *why,* and that's the important bit. Will you trust me?"

They all exchanged glances. Stone could tell none of them were happy about it—some less so than others. Ian and Verity didn't look like they were planning to go along with him.

Before they could say anything, though, Eddie spoke up. "I trust you, Stone. You know I'm as curious as a whole roomful o' cats, and I'm dyin' to know what kind of enemies you've got who'd 'ave not only the desire, but the power to put somebody as strong magically as you are on ice for three years. But I also know not everythin' in the world is my business. I won't lie—I do want to know. But I gotta respect your right not to tell me."

Next to him, Ward nodded. "I have similar concerns and questions, but I concur."

Jason shrugged. "This is all above my pay grade anyway, and I've got a feeling even if I knew the answer, I couldn't touch this person. So I don't really have a choice. You do what you need to do, Al."

"Yeah," Amber said.

Stone looked at them gratefully. He had a feeling he'd be getting a pass for a while with Jason and Amber, but best not to push things too far. And Eddie and Ward had known him a lot longer than any of the others—they were used to his secretive ways, and it wasn't like they didn't have secrets of their own.

That left Ian and Verity. "What do you say, you two? Will you trust me? Give me some time to sort this out?"

Ian didn't look at him. His jaw was tight, his body tense. "I will—for now—if you promise me two things."

"What things?"

"First, that you won't go after whoever it is alone. We just got you back—I don't want to lose you again."

Stone took a breath. "I...can't promise that, Ian. Not entirely. But I will promise you that I don't plan to 'go after' them. Not in the way you think."

"What does that mean?"

"It means there isn't going to be a fight. I'm not reckless enough to go against them on my own. I wouldn't have a chance." He softened his gaze. "That's all I can give you for now, Ian. I'm sorry. What was the other thing?"

"That you'll tell me everything eventually. When you can."

Ian wasn't making this easy—but then, he never did. Stone shouldn't have been surprised; he *was* his son, after all. "I can't promise that either, because I won't lie to you. I'll promise to tell you as much as I can...*if* I can. It's not completely up to me. There are things involved in this that aren't mine to tell. Is that good enough for you?"

"I guess it's going to have to be, isn't it?"

Stone decided that the best course of action was to take Ian's words at face value for now, even though it was obvious his son wasn't satisfied. "What about you, Verity?"

Her gaze was level, and so was her voice. "I have some questions too, before I say yes."

"Why does that not surprise me?" When she didn't answer, he spread his hands. "Same deal as with Ian. I'll answer them if I can."

She nodded once. "Okay. Do any of us know this person?"

Oh, good. An easy one, for a change. "No."

Brief surprise flashed in her eyes. "So it's not one of your old enemies that we've dealt with before?"

"That any of you have? No."

"Or any of your friends? Kolinsky? Madame Huan? Harrison?"

"Gods, no."

"What about Brathwaite, or Elias Richter? Trin, or the demon who was pulling her strings?"

Verity had a good memory, Stone had to give her that. "Not Brathwaite or Richter. I'm fairly sure Richter's dead, anyway. I *know* Trin is dead, and even if Razakal isn't, he's agreed not to mess with me or any of my family or friends again."

She rolled her eyes. "Like a demon's word means anything."

"Good point. But no, this isn't Razakal. I promise you, Verity, you've never met the one responsible for this."

"So, not any of the Evil?"

"Verity—"

"Is it?"

"No. It has nothing to do with the Evil. And before you ask, it's got nothing to do with the Changelings, either."

"So, you've got some enemy that none of your friends or family know anything about?" Ian looked doubtful. "Are you leading some kind of double life, Dad?"

That was an interesting question. "I…have some things going on that none of you know about—or don't know *much* about." He glared at his son, but there was no fire behind it. "And you, especially, would be quite the hypocrite if you had a go at me for keeping secrets. I'd be willing to bet you don't tell me a fraction of what you and Gabriel get up to when you're off gallivanting around the world. Am I wrong?"

"No, but that's only because I didn't think you'd be interested."

"Perhaps you should let me be the judge of that—or, even better, accept the fact that I've got things I can't, or won't, tell you, and let it go at that."

Ian held his gaze for several seconds, then sighed. "Yeah. Fine. Believe it or not, I *do* trust you, Dad. But you have to understand this whole thing—having you disappear for three years, and especially me being the bait that got you captured in the first place—has been pretty hard on me."

Stone bowed his head. Ian was right, of course. It wasn't fair that he couldn't tell any of his closest friends about Aldwyn—but sometimes things weren't fair, and there wasn't anything that could be done about it.

"I know, Ian," he said softly. "I get it. If it makes you feel any better, nobody's holding it against you, least of all me. I can say with certainty that nothing about this was your fault."

"I could have questioned the text you sent me," he grumbled. "I could have called you."

"No. It wouldn't have mattered. The person behind this is so powerful and relentless, he would have worked out another way to snatch you if you hadn't gone along with his plan." It seemed strange calling Aldwyn a "person." "And anyway, why would you have? Do you ever question any of the other texts I send you?"

Ian didn't seem convinced, but finally he nodded. "Yeah. If you say so. I'm still going to feel guilty, though. Nothing you can do about that."

"Well, I'm back now, so the best thing is probably to do our best to put all this behind us. I'll be counting on you lot to get me up to speed with what's happened while I was away, and I've got several people I need to check up on. Starting with Aubrey, I think. I—"

The phone rang. Not Stone's mobile, which he hadn't recharged yet, but the landline.

Without thinking, Stone raised his hand and summoned the handset to him. "Probably a telemarketer. But if not, here's my first chance to reconnect with the world." He tapped the button. "Yes, hello?"

"Welcome back, Alastair."

The voice was immediately familiar, and sounded amused. Stone tightened his grip until his knuckles whitened.

Aldwyn.

CHAPTER FIVE

THEY WERE ALL LOOKING AT STONE. He caught himself before he spoke the dragon's name, and rose from the chair, stalking away. "We need to talk," he said when he reached the kitchen, removed from prying ears.

"Yes, I believe we do."

"On *my* terms, though. Not yours. So if you've got any plans of hijacking my portal or my teleport, don't even think of it."

"I have no intention of doing that." Aldwyn still sounded unruffled. "Take some time to re-acclimate yourself. You've been away a while."

Stone couldn't tell if there was a mocking edge to his tone, but he wouldn't put it past the old dragon. "And while you're at it, don't think about messing with any of my friends or family. If you do, I promise you I *will* find a way to make you regret it."

"Empty words, scion."

"Maybe not so empty," he growled. "Remember, Brathwaite and Cyrus put you down once. That means it's possible." He thought about the black obelisk he'd left in Stefan Kolinsky's care.

"You may continue to think so if it comforts you."

Stone glanced behind him, to make sure no one from the other room had followed him. Then he bent to the phone and whispered furiously, "I want to know why you did what you did. What purpose did it serve?"

Aldwyn chuckled. "All will be revealed in time. I will give you two weeks to get your affairs in order. Then we will discuss our next steps."

"Next steps? What next steps?"

"Have you forgotten so soon, Alastair? We have unfinished business. You made certain...agreements, and I have every intention of holding you to them."

Something wrenched in the pit of Stone's stomach.

Agreements.

In all the confusion surrounding his return, he'd forgotten about the oath he'd sworn to Aldwyn—the one that bound him to the dragon for five years or three tasks, whichever came first. Even after all the time he'd been out of commission, that still left two years.

"I'll find a way around that," he growled.

Again, the dragon chuckled. It seemed as if he was finding this entire conversation—or perhaps only his scion's discomfort—highly amusing. "I doubt that. The oath is binding, and I held up my side of the bargain. Your son was returned, safe and well, just as I promised."

Unfortunately, he was almost certainly correct. Breaking a magical oath was hard enough. Breaking one made by—and to—a dragon would be nearly impossible.

But that didn't mean Stone didn't plan to give it his best shot. "I'll find a way," he repeated stubbornly. "I'll find Kolinsky, or Madame Huan. They'll have ideas."

He expected Aldwyn to reiterate his threat of dire consequences if he revealed any of this to anyone. Instead, he said, "Find them if you like. Tell them everything. It doesn't matter. They will not help you."

"Why not?" His voice rose a little, and he lowered it again with another glance toward the sitting room. Ian and his friends were all still there, still seated, but they too were shooting looks in his direction.

"I will be in touch, Alastair. Best for you to get back to your friends. Good day."

"Wait! You can't—"

The line went dead.

"*Bugger!*" Stone nearly threw the handset across the room, but caught himself.

"Dad?"

He wheeled to find Ian standing in the kitchen doorway.

"You okay?"

"I—" He tossed the phone on the counter. "I'm fine."

"Who was that on the phone?"

"Nobody important."

"Dad…" Ian's tone grew suspicious, and so did his expression. He wasn't buying it.

Of course he wasn't. He was highly perceptive under normal circumstances, and Stone wasn't exactly putting up his best poker face. He let out a loud sigh. "Okay. No, that isn't right. It *was* somebody important. But there's nothing I can do about it now."

"Wait." His gaze sharpened. "That was the guy, wasn't it? The guy who did this to you?"

There was no point in lying about it. "Yes."

"So he knows you got loose."

Stone considered that. "I think he intended all along for me to get loose."

"Huh?" Ian followed him back to the sitting room, where the others were waiting. "Why do you think so? Why the hell would he do that?"

"Trust me, Ian: your guess is every bit as good as mine. This man is…inscrutable. I haven't got a clue about his motivations." That was true. What was the point of Aldwyn tricking him into a trap that kept him out of commission for three years, when he'd just sworn a magical oath to do the dragon's bidding? It didn't make sense.

"Whose motivations?" Verity asked.

Before Stone could answer, Ian said, "That was the guy who's responsible for all this."

"*What?*" Several of them spoke at once, and all of them looked shocked and surprised.

"What did he want?" Jason demanded.

Stone shrugged. "Probably just to let me know he's aware I'm back."

Eddie looked around nervously. "Does that mean 'e's comin' after you again?"

Stone dropped back into his chair. "I doubt it. As I just told Ian, I think he expected me to get loose eventually." Perversely, he wondered how he'd done. How long had Aldwyn expected him to take? *Yes, because that's the most important thing right now—how well you scored on your mad dragon ancestor's test.* Some things never changed, he supposed.

"So…what now?" Verity was watching him with concern. "What are you going to do?"

"Right now, I'm going to concentrate on getting back into the world." He levitated his half-finished beer over and took a drink. "I've got a lot of catching up to do."

Ian tilted his head. "So you're not going to try finding him?"

"I haven't got a clue how to do that, even if I wanted to."

"How powerful *is* this man?" Ward asked.

"And 'ow the 'ell did you get on his bad side?" Eddie added.

"That's the thing." Stone set the empty bottle down. "I'm not sure I *am* on his bad side."

"What the hell?" Amber's eyes flashed. "Alastair, you might still be a little addled from your time away, but trust me: anybody who kidnaps your son to lure you off so he can put you in suspended animation for three years isn't your friend."

"He's not my friend. That much you're right about. But...it's complicated." He stood. "Listen—I know this sounds ridiculous after waking up from a three-year sleep, but I'm tired. I think I need a bit of time to...just get re-acquainted with the house. I'm not going anywhere, trust me."

"How do you even know that?" Ian asked darkly. "He's still out there—how do you know he won't do the same thing again?"

"I can't tell you how I know. But I *do* know. Will you trust me?"

They all grumbled, but stood. "You better come over to Caventhorne soon," Eddie said. "You wouldn't recognize the place, now that it's bein' used for all sorts o' new things. Plus, you owe us a round at the Dragon."

"For what?"

"For disappearin' for three bloody years. Actually, you owe us a *lot* of rounds. And we owe you a few, too."

Stone grinned, feeling genuine pleasure for the first time since his return. "I'll take you up on that, Eddie, I promise."

"Too right you will." He pointed down. "If you don't, we'll come after you. Remember, we've got the keys to your 'ouse now, so we can pop in whenever we like."

That was a good point. He'd need to find out how many people had access to that portal, but as long as it wasn't anyone else besides those in this room, he didn't mind.

Eddie and Ward left first, heading downstairs.

"You should come by and see us too," Jason said, his arm around Amber. "Gina will want to see you at the agency."

"And you need to meet Alice and Jaden," Amber said. "We've been telling them all about their Uncle Alastair. Alice knows she was named after you, so she's obsessed with meeting you."

Before, Stone would have found the thought that a three-year-old was "obsessed" with him terrifying, but right now all he felt was a deep warmth. He still doubted he was going to become a fan of small children, but perhaps he might make an exception for these two. He'd give it a try, anyway. "I will. Give me a couple of days to get myself sorted, though."

"We'll invite you over for dinner," Jason said. "You need to see the house—*it's* changed a lot, too."

Stone wondered if anything in his life *hadn't* changed, but didn't say it. "It's a plan. I'm looking forward to it."

After they left, only Ian and Verity remained.

"Stay in touch," Ian said, almost in the tone of a warning. "We kept all your accounts active, so your phone should still work once you charge it up."

That was good to know; he'd wondered about that. "Where are you living these days? It sounds like you and Gabriel are still together, since he's taught you portal science. Are you still…running around the world going to parties?"

His son's smile was amused, not mocking. "What kind of answer are you looking for?"

"Ian, I just want you to be happy. However you define that. As long as you're not hurting anyone, you're an adult. It's none of my business what you do."

His son held his gaze for a few seconds, then nodded. "Fair enough. Yeah, we're still together. I've passed my apprenticeship by now, but he's still got a lot to teach me and I want to learn. And yeah, we're still going to parties. But I've settled down a little more, too. I've had to, running your life and all."

Stone returned the smile. "So now I've got my life back, you're planning to go back to the way things were?"

"Who knows? I'm not kidding—I want a piece of this guy who did this to us. And you know you can always get in touch with me if you need me for anything."

"I'm glad to know that, Ian." He stepped forward, gripped his son's arm, then pulled him into a hug. "I'm so sorry you got caught up in all this nonsense."

"Eh, we're mages. Nonsense is kind of our lives." Ian returned the hug, but didn't squeeze hard enough to crack ribs this time. "We'll talk soon."

"Yes. You *and* Gabriel."

Verity watched Ian's tall figure recede from the room. "It really is good to have you back, Alastair."

He studied her a moment. "You know what I'd like right now?"

"What's that?"

"Believe it or not, I miss Raider. I'd like to have him back, if you haven't grown too attached to him."

"I kind of have," she admitted. "He's a great cat, and he gets along great with Luna, my other one. But I know he misses you. You can come pick him up now, if you want." She stabbed a finger up. "Oh—forgot to tell you. I've moved."

"Have you?"

"Yeah. With what Scuro pays me plus all the other stuff I do, I saved up enough to buy a little loft in San Francisco. Got really lucky and found a nice one. It's not big, but it's in a decent area and it's mine." Her smile widened. "And it's closer to a ley line than the old one."

"Verity, that's…brilliant." He looked her over again, still marveling at her new maturity—not only in her appearance, but the whole way she carried herself. A long way from the frightened, confused seventeen-year-old he'd taken as his apprentice all those years ago. Pride swelled in him, that he could have been even a small part of everything she'd become. "Congratulations. I owe you a housewarming gift."

"It's okay. Having you back is the best gift I could have asked for." Almost as if realizing he might take that wrong, she patted his arm. "How about it—want to go get the furball? It'll take me a little longer to get there, since I can't travel to the dedicated portal at the shop."

He thought about it. "No...on second thought, suppose I come up there tomorrow and pick him up? I wasn't kidding about being tired."

"Sleeping for three years will do that," she teased. Tilting her head, she said, "*Were* you sleeping, though?"

"I'm...not sure. I remember odd dreams, but only snippets. I was a mundane, living a completely mundane life. I had a girlfriend and a job I didn't like, and...I think I was seeing a therapist."

"Huh. So you were kind of like in the Matrix, living a whole different life?"

"Who knows? I suppose I'll never know." He doubted Aldwyn would give him the details of whatever magic he'd used.

"Maybe not. But that's some powerful magic. *Really* powerful magic." Her eyes narrowed. "Are you sure Harrison isn't involved with this? You didn't have a fight with him or something, did you?"

"No. I'm certain it's not him."

"You wouldn't lie to me, would you?"

"I would never lie to you, Verity. That much hasn't changed. I might leave out relevant details or refuse to answer, but I won't lie."

She studied him for a few seconds, obviously trying to decide if he was telling her the truth. "Okay," she finally said. "I remember I used to say before that you were moving away from me—from all of us—and going to a place we couldn't follow. I still think that's true, but I've grown up a lot since then. Enough to accept that it's none of my business, even if I want it to be. I've got my own life to live, and you have yours. So all I can say is, be careful."

"That much I can promise you. Believe me, I've got no intention of losing any *more* time from my friends' and family's lives."

Her smile now was bittersweet. "I notice you didn't say *yours*."

"Yes, well, that's something I'm going to have to deal with too, at some point. But not right now. One thing at a time."

She stood on tiptoe and kissed his cheek. "I'll leave you alone so you can get some rest. Let me know when you're ready to pick up Raider."

After she was gone, he stood a moment in the foyer, looking at the closed front door. A warm, satisfied feeling spread through him, and he smiled. He had a lot of problems to deal with, and getting caught up with three years' absence wasn't going to be easy. But he still had his friends, and Ian. Their loyalty had never wavered. Not for the first time, he wondered what he'd done to be worthy of such loyalty, but he didn't question it.

He suspected he was going to need it.

But for now, he had other things to do—things none of them could help him with.

CHAPTER SIX

HE FOUND HIS BLACK BMW IN THE GARAGE, covered with a soft tarp, and wondered if it was still drivable. To his surprise, it was. It even had nearly a full tank of gas. He assumed Ian or Verity had taken it out periodically and kept it maintained.

Might be time to look for a new one, he thought has he drove out through the front gate. On his way to his destination, he thought fondly of the time when he'd first bought it. He, Jason, and Verity had barely known each other back then, and they'd been in the middle of the whole Evil situation. It seemed like another lifetime ago.

To his surprise, not that much looked different. Even though three years had been a long time to be asleep, it wasn't that long in the greater scheme of things. He noticed a few familiar businesses and shops were gone, and a few new ones had taken their place, but for the most part everything was as he'd remembered it.

He found an important exception when he stopped in front of the shabby shop in East Palo Alto. For one thing, it wasn't shabby anymore. The whole neighborhood had taken a definite step up, which didn't surprise him too much when he thought about it. Prices in the Bay Area had been going nowhere but up for years, so it had become profitable to buy lower-income areas and gentrify them, replacing the low-end businesses and apartments with ones that appealed to the burgeoning population of high-tech workers and their support systems. He remembered hearing Verity complaining about it on occasion.

He found a parking place down the block and walked back to the shop. It was a women's clothing boutique now, with a big picture window replacing its formerly unwelcoming façade.

After hesitating a moment, he pushed open the door and walked inside, even though he already knew there was no point to it.

"Good afternoon. May I help you?" called a voice from further in.

Stone paused, looking around. The place had been so heavily remodeled that he didn't recognize anything of the familiar shop. Even the door leading to the downstairs area wasn't immediately visible. A faint, pleasant floral scent hung in the air.

"Er," he began. "I'm looking for someone, actually. But I think I might be in the wrong place."

The woman stepped out of the shadows. She was young, pretty, and wore trendy clothes similar to those on the mannequins and racks. She looked him over, obviously liking what she saw. "I'll help if I can."

He was glad he'd changed out of the tuxedo and back into his more customary style. "You probably can't, actually, but thank you. How long have you been here? This shop, I mean?"

"A couple of years, I think. I only started working here last year, but I remember the grand opening."

"Do you know what was here before that?"

Her brow furrowed. "Not…really. I think it might have been abandoned. They redid this whole block around the same time we opened. Why?"

"It wasn't abandoned. There was another shop here, but it was very…exclusive. Open by appointment only. I was looking for the proprietor."

"I'm sorry, but I can't help you." She sounded like she really was.

He thanked her and headed back out, frustrated. Stefan had abandoned the shop? What did that mean? Had he decided that, with Stone missing, there was no need to keep up the pretense any longer? Had he even made any effort to look for Stone, or had he not cared enough to put himself out?

He pulled his phone from his pocket. He'd put it on the charger while he showered, so it only had a little power. As he walked back to the car, he texted Ian. *Are you there?*

The answer came quickly. *Yeah. What do you need?*

Can you get me in touch with Gabriel? I need to talk to him.

The pause was longer this time. *About the guy you're after?*

Not directly, no. I have some questions for him. Can you ask him to contact me?

Yeah. I'm not sure where he is, though.

Give it your best go. Thank you, Ian.

He reached the car and considered his next move. He didn't feel like going to the University yet. That would take some mental preparation. Finally, he drove back to Palo Alto and cruised up University Avenue, checking out what had changed. He let his mind wander, and by the time he dropped out of autopilot, he was across the street from Madame Huan's shop.

It was closed, but at least it wasn't gone. That was something.

His phone buzzed in his pocket.

Welcome back, Dr. Stone, the incoming text read. There was no name associated with it, but Stone knew who it was.

Ian must have told him the latest. He didn't waste any time with greetings. *I need to talk to your father. His shop is gone.*

Is it? I'm not surprised.

Stone was in no mood for playing games. *Can you please just tell me how to reach him? Or ask him to contact me? I assume he knows I've been gone.*

No doubt. We don't talk much. Nothing has changed there.

Stone gritted his teeth and growled under his breath. Dragons were the most frustrating beings around—and that was saying something, given some of the people he'd met. *Do you know how to contact him? I'm serious—it's important.*

The reply after a long delay. *I will try to reach him. If I can, I'll ask him to contact you. I don't want to get involved, though.*

That was an odd thing to say. *Involved in what?*

But this time, there was no reply.

Nothing else happened until later that evening. He returned to the Encantada house, stopping at his favorite downtown sandwich shop to pick up something for later. Nobody recognized him, which didn't surprise him—shops like that had a lot of turnover. When he got home with the sandwich, he thought with a twinge of sadness about all the times he'd picked meat out of these very same sandwiches to give to Raider. Would the cat even recognize him after three years? Would they re-establish their easy relationship, or would Raider treat him with suspicion? Three years was a long time in a cat's life. He'd be around eight by now—not exactly old by feline standards, but not young, either.

Stone slammed the refrigerator closed, anger at Aldwyn welling up again. What had he done to his dragon ancestor to cause this kind of treatment?

Deliberately, he shoved the anger aside. It wasn't helping him now, and he knew it would be right there, smoldering in its safe place, when he was ready to unleash it. For now, he felt guilty. He should be contacting the other people who no doubt missed him, not sitting here on the sofa like a lump. Aubrey, especially, would want to know. He wondered if Verity or Ian had told him. It was too late to call him now, though, since it was the middle of the night in England.

He'd dozed off when a knock on the door jerked him awake. *That's odd. Who would be coming by at this hour?* Verity, Ian, Eddie, and Ward had all left via the portal, so if they returned they would come the same way. And Jason and Amber had no doubt returned home to their house in the Santa Cruz Mountains and their two children.

A young man in a dark suit stood patiently waiting when he opened the door.

Stone smiled. *Gabriel must have made contact after all. Some things never change.* "Good evening. I think I know who sent you."

"Yes, sir." The young man held out a cream-colored envelope sealed with a blob of black wax.

Stone took the envelope. "Is he waiting for a reply?"

"No, sir. Good evening to you." He bowed slightly and left.

Stone watched him go until he disappeared into the darkness, then carried the envelope back inside. He retrieved one of the leftover beers from their lunch and resumed his seat on the sofa, missing Raider's soft furry form on his lap.

The stiff card inside the envelope was blank to normal sight. Switching to magical sight revealed a series of figures.

Stone recognized them immediately: they were a way for mages to describe ley-line locations, similar to the mundane method of using longitude and latitude. When he hurried to retrieve his ley-line reference book from the library and compared it to the figures on the card, he discovered they corresponded to a small town in central Mexico. Closer examination revealed the exact location to be a cantina just off the town's main street.

Well. That's an interesting place for a meet. At least he's keeping things interesting. And the food's likely to be good.

Stone had never been to Mexico, but the cantina he arrived behind had the unassuming look of a place that got passed over by tourists looking for something glitzier, but was beloved of the locals.

Several customers looked up as he entered, but quickly returned to their own business even though he didn't even begin to look like he fit in. The lazily spinning ceiling fans overhead did next to nothing to move the warm air around, but they did help fill the place with the mouth-watering aromas of spiced meat.

Stefan Kolinsky didn't look any different, and Stone found that oddly comforting. The dragon sat at a table in the back of the cantina, with a tall, half-finished drink in front of him. His sleeves were rolled up, revealing the elaborate tattoos on his powerful forearms.

Stone approached the table. "Did you ever even need those?"

Kolinsky didn't seem surprised to see him. He flicked a quick glance down at his arms and didn't respond. Instead, he nodded a greeting. "Alastair. It is good to see you."

"After all this time." Stone recalled that the dragon—all of the dragons, in fact, except for Gabriel and Aldwyn—had disappeared well prior to his own absence. They'd been off somewhere to convene a rare conclave, at least partially to discuss what, if anything, they planned to do about the Changelings.

"Please. Sit down."

Stone took the chair across from him. Normally he didn't like sitting with his back to the door, but he figured if anything threatened them, Kolinsky could deal with it before it reached him.

Assuming Stefan's not the threat, his perverse little voice pointed out, but he didn't listen.

As soon as he'd sat, a server came over and set a drink on front of him. He wasn't sure what it was, but that was all right. Anything alcoholic would be welcome right now. He waited for her to leave and faced Kolinsky. "You look good. But I suppose three years wouldn't make much of a difference to you, would it?" He cocked a questioning eyebrow back toward the bar.

"You may speak freely here. No one can hear us."

"That's good, because I've got a lot to say. I take it your son managed to find you?"

"He passed on a message that you wished to speak to me, yes."

"Did you even know I was back?"

"I did not."

That was a surprise too. He took a slow deep breath and sipped the drink. It tasted good—cold and tart, with a hint of a fruity aftertaste. "You *did* know I was missing, though, didn't you?"

"Yes. I was aware." Kolinsky's face remained utterly calm and unreadable. He certainly didn't seem to be overwhelmed with relief that Stone was back. No crushing hugs would be forthcoming this time, which was also a relief.

Stone wasn't entirely sure he wanted to ask the next question, because he wasn't sure he wanted to know the answer. "Did you know where I was? Who was responsible for my absence?"

"I did not know where you were. I did know who was responsible."

Stone frowned. "You knew it was Aldwyn?" He looked around, almost as if expecting a lightning bolt to strike him down for saying the name. But Aldwyn *had* said he didn't care if Stone revealed the details to Kolinsky or Madame Huan. With a chill, it occurred to him why that was true. "You *did* know."

"I did." Kolinsky still showed no reaction. His black eyes met Stone's, level and emotionless.

An uncomfortable knot formed in Stone's stomach. For a second, he wondered if it was the drink, but it wasn't. "Wait. You...*knew* he did this to me, but you didn't make any effort to stop him? To find me? To at least contact my friends and let them know?" Despite their close working relationship over the years, he had no illusions that Kolinsky had any particular personal feelings for him, but this was a bit hard to swallow. As far as he would have believed, the dragon would have looked for him for no other reason than to mess up Aldwyn's plans.

Was that the slightest bit of discomfort? "No. I did not."

"But...*why?*" Stone shoved the drink aside and gripped the edge of the table. "I mean, I know we're not best mates or anything, but I'd like to think we're friends at least on some level. Professional respect, if nothing else."

"That is true. I have always valued our association, and that has not changed."

"But yet you'd let me languish under some sort of magical suspended animation for three *years?* It could have been even longer if I hadn't managed to break out of Aldwyn's little mind-prison. I could have been in there for bloody *centuries,* Stefan."

Kolinsky inclined his head.

Another chill ran through Stone. He'd been indulging in a bit of hyperbole—or so he thought.

Aldwyn was down there for nearly two hundred years...and he's stronger magically than you are.

"I want to know what's going on." He narrowed his eyes. "You weren't...somehow *involved,* were you?" That was a new—and even more chilling—thought: had he done something to piss off the dragons in general? Had they decided something about him at their conclave, and left it to Aldwyn to implement? That seemed unlikely, since his dragon ancestor hadn't even attended the conclave.

"No. I was not involved. None of us were."

Well. That was comforting, at least. "None of you. As in, the other dragons."

"Yes."

"The others knew?"

"Some of them did."

"Madame Huan?"

"Yes."

"What about Gabriel? Did he know?" The knot in Stone's stomach churned. If Gabriel had known, that meant he hadn't told any of his friends…or Ian.

"He did, eventually."

Stone's bottled anger bubbled up again. He slammed his fist down on the table so hard his drink made a little jump. "Bloody *hell*, Stefan! I thought you lot hated Aldwyn! But yet you let him get *away* with this? You didn't even *try* to stop him?"

He glanced around, wondering if his outburst had attracted any attention, but the cantina's few other customers were going about their conversations as if nothing had happened. He turned his glare back on Kolinsky. "I want to know what's going on. You owe me that much, at least."

"I do not 'owe' you anything." Kolinsky spoke mildly, but his eyes were serious.

"You—"

"But," he continued as if Stone hadn't spoken, "there is no reason for me not to tell you. I am no more pleased about it than you are, nor is Madame Huan."

"Pleased about what? Not getting involved? Not looking for me?"

"Yes."

Stone shook his head, not following. "So why *didn't* you? You're not afraid of Aldwyn, are you? He isn't so much more powerful than the rest of you that pissing him off would be a risk?"

"No. Although, as I told you before, he is very powerful—as well as unconventional. To put it in terms you would understand, he does not play by the rules."

"The rules. You mean the dragons' rules."

"Yes."

"Well, then, what's the point of *having* rules?" Stone sharpened his glare. "Why do the rest of you follow them, if you're just going to let Aldwyn go on his merry way and do whatever the hell he likes?"

"It is not precisely like that. He does not participate in our society by his choice, but for the most part he keeps to himself and does not test us. He is highly intelligent and devious. Most of his actions skirt the edges of our agreements, but do not outright defy them." He looked down, then back up. "That, combined with the fact that a subset of our community is beginning to believe that our agreements no longer reflect the reality of modern times, makes many things more difficult."

"Difficult?" Stone wasn't sure he was hearing what he thought he was hearing. "You mean he's got some of the other dragons convinced he's right? That the rules don't matter anymore?"

Kolinsky inclined his head. "Just so. Much has changed during the time you were out of communication, which is unusual for us."

"I remember. You lot usually move at about the speed of continental drift, right?"

"I would not put it so fancifully. But yes. There is no need to move quickly. Most of us prefer…the long game."

"Yes, I can see that. Immortality does that, I suppose. But what, if anything, has this got to do with me?" A thought occurred to him. "I'm not the cause of this…whatever happened, am I?"

"No. You are aware of our conclave."

"Yes. You all took off to parts unknown and dropped out of communication, except Gabriel who didn't care, and Aldwyn, who didn't want anything to do with the rest of you. I don't know for sure what it was about, though. Gabriel didn't tell me anything. Did he know?" Stone was fishing a little, since Aldwyn had already told him the main purpose of the conclave was to discuss the impact of the Changelings on dragon society. He wanted to see if Kolinsky would give him the same answer.

"Not at the time."

"So, what was the point of it? What happened that made you all decide to get together for the first time since Aldwyn disappeared? It wasn't him, was it? You already knew he was back a while ago."

"No. It was not him."

"What, then?"

"I should think it would have been obvious."

Fair enough. "The Changelings."

Kolinsky inclined his head.

Stone looked at his drink again, but didn't pick it up. "They're something new. Newer than anything else that had happened in the world for a long time."

"Yes."

"Did you ever figure out what caused them?"

"We did not. A few of us chose to examine some of them, but all we discovered was that the cause was extradimensional in origin. This was later confirmed by conversations with the researchers your friends gathered at Caventhorne. That is the extent of our knowledge, however."

"A few? You mean you grabbed Changelings off the street and…what…experimented on them?"

"They were not harmed. The experiments did not require a great deal of time, and when they were completed, the subjects were returned with proper magical safeguards in place."

"You wiped their memories of being experimented on." Stone sighed. "And you were part of this 'few,' weren't you?"

"I was." There was no apology in the dragon's tone. "And yes, we used magic to prevent the subjects from recalling the details of their time with us."

Of course there was no apology. Stone reminded himself once again that, despite their long association, there was nothing cuddly about Kolinsky. He did what he did, and he didn't make excuses for it. Stone didn't like it, but there wasn't anything he could do about it beyond breaking off his association with the dragon, and that wasn't something he was ready to do yet.

He considered for a long moment, staring into his drink while he tried to decide how much he wanted to reveal. Finally, he decided it couldn't hurt anything at this point. Kolinsky, as always, operated on a *quid pro quo* model, so giving him some harmless but valuable information might loosen the dragon's lips.

"I know what caused it." He brought his gaze up and fixed it on Kolinsky.

Kolinsky regarded him in silence for long enough to make him uncomfortable. "Do you?"

"I do."

"How do you know?" His eyes narrowed. "Did you cause it, Alastair?"

"No. But I know who did."

Something changed in the dragon's gaze. "Of course. I should have guessed."

"You've figured it out, then?"

"Not completely. We closed the rift your friend and her son caused. I am certain of that."

Stone wasn't surprised he'd picked it up so quickly. Dragons were a bright lot, overall. "We did. But we didn't think there might be *another* one."

"Indeed."

Clearly, he had Kolinsky's undivided attention now. "You weren't keeping tabs on me at the time, because you were off doing your little conclave thing. Believe me, I'd have been happy to have your help with it. You might think about that next time you disappear without a trace."

"I will keep that in mind."

Stone didn't believe it for a moment. "In any case—do you want to know?"

"I do."

"Then I expect you'll fill me in on what you know about what Aldwyn's up to, and why the rest of you lot either couldn't try to find me, or chose not to."

Kolinsky nodded. "Agreed."

Well. That was easy. Stone decided the dragon had already been planning to tell him, with or without his information. But that was all right. He had no reason not to share the details with the dragon.

Quickly, without including a lot of interesting but unnecessary detail, he explained about the second rift Jeremy had spawned in the back room at the Rochester hotel, and how it had pumped out some kind of extradimensional "virus" that affected those with magical blood but no powers. "We found it eventually and closed it, but not before it had enough of a hold that there was no putting the genie back in the bottle. I don't know much about it beyond that, since that was around the time I did my Rip Van Winkle impersonation. But I'm guessing you probably already *have* the rest of the information."

"We do. We have access to detailed studies about the condition—including the fact that it is not curable or reversible. The so-called 'Changelings' appear to be here to stay."

"Which returns us neatly to your conclave. According to Aldwyn, you lot hadn't got together for a meetup like this since before he got sealed under my house. Why now? What is it about the Changelings that got you all so wound up?"

"Very simple—they aren't human."

"What?" Stone glared at him. "Of course they're human. They're just…enhanced."

"For the purpose of our agreements, they are not." Kolinsky finished his drink and made a vague gesture in the air. Almost instantly, the server hurried over and replaced it with a fresh one.

"What do you mean by that?"

"Our agreements are very specific about what we are and are not permitted to do—and to whom we are permitted to do it."

Stone tilted his head. "Sorry, I'm not following. Maybe because I've got no idea what's actually *in* your agreements, and I doubt you're planning to share the details with me."

"That is correct. But in order to prevent…unavoidable conflict between us, we have sworn to avoid any direct interaction with humans—including human mages."

"But not including scions."

"Scions are a different subject." Kolinsky sipped his new drink. "Our agreements stipulate that we are not permitted to involve ourselves directly in human affairs. We cannot directly harm humans without provocation, nor use our greater influence, wealth, and experience to manipulate them or their institutions, most specifically in any way that involves magic."

"So…no mucking with the stock market or blackmailing the President."

"Yes. As you might suspect, these agreements have been…tested…in many ways over the years, usually by involving proxies, knowing or unknowing, to do our bidding and ensure desired outcomes. For the most part, we ignore these minor transgressions. Each of us has carved out a sphere of influence in the world."

"And you keep your noses out of each other's business in your own spheres, as long as nobody pokes their heads up too high or causes too much trouble."

"Yes. This is as much for our own protection as others', especially in modern times. Advances in technology—communication, travel, intelligence, and weaponry—make humans more of a threat to us than they have ever been in the history of the world."

Stone snorted. "You dragons aren't scared of a bunch of humans, are you?"

"Of course not. Even with their technological advances, it would be difficult for them to affect us enough to cause more than temporary inconvenience. But, as I am sure you are aware regarding mages, it is preferable to keep mundane humans—and especially human mages—unaware of our existence."

"Makes sense." Stone couldn't argue with that. Mages had been hiding themselves and the existence of magic from the mundanes for centuries. "But what's this got to do with the Changelings?" Once again, though, he saw the answer before Kolinsky replied. "Hang on. You're saying that, since they're not human, they're not subject to your agreements."

"Yes. Or rather, some of us are."

"Some of you. You mean, some of the dragons are arguing that the agreements don't cover them, and others are saying they do?"

"Yes."

"That was what the conclave was about?"

Kolinsky inclined his head.

"And it took you weeks—months, maybe—to sort this out?"

"We do not move quickly. Especially, as you might surmise, on subjects regarding agreements that have been in place for over a thousand years."

Stone let his breath out. "I suppose you've got a point there. Given how long it takes human governments to agree on anything, I'm not surprised." He looked up. "So...which side did you land on? And what was finally decided?"

Kolinsky didn't answer right away. He appeared to be trying to decide whether he would do so at all.

"Come on, Stefan—you've told me this much. Might as well go for the whole thing. You should know by now that I'll keep my mouth shut."

Still, several more seconds passed before he replied. "I chose to uphold our agreements, and to extend them to include the Changelings."

"That surprises me a bit, to be honest. I thought you've always been looking for ways to advance your agenda."

"I am. All of us are, in our way. But I am well capable of doing that with conditions as they currently are."

That *did* surprise Stone. He was nearly certain that Kolinsky's wealth, power, and influence were all far more extensive than he could ever suspect. You didn't hang about for a thousand years with the kind of magical ability the dragons had without amassing a lot of all three. Hell, a smart and long-lived human could do the same thing with ease, even without doing anything nefarious to influence the course of world events. "So you think it's better to keep things as they are."

"I do."

"I assume Madame Huan feels the same way."

"She does. She made some of the strongest arguments in favor of the status quo."

That was a relief. When dealing with the dragons, even Kolinsky and Gabriel, Stone often felt as if he was standing on shifting footing, and that he could never be certain his assumptions about them were accurate. It was nice to know the kindly Madame Huan, at least, was living up to his expectations. "What about the others?"

"Of those you know, Morathi and…" He paused a moment, as if trying to recall something. "—the one you know as 'Vic' both sided against altering the agreements."

Stone thought back to his meeting with the dragons. "Vic," who'd looked and spoken like someone's suburban dad, had been difficult to read. He'd seemed amiable enough, but with dragons you could never tell. "Huh. The one I *know as* Vic. I guess that shouldn't be a surprise. 'Vic' doesn't sound very much like the sort of name a dragon would choose."

Kolinsky didn't favor that with a reply.

"Okay, moving on. So that's four. Who came down on the other side?"

"As you might suspect, Thalassa Nera did."

"Big surprise there. That woman still scares me, if I'm being honest. I'd be surprised if she *didn't* come down on whatever side got her the most potential power. I'm guessing Cassius landed on that side too."

"He did, yes."

Stone ticked them off on his fingers. "That's six. Gabriel told me he didn't attend the conclave, and neither did Aldwyn, so they didn't get votes?"

"Their opinions were not considered."

"Okay, so it sounds like we've got four in favor of the status quo, two against, and two abstentions. If I recall correctly from our meeting, there are somewhere around twenty of you in the world. So that leaves around twelve unaccounted for."

"And so they shall remain. Many of us do not wish to have our identities revealed, and I will respect their wishes."

"Fair enough. But you can't even tell me how they voted?"

Kolinsky's jaw tightened.

"Stefan?"

Once more, the dragon didn't look as if he wanted to answer. When he spoke, it was with clear reluctance. "There was a... schism."

Stone stopped in the act of lifting his drink. "What?"

Kolinsky looked suddenly tired. "We are not a democracy, Alastair. Our original agreements were adopted not because they were peacefully voted upon—but rather as a last-ditch attempt to keep us from each other's throats. As I have told you before, we are a contentious lot. It is not surprising, given our power and our thirst to better ourselves. Our agreements were put into place due to self-interest, so we could all choose to pursue our own aims without the constant concern that our fellows were plotting against us. The decision not to involve ourselves in human affairs wasn't made to protect the humans—it was made to protect *us*. From each other."

"I...see." Stone remembered something Gabriel had told him before, about how the dragons protected the Earth from extradimensional threats—but not because of any altruistic feelings for humans. They did it because, after their exile, they were stuck here, and thus it was in their best interests to keep the place threat-free. "So...a schism. What does that mean? Was there a fight? Did you throw the agreements out the window?" That was a chilling thought. Twenty dragons without anything preventing them from doing whatever they like could cause a lot of trouble in the world.

"Not...precisely. As I said, all of us, regardless of our opinions about the Changelings, recognize that revealing ourselves to the humans directly would not be a wise decision."

"That's not saying much. They—you—could do a lot of harm behind the scenes."

"That is true. So far, however, it has not come to pass to any significant degree. We are nothing if not subtle, since there is no need for us to act quickly."

Stone went over Kolinsky's words. "But some of you—the ones who argued against the Changelings being human for the purposes of the agreement, don't see any problem with manipulating *them*."

"Correct. Some of us, including Thalassa Nera, have already made inroads into making use of Changelings to advance their interests."

"Making use of them? What's that mean?"

Kolinsky shrugged. "It depends on the individual. Some are more direct than others."

Stone mulled that over. "Okay. I don't like it, and it sounds like you don't either. But it doesn't sound like there's much I can do about it."

"There is not. I am merely informing you because you asked, and because if you look carefully, you are likely to see signs of its effects."

"Like I haven't got enough to be getting on with, without worrying about a bunch of dragons trying to one-up each other." He sighed. "What about Aldwyn? Where does he stand in all this? Is he still on his own, defying anyone else to get in his way?"

This time, there was no hiding it: Kolinsky looked uncomfortable. "No."

"No, what?"

"He is no longer alone."

"What the hell does that mean? I thought the rest of you believe he's stark raving mad."

"Opinions have...changed."

A chill ran up Stone's spine. This wasn't good. Kolinsky had always implied Aldwyn was one of the most dangerous of the dragons, precisely *because* he carefully flouted the rules and agreements the others followed. And now he'd lured *other* dragons to his side? "Opinions."

Kolinsky spread his hands. "It was inevitable, given how long we live. It happens with you humans, after all: a powerful political, entertainment, or athletic figure can commit a horrific crime or experience some scandal, but after a time, emotions begin to cool and the horror is softened. Why does it surprise you that it might occur with us?"

"I don't know," Stone muttered. "Maybe because I thought you lot might have more sense than we do?"

"That is not an accurate assessment."

"That's frightening. Considering the level of power your bunch is wielding, it was comforting to think you had your ducks in a row. Except for Aldwyn, of course." He shuddered. "And speaking of Aldwyn, let's get back to the sixty-four-thousand-dollar question: *Why,* if you knew I was missing and you knew Aldwyn was responsible, didn't you do anything about it? Has it got something to do with the fact that he's got allies now? You were afraid to go against him?" He snorted. "I never flattered myself to think I meant enough to you to bother putting yourself out, but I would have thought Madame Huan and possibly Gabriel might have done *something*."

Kolinsky continued to look unsettled. "They wanted to. *I* wanted to."

"So why the hell *didn't* you?"

"Because of another part of our agreements—one that, even after the schism, no one was willing to defy."

"Is that right? Are you going to tell me what it is?"

"It is concerned with the relationship between us and our scions."

That hadn't been what Stone was expecting to hear. He jerked his head up. "I thought none of the other scions *knew* they were scions."

"They do not. But that does not mean those who have them—a vanishingly small number, as I believe I mentioned before—do not keep track of their whereabouts, and in some cases make certain efforts to aid or manipulate them without their awareness."

More surprises. "Okay, but I still don't see—"

"One of our most stringent rules is that none of us are permitted to interfere with the sire-scion relationship."

Stone narrowed his eyes as things became clearer. He remembered Kolinsky had told him before that he couldn't get directly involved in his search for Elias Richter. He'd implied it was because Richter was a scion too, but hadn't said anything directly. "So...you *knew* Aldwyn had done something with me, but you couldn't get involved."

"Yes." Kolinsky didn't look at him. "If it is any consolation to you, I, Madame Huan, and Gabriel, both separately and as a group, spent a significant amount of effort looking for loopholes in the agreement. But in the end, there were none. We were very careful when we originated it. The sire-scion relationship is inviolate."

Stone supposed he should be pleased that his dragon allies tried going to bat for him, but all he felt was tired. "Did you talk to him at all? Did he tell anyone *why* he did what he did? I still haven't worked that out."

"We did not. At that point, following the schism at the conclave, he was focused on forming alliances with some of those who chose not to recognize the Changelings' humanity. I believe he avoided us *because* he did not wish to discuss your fate."

"I see." He didn't, not entirely, but that was all right. A lot of what dragons got up to didn't make sense to him. "Well, *I* haven't got a clue about why he did it. In fact, I can't discuss my reasons for thinking so, but I would have thought he'd have more reason for wanting to keep me around, not get me out of the way."

He'd been wondering about that ever since he'd spoken with Verity: if Aldwyn had gone to the trouble of kidnapping Ian to compel him to swear the oath, why put him out of action for three of the five years? For that matter, had Aldwyn intended for Stone to get out? Perhaps even *let* him out? Or had the whole thing been a test to see how long it would take him to break free?

"I do not presume to comprehend his motivations." Kolinsky looked past Stone, scanning the crowd.

"Yes, that's what I was afraid of." Stone finished his drink. "I guess that's about it, then. Thank you for what you've told me, but you can't help me with Aldwyn, and it sounds like there's no point in tracking down Gabriel or Madame Huan because they can't either. I'm on my own with this." He glared at Kolinsky. "He's going to pay for what he did to me—and to my son."

"I would advise you to be careful, Alastair."

"Of course you would. But I'm quite finished with being careful. He might find I've got more options than he's aware of."

They were mostly, as Aldwyn had said, empty words, and he knew it. Unless he could figure out how to get around a dragon-level magical oath—or how to kill Aldwyn, which might not even be possible—his options weren't looking good.

He'd have to play it by ear. But fortunately, he was good at that.

CHAPTER SEVEN

H E TEXTED VERITY when he returned home. *Up for letting me pick up Raider? I miss having the little furball around the house.*

Sure, she replied. *It will have to be this evening, though. Busy all day.* There was a pause, and then she added: *Let me make you dinner. I'll show you my new place.*

Sounds like a plan.

She sent him the address. *It's on a ley line. Seven okay?*

Looking forward to it. I'd better drive, though. Not sure how my travel method would agree with Raider.

As he settled back and put the phone away, it occurred to him how strange he felt right now—almost as if the three years hadn't passed. Despite Verity's new maturity, the two of them had fallen back into their old-friends relationship with barely a ripple.

Don't get too complacent, though, he told himself. A lot of things had changed, and until he'd dealt with all of them and got his feet back under him, he'd have to be careful.

Verity's loft was in San Francisco's Castro District, just south of Lower Haight and less than a mile from her old place. The neighborhood wasn't fancy, but it did have a bohemian, industrial-artsy vibe to it that Stone knew would appeal to her. It also, as she'd mentioned, had a ley line running through it, which he was sure was part of the reason she'd chosen it.

She must be doing all right for herself, he though as he headed upstairs. Even severe fixer-uppers in bad neighborhoods weren't cheap in the City, and this place was several steps up from that.

He reached her third-floor door and knocked.

She answered quickly, with a big smile. "Hi. Right on time, as usual. Come on in." She was dressed more casually than before, but clothes were still obviously carefully chosen and of higher quality than she used to wear.

Stone sniffed appreciatively. "I've got no idea what that is, but it smells delightful."

She laughed. "It's nothing special, honestly. I didn't have a lot of time to cook today. But I think you'll like it. Come on in, and let me show you the place."

He looked around as she led him further inside. "This is quite nice, Verity. I'm impressed."

He wasn't just being polite. It was a two-level loft, with a large, open living room, small but well-stocked kitchen with modern appliances, a dining area, and a big window with a glass door leading out to a balcony lined with various plants in pots. The rest of the walls were a combination of white-painted wood and weathered brickwork. Two closed doors led off from the living room on the ground floor, and a modern staircase ascended to an open bedroom bounded by an industrial-cable barrier. High above, a large ceiling fan turned slowly, blowing the delicious aromas of the cooking meal all around the space.

Her proud smile widened. "Yeah, I was really lucky to get it. One of Scuro's clients was selling it, so I pounced. It needed some work, but Jason and Amber helped me fix it up nice. I got it two years ago, and it's already nearly doubled in value." She pointed at the walls. "Before you ask, that's not really brick, but it's hard to tell. And the place has two bedrooms, so I can set up the alchemy lab downstairs. Hang on—I need to check on dinner. Feel free to look around. Raider's around here somewhere. Probably upstairs sleeping with Luna."

Stone felt a twinge of regret at her words. Before he'd done his three-year disappearance, Raider usually came running when he got home. He knew it was a small thing in the greater scheme of everything else that was happening, but the thought of losing his feline friend's affection bothered him more than he wanted to admit.

To hide this, he wandered around the downstairs area, taking it in. Verity had hung a few framed art pieces on the walls. They looked like originals rather than prints; he wondered if she'd befriended some local artists and bought some of their work. A small desk near the glass door held a closed laptop, and next to it was a cat tree made of wood and carpet-wrapped platforms. Overall, the place had a neat but lived-in feel. Shifting to magical sight reinforced this impression. She obviously loved the place and felt at home here. He was happy for her. *See? She doesn't need you to help her anymore. She's got her life under control—probably better than you do.*

"You can go upstairs and look for Raider if you want," Verity called from the kitchen, where she was stirring something in a large pot. "I cleaned up before you got here."

He considered not doing it, figuring he wanted the cat to come to *him*. But trying to compel cats to do anything they didn't want to do remained, as always, an exercise in futility, and competing with them for stubbornness was doomed to failure. If this reunion was to happen, he'd have to be the better man.

He mounted the staircase to the second level, glancing at more dramatic, abstract paintings hung along the walls on the way up. The bedroom was large and airy, beneath a high, slanting ceiling with a dusty skylight. A queen-size bed was against the far wall, with a single nightstand, a heavy wooden armoire and dresser, an overstuffed chair, a tapestry, and another framed painting comprising the rest of the décor.

Stone didn't spend much time looking at any of this, though. His attention immediately fell on the two small, furry figures intertwined on top of Verity's deep-red comforter.

"Raider…" he murmured, once again struck with the odd, disorienting feeling of having seen the cat only a couple of days ago while, by Raider's reckoning, he'd been gone for years. So much longer for a cat than a human. It might as well have been a lifetime.

Raider, hearing his name, lazily raised his head and opened his eyes. His green gaze settled on Stone for several moments. Then he closed his eyes again and lowered his head back to where it had been resting on the flank of another cat, this one sleek and gray. The other cat didn't stir.

He swallowed, trying to get rid of the lump rising in his throat. "Hello, mate…" he whispered, moving to sit on the edge of the bed. He held a hand out, but not too close.

Raider cracked his eyes open again. He studied Stone before looking at the outstretched hand. For a long time, he didn't move. Then, oozing upward with languid slowness, he disentangled himself from the gray cat, padded across the bed, and sniffed Stone's hand.

"That's it…you remember me, don't you?" Stone didn't move his hand, even though the compulsion to pet his old friend's head was nearly overwhelming. This had to be Raider's decision.

The cat took another sniff, then tentatively walked forward until he was standing right next to Stone. Something in his expression shifted. He rose onto his back legs and head-butted Stone, purring loudly.

"That's it. That's the way." Stone's voice shook, and he was surprised at the faint prickle of unshed tears. He pulled Raider into his arms and stroked him. "You haven't forgotten me."

The other cat, clearly offended at being left out of the love-fest, lazily stood and stalked over, dropping down to press herself against Stone's leg.

"The reunion was a success, I see," came a dry voice from the stairway.

Stone knew he was grinning like an idiot as he twisted around to face Verity, but he didn't care. "He remembers me."

"Well, you *are* pretty hard to forget." She reached the top of the stairs and came over to sit next to him on the bed. She nodded at the other cat. "She's going to miss him, though. He kind of raised her."

Stone stroked both cats, one with each hand. "She's lovely. I know you've been saying you wanted one. We'll have to set up play dates. Perhaps I'll see if I can find out if the ley lines are safe for him."

"We'd like that. I'll miss him too. He's been a great houseguest." The gray cat ambled over to her and plopped into her lap. "Luna is great too. I take her to work at the shop when I'm there, and she seems to like it. Gives Raider some alone time."

Stone chuckled. "A shop cat."

"Yeah, got the idea from Bron. She takes her cat to her bookstore every day. Rides her in a carrier on her motorcycle. I don't think Luna would go for that, though. Anyway, dinner's ready if you want to come down. I'm sure these two goofballs will be along to step in your food any time now."

Dinner, lobster mac and cheese with a green salad, was a complete success. It wasn't one of Verity's usual complicated dishes, but that was fine with Stone, who found he felt more relaxed than he had since he'd returned. Part of it was letting go of the stress of worrying whether Raider would remember him, and part was his easy camaraderie with Verity. Every time he spent time with her, he thanked the gods that their romantic breakup hadn't affected their deep friendship, and the three-year hiatus seemed not to have mattered. Their conversation was light, mostly discussing events that had occurred in the world during Stone's absence.

"So much to catch up on," he commented as he poured another glass of wine (Verity's taste in wine had improved since he'd been gone as well). "I suppose I'll pick it up as I go, but I expect I'll be rubbish at current-events pub trivia for a while."

"We all have to make our sacrifices, I guess." She used magic to gather the plates, making them do a little dance to amuse Raider and Luna.

"It's all a bit overwhelming. So much to do—I need to visit Jason and Amber and meet their children, which I'll admit sort of terrifies me…"

She laughed. "I wouldn't worry too much about it. They're good kids. Just think of them as mostly-hairless cats."

He shot her a sideways look, and continued as if she hadn't spoken. "I also need to go back home and see Aubrey. I hope I don't shock him too much. You—er—didn't already tell him I'm back, did you?"

"Me? No. I don't think Jason or Ian did either. That's your business, when you want to do it."

"I'm wondering if perhaps one of you *should*. Remember how shocked *you* were when you heard my voice. I don't want to give the old man a heart attack or something. Susan would flay me alive." He spoke lightly, but it was a genuine concern.

She seemed to pick up on that, and her expression grew sympathetic. "You want me to?"

"I'd appreciate it. Don't give him any details—just let him know I'm back. Once I know he's got over the initial surprise, I'll pop over there to see him."

"Sure, I'd be happy to."

The stress was starting to get to him again, so he stroked Raider, who'd jumped up on the table a while ago. "So much to do. The University, Gina…"

"It'll be fine," she said gently. "Take your time. You don't have to do it all at once. Oh—speaking of Gina. You don't have to be home early tonight, do you?"

That was an odd question. "Er—no. Why?"

"You mentioned you wanted to see what was up with the Changelings. There's a decent-sized group of them here in town. If you want, we can go over there."

"Go...over there? Oh, that's right—you mentioned they've formed themselves into little enclaves."

"A lot of them have. It makes sense—since they're the only ones who can see each other's true forms, they tend to gravitate toward each other. In San Francisco, they've taken over a section of the Tenderloin."

He tilted his head. When he'd left, the whole Changeling phenomenon had barely gotten started, and now there were enough of them to form neighborhoods. "How many of them are we talking?"

"Not *that* many as a percentage of the general population. Less than one percent, as far as anybody can tell. But that's still a lot of people. If you figure there are almost nine hundred thousand people in San Francisco, even half a percent of them is a few thousand."

"Bloody hell."

"Yeah. It's hard to be sure because a lot of them don't want to be tracked, but the majority have definitely gravitated toward a few larger cities. There are big groups of them here in San Francisco, Chicago, Seattle, Los Angeles, New York City, Atlanta, Dallas, Las Vegas, Boston..." She trailed off and spread her hands. "And that's just in the US."

"Do you know any of them? Aside from Gina, and Jason and Amber's son?"

"Oh, sure. I have a few friends over there. Met them through Gina. Most of them don't trust mages very much, but her friends figure I'm okay because she trusts me."

"They know about mages?"

"Not most of them—and some of the ones who've heard of us don't believe it, or haven't ever met one. But the ones who *do* know don't like how we can see their true forms. It makes them nervous, since there's nothing about us *they* can see unless we reveal ourselves."

"I suppose that makes sense." He finished his wine. "Do they even *want* us over there?"

"Eh. They're just people. They run businesses and work at jobs like everybody else. As long as we don't mess with them, it'll be fine. I can introduce you to my friends."

"I have to admit I'm curious."

"Of course you are." She smiled fondly. "Because you're *you*. As long as you don't say anything about trying to 'cure' them—that pisses them off—you'll be fine."

"Yes, I think I've got it through my head that that horse has well and truly left the barn."

"And it's probably best not to do any magic around them, but that shouldn't be a problem. I know how good you are at hiding when you do magical sight." She gathered the rest of the plates. "Come on—I'll dump these in the dishwasher and we can head out. You can grab Raider when we get back."

CHAPTER EIGHT

A	T FIRST, Stone couldn't put his finger on what felt different about the area Verity drove him to. As they cruised around looking for a parking garage, he watched the scenery go by with mundane sight, noting the usual mix of ground-floor businesses, apartments on upper levels, vacant lots and abandoned spaces, and a familiar collection of homeless people lining the streets with their tents and makeshift cardboard shelters. It took him until they'd pulled into a narrow space on the third level of a structure on Jones Street before he got it: a subtle feeling of suspicion permeating the air, even before he switched to magical senses.

A feeling that he wasn't welcome here—and that he was being watched.

He got out of the vehicle—Verity had traded her black SUV for a sporty red Toyota—and paused, looking around. "Do you feel that?"

"Feel what?" She locked the Toyota and paused to put a disregarding spell on it.

"Not sure exactly. A kind of…tension."

"Oh—yeah. The Changelings don't encourage non-Changelings to be in their area, especially this time of night. Even some sensitive mundanes can feel it." She hurried down the stairs toward the ground level. "It's not really safe for mundanes to come here at night. Most of the Changelings are fine, but some of them just want to be left alone. This area has developed a reputation for being kind of a no-go zone after dark."

"That seems a bit…odd. It's not as if the mundanes have any idea who or what they are."

"That's true—and of course they don't mind people coming around to patronize their businesses. Think of it as kind of like a heavily ethnic neighborhood, though. Anybody who doesn't belong is going to stand out like a sore thumb, especially at night." They reached the street level, and Verity paused a moment to look around. "I'm probably making it sound worse than it is. Like I said, mostly they just want to live their lives and be left alone. But just like there are some bad folks in the magical community, the Changelings have them too. Come on—let's go. And remember to be subtle if you use magical sight. We're right on the edge of their area right now, so that being-watched feeling will probably get worse."

Curious and intrigued, Stone followed her up the street. He still didn't use magical sight, content for the moment to scan the businesses along both sides. This area was clearly an entertainment district; bars, nightclubs, restaurants, and tattoo parlors lit with bright neon were all open, along with all-night convenience stores and liquor stores. To his surprise, though, he also saw a few other open shops: clothing stores, bookstores, even a kitchen-gadget shop. "Do they work here, too?"

"Some of them do. For whatever reason, a lot of Changelings prefer being out at night. Sometimes it's because the sun hurts their eyes, and sometimes it's just that they prefer not to be seen. Even though mundanes can't see their true forms, quite a few of them have developed mannerisms consistent with who they really are. It can creep out the uninitiated—and some of the Changelings have kind of taken that as a point of pride."

Stone shook his head, amazed at how much things had changed during his absence. "This is a lot to get my mind around," he admitted. "It's fascinating, though."

"It is. Just—" She stopped and appeared to be considering how she wanted to continue. "—don't take this wrong, but I'd advise you to rein in your inner cat. The one thing that really sets them off, especially with mages, is being looked at like they're zoo animals, or experimental subjects."

If it had been anyone else, Stone might have been offended by her words. As it was, he nodded. "I understand. Believe me, as I said before, I've well and truly internalized the idea that they've got as much right to be here as the rest of us, and they don't want to be cured."

She smiled in relief. "That's all I'm saying. Come on—let's find my friends. I gave them a call, so they know we're coming."

The uneasy feeling grew as he followed her up the street. More people were visible now, patronizing the businesses, loitering outside the bars and nightclubs, walking along in pairs or small groups. As Verity and Stone passed them, he felt their gazes burning into both of them. Nobody bothered them, but the impression of not being welcome was nearly palpable at this point.

"They *don't* like us, do they?"

"Not really. They can tell we aren't Changelings because they can see we don't have true forms, which means we're either mundanes or mages. Probably mundanes, since they don't get too many mages around here. Just keep walking and be cool."

Stone often felt out of place in crowds, but never this much. Every moment they remained on the street, he expected someone to jump them—especially since he'd chosen not to use his magical shield in case any of the Changelings could spot it.

"How many different types of them are there?" he asked under his breath, leaning in close to Verity. "Are there...classifications of them? A finite number of types? Do any of them have powers?"

"Probably not the best time to ask those questions," she murmured back, nodding toward another small knot of people lounging in front of a tattoo parlor, smoking. "Some of them have enhanced hearing, and you never know who's listening."

Stone looked around, directing his gaze not only down the street but up toward the sky. He wasn't surprised to see a few shadowy figures in windows, and wondered if they were watching the strangers. Without magical sight, he couldn't tell if anyone aside from himself and Verity weren't Changelings, but he suspected the two of them were the only ones. Though he remained apprehensive, his fascination eclipsed that. His academic discipline, Occult Studies, was a subset of Cultural Anthropology, and it wasn't every day that an entirely new culture emerged this quickly. The Changelings could have developed a lot of traditions and ways of interacting with both each other and the larger world in three years. It was too bad the mundanes knew nothing about them, and probably wouldn't believe it if they did. He made a mental note to ask Eddie and Ward if any of the magical community had managed to do any research.

They passed a couple of closed storefronts in an older building, with their doors set back in alcoves from the street. Stone noticed a few homeless people huddled under blankets, but he didn't see the other figures—three of them—until they stepped out and surrounded him and Verity.

"Hey," one said. He was a hulking young man, a few inches taller than Stone, with broad shoulders, a bald, tattooed head, and a ripped denim jacket covered in patches. His voice, deep and rumbling, didn't sound aggressive.

"Hey," Verity She stood straight and tall, confident but not confrontational.

"You two don't live around here." A woman, thin and gangly with green hair and a thin, ratlike face.

Stone didn't say anything, since Verity obviously had this under control.

"Nope," she agreed. "We're visiting some friends."

The third member of the group, a teenage boy who moved with an eerie fluidity, paced back and forth behind them. "You got friends here?" His tone made it sound like he thought that was a ridiculous idea.

"Are you surprised?"

"Yeah, kinda," the bald man admitted. "If you did, they'd'a told you not to visit 'em at night. Ain't safe around here for your kind."

"Our kind?" Stone couldn't help it. "And what kind is that?"

Verity shot him a warning look.

The green-haired woman narrowed her eyes. "You tell us."

"Who's your friends?" the kid behind them asked. He drifted around toward the front. "Where do they live?"

Verity's expression hardened. "You want to tell me why that's any of your business?" Though she didn't say anything to Stone, he nonetheless had no trouble picking up her unspoken *let me handle this.*

"Everything around here's our business," the bald man said. His voice didn't rise, and he didn't demonstrate any overt threat, but something about his physicality seemed off—almost as if he were bigger and took up more space than it seemed he should.

"This is our place," the green-haired woman added. Unlike her larger friend, she looked stressed and twitchy.

"Look," Verity said, "we don't want any trouble. I'm serious. All we want to do is visit our friends for a little while. We'll be out of here in a couple hours."

Stone couldn't resist any longer. While the three were focused on her, he switched to magical sight for less than five seconds.

He didn't let his reaction reach his face, but it wasn't easy.

Back when he'd encountered the first Changeling he'd ever met, a satyr named Wayne Carter, Carter had spoken of seeing what he described as an "ogre"—a massive, muscular creature with a bald head—stepping out of a MUNI train. Stone wondered if the man in front of them was the same one Carter had seen, or just another of the same type. Either way, the reason for the odd physical sensation he'd been feeling became immediately clear: the man's astral Changeling form was nearly seven feet tall, his heavily muscled shoulders and torso straining his denim jacket. His face had morphed into something that was still mostly human, but the heavy, ridged brow, squashed nose, and especially the two long, silver-capped teeth poking up from his lower jaw made him look like something else entirely.

Like an ogre, in fact.

Carter had described the man he'd seen as putting out "anger vibes." Stone wasn't getting that—perhaps the man had calmed down in three years—but there was still an overwhelming sense of intimidation.

Next to the ogre, the other two were less immediately frightening, but every bit as strange and interesting to look at. He didn't get much in five seconds—only that the green-haired woman had a skinny, hag-like face with a faint green tint and eerie eyes, and the sinuously-moving kid's visible skin was covered with small, even scales.

"Hey! What're you doing?"

The scaly kid was looking straight at Stone.

Verity gripped his hand and squeezed.

"What are you talking about?" Stone spoke with confidence.

"You were lookin' at us funny." He narrowed his eyes, leaning in to study Stone more carefully.

"Come on," Verity said. "Nobody was looking at anybody funny. You guys must have better things to do than hassle us, don't you?"

"Not really," the green-haired hag admitted.

Stone tensed. This was getting ridiculous.

Verity squeezed his hand again.

"Tell ya what," the ogre said, glancing at his watch. "How 'bout you turn back around and get outta here. You can call your friends and they can meet you someplace else. Everybody's happy."

Stone half-expected Verity to go along with his request to keep the peace, but she remained resolute.

"I don't think we're going to do that," she said in a conversational tone. There still wasn't anything confrontational in her demeanor. "We came all the way over here to visit our friends, and that's what we're going to do. Would you please move so we can get out of your way?"

Before any of them could answer—or potentially start something—another voice spoke from behind them. "Is there a problem here?"

Stone turned along with Verity. Two other figures were approaching, stopping a few feet away. The man was in his late twenties, pale, of medium height and long-limbed, while the darker-skinned woman looked about ten years older. She was tall and broad-shouldered, even to mundane sight. A quick glance with magical sight revealed both of them to be covered with fur. The man had abnormally long fingers and a graceful prehensile tail, and the woman could have been another of Amber's bear-shifter clan. Both wore leather jackets, T-shirts bearing a symbol that looked like a stylized, furry hand, and baseball caps with the same symbol.

"No trouble," the ogre said quickly. "Just talkin' to these folks here a little." He didn't sound scared, but his voice held healthy respect.

The muscular woman looked Stone and Verity over. Recognition dawned on her face and her stern expression changed to a wide smile. "Oh, hey, Verity."

Verity grinned. "Hi, Ellie. Haven't seen you for a while."

"Yeah, been busy. You know how it is."

Next to Verity, Stone let himself relax, at least a little. He wanted to turn around because having the three others behind him made him uncomfortable, especially without his magical shield up. But it was obvious the situation was more in hand now than it had been before the newcomers showed up.

"What are you doing here? Little late for you, isn't it?"

Verity jerked her head, indicating the three. "We were coming by to visit some friends, but these three wanted to talk."

"Pfft, talk." Ellie looked like a mother whose kids had been caught tossing water balloons at passing cars. "C'mon, Carlos, take your two buddies and stop hassling people."

"We weren't hasslin' 'em," the hag protested. "They don't belong here."

"Not gonna say it again. Go on, go bug somebody else. Verity's cool, and whoever this guy is, if he's with her, he's cool too."

The three grumbled among themselves, obviously not wanting to give up, but finally the ogre said in a reluctant growl, "Okay, whatever." He gripped Stone's shoulder with his big, meaty hand, not quite hard enough to hurt but definitely hard enough to *promise* pain. "But don't make any trouble or we'll find you."

"That ain't your job, Carlos." The monkey-man spoke for the first time. "Get on outta here. Now."

The three sloped off, still muttering darkly and glancing over their shoulders as they went. When they disappeared around a corner, Ellie let her breath out.

"Don't mind them," she told Verity. "They're good folks, but a little...oversensitive."

Verity nodded. "I get it. Have you been having any trouble?"

"Eh, it happens." She looked at Stone. "Who's this?"

Stone didn't miss the slight suspicion in her voice. Even though she'd told the three other Changelings he was all right because he was with Verity, now that the threat was past she seemed inclined to verify that.

Verity didn't appear bothered. "His name's Alastair Stone. He's a good friend of mine, and he won't cause any trouble." She shot him another warning look, as if to say, *don't make me a liar.*

The two Changelings exchanged glances. "Is he...like you?"

"Yeah. But he's cool. Trust me."

They studied him again with narrowed eyes. "You know we don't like mages around here," the monkey-man said. "Nothing personal, but they make folks nervous."

"Yeah. I know. That's why I haven't come by in a while. Are you going to tell us to leave?" Her words took on the slightest hint of a challenge—not intimidating, but making them own up to it if they were going to imply it.

Ellie shook her head. "Nah, you're good. You know how to act." She shifted her gaze to Stone again. "I don't know if Verity told you, but we're kind of the unofficial law around here."

"The...law?" Stone tilted his head.

"Do you remember the Guardian Angels?" Verity asked. "Group of folks who took on citizen-based law enforcement in areas where the cops were having trouble?"

"Vaguely." He studied the two in a new light, paying more attention to the symbol on their T-shirts. "So, you two do that? Keep people in line around here? What about the police?"

"What about them?" The monkey-man's voice dripped with contempt. "They don't come around here much. We scare them."

"Not without reason," Ellie added. "Even though they can't see our true forms, they still sense there's something odd about us. The problem is, even we can't keep a lid on everything around here." She indicated the monkey-man. "There aren't enough of us willing to do it. Fortunately, most people go along with us because we're better than the cops. We live here, we're dealing with the same challenges, and most folks recognize we need law and order one way or another or nobody will be safe."

"They're afraid if the Watch doesn't keep things under control, the cops will finally get brave enough to come in and try to do it themselves," the monkey-man said sullenly. "And that won't be pretty for anybody."

Stone found all this fascinating, and he was itching to take notes. He didn't, though. As Verity had said, letting his "inner cat" run free here was clearly a bad idea. "I know you don't like us," he said, trying to sound as harmless and persuasive as he could, "but I promise, we won't cause any trouble. I've been…out of town for an extended period, and Verity had offered to introduce me to some of her friends. We won't be staying long."

The two Changelings looked at each other again. "Yeah, okay," Ellie said. She didn't sound happy about it. "Go on. We'll alert the other Watch to leave you alone. But don't stay too long." She shot Verity an apologetic glance. "I know, it sucks. I wish it wasn't this way. But you know how it is."

"Yeah, I do." Verity looked as unhappy about it as she did. "Thanks, Ellie. You should come over one of these days. I owe you lunch."

"We'll see. Been keeping pretty busy around here lately. A couple of gangs on the edge of our space are stirring up trouble, and some of the younger Freaks aren't handling it too well." She tensed and pulled her phone from her pocket. "Anyway, gotta go. There's a problem at one of the bars. Some lost norm tourists wandered in and the kids are bothering them. Take care, Verity. Nice meeting you, Alastair."

The two hurried off, leaving Verity and Stone alone.

"'Freaks'?" Stone whispered. He leaned in close to Verity, looking around in case anyone was listening.

"Yeah." She started walking again, motioning for him to follow. "Some of them call themselves that, especially the younger ones. It's sort of a take-back-the-power thing, like LGBT people calling themselves 'queer,' or black people using the N-word among themselves."

Stone nodded. "So not something I ever want to use."

"No way. Not unless you want somebody to bite your head off. Maybe literally."

That brought up another question. He risked a 'Cone of Silence' spell, using extra power to make it as subtle as possible. "Do we need to worry about them? Do any of them actually have abilities that can hurt us?"

"Oh, yeah. It'd be harder with A's like you, but there aren't many of those around. And even so, if you're not paying attention, there's a lot of ways they could make your life miserable."

Stone had mostly stopped listening near the beginning of her sentence. "What did you just say? 'A's'?"

"Oh, right, you don't know about that. Remember before, we were telling you about how they've started classifying magical power levels?"

"Yes…"

"It's on a five-point scale, A to E. A's are people like you and Harrison and Kolinsky. Shitloads of power and full training. You three are probably A-pluses, actually. I'm a high B—higher than average power, fully trained. C's are your garden-variety talents with some training and middling power, like Hezzie. D's have a basic level of power but little or no training. E's have the lowest power and no training. Oh, and there's also Xes."

"And those are?" Stone was still maintaining the spell, keeping an eye on their surroundings as they continued walking, but he found this whole classification thing almost as interesting as the Changelings.

"Wild talents. People who have a single ability, or a small cluster of related ones. They're sub-classified one to five, highest to lowest, depending on how impressive that ability is. Like Bron's friend Nick—remember him, the guy who messes with magic? He's an X-1."

"I'm not surprised." A stray thought struck him—a fleeting speculation about whether Nick Happenstance's uncanny ability to interfere with magic had any connection to the magic-damping obelisk currently in Stefan Kolinsky's possession—but he pushed it aside. He had a lot more immediate problems to occupy him right now, without adding more.

"Your guy who can get through wards is probably an X-1 too."

"Ah, right. Zack. I doubt he'd submit to getting tested, though." *Or rather, I doubt Kolinsky would allow him to get tested, assuming he's still got him in his pocket.* He shook his head. "I can see I'm going to need a lot of updating."

"I'll write a few things up for you when I get a chance. I—" She stopped when a loud *crack* sounded in the distance, followed by yelling voices.

CHAPTER NINE

"DID YOU HEAR THAT?" Stone glanced around, trying to home in on the source of the sounds.

"Yeah." She was doing the same thing. "It's up ahead, I think."

"Should we investigate? Could it be near your friends' place?"

She hesitated. "We shouldn't get involved. The Watch—"

"They went the other way." Stone hooked a thumb over his shoulder at where they'd just come from.

More muffled sounds came from up ahead: another *crack,* followed by a soft *boom* like something heavy being dropped from a great height. Then a piercing scream.

Stone increased his pace to a jog. "I'm sorry, Verity, but I can't just walk past this. Are you coming?"

"Alastair—"

He didn't stop; in fact, he moved faster. "I won't get involved if they have it under control."

He heard her loud sigh behind him, then her footsteps quickened. He wondered if she was regretting bringing him here, but the thought left his mind when two more quick *crack*s split the quiet night. Gunshots? Something else?

As soon as he rounded the next corner, Stone got a good look at what was going on. A short block ahead, an intersection was choked with people and cars, several of the latter parked at odd angles to block the way through. There were no more *crack*s or *boom*s at the moment, but a small crowd of people were still yelling something he couldn't make out. They all appeared to be focused on a three-story building on the intersection's far corner.

He skidded to a stop well before he reached the crowd, and switched to magical sight.

Bright, colorful auras sprang up around the crowd in the street, all of them tinged with red patches indicating their agitation. But nothing else.

The crowd members were mundanes—or at least non-Changelings.

As he watched, one of them flung something at the building with a loud, inarticulate roar. The window shattered, and another *whump* followed immediately. From here, it sounded less like something hitting the ground and more like some kind of explosive.

Verity gripped his arm. "Look—I think it's one of those gangs Ellie was talking about."

Stone hadn't noticed it at first, figuring if they were a gang they'd all be wearing the same jacket or something. But now that she mentioned it, several of the milling crowd members—almost all of them young men—wore red hoodies or sports jerseys.

"Come on out, freaks!" one of them yelled. "Next one won't just be smoke!"

Stone glanced up again. Black smoke was billowing from the broken window, but he didn't see any sign of fire.

From the back of the group, someone emitted a high, shrieky scream. *"My eyes!"*

Stone and Verity both spun. They were standing on the periphery of the crowd so it was hard to get a clear read on the situation, but magical sight revealed the answer: several Changelings, also wearing red, had surrounded the mundane group, and not just on the ground. Several of them were either clinging to the sides of buildings or leaning out of upper-story windows. One of the mundanes, a husky young man, writhed on the ground, still screaming, clutching his face. The rest of the group were spinning around, confused, trying to spot who was responsible.

"They can't tell," Stone murmured, getting it. "They can't see the Changelings." To him they were obvious: one with snakelike features, another who looked like a fox, and a third with unnaturally smooth, spotted skin and bulging eyes.

"Yeah." Verity sounded grim. She looked around. "Where are the Watch?"

"I heard gunshots. Will the police show up for that?"

"Don't know. They're supposed to, but—"

Stone didn't wait for the rest of her answer. One of the red-clad mundanes had backed off, obviously catching on that something was up. Stone reached out with magic and yanked the young man closer. "You! What's going on here?"

"Fuck off!" the boy snapped. He was maybe fifteen, skinny and pimply with a mop of dirty-blond hair under makeshift mask covering his lower face. He wore an oversize 49ers jersey over sweatpants and basketball shoes. "Let me go!"

Stone held him fast with magic. "I'll let you go after you answer my question."

"Doc—" Verity began.

He barely noticed she'd deliberately not used his name. "Tell me!" he ordered. "Why are you doing this?" Beyond them, the Changelings were moving in, using their various abilities against the mundanes. An ogre had arrived and was wading in, knocking crowd members to both sides.

The boy struggled harder. When he couldn't get loose, his eyes got big. "You're one o' them freaks!"

"No, I'm not." He gripped the kid's arm, shifting his magic to make it appear that his grip was strong enough on its own. "Last chance. Why are you here?"

The boy held his gaze for a couple more seconds. Anger still blazed on his thin face. "Fuckin' freaks moved in on us. Took over the Blackbird."

"What the hell is the Blackbird?"

"It's a bar," Verity said. "On the edge of their territory." She nodded toward the Changelings.

"So they're expanding?"

"Sounds like it." She was looking around again, more concerned this time. The mundanes were fighting back. So far there was no sign of firearms, so the *crack*s must have come from something else. But it was already clear that the Changelings had the upper hand. The ogre had picked up one mundane kid in each hand and thrown them to two different sides, slamming one into the side of a building and the other into a parked car. Three more mundanes had piled onto him, trying to bring him down. From above, a long-limbed, furred figure hung from the top of a streetlight and was throwing something into the crowd.

"They fucked up Juan and Kosal!" the kid shrieked, renewing his efforts to get free of Stone's hold. "Put 'em in the hospital! They're gonna pay for that!"

Verity touched Stone's arm. "Let him go," she murmured.

Stone didn't want to let him go, but she was right. He couldn't hold the kid all night. He released his magical grip and shoved him away. "Get out of here."

"Fuck you!" The kid flipped him off and took off, disappearing into the crowd.

Stone scanned the crowd again. "Are we just supposed to let this happen? Stand by and do nothing?"

Verity didn't look any more comfortable about it than he did, but she nodded. "We can't do much—this isn't our fight." She pointed. "Look—the Watch is showing up."

From three sides of the fray, Stone spotted leather-jacket-clad figures moving closer. Magical sight showed him two of them were

Ellie and her monkey-man partner. Another group of three coming in from the near side had a megaphone, currently held by a tall, muscular man with thick, green scales along his bare arms.

"Everybody calm down!" the beefy lizard-man yelled. "We aren't gonna solve anything by fighting! Somebody's gonna get hurt!"

A chorus of "Fuck you, freak!" and "Take 'im down!" and "Take back our space!" came from the mundane crowd.

"They don't have any weapons," Stone muttered to Verity. "How are they going to deal with this? He's right—someone's going to get hurt. People already *have*." From where he stood, he could see at least five people, all of them mundanes, lying prone in the intersection. They still had auras so none of them were dead, but two flickered dangerously, indicating more severe injury.

The Watch members didn't seem intimidated by the crowd. They waded in, but Stone noticed they did their best not to hurt the mundanes. Though none of them had weapons, several used their various abilities to avoid or shrug off the crowd's attacks. The monkey-man moved like a blur, seeming to flow around the punches and kicks the mundanes were trying to rain on him. Bearish, furry Ellie simply kept walking, shoving kids to the side like a ship's prow slicing through water. It looked impressive to magical sight, and even more so to mundane vision, where she simply appeared as a stocky, unenhanced woman shrugging off attacks that would have dropped a full-sized man.

"We should get some height," Stone said. "If there's any way we can help, it won't be from here. And we'll have to be subtle."

Verity looked like she might protest, but finally nodded reluctantly. "This looks bad." She pointed. "Look—more mundanes are coming. It's gonna turn into a full-blown riot if this keeps up. I don't think the cops can ignore it this time."

"Let's get on the roof of that—" Suddenly, Stone couldn't remember what he was about to say. The scene in front of him began to shift, the writhing crowd turning to hypnotic, brightly-colored patterns. They were so beautiful—

From somewhere far in the distance, he thought he heard someone calling his name. Or *was* it his name? Maybe it was somebody else's name. Maybe it wasn't even related to him. It didn't matter anyway—the undulating colors had claimed his full attention. The sounds appeared in front of him as splintered, jagged fragments, swirling in the air around his head, trying to find their way into his ears.

Something grabbed his arm, tugging at him. He wrenched free. The swirling colors were moving away now, and he had to follow them. He couldn't let them get away. They had something to tell him, if the noise around him would only quiet down so he could listen—

A sharp pain smacked him in the face, followed immediately by a loud voice in his ear. "*Alastair!*"

Alastair? Who was that? The voice fragmented into a cloud of bees buzzing around his head, all of them echoing the sound in their high, piping voices: *Alastair…Alastair…Alastair…*

The pain struck again, even harder this time. The colorful fragments splintered and scattered in all directions as if fleeing from a threat, leaving Stone confused and muddy-headed. "…what?"

Something gripped his arm. "Come on!"

Regretful that the beautiful colors had departed, he allowed himself to be dragged further from the fray. As he stumbled along, his heart beat faster and the muddy feeling began to recede. "Verity!"

She stopped, looking relieved, but didn't release his arm. "Are you back?"

He glanced back over his shoulder. "What *was* that?"

"One of them probably got you. A few of the Changeling types have chemicals that can affect the mind. Saliva, or something they exude from their skin."

Stone didn't remember being spit on or grabbed by anyone else, but the whole scene had been chaotic enough that he might not have noticed. "Bloody hell…" he murmured. "So they can even affect *us*?"

"Yeah, some of them. Come on. Are you together enough to do an invisibility spell?"

"I think so."

"Make sure. If they spot us using magic it could cause more trouble."

"I can do it," he said with more certainty. "Come on."

Together, they ducked into an alley, faded to invisibility, and levitated to the top of the two-story building next to them. After looking around to make sure no Changelings already occupied the space, they settled next to the edge, ducked low, and observed the scene.

It actually looked worse from up here. Stone estimated there had to be about twenty to thirty mundanes in the intersection, along with their haphazardly-parked vehicles and the innocent by-standers who were merely trying to get away from the scene. About the same number of Changelings—at least the ones he could see with magical sight—ringed the area, some on the ground and some on tops of buildings or leaning out windows. A couple stuck to the sides of the buildings and were tossing things down into the crowd. As he watched, a loud *crack* sounded above the shouting crowd, and one of the Changelings fell off the building and hit the ground. Immediately, several other Changelings converged on the area, some surrounding their fallen friend, others swirling around the shooter.

"Look." Verity pointed. "More Watch have shown up. I hope they can handle this."

Stone wasn't used to standing on the sidelines during situations like this. "We've got to help them. What good are we doing up here?"

She didn't look happy. "We can't help. It's too dangerous. This is bad enough now with the Changelings and the mundanes. What do you think will happen if mages show up?"

"They're killing each other down there." He pointed at the fallen Changeling, whose true form looked like some kind of lizard. His orange aura flickered, fading noticeably even as Stone watched.

"What do you want to do?" Her frustration was evident. "We can't just wade in and start firing off concussion spells. You saw what that guy did to you. You might think you're invincible, but what the Changelings do isn't strictly magic. It's harder for us to defend against some of their abilities."

That was news to Stone. One, he could possibly accept—but multiples of them? And not magic? He narrowed his eyes. "Is that right?"

"Yeah. Not a lot of them, but their abilities are still being cataloged. That's what can be so dangerous about them—you never know what you're dealing with until you're in the middle of it."

Stone had to stop himself from growling aloud. Down below, the Watch seemed to be getting the situation under control, but not fast enough. The mundane bystanders had mostly abandoned their cars and taken off on foot, but more angry young mundanes were starting to show up. Even if they outnumbered the Changelings, though, the locals seemed to be better organized. This wasn't going to end well for any of them unless the Watch—or the police, if they ever showed up—got it under control. Stone couldn't hear any approaching sirens. Did the police really avoid this area? He made a mental note to ask Leo Blum about it later.

Now, though, they had more pressing concerns. "Okay," he said grimly. "If we can't do anything direct, maybe we can do something *in*direct."

"Like what?" She looked dubious.

He looked around, scanning first the crowd and then the area around them. When he spotted a transformer pole across the street, the beginnings of a plan started to form.

Verity grabbed his arm. "What are you going to do?" Her voice held a warning edge.

"Cause a distraction."

"Alastair—"

Without answering her, he focused his attention on the pole. It was a little harder to do what he was planning than to cast a lightning spell directly at it, but doing it that way would be far too noticeable—a beacon that screamed "Look at me! I'm doing magic!" to anyone who cared to look. He concentrated, gathered Calanarian energy—thank the gods nothing had happened to Calanar's relative location to Earth's dimension in the last three years—and released it around the top of the pole.

A deafening *boom* sliced through the shouting combatants, followed by an equally loud *bzzzt* as the transformer exploded. All around them, the lights in the buildings winked out.

Cries went up from the crowd down below. Stone, watching with magical sight, saw some of the mundanes' auras flare in surprise and fear. There wasn't much of a moon tonight, so now the only light came from any car headlights that were still on. A few of the mundane gangers yelped and took off running, but the Changelings were close on their heels. Around them, the Watch—it appeared there were ten or twelve of them on the scene now—did their best to control the situation.

"I'm not sure that helped," Verity said.

"I'm not done yet." He concentrated again, this time summoning an auditory and visual illusion of several approaching police cars, their red and blue lights whirling and sirens shrieking.

That had more of an effect. The mundane gangers yelled to each other and ran faster. A few of the Changelings tried to follow, but the Watch members got in their way and rounded them up. A few moments later, the intersection was clear of mundanes, except for the ones who'd fallen in the fight.

Stone half-glared at Verity. "Can we help them now? Do you think they'd appreciate some healing?"

Verity was already levitating. "Yeah. Can't let them die if we can do something about it. Come on."

They used their invisibility spells to get them to the ground without being seen, then strode toward the intersection. Stone slowed his long strides to let Verity take the lead, since she knew the situation better than he did, but he stayed close to her.

Several Changelings were huddled around a couple of fallen forms, one in the middle of the intersection and the other—the lizard-man—on the sidewalk near one of the buildings. Several more prone mundane figures lay scattered among the cars, but the Changelings near them appeared more interested in guarding them than helping them.

"We can help if you let us," Verity called.

Several suspicious gazes immediately fell on her and Stone. "Get out of here," one man growled. "This isn't your business."

"It is if you don't want your friend to die." She held her ground, meeting their gazes head-on.

"You're not one of us," a woman said.

"She's a friend," came another female voice, strong and clear. "Let her help."

Stone scanned the crowd and spotted Ellie, the bearish Watch member, approaching.

"How can she help?" a man asked.

"I can heal him, if you let me get to him." She moved closer to the fallen lizard-man.

A rumble started among the crowd. Stone heard snippets of conversation: "—what is she?—" and "—how can she heal—" and "—doesn't belong here—"

Then, rising above the rest of the voices, came an accusatory declaration: "She's a mage!"

The rumbles got louder, and Stone, who was watching the crowd with magical sight, noticed dangerous red flashes forming among the auras. Several people took steps closer.

He knew it was better to stand back and let the others handle this, but if the mundane kid could be believed, this altercation was as much the Changelings' fault as the mundanes'. "Stay back!" he boomed.

Most of the group had been watching Verity, but every gaze now swung to him.

"Who the hell are you?" demanded the ogre. His huge, muscular torso was streaked with blood.

"He's a mage too!" a woman yelled.

The crowd rumbled louder.

"We're not here to mess with anybody!" Verity called, shooting a warning glance at Stone. "Do you want your friend to die?" She gestured at the lizard-man, whose flickering aura was fading.

More rumbles.

"She can heal him," Stone said, using a little magic to amplify his voice. "Can any of you lot do that?"

"You know we can't," Ellie called to the crowd. She didn't need magical amplification. Her voice was plenty loud enough to get over the general hubbub on its own. "I know her. Let her help unless you want Keegan to die."

The rumbles became less united, as some of the crowd seemed more willing to allow a mage access to their friend to save his life, and others still didn't want any outsiders messing with their business.

Finally, Ellie and her monkey-man partner moved forward and stationed themselves on either side of Keegan. "Stay back," Ellie said. "Let her work."

When no one approached immediately, Verity took that as permission. She hurried forward and dropped to her knees next to the lizard-man. "Let me concentrate."

"What about Kyle?" another voice called. "He's hurt too."

Stone looked around. "How badly?" Unless this was a life-or-death situation, Kyle would be better off waiting for Verity than settling for his middling healing skills.

"His arm's busted up." Whoever answered sounded grudging, as if he didn't even want to talk to the outsider.

"My friend's a lot better at healing than I am. Best if he waits for her."

"What, you're too good to heal him?"

Stone sighed. This bunch was starting to annoy him. First they were complaining about mages even being near them, and now they were complaining the same mages didn't want to drop everything and heal their friend. He understood their reluctance to trust strangers, but now it was getting irrational. "That's not what I said. *You* don't want me to heal him. He'll have a better outcome if Verity does it."

"Hey, at least you can take a look at him. You're not doin' anything else."

He shot Verity a withering look, but she was too focused on Keegan to notice him, or anything else. Fortunately, Ellie and her partner were keeping a close watch on the situation, so Stone was confident they would keep any disgruntled crowd members away from her while she worked.

"Fine," he said. "Show me where he is."

A couple of them broke away from the crowd and pushed past two parked cars. Stone followed them to a cleared area, where a young man lay, cradling his left arm. Somebody had taken their jacket off and put it under his head as a pillow. To magical sight, his smooth skin was covered in shaggy dark fur.

Stone was about to kneel next to him when a red flash near another parked car caught his eye. A closer look revealed yet another fallen figure, this one mundane. His aura flickered even worse than Keegan's.

He rose again, focusing on the new figure.

"Hey," one of the Changelings snapped. "Pay attention."

"Just wait." Barely acknowledging him, Stone hurried over to the other victim.

It was one of the mundanes. He lay in a fetal position in front of one of the cars. Its headlights showed a spreading puddle of blood beneath him on the street.

"Hey!" Somebody grabbed his shoulder and spun him around. "Get back over here and help Kyle!"

Stone wrenched free of the grip. "Get away from me!" he snapped. "This boy is dying." He wasn't even thinking about whether he'd be able to do anything about that. Verity was busy, and there was no way the Changelings would allow her to abandon one of their own gravely injured number in favor of a mundane.

"Who gives a fuck?" another one growled. "They came over here to fuck with us, they deserve what they get."

"Yes, well, it doesn't work that way, does it?" Stone dropped to his knees next to the fallen boy. He'd already lost a lot of blood, but the headlights' harsh glare made it difficult to pinpoint the source of the injury. If this was more than a slash and involved his internal organs, the best Stone could hope for was to stabilize him until Verity could get to him.

"Get away from him, man." A deeper voice.

Stone looked up. The ogre from the confrontation with Ellie and her partner was there now, looming.

Damn. This situation could get ugly in a hurry. Stone had no idea what most of these people's Changeling abilities were, but he was pretty sure the ogre could pick him up in one hand and toss him across the intersection. If the one who'd messed with his mind was there too—

He stood and glared at the ogre. "Listen. This isn't my problem. I was just coming here tonight with my friend to visit a couple of *her* friends. I'm not involved in your little vendetta. But I'm not going to let someone die because you lot can't see a little reason. Do you *want* one of you to be a murderer?"

"They started it," said a sullen voice from somewhere behind the ogre.

"Did they?" Stone glanced down at the bleeding victim, magical sight still active. He was fading fast. *Hang on a bit longer...* he pleaded silently. Maybe Verity would finish soon and come over— but a quick look across the intersection dashed that hope. She was bent over the prone Changeling, her aura alight with concentration.

"What are you talkin' about?" A woman, this time—the hag-faced one who'd been with the ogre before.

"Your Watch friends told us some of you took over one of their bars."

"Hey, man, they got no right to keep us in no small space." There were five of them now, ringing Stone and the mundane boy. "We need room."

"Yes, so said every invading force in the history of the world." Stone sighed. "Listen—I don't know which of you did this—" He indicated the boy again. "—and I'm not sure if you've noticed, but this is a teenager. A bloody *child*. Okay, maybe he made a mistake. Maybe he's an idiot. Certainly seems to be no shortage of *that* around here tonight. But if you've got consciences at all, do you want his death on them? And even if you don't care about that, do you honestly think the police are going to stand by and leave you alone if you start killing people?"

"Cops is *scared* of us, man," someone said with obvious pride. "They don't come around here."

Stone shook his head in disgust. "You don't *learn*, do you? Do you pay any attention to the world around you?" He made a sweeping gesture at the buildings. "How many of you live around here? How many of you work and go about your days and just try to be left alone? Maybe the cops are scared of *you*. But are they scared of *all* of you? Of your mothers and children and old people? You don't think they don't have enough firepower that if it becomes enough of an issue, they won't roll in here and level this whole place? You don't think they'll differentiate between a bunch of troublemakers and the people you give a damn about?"

He glared at them. "Like I said—I don't have any issue with you. Probably best if you keep it that way, because you don't want me for an enemy."

"That a threat?"

"No. It's a fact. And even if you do manage to take me down, I've got friends who are as powerful as I am, and they won't be terribly patient with you. Or, you can show some sense and let me help this boy before he dies. Your call, but make it quickly. Otherwise, you'll just have to do your best to stop me, and I'll have to do my best to make sure that doesn't happen."

This time, he stood tall and swept a challenging gaze around the crowd. He hoped none of them could sense how hard his heart was pounding, or the sweat that was starting to run down his back. Sure, he could put up a barrier around himself and the boy, but who knew if they could punch through it? And in any case, he'd need all his concentration if he had any change of helping the boy. "What's it going to be?"

The tension hung in the air for what felt like several minutes, though it was probably only a few seconds. "Fuck it," the ogre finally said. "Go ahead. Fuckin' kid deserves what he got, but you're right—it'll just go bad for us if he dies."

Several other crowd members grumbled in protest, moving in closer.

The ogre stretched his arms to his sides, his eight-foot wing-span doing a good job of blocking most of them. "You heard me. Back off."

"But Kyle—"

"Kyle's got a broke arm. He ain't gonna die." He jerked his chin at Stone. "Better hurry, magic man. Can't hold these guys off forever."

It wasn't as easy as Stone might have hoped for him to turn his back on the still-angry crowd and focus his attention on the boy. But mobs were dangerous, and this one's agreement was fragile. If he showed any weakness, who knew what they might do, either to him or to the young victim?

Forcing himself to concentrate, he knelt next to the boy again and studied him with magical sight. He was barely alive at this point. The blood pool beneath him had spread even in the short time Stone had been addressing the crowd. He didn't know if there was anything he *could* do at this point, but Verity was still busy with the Changeling. He cut his gaze up toward the ogre. "Send somebody to bring my friend over here as soon as she's done with the one she's working on."

He didn't wait for an answer, but instead turned back to the kid. He rolled him over on to his back and stared at him in shock. He hadn't been wrong before: this *was* a kid. Shaggy-haired and pimply-faced, dressed in an oversized, blood-soaked Tony Hawk T-shirt and baggy jeans, the boy looked barely fourteen. He didn't move or even groan when Stone moved him.

Bloody hell, why do I keep getting myself into these situations?

No time for second-guessing now, though. He focused his attention and his magic on the kid's slashed abdomen. He knew there was no chance he'd be able to heal the boy to full health, so he concentrated instead on stopping the bleeding and stabilizing him until Verity could get to them.

Even so, it wasn't easy. He was good at ignoring distractions—all good mages were—but this kind of distraction was harder. Some small part of his mind constantly kept reminding him that mobs were dangerous by definition, and if one of the Changelings decided to do an end run around the ogre and go after him, there wasn't much he could do to stop it.

But on the other hand, if he didn't give this poor kid his full attention, there was a very real chance he'd die. Stone apparently couldn't, so even if somebody did club him over the head or stab him in the back, it would be a painful inconvenience at worst. He shoved the lingering thoughts aside and redoubled his focus on the boy's wound.

He had no idea how long he remained like that, hunched over his work and blocking out the world around him, when a gentle hand touched his shoulder.

"What?" By this time, he'd managed to stop the bleeding and was now working on closing the wound. It wasn't easy work—closing portals was a lot easier than closing wounds, at least for him—but at least he was making progress. The kid would still need medical attention, but Stone didn't think he was in imminent danger of death.

"You okay?"

Relief flooded him at Verity's voice. He let his breath out in a loud *whoosh* and let his shoulders slump. "Can you take over? Is the other one all right?"

"Yeah—he'll live. Ambulances are on the way, along with the cops. If this guy's stable, we should probably get out of here before they get here."

Stone looked up at her. More suspicious-looking Changelings were spread out behind her, but the ogre, Ellie, and her monkey-man partner were keeping them back. Verity looked as tired as he did. When he stood, he noticed most of the other Changelings had taken off, probably to avoid the police. The ones who remained, picking through the area, wore the same leather Watch jackets as Ellie and her partner.

He ran a hand through his hair, looking around for more victims. "Is everyone else all right?"

"No, but they'll live," Verity said. "Nobody else is as bad as these two were." She regarded the boy. "Nice job."

"You'll probably want to check my work. I did the best I could, but—"

She was obviously using magical sight. "No, it looks fine. You did what you could to keep him from dying. Can't ask for much more than that in a situation like this."

Her words warmed him. Maybe all his association with her had finally rubbed off on him, and he was beginning to get a slightly better handle on healing. Probably not, but he could hope. "We should go. These people don't want us here. Sounds like we'll need to give your friends a rain check."

"Yeah. I already texted them. I guess I'll have to introduce you later."

Stone turned to Ellie. "Are these mundanes going to be all right? No one will bother them?"

"We'll make sure of it."

In the distance, the approaching sound of sirens rose above the murmurs of conversations. Several of the Changelings began muttering about cops, and in a few seconds only the Watch members remained.

"You better get out of here," the monkey-man told Stone and Verity. "Unless you want to answer a lot of uncomfortable questions."

Ellie touched Verity's arm. "Thank you for taking care of Keegan." To Stone, she added, "and that kid, too. We don't want trouble around here."

Stone almost said, "Then maybe you should keep your people from taking over places where they don't belong," but he didn't.

R. L. KING

Not only would it not be helpful, but he didn't have a full appreciation for all the variables in this situation.

They said their quick goodbyes and pulled up disregarding spells. Even so, Stone was certain he sensed attention on both of them as they left the neighborhood and headed back toward Verity had parked.

"Well," he said. "That wasn't what I expected."

"No."

She seemed pensive about something, walking along next to him. "Something wrong?"

She continued to walk in silence for a while longer, then shook her head. "Part of me feels like we shouldn't have gotten involved back there."

He narrowed his eyes. "If we didn't, those two boys would have died."

"I know. That's why I'm so torn about it."

"You think I shouldn't have caused the distraction."

"I don't know. They don't want us around there, so part of me thinks you shouldn't have. But on the other hand, you distracted them from hurting each other, so that's a good thing." She sighed. "It's a complicated situation all the way around. You're lucky you missed most of it."

"I wouldn't say I'm lucky. I think I'd rather have seen it than to miss three years of my life."

She stopped, and her eyes were big. "Oh, God, Alastair, I didn't mean it that way. I'm so glad you're back. I wish none of this had happened to you."

He gave her a faint smile and gripped her shoulder. "I know. I get it. And I do see where you're coming from. Believe me, as an anthropologist, I'm finding this all fascinating. But also feeling a bit guilty about it. It's probably a good thing I'm not strictly an anthropologist anymore. How do you study a society most of the world knows nothing about, even though they live right in our midst?"

They resumed walking. "Are you going back?" Verity asked.

"Back? You mean to the University?"

"Yeah."

He thought about it. "I...don't know yet, to be honest. I suppose I don't have to figure it out right away."

They reached her car, which no one had bothered while they were gone. She unlocked it and got in. "I guess you've got enough to keep you busy for a while, between dealing with whoever did this to you, and getting used to the way the world is now, and maybe even getting more involved with what's going on at Caventhorne."

"That isn't the full question, though." He slumped into the passenger seat and watched the streetlights as she drove. "I'm not even sure whether they'll *want* me back. I do enjoy teaching students, but..."

She patted his hand. "Don't worry about it. Like you said, you have time. For now, let's get Raider back where he belongs."

"Yes...good idea." Stone didn't say anything else on the way back to Verity's condo. Instead, he remained deep in thought about the Changeling situation. She'd said they didn't like mages, but he hadn't gotten such a visceral taste of how *much* they didn't like them until he'd been in the midst of them. It hadn't occurred to him that their abilities could affect him, though he supposed it should have, given the way Michele Berry's seduction aura had touched him after his talk.

Michele's been dead for three years, but it still feels like a short time ago for me.

A new world, indeed. He'd need to spend more time getting up to speed about what had changed, and start getting a feeling for how those changes would connect to his own life.

He was beginning to think being out of circulation for three years wasn't the hardest thing he'd have to deal with, at least in the near term.

CHAPTER TEN

ALL THINGS CONSIDERED, Stone had an easier time returning to society over the next two weeks than he'd expected. He made a mental note to find proper tokens of appreciation for Ian and Gabriel—their efforts to impersonate him and keep the day-to-day minutiae of his life moving smoothly ended up preventing a lot of uncomfortable questions when he re-contacted the important people in his life.

His first stop, of course, was Aubrey. He was glad he'd asked Verity to prepare his old friend for his return, since the caretaker was one of the few people who knew the real story and thus had no idea whether Stone would ever resurface. The reunion, conducted when Susan was out visiting friends, was heartfelt and emotional.

Stone didn't make a big deal of it, but merely showed up in the garden one afternoon. He stood silently, watching Aubrey push a wheelbarrow down one of the narrow dirt pathways that wound through the wild space, noting with pleasure that while the caretaker did look a little older and perhaps a little thinner, he walked with confidence and no sign of a shake. Verity had told him she and Hezzie had, with Aubrey's dubious permission, taken a blood sample from him and concocted an elixir designed to hold back the worst effects of the Parkinson's.

"We can't cure it," she told Stone soberly. "I don't think any alchemist can do that. But we've been monitoring his reactions to it closely and it seems to be working. His doctors are confused, of course, but they're just chalking it up to a strong constitution."

Another thing Stone had to be grateful to Verity for. He'd amassed quite a list these days.

When Aubrey finally turned a corner and spotted him, his craggy face slowly split into a wide smile. He dropped the wheelbarrow handles and hurried over, and once again Stone found himself the recipient of a vigorous hug. He'd never been much of a hugger, but under the circumstances he was willing to suspend his reluctance.

"Hello, Aubrey. It's so good to see you. You're looking well."

Aubrey didn't let loose. He buried his face in Stone's chest and gripped even tighter. "Oh, sir. I...don't even know what to say. When Verity told me, I almost didn't believe her."

"Yes, it's been...quite an unbelievable situation." Stone returned the hug, because it was impossible not to. "But I promise, I'm really back, and I'm fine." He patted the old man and took a step back, indicating the garden. "You don't have to work anymore, you know. Didn't I give you enough money so you never have to work another day in your life?"

Aubrey chuckled. "There isn't that much money in the world, sir. I *like* to work. In the garden, at least. I find it peaceful, and it keeps me feeling useful. Susan likes it too. You might notice we've made some changes—I hope you don't mind."

Stone *hadn't* noticed, but when he looked again he saw that some of the garden's wildness had been tamed and given a bit more structure, and there were more bright flowers than before—probably Susan's doing.

"No—I like it. You just go on doing whatever makes you happy. I suppose I can't picture you stretched out on some beach somewhere, sipping something with an umbrella in and soaking up the sun." He looked the caretaker over now that they were closer. "I wasn't kidding—you *are* looking well. All's well with you and Susan, I trust?"

The smile was different now—fond and loving and utterly happy. "I couldn't ask for a better life, sir—except to have you back. And now I've got that as well."

"Now, come on—don't get sappy on me."

"I wouldn't think of it, sir." He indicated the house. "If you'll come inside, I'll be happy to fix you some—"

"No." Stone gripped his arm. "I'm serious, Aubrey—your days of fixing me anything are over."

"Even if it makes me happy to do it?"

Stone rolled his eyes. "You're incorrigible, do you know that?"

"You've always told me so, sir."

And that was it—three years' absence erased as if it had never occurred. Stone smiled as the two of them walked back toward the house. Someone had once told him that was how you judged a true friendship: by the way time apart disappeared as soon as you were together again. If that definition was correct, he was lucky to have quite a number of true friends. Okay, maybe it was a little different when magic was in the mix, but he'd take it.

Aside from Aubrey, Stone had three other people or groups on his list to contact soon. The first one was easy—all he had to do was show up to Jason's office late one afternoon. Verity had given him the new location, but he was still surprised to see how much bigger it was. Thayer Investigations must indeed be doing well for itself.

They even had a receptionist, a cheerful young man he didn't recognize—and who didn't recognize him. "May I help you?"

"Er—" Stone glanced at the nameplate on the front of his desk: *Derik.* "Good morning, Derik. Is Jason here? Or Gina?"

"Doc!"

Derik's head snapped around as Gina erupted out of one of the back offices, a big grin on her face. She hurried forward, appeared poised to add to Stone's collection of bone-crushing hugs, but reconsidered at the last moment.

"*Damn*, it's good to see you!" Her grin didn't falter in the slightest. "Jason told me you were back. I was hoping you'd come down to see us."

Derik looked like he was watching a sporting match where he had no idea of the rules—or even what game was being played—but he recovered quickly. "Guess you don't need an appointment," he drawled, amused. "Whoever you are."

"Oh, right!" Gina seemed as frenetic as ever—possibly more so. Apparently, her transformation into a cat-Changeling continued to be a positive thing for her. "Doc, this is Derik Brody, our new receptionist. Well, maybe not new—he's been here for like a year. Derik, this is Dr. Alastair Stone."

Derik's eyes narrowed. "Wait a sec. I know that name."

"You should. He's part owner of this place. He's been…away for a while. You know, off knocking around the world, doing rich-guy stuff." She shot Stone a sideways look full of question.

He wondered how much she actually knew about what was going on, and especially how much Jason, Amber, and Verity had told her following his return. "Er. Yes. But I'm back, now. Pleasure to meet you, Derik."

"Always nice to meet one of the bosses."

"I'm not exactly a 'boss.' More of a silent partner, and old friend of Jason's. Speaking of—is he here?"

"Nope." Gina shook her head. "He's out on a case. Did you tell him you were coming?"

"I didn't. It was actually you I mostly wanted to see."

Her grin widened and grew mock-flirtatious. "Why, Doc, I'm flattered." She hooked a thumb behind her. "I actually have an office now, so come on in. Hold my calls, Derik," she added in an obviously affected pretentious tone.

"You never *get* any calls."

"Oh. Right. Well, then, your job will be easy, won't it?"

Amused, Stone followed her back to her office. It was small, with every flat surface covered in computers, computer parts, and geeky toys. A whiteboard scribbled with notes took up one wall, and the others had anime posters.

"Have a seat," Gina said, indicating the single guest chair, which sported an empty pizza box and an iPad. "You can clear that stuff off. And before you ask," she added as Stone moved the items to her desk, "I never get any visitors in here, so it doesn't look bad for the agency that I'm a slob. The IT nerd is supposed to have an office like this, anyway. It's expected."

Stone had no idea about that. "I thought cats were neat and fastidious."

She snorted. "I'm not a cat. I'm a Changeling. And we don't fit into little boxes." A grin lit up her face. "See what I did there? Cats? Boxes?"

Stone sighed, but her words had brought his experience in San Francisco with Verity back to mind. "Yes, I'm beginning to get that impression."

Her eyes narrowed. "I heard about your little adventure up in the City. I hope you didn't try telling anybody they needed to be cured."

"I'm not an idiot—Verity explained things to me fairly well, even though I've been…away, and haven't had any chance to interact with anyone, let alone Changelings."

"What's that mean?" She frowned, her brow wrinkling in suspicion. "You know, nobody ever told me exactly where you *were.* Just that you'd gone away for a while and nobody knew when you were coming back. Are you gonna tell me what happened? I thought I'd never see you again."

"Yes, well, that was a possibility." He considered. "It's…hard to explain." He lowered his voice, to make sure there was no chance Derik could hear them. "I think Jason's old expression, 'MFM,' will have to suffice."

Her eyes got big. "Magic?" she whispered. "You were gone because of magic?"

"Yes. But I'm not going to tell you the details, so please don't ask. I'd like to talk about you, anyway. I hear you've become quite active in the Changeling movement."

"We're not exactly a 'movement.' It's hard to be, when nobody but us and mages can even see us. But yeah, I'm pretty involved." She nodded toward the open laptop on her desk. "It all started back when this whole thing first happened. Remember how I was tracking the instances?"

"Of course." He almost said something about it only being a short time ago for him, but stopped himself. "You were working with Eddie and Ward to trace the emergence of Changelings around the world."

"Yeah. It sorta spiraled from there. Somehow, I ended up as kind of an expert for a while. I still keep up the original message board, though there are a lot more of them on social media now, of course, but aside from that, I kinda switched to…" She glanced upward, as if thinking, "…I guess you could call it more 'activism.'"

"Activism."

"Yeah. Helping Changelings connect with each other, helping them set up areas in cities—mostly San Francisco and San Jose around here—and working with people in other cities to do the same thing."

"That must keep you fairly busy, on top of your work here."

"It does, but that's okay. Jason gets it, so he's sympathetic. You do know they have a Changeling kid, right?"

"I do. I haven't had the chance to meet either of their children yet, though." He pondered. "Do you get involved in the conflicts the Changelings have with the people around their areas? How do you deal with that?"

She looked down, and closed her laptop screen. Suddenly, she looked older. "It's not easy. You saw what it's like. I'm glad you were there, by the way. Saving the Changeling kid and the other one from dying probably headed off a lot of potential problems. The last thing they want or need is the cops coming in and stomping all over their space, especially since most of them—the cops, I mean—don't even have a clue about what they're dealing with."

"There aren't any Changeling cops?"

"Not many. Some of them quit the force, and the ones who stayed on trying to make a difference are having a lot of problems."

The anthropologist in Stone raised his head in interest. "Is that right? What sort of problems?"

She spread her hands. "It's tough, Doc. A lot tougher than most people—even us—thought it would be. I mean, we've got these Changeling neighborhoods, but even though they're kind of like ethnic areas, they don't work the same way."

Stone was about to ask why, but the answer came to him quickly. "I think I get it. Other sorts of areas where similar people gather, it's easy to see that everyone's Chinese, or Italian, or Ethiopian—if not necessarily by looking at the people, then by the businesses, the decoration styles, the entertainment—"

She nodded approval. "Exactly. Even in LGBTQ areas, it's pretty obvious unless you're totally oblivious that you're not in Kansas anymore. But Changelings…we're all different. We come from all races, ethnic groups, sexualities—and we all have different traditions. Hell, there's even starting to be a little friction between different *types* of Changelings. You know, the frogs and the lizards and stuff are staying away from the wolves and ogres, and some of the more quote-unquote 'normal' or 'pretty' ones start thinking they're better than the weirder-looking or 'ugly' ones, and…" She shook her head. "Mostly everybody gets along because they have more in common than not, but you saw the situation in the City. There's definitely conflicts."

"There are always going to be conflicts among humans." Stone was definitely looking at Gina in a new light now. Like Verity, she'd done a lot of maturing in the last three years. "Sadly, we do like to highlight differences."

"Yeah." She stared down at her closed laptop for a few more seconds, then brightened and focused on him again. "Anyway, it's really good to have you back. You don't look like you've aged at all. Must be nice."

"Eh. Good genes, I suppose, since I can't attribute it to clean living." He stood. "I should go, and let you get back to whatever you were doing. It was good to see you."

"I'm really glad to have you back." She leaned forward and dropped her voice again. "Take a look at Derik on the way out."

It took him a second to catch her meaning. "Really?" he mouthed.

She gave an exaggerated nod, accompanied by a grin. "He doesn't know about the other stuff, though." She waggled her fingers, indicating magic. "He's heard of it, but he doesn't believe it. So be good." Louder, she added, "See you later, Doc."

On his way out, feeling once more overwhelmed, Stone paused in front of Derik's desk. "Pleasure meeting you. I'm sure I'll be by again soon."

As he spoke, he shifted to magical sight. Instantly, the handsome, dark-skinned young man morphed into a humanoid shape covered in glittering, jewel-like feathers. His eyes went solid black, and his neck lengthened. He looked like a human peacock, except without the extravagant tail. Stone was so startled by the sight, he almost forgot to switch back.

"Great to meet you!" Derik's voice was as bright and cheerful as his hidden appearance. "Have a good one."

Aside from meeting Jason and Amber's children and reconnecting with the University, the only other person on Stone's immediate priority list was Leo Blum. He waited until he got back to Encantada to call, but was disappointed to get voicemail saying that Blum was on vacation and wouldn't be back until the following week. He was surprised when he felt relief along with the disappointment, though. As good as it was to be back, he'd been feeling a bit like his life had been tossed in a blender over the past few days. He supposed he could use a bit of downtime.

Raider greeted him with his usual enthusiasm as he entered. Like his other friends, once he'd gotten past his initial confusion the cat had warmed to him and gone about his business as if nothing had changed. He did seem to miss Luna, though, and Stone made another mental note to ask Kolinsky if it would be safe to leyline travel with animals. He definitely knew what it was like to miss his friends.

He'd got himself a Guinness and settled on the couch with Raider on his lap, ready to spend a quiet evening if his brain would slow down enough to let him, when his phone buzzed.

Before he even pulled it from his pocket, his whole body went tense. Contrary to what he sometimes told mundanes, Stone wasn't psychic—not in the conventional sense, anyway. But even so, he knew with a certainty he didn't question who was behind the blocked number on the display.

He considered not answering. That was an option, after all. But the consideration didn't last long. The faster he got this over with, the faster he could get on with his life.

His heart beat faster as he punched the button. "Yes, hello?"

"Alastair."

Well. It was good to be right, at least, even though he'd been hoping he wasn't. "Hello, Aldwyn. Pleasure as always to hear from you." He kept his voice even, utterly emotionless, but still managed to convey his sarcasm.

The dragon, on the other hand, sounded amused. "I trust you've been enjoying your return to the world."

"No thanks to you. What do you want? I was having a pleasant evening until you called."

"There is no reason why you cannot continue to do so."

Stone didn't reply.

"I gave you two weeks to resume your life. As I'm sure you are aware, tonight marks the end of that period."

"Slipped my mind." Of course it hadn't, but Aldwyn didn't need to know that. "Been a bit busy."

"Understandable, which is why I am reminding you."

He sighed. "What do you want, Aldwyn? Let's get it over with, shall we? I've got many more interesting things to do than waste time talking to you. Like taking out my rubbish bins and scheduling a dental checkup."

If Stone's words affected Aldwyn, he didn't show any sign of it. "Return home."

"What, now?"

"Yes."

He looked down at Raider in his lap. The cat was regarding him with a quizzical expression, obviously picking up on his tension. "You could have given me a bit more notice."

"I gave you two weeks. Return home."

"I—"

But the line was dead.

"Bloody hell, Aldwyn, you're annoying."

"Meow?" Raider was still watching him, concerned.

"No, there's nothing you can do about it." He stood, gently tipping the cat off, and ran a frustrated hand through his hair. "I hope I'll be back soon, but who the hell knows?"

CHAPTER ELEVEN

S TONE DIDN'T WANT TO ADMIT IT, even to himself, but the idea of traveling home at Aldwyn's order made him nervous. What was to stop the dragon from doing the same thing again—hijacking him somewhere and putting him back into his little suspended animation trap, maybe for a much longer period this time?

Sure, it didn't make sense—but then again, doing it the *first* time hadn't made sense, either. Who could tell with dragons? Their motivations were often inscrutable, and most of them got off on messing with humans because they could.

Still, there was no way he would give his problematic dragon ancestor the satisfaction of *knowing* he was nervous. He'd rather risk the possible consequences than to do that. So, with one last look at Raider, he formed the familiar pattern in his mind and released the energy.

He wasn't surprised in the least when he didn't reappear in the great room of the Surrey house. He would have been surprised if he *did* appear there. Instead, the familiar room formed around him, with its pair of elegant chairs, priceless artwork, and total lack of obvious exits.

Aldwyn sat in one of the chairs, watching him with a faint, mocking smile. He was dressed in his version of "casual," which meant his bespoke suit didn't include a tie. "Good evening, Alastair."

"It's really not." Without invitation, he dropped into the other chair, turning it to face Aldwyn. "Let's get this over with. I haven't got all night."

It was clear the dragon knew he had the upper hand, because he displayed no sign of anger or annoyance at Stone's flippant words. "How is your re-acclimation proceeding?"

"Well, you're lucky nobody's died. But don't think I'll ever forget what you did—kidnapping my son, taking me away from my friends and family for three years—I owe you for that, Aldwyn. And I *will* pay you back for it."

Aldwyn shook his head, his mocking smile growing a bit wider, like a doting father amused at a toddler threatening him. "We shall see. I invite you to try. But not yet. First, we have business to discuss. You have made certain promises, and it is time to keep them."

Stone sighed. "Yes, yes. I'm still trying to work out a way around *those*, too."

"Pray, continue to do so. But until you do, you are still bound by the oath you swore."

"So what do you want? I'm not going to play games. Tell me what you've got in mind, and I'll decide whether to laugh in your face."

Something brief and dangerous flashed across the dragon's expression, and then the smile was back. "I would not advise that. My patience with you is not infinite."

"I suppose I should stop trying to work out what the hell's going on in that twisted brain of yours. Just tell me what you want me to do. And I hope you remember that part of our agreement means I won't do anything that affects my family or friends."

"I remember everything, Alastair." Aldwyn leaned back in his chair and crossed his ankle over his knee. "I also remember that I agreed not to give you any tasks you would be unable to complete. In any case, I do not think you will find this one distasteful."

"Brilliant. Saving the distasteful ones for later, are you?"

Aldwyn didn't reply.

Stone didn't either. The two of them regarded each other for several seconds in silence.

As if nothing had happened, Aldwyn uncrossed his ankle. "At its essence, the task I wish you to complete for me is a theft."

Stone narrowed his eyes. "A theft? Of what?" Immediately, his mind went back to when he'd broken into Thalassa Nera's New York City penthouse apartment a few years ago to steal a magical chess set, along with a scroll Kolinsky had wanted in return for his assistance. Would Aldwyn ask him to steal from another dragon? Obviously it was something he was capable of, since he'd done it before. That had happened before Aldwyn had resurfaced, though. Had one of the other dragons told him about it, especially now when apparently some of them—including Thalassa Nera—had rethought their opinions on him?

"Of a tapestry—or rather, a section of one."

"A *section* of a tapestry? You mean, you want me to cut a piece out of it?"

"No. The tapestry is quite large, and constructed of multiple sections sewn together. I want one section of it. I do not care which one."

Stone didn't bother trying to conceal his confusion. "I said I'd stop trying to work out what's going on in your brain, but you've got to give me more than that. Why do you want this piece of a tapestry? Is it magical?"

Aldwyn didn't reply. "The tapestry in question is located in the western United States, in a small town called Rydell, Oregon. I am not certain exactly where, but with your proven investigation skills, you should have no trouble discovering this on your own. You will find it, remove a section, and return it to me."

"That's it? And that completes the task?" Stone wasn't believing it for a moment. It sounded far too easy, so there had to be more to it. "Who or what is guarding this thing? Are there other dragons involved?"

"No other dragons are involved."

That was a surprise. "Your word on that? This thing isn't part of some other dragon's hoard, or another one is after it?"

"You have my word. It is not in any dragon's possession, and to the best of my knowledge, no other dragon is even aware of its existence."

"To the best of your knowledge." There were the lawyerish wiggle words Stone had come to expect from dragonkind.

Aldwyn made a minimal shrug of one shoulder. "I cannot be certain, of course. The activities and motivations of my fellow dragons are often inscrutable, even to other dragons."

"You can say *that* again," Stone muttered.

"However," he continued as if he hadn't been interrupted, "As I said, I am reasonably certain no other dragon is even aware of the tapestry's existence, let alone its significance."

"What *is* its significance?"

"That is irrelevant to the task." He narrowed his eyes, and his expression grew colder. "You have sworn an oath to me, Alastair, that you would complete three tasks within five years. Nothing was included as to my requirement to explain my reasons for them."

It was true, and Stone suspected nothing he said would get him around that. "Fine. But you've got to give me more than 'it's in Rydell, Oregon.'"

"I think not. You are intelligent and resourceful, so I have little doubt you will have no trouble locating it." He returned to his relaxed position. "However, I *will* give you one more bit of information, which you will need in order to fulfill an additional requirement for your mission."

"Oh, there's more. Lovely. Why does that not surprise me?"

Once again, Aldwyn didn't acknowledge his words. "The additional requirement is this: I do not merely wish you to steal the tapestry section. You must make it appear as if someone else has done it."

Now, things were starting to get interesting. Not in a good way, though. "You want me to frame someone else for the theft."

"Yes." He gestured, and the three-dimensional, illusionary image of a man appeared in the center of the room. "His name is Chase Cassidy."

Stone studied the image. Chase Cassidy was in his middle thirties, stout and sturdy with a receding hairline. He wore slacks and a sweater. There was nothing impressive or noteworthy about him, though his eyes held a sharp intelligence. "Okay, who is this bloke? I assume you don't plan to tell me *why* you want to frame him for the theft."

"I do not. That is none of your concern."

I beg to differ, he thought, but didn't bother saying it aloud. "Is he in the area? It will be a lot harder to frame someone who's halfway around the world."

"He is in the area, yes."

Stone drew breath to ask another question, but Aldwyn raised his hand.

"No more questions. This is not a negotiation. You will perform this task. You have one week to return the tapestry to me." He rose, and indicated the other side of the room, where the familiar, swirling teleportation portal had appeared. "Good evening, Alastair."

Stone's mind still spun with both questions and frustrations. *Damn,* but this man was irritating. Why couldn't he have had a *reasonable* dragon for an ancestor, like Kolinsky or Madame Huan? Instead, he got Mr. Enigma.

He spun toward the portal, but then turned back. "Wait."

Annoyance flickered across Aldwyn's face. "Yes?" It was clear Stone had been dismissed.

"You said I had to complete this task, and in your little note from before, you told me I couldn't tell anyone else about my involvement with you."

"Yes, that is correct." There was a definite *get on with it* edge to his tone now.

"Can I enlist any help with this job if I *don't* say anything about why I'm doing it?"

"I am surprised you would wish to involve any of your friends in such an endeavor."

"Suppose you answer the question."

Aldwyn held his gaze for several seconds. "You specified in your oath that you would only agree if your friends and family were not involved. That works both ways. So, no. You cannot involve any of them, so I suggest you get to work devising a cover story to explain your absence. Now go, and do not stall any longer. I expect to hear from you no later than one week from now."

CHAPTER TWELVE

B Y THE TIME STONE RETURNED to the Encantada house through the portal, he'd already gone through an entire creative lexicon of expletives about Aldwyn. He'd managed to insult everything from the dragon's parentage to his taste in clothes, his bathroom habits, and his amorous activities with several local species of animal before realizing Raider was looking at him like he'd suddenly gone insane. He snapped out a couple more, this time in Latin, and then regarded the cat.

"Well, that was fun."

Raider didn't answer, but Stone knew that expression. "Yes, I know. You want to eat, and that's more important than anything else. But I'm afraid you're going to have to stay with Auntie Verity again for a little while. I'm sure you're gutted about seeing Luna again so soon, but there's no helping it."

He didn't bother trying to figure a way out of Aldwyn's task. He suspected there wasn't one, and if he took too long to arrive at that conclusion, he risked not leaving enough time to complete what he needed to do. He'd have to leave right away, which had its own whole new set of problems. He'd just got back—how was he going to explain to his friends that not only did he have to leave again, but he couldn't tell them where he was going or what he was doing? All he knew for sure was that he couldn't simply disappear for a second time. If he did that, he wouldn't blame them if they decided he wasn't worth forgiving this time. He wasn't sure he'd forgive *himself* if he did that.

At least there was *someone* he could talk to about this.

He pulled out his phone and sent a text. *I need to talk to your father again.*

The reply didn't come back right away. He was in the middle of packing a small bag while trying to keep Raider from packing himself along with it when the phone beeped.

You two need to set something up. I don't want to be your go-between.

Fair enough. Get me in touch one more time and we'll do that. Thank you.

Another ten minutes passed, and the phone chirped again with an address. This time, at least, it was local—a bar in Palo Alto.

Thanks. Oh—is it safe to LL travel with animals?

Odd question.

Raider needs his play dates with Luna.

Ah. Yes. Enclose him in a carrier, though.

Got it. Thanks. One relief, at least. It wasn't much, but he'd take what he could get.

Stone had never been to the bar Gabriel had named. It was a tiny place on the far end of California Street, an area he'd never frequented much, and he suspected it might have popped up during the time he was away. It was one of those kinds of places you'd probably never see unless you were looking for it.

Kolinsky was already there when Stone arrived, seated in a dim alcove. The place was crowded but nobody got near the dragon's table.

Stone slid in across from him. "Thanks for showing up. We've got to find some new way of communicating. Gabriel's getting tired of playing messenger, and I can't very well turn up at your shop anymore, unless you've got out of the magic business and started selling high-end dresses."

The dragon's eyes narrowed. "I hope you do not plan to begin the habit of summoning me without a very good reason."

Stone sighed. Dragons. Couldn't live with 'em, couldn't drop-kick 'em to another dimension. "I don't plan to *summon* you at all. I thought we were friends. Friends do have ways to contact each other, generally. But since you refuse to even enter the twentieth century, let alone the twenty-first, that leaves out most of the common methods, doesn't it?" He spread his hands. "Look—if nothing else, give me an address where I can send things. That way you can get to them on your own time, and I don't have to keep bothering your son."

Kolinsky's jaw tightened at the word *son,* but only for a second. "What do you want, Alastair?"

"I need to talk about something, and you're the only one I can safely do it with."

"Safely?"

"Yes—well, you or Madame Huan, and I've got no idea how to reach her."

"I see." The dragon sipped his drink. "What is this about?"

"Aldwyn."

He inclined his head as if he suspected that. "What about him? As I told you before, I cannot, and will not, involve myself in whatever affairs are between you. It is unfortunate, but it must remain so."

"Yes, I get that. I'm not asking you to help me. Not directly, anyway. But I was hoping you might at least give me some advice."

"Regarding what, specifically?"

The server appeared, and Stone ordered a Macallan. Guinness wasn't going to do the trick tonight. "I can't tell you everything, but he's asked me to do an…errand for him."

Kolinsky's expression hardened. "An errand. You are hardly an errand boy, Alastair."

"Yes, well, there's a bit more to it than that. Please don't ask for details, but I'm guessing you're bright enough to work out at least some of them on your own."

"He has compelled you under an oath." It wasn't a question. "Probably as a condition for returning your son to you when he had gone missing."

One thing that was occasionally nice about dragons was that most of them were quicker on the uptake than most humans. It could be inconvenient when you *didn't* want them to figure something out, but useful when you did. "I can neither confirm nor deny that, and I'm not sure what would happen to me if I tried. So let it go, all right?"

"Of course." He didn't seem ruffled; in fact, he appeared satisfied that something had been confirmed.

"So, the first thing I wanted to ask you was whether your friend kept my little bogus corporation going during my absence."

"I did not involve myself directly in the transaction, but I see no reason why not. Especially since it is my understanding that Gabriel and your son made some effort to maintain your identity during your absence."

Stone's drink arrived. He wondered if the service here was always that good, or only for certain customers. He paused for a sip, savoring the sweet, spicy bite of the aged whiskey. "That's good, at least. I was also hoping I could ask you for some specific advice about the...errand. But it sounds like you're not willing to help me there."

"It is not a question of willingness. There are larger forces at work here that limit my options."

"Fine. I get it." He stared into the glass, watching the faint reflection of the overhead light in the swirling amber liquid. "I can't tell anyone else about this. He was clear on that. I'm not allowed to involve any of my family or friends—aside from you and Madame Huan. And now I know why he didn't seem to care if I mentioned any of this to you. Because you can't do a damned thing about it."

"No doubt."

Stone let the silence linger a while longer, focusing on his drink. Finally, he raised his head. "Okay. You can't help me with anything specific, and it's probably best if I don't *tell* you anything specific. But can you give me any general advice? Anything you might know about Aldwyn that would make this easier for me?"

Kolinsky pondered. "Do not trust him."

"Yes, I get that. I don't trust him as far as I can throw him—and that's *without* using magic. But I'm a bit constrained here. He's given me directions, but refuses to provide me with much detail."

"I see. That does not surprise me in the slightest." Kolinsky finished his drink and set the glass aside. "And thus I reiterate my advice: do not trust him. Do not believe that what he has told you is the full truth."

"So you think he's got an ulterior motive for what he wants?" Stone thought about the instructions Aldwyn had given him. They weren't much: steal the tapestry and frame somebody else for it. On the surface they seemed fairly straightforward, but this was a dragon he was dealing with—and a particularly devious one at that.

"I would be disappointed in you if you did not."

"Well, of course I do. I mean, the bloke's like a diseased onion. He's got layers I'll probably never get to. But I haven't got a lot of choices here, Stefan."

"I understand. I truly wish I could help you further."

"No chance of sending Zack along?" Zack Beeler, the former stoner who'd tried to steal some tomes from Kolinsky's shop many years ago, had a highly useful wild talent: he could get through almost any ward. Instead of killing him, Kolinsky had made him the proverbial offer he couldn't refuse, turning him into a masterful cat burglar and B&E artist. "Do you still have him on your payroll?"

"I do. But no. Not only do I believe it would violate the spirit, if not the letter, of our agreements, he is currently otherwise engaged."

"I was afraid of that." He drained the last of the Macallan, smacked the glass down on the table, and stood, tossing enough cash down to cover his drink and Kolinsky's current one. "Well, thanks anyway. And please—give me some way to contact you so I don't have to keep pestering Gabriel. I think our partnership has come far enough that that's not an unreasonable request."

"I…shall consider it." He looked up at Stone, and his expression was sober. "Be careful, Alastair. Remain on your guard at all times, and examine your every action for possible ramifications. I do not wager, but if I did, I would feel safe in risking a great deal on the near-certainty that whatever he has asked you to do on the surface does not represent his true motivation."

"Tell me something I don't know."

Stone's mood didn't improve on his drive home. He supposed he should have expected Kolinsky wouldn't, or couldn't, be much help, but consulting him at all seemed now to be a wasted trip. "Don't trust him." If that was the only wisdom Stefan had to impart, he could have saved the gas.

In an attempt to put the annoyance behind him, he punched in Verity's number.

She answered immediately. "Hi. Didn't expect to hear from you tonight."

He listened a moment, trying to pick up any auditory clues to her current location, but got nothing. "Are you home?"

"At the moment. I was about to head over to the shop. Hezzie and I are working on a couple of new projects. Why?"

"I need to ask a favor."

"What kind of favor?"

He wasn't sure he heard faint suspicion in her voice—it might have been in his head. "I need you to look after Raider for me for a few days."

"Look after him? Why? Are you going somewhere?" Now there was no mistaking the suspicion.

"Yes. Not for long. A week at most."

There was a long pause. "Alastair…you just got back. And you're leaving again?"

Stone paused to consider. She was right—as far as she was concerned, he'd been gone for three years, and back for less than a month. He had a chance to make a fresh start with her, to be more truthful about his activities, at least to the limits of his annoying constraints. "Listen—Verity—can your session with Hezzie wait for a bit? I can come up there and we can talk. Will you look after Raider? I can bring him with me and be there in a few minutes."

"Of course I will. I told you already, Luna misses him. But a few minutes? That means you're coming up here…your way. Are you sure it's safe for him?"

"I checked with Gabriel, and he said it is, as long as I put him in a carrier. Raider, I mean. Not Gabriel." He smiled as the mental image of the handsome young dragon glaring at him from the inside of a cat carrier.

Instantly, she sounded more relieved. She chuckled. "Okay, then, if he says so. Don't tell him I told you, but he's a total cat guy. So is Ian. They'd die before they admitted it, but I swear, they used to come by my place sometimes just so they'd have an excuse to see Luna and Raider."

Stone smiled as the cat-carrier image was replaced by one of stylish and hyper-cool Ian and Gabriel stretched out on the floor playing with the two felines. "So, can I bring him, then?"

She sighed. "Sure. I'll call Hezzie. But you've got to tell me something about what's going on, Alastair. No more secrets."

Despite Gabriel's assurance, traveling with Raider still made Stone nervous. If anything happened to that cat, he'd never forgive himself. But aside from his usual reluctance to enter his soft-side carrier, Raider weathered the trip with no ill effects. As soon as Stone let him out inside Verity's loft, he dashed out and hurried across the room to sniff Luna. An instant later, the two of them disappeared up the stairs.

"Well. I can see where I fall in his hierarchy these days." Stone watched them, amused, until they were out of sight.

"I think he has a crush on Luna." Verity was dressed for going out, but not anywhere fancy.

"He's fixed."

"So is she, but who can tell with cats?" She gave him a critical once-over. "So. What's this about leaving for a week?"

"It's just…something I've got to do. Came up suddenly." That wasn't strictly true, since he'd known all along that Aldwyn would be reconnecting with him soon.

She indicated the sitting area, and took a spot on the end of the couch. Nineties rock played softly on a high-tech modern speaker designed to look like an old-fashioned wooden radio. Her eyes narrowed. "We're not starting the secrets again, are we? I thought it would at least take a little longer."

"Verity…" He sighed. He didn't want to do this anymore. He was tired of secrets, and even angrier than before at Aldwyn for forcing him to keep more of them. "Okay. I'll tell you as much of the truth as I can. But I can't tell you everything."

Her gaze sharpened. "This has something to do with the person who took Ian, doesn't it? The guy who was responsible for…"

He nodded reluctantly. "It does. And I can't tell you any of the specifics. Believe me, I want to. I don't *want* to keep secrets from you—from any of you. And I won't, if it's possible. But there are things I'm not allowed to say, no matter how much I want to."

"Like the rifts…" She jerked her head up. "This doesn't have anything to do with those, does it?"

"No." He struggled to gather the right words. "But…the same considerations are involved."

She was as quick as ever, thank the gods. "The same considerations. You mean…it involves an oath? You won't tell me because you literally *can't* tell me?"

"Yes."

"He's making you go somewhere."

Stone didn't answer.

"You can't even tell me that?"

Raider poked his head over the edge of the second level, and an instant later, Luna's green-eyed, silvery-gray face joined it. Stone smiled. "They're good together. It's almost too bad they're fixed—they would have had lovely kittens."

"Alastair…"

"Yes. He's given me a task he wants me to do, and I'm not allowed to involve anyone else. Not any of my friends or family, anyway." He waited, half-expecting some magical consequence to strike him down for even revealing that much.

She frowned. "A task? And you can't say anything about what kind of task."

"No. I think that would be ill-advised."

"Is it something dangerous?"

"Who knows?" He got up and began pacing the room. "He hasn't told me much about the details. On the surface, it seems fairly straightforward. But this particular person doesn't ever do anything on the surface."

She remained silent for a while, watching him pace. "I hate this, you know."

"I know."

"No, I don't think you do. It might only feel to you like you've been gone for a day or two, but for us it's been three *years*. Whoever this guy is, he's obviously powerful enough to do this to you, and he obviously doesn't like you very much. So what's to say he isn't sending you off into another trap?"

Stone wished he could give her more detail to set her mind at ease. In truth, he *didn't* know for sure that Aldwyn wasn't sending him to another trap, but something in his gut told him that wasn't the case. "I'm...not sure that's true."

"What isn't? That he's sending you into another trap?"

"No. That he doesn't like me very much." He chose his words carefully, holding Verity's gaze as he spoke.

She tilted her head. "What do you mean? Are you saying he *does* like you? Damned fucked-up way to show it."

"I'm...not sure I can say he *likes* me, exactly. But I am sure his motives are complicated, and I don't think I've figured them out yet."

"That says a lot. You're usually pretty good at that sort of thing."

Yes, when dealing with actual humans, he thought bitterly. Lately, that didn't seem to be the case as often as it used to. "What can I say, Verity? I've got to go—there's no way around it. And I can't take any of you along with me. Would you tell the others? Make some excuse for me so they don't worry—especially Jason. It sounds like he's got quite enough to be getting on with already, without adding my issues to his."

"You'd be surprised," she said fondly. "He's taken to this whole 'dad' thing like he was born for it. Amber, too, which doesn't surprise me at all. I'm convinced now that the whole Mama Bear cliché originated with shifters. They're great at balancing work and parenthood." She chuckled. "It's kind of exhausting, if you want the truth."

Stone smiled, which surprised him since he didn't have much to smile about at the moment. Even after all this time and the definitive end of their romantic relationship, she still had a knack for smoothing over his rough patches. He returned to his seat and settled back, and a moment later something soft landed in his lap.

"Wow," Verity said in a tone of near-awe. "She doesn't do that with anybody."

He looked down to find not Raider, but Luna settling into his lap. Her huge, emerald-green eyes were fixed on him and her shimmering fur shone like liquid silver as she shifted around to get comfortable. A moment later, a soft, whirring purr rose.

"Well…" he murmured. "Guess I'm not going anywhere for a while." He gently stroked her flank, and she tucked her head under her leg and relaxed into him. "I can see why Raider's so smitten with her."

"Yeah, she's quite a charmer." Her expression shifted from loving to serious. "You need to be careful, okay? Can you at least contact me and let me know you're okay every now and then? Don't just disappear off the face of the earth again."

"I think I can do that. I'll be using one of my false IDs, including the phone connected to it, so I should be able to call or text without arousing any suspicion. I will if I can—that's all I can promise."

"I guess that's all I have a right to expect." She looked at her hands in her lap. "I don't like it, though. Part of me wants to tie you up and make you stay."

He gave her a sly smile. "I thought those days were long past." When she didn't reply, he took a more serious tone. "Verity, if it's any comfort, I hate this as much as you do. I want to be done with secrets. The only problem is, the secrets don't want to be done with me—and I think it's going to get worse before it gets better, unfortunately."

"Yeah. Me too." She sighed and stood. "I'll make your excuses, and I'm always happy to take care of Raider. But I can't say it isn't frustrating. I love you, Alastair—I always will. But being around you is like trying to play chess in the dark. You think you're doing the right thing, but you never can tell for sure."

He thought that was a fairly apt metaphor—not just for this, but for his life in general. And lately, Aldwyn was doing a great job of filling the role of chessmaster.

CHAPTER THIRTEEN

STONE DID A LITTLE RESEARCH ON RYDELL before he left the next morning. A small, remote town located in the mountains of west-central Oregon, it had fewer than three thousand residents. Its nearest neighbor was a similarly-sized town named Tuttleton, ten miles to the west along a narrow, snaking two-lane road. Aside from that, no other settlements existed for more than thirty miles in any direction.

Unfortunately, neither town was anywhere near a ley line. The closest one that passed through a city large enough to include a rental-car agency was nearly a hundred miles to the south.

Better than nothing, Stone supposed. It beat driving, or even flying. He gathered his overnight bag, his black leather ritual-materials bag, and the small pack where he'd stashed a few magical references including a ley-line map, then paused in his living room before forming the pattern that would take him to his destination.

To his surprise, last night's internet search had actually located some information about Chase Cassidy, the man Aldwyn wanted him to frame for the theft of the tapestry. Unfortunately, there wasn't *much* information to be had, and what little he could find didn't make a lot of sense. Not only did Chase Cassidy not seem like a very interesting guy—he was a local businessman who owned a real-estate agency—he didn't even live in Rydell. Instead, he was a resident of Tuttleton, where his agency was located.

Before Stone had disappeared, Gina had helped him set up a better way to do anonymous web searches than using the browser's incognito mode. Surprisingly, it still functioned after three years, so he used it to search the town's name and *tapestry*, thinking perhaps there might be a local museum or that some locally famous tapestry might exist. No luck, though. On a hunch, he checked Tuttleton, but nothing turned up there either.

Of course. He's not going to make it that *easy for you.* Not for the first time, Stone wondered if Aldwyn was either trying to get him out of the way for a while, or testing him with some busywork job to see if he could handle it before giving him something bigger.

He didn't care, though. If it was a pointless job, that was actually a good thing. It not only meant one of his three tasks would be complete, but also that whatever he was doing wouldn't cause any additional trouble for anyone down the line—including himself.

He didn't believe it for a moment, for exactly that reason. Aldwyn was all *about* causing trouble, pulling strings behind the scenes, unraveling the status quo, and thinking ten steps ahead of whoever he had in his sights. This job meant *something,* and Stone planned to figure out what. Aldwyn hadn't told him he couldn't do that.

He used his invisibility spell when he traveled, since he had no idea where he'd end up. So far, he'd been lucky—he hadn't popped into existence in the middle of a busy street—but a few times he *had* shown up in a crowded area. The spell's magic ensured he wouldn't materialize inside any solid objects, but that was where its protection ended. The best he could do was try to identify a spot along the ley line that didn't pass through a populated area, but he had to balance that against having to walk for miles to find some-place he could get a vehicle. He smiled wryly as he released the energy. People in books never had to think about things like this.

When the world re-formed around him, he was standing in the parking lot behind a convenience store. A few cars were scattered around the small space, but he didn't see any people. Beyond the edge of the lot, he saw nothing but trees, undergrowth, and a single curious squirrel watching him from a high branch. It immediately skittered off and disappeared as soon as he spotted it. Stone liked to think he was getting better at finding landing spots, but the truth was, it was all luck. The ley-line maps weren't precise enough for pinpoint locations. He wondered if there was a way to superimpose them over the more accurate satellite maps online, and made a mental note to ask Gina about it when he got back.

He pulled out his phone and checked the map, grateful again that he'd finally gone through the process of having Kolinsky's friend set up a solid fake ID for him, complete with bank account and credit cards. The phone he had now wasn't quite as nice as his normal one—or at least it wouldn't have been, since what had been top-of-the-line three years ago was probably nearly obsolete by today's standards—but at least it was a smartphone instead of a flip phone. He texted Verity: *I've arrived. Nothing exciting happening yet.*

She replied quickly: *Be careful. Update if you can.*

He sent back a thumbs-up emoji—he was getting better at this texting thing, too, though he doubted he'd ever sink to the level of using 'text speak'—and called up his rideshare app. He'd already scoped out the location of the rental-car agency last night, and made a reservation in the name of Michael Townes.

Less than half an hour later, he was driving west out of Salem, behind the wheel of a silver Jeep Cherokee. He'd picked the four-wheel drive version just in case, but hoped he wouldn't have to do any off-roading.

The first half-hour of the drive went smoothly and quickly. There was a fair bit of traffic this time of day, but not enough to slow him down. It was only when he left the main highway and began driving along a series of increasingly smaller roads that he was forced to decrease speed. He glanced at the phone, which he'd plugged into the Jeep's nav system after entering Rydell as his destination. The road on the map looked like a squiggled jumble of yarn someone hadn't been very successful in untangling. To his surprise, however, Rydell hadn't shown up as a possible destination. Neither had Tuttleton. They were on his paper map, and even showed up on his Google map search, but as far as the electronic nav was concerned, they didn't exist. He thought perhaps they were too small to be included, but he had no trouble finding directions to far smaller towns.

Odd. But then, he'd been expecting odd. He compromised by entering the name of the closest town, thirty miles away, and memorizing the route from there. It would have to do.

Whatever else was going on around here, the area was pretty. The air, which smelled of pine needles and tree sap through the Jeep's vents, held a comfortably chilly bite, cool enough that Stone was glad he'd worn his coat but not cold enough so he had to run the heater. The trees, towering pines and spruces, grew thick and tall on either side of the road, giving the whole area a comfortably enclosed feeling, almost as if the tops of the trees were leaning in to form an archway with only a narrow strip of bright blue sky far overhead. It felt good to be out in the world again. He almost wished he'd had to walk further—he hadn't had a chance to go on any long runs since his return, but he was pleased to discover on a few short ones that his three-year nap hadn't caused any obvious degradation in his physical abilities or endurance. Whatever else Aldwyn was—and Stone continued to have many choice words in a selection of languages to cover his thoughts on *that* matter—he was without question a master mage. If the situation had been different, Stone might have wanted to study with the old dragon. Aldwyn could probably teach him a lot.

But only at a price, he reminded himself. He'd already tied himself to the dragon until the three tasks were complete—there was no way in hell he was going to do it again. Not for all the fancy magical techniques in the world.

No cars were passing him now, but that didn't surprise him. Rydell and its sister town of Tuttleton weren't near any major roads, and both were far enough from civilization to make them inconvenient tourist destinations. Last night's internet search had shown him that neither encouraged tourism. Their main draw, such as it was, seemed aimed at unconventional types: artsy people who wanted to escape the rat race, hikers who wanted to get away from it all and commune with nature, and retirees looking for a place to live out their golden years amid natural beauty.

The area reminded him a bit of Encantada, in a way: the narrow road he was driving on now was the only way to reach the two towns, and there were no exits out the other side. If anyone wanted to go to Rydell or Tuttleton, at least by road, this was the only way to do it. The location where the towns should be didn't show up on the nav screen yet because he still had at least ten miles to go before he reached it, but Stone remembered from last night's map examination that the road north hit a crossroads, with its northernmost route petering out into an abandoned campground a few miles further up, while the eastern and western directions ended in Rydell and Tuttleton, respectively.

The road was twisty enough that it took him nearly an hour to cover the ten miles to the crossroads. Aside from a weathered stop sign on the near side of the intersection and an even more weathered *Road Closed* one on the far side, there were no other indications of what might lie to the left or the right. Stone didn't bother to pull over when he stopped the Jeep for a few minutes to scan the area with magical sight—it hardly seemed necessary since he hadn't seen a single vehicle in over an hour.

Strange that there were no signs pointing toward either of the towns, but maybe not *that* strange. If the locals didn't encourage visitors, they probably didn't prioritize anything that might lead anyone there.

Curious, he got out and paced around, thinking perhaps the sign had fallen (with or without help) and now lay rusting in the heavy undergrowth beneath the towering trees. Even Encantada, which likewise didn't encourage visitors, had a sign, though most of the time it was hidden behind bushes or low-hanging branches. He wasn't sure why it mattered so much, but he was in no particular hurry to reach his destination. It might be best to do a little recon before he got there.

To his surprise, a faint feeling of tension began to grow as he crossed the intersection and approached the densely packed forest on the other side. It wasn't anything strong—he didn't even notice it at first—but as he drew closer something made him uneasy. He stopped, shifting to magical sight again and trying to peer through the trees, but the growth here was old and the overlapping green auras made it impossible to spot anything. Instead, he closed his eyes and took several deep breaths, clearing his mind to make it more receptive to the feeling, whatever it was.

At first, nothing happened. But then, gradually, the sense solidified:

Despair.

Longing.

Futility.

A sense of something very old that had given up—or perhaps that *he* should give up. He should get back in his car, turn around, and return home. Tell Aldwyn to pound sand.

He turned in place, eyes still closed. The feeling faded. Whatever it was, it was stronger on the far side of the intersection.

A horn blared, followed by the screech of brakes.

CHAPTER FOURTEEN

STONE SNAPPED HIS EYES OPEN AND SPUN.

A large box truck was in the middle of the intersection, its skid marks clearly indicating it had braked to avoid him. It was only a few feet away from the Jeep, still parked at the stop sign.

The sound of the truck's door flinging open was quickly followed by the thump of feet, and then a red-faced, muscular man in a T-shirt and cargo shorts was glaring at Stone.

"What the hell, man?" the guy yelled. "What the fuck you doin' standin' in the intersection? I almost hit you!"

Stunned, Stone tried to get his bearings. The vehicle was one of those big delivery types, shorter than a semi but every bit as loud. How had he not heard the approach of a truck that size out here in the middle of nowhere?

"Er—sorry. Sorry." Stone quickly stepped out of the road in case any *other* vehicles might be on their way. Perhaps he'd been wrong about the frequency of traffic through here.

The driver didn't seem inclined to let him off the hook yet. "What were you *doin'* out there? You an idiot or somethin'? One o' those freakin' hippies, wanderin' around high as a kite?"

Stone looked him over. He was in his late forties, with big nose, thinning hair, and heavy brows. His stained T-shirt read *FBI – Female Body Inspector*. "I'm sorry," he said again. "I was just…admiring the scenery." Before the man could reply, he fixed him with a glare of his own. "But I'd think I'd be a bit hard to miss if you were paying attention, wouldn't I? Not like you see people in the road every day out here in the middle of the great bugger-all."

"Yeah, exactly. I *don't* see anybody out here. But don't give me that crap. I *was* lookin'. I didn't see a fuckin' thing until I was practically on top of you."

That hardly seemed likely. Stone decided the man was probably making an excuse for texting, or fiddling with his musical selections. "Are you from around here? These roads are a bit narrow for a truck that size."

"Yeah, tell me about it." The man pulled a gaudy red cloth from his back pocket and swiped it across his sweat-dotted brow. "You nearly gave me a heart attack. I'm guessin' *you* ain't from around here."

"What was your first clue?" Stone glanced around again. The strange feeling of futility had vanished, probably driven off by the adrenaline rush of nearly becoming road pizza. He decided to play dumb and see if he could get any useful information from the driver. "If you must know, I was trying to find Rydell. I assume it's up one of these roads, but it's not showing up on my nav. I thought perhaps I might find a sign in the weeds somewhere."

The man snorted. "Good luck with that." He gestured to the road pointing east—the one he'd just come from. "Rydell's that way. Though I ain't got a clue about why you'd want to go there. Ain't exactly tourist territory."

"Oh? Why not? I was led to believe it was a nice place to get away from it all."

The driver tilted his head, as if trying to figure out what to make of this strange Englishman in a long black coat. "You one of those artsy types, up from California?"

"I...suppose you could say that."

He mopped his forehead again, and Stone got the impression the 'heart attack' comment hadn't been entirely flippant. "Well, whatever. You do whatever you want, but I'm tellin' ya, you could find a lot better places to get high and watch the stars. Place is fuckin' *weird* if y'ask me." He turned toward his truck. "Anyway, I gotta go. Still gotta drop off a load in Tuttleton before I can get the fuck back to civilization. Stay outta the road, or you maybe won't be so lucky next time."

"Wait a moment." Stone approached him, but stopped before he got too close to the truck. "Why do you say it's weird? Did something happen there?"

"How the hell should I know? I just deliver shit, I don't ask questions." He glanced at Stone before rounding the front of the cab, and let out a long sigh. "Look, I'm not sayin' the town's haunted or fulla serial killers or nothin'. It ain't like that. The people are just regular nice people, far's I can tell. They just…don't seem to be that interested in visitors, y'know?"

"Fair enough."

He watched the man climb into the truck, fire it up, and drive off. On a hunch, he shifted to magical sight, scanning both the truck and the area around it, but saw nothing of interest. He hadn't expected to, though. The guy looked like the type of bored driver who'd been paying attention to something other than the road in front of him, and it was only both their good luck that he'd looked up and spotted Stone before running him over.

But why didn't I hear the truck approaching?

That was a question to ponder as he headed back to the Jeep. It was true, he sometimes tended to lose track of the world around him when he was deep into a magical-sight investigation, but he hadn't thought he'd done that this time.

He glanced across the intersection, to the north side of the crossroads. Still nothing there but trees. He supposed he should check out what was beyond and try to locate the source of the strange, despairing feeling, but decided to leave that for later. Rydell was only a few miles away, so he could always come back.

The road to Rydell was even twistier than the one that had brought him this far, so it took him another twenty minutes to get there. Once again there was no sign—in fact, he almost missed the turnoff because nothing indicated what it was. The only way he could tell he'd finally reached his destination was the familiar small-town billboard showing the local fraternal organizations—Masons, Oddfellows, Lions Club, and such, with a few others he couldn't make out on his way by. Beyond it, small clusters of buildings spread out along both sides of the main street, called Rydell Road. He slowed—there still wasn't much traffic, even here—and scanned them as he drove by.

Almost immediately, he noticed there weren't any chain businesses. Another thing the place had in common with Encantada, whose citizens had voted many years ago not to allow any within its city limits. Stone saw no familiar golden McDonald's arches, no Starbucks, no Holiday Inn. Instead, he passed several local restaurants, coffee shops, a market, a hardware store, a non-chain gas station, and similar businesses. By the time he'd reached the end of Rydell Road—which terminated in a dead end—he'd identified a couple of churches, a community center, a school, a tiny medical complex, three bars, and two rustic clothing stores. Several smaller roads crossed Rydell Road, and as he glanced down these he spotted not only a few more local businesses, but also a number of homes.

What he didn't see, oddly, was any sign of decay or crime. No graffiti, no homeless people, no boarded-up windows—hell, no empty shops or abandoned buildings. Everything he passed had a freshly-scrubbed, storybook quality that made it look like it wasn't quite real. Strange, he supposed, but not *that* strange—some small towns took tremendous civic pride in keeping their space as pristine as possible.

Another thing he didn't find was a place to stay. He'd been looking carefully for any sign of a hotel, motel, or even a bed and breakfast, but nothing showed up. He hadn't checked last night during his internet search, because it hadn't occurred to him that it wouldn't exist. Every town had at least *one* place for visitors to stay, right?

He turned the Jeep around and pulled into the parking lot of one of the restaurants, turning so he could park facing the street, and then pulled out his phone. He could probably find something with a quick internet search—perhaps they were located in more picturesque areas off the beaten track.

No Service.

The words flashed across the top of the screen, next to four ghostly gray rectangles indicating the bars that weren't there.

Bugger. What kind of town in modern-day America didn't have cell service? Even Encantada had cell service.

Yes, but Encantada is in the middle of the bloody Silicon Valley, not out in the armpit end of nowhere.

Well. That was going to make things more difficult. He remembered reading once that modern cell phones needed to be within five to seven miles of a tower to function. If Rydell didn't have one, chances were that unless Tuttleton did, he was out of luck. So much for texting Verity to let her know he'd arrived—and so much for contacting anyone in the outside world for further information, unless he wanted to drive all the way back to civilization.

No wonder Aldwyn had wanted him to do this. With no ley lines, no cellular service, and only one other small town within thirty miles, this was a place that would lend itself to a self-contained investigation. Hardly the sort of thing the lofty dragon would want to waste his time on.

Okay, first things first—finding a place to stay. After considering a moment, he decided to try one of the coffee shops. As he pulled out of the parking lot, he thought he noticed a few people glancing at him, including two coming out of the market. The glances weren't hostile or suspicious; merely curious, as if they didn't see

R. L. KING

strangers very often. Stone shrugged it off and continued on his way. Plenty of time to delve into the mysteries of this weird little town once he'd secured lodgings.

He chose a coffee shop called Rydell Roast because it had the most cars parked in front of it. A rustic wooden building with an inviting-looking glass façade, it had a tall sign out front featuring a wide-eyed owl carved into a slab of wood.

The inside was equally inviting, with a dozen small, rough-carved tables, a counter along the back, a bar with several stools along one side and a large, free-standing fireplace, currently unlit, in the middle. Old band posters covered the walls, and folky indie rock played from an old stereo at the front. The air smelled strongly of rich coffee, with a faint undertone of pot smoke. The only thing that struck Stone as odd was that there were no TVs showing sports or news. Nowadays, it seemed like every establishment where people gathered had at least one.

Four of the tables were occupied—one by three older men, two by what looked like pairs and trios of mothers, and two by teenagers. All of them looked up when Stone entered, their conversations stalling, but quickly—perhaps almost *too* quickly—returned to their own business.

Stone was fairly sure none of the people here looked like fellow tourists. *Were* there any other tourists in town? He was beginning to doubt it. He strode with confidence to the counter and addressed the woman there, who'd been watching him since he'd come in. "I'll have a cup of whatever your special is, please."

The woman, middle-aged and comfortably chubby with shoulder-length, brassy-red hair, sized him up and smiled. "Coming right up."

He watched her while she puttered around, pulling a solid-looking cup with the shop's owl logo from a stack and pouring his coffee. Her movements were efficient and practiced—and more importantly, her aura was a steady, unruffled gold with only a few faint flashes indicating her curiosity. She wanted to know what he was doing here, but didn't seem disturbed or upset by his presence.

"There ya go," she said, setting the steaming cup in front of him. "Cream and sugar?"

"No, thank you." He paid with his Michael Townes credit card, including a tip generous enough to catch her attention but not enough to arouse suspicion. "Actually, I'm guessing you've probably figured out I'm not from around here."

She smiled. "I know pretty much everybody in Rydell, and I haven't seen you around. Most people who turn up here are lost."

"Oh, I'm not lost. I'm actually right where I want to be." He hadn't bothered using his American accent. Using the Townes ID, and especially since he'd dropped off the face of the Earth for three years, he was all but certain nobody would recognize him.

"Is that right?" She tilted her head.

Stone sensed some of the other customers might be paying more attention to him, but he didn't turn to check. "It is. A friend recommended Rydell to me as somewhere to go if I wanted to…get away from it all."

Her smile widened. "Well, it is that, I guess. Depends on what you're looking to do, I guess. How long are you planning to be in town?"

"I suppose *that* depends on whether I can find somewhere to stay. When I looked the town up on the internet, it appeared you attract retirees, artists, and other sorts who are looking for a remote place to…unplug." He pulled out his phone. "I didn't realize they meant it quite so literally."

Her smile turned to a laugh. "Oh, yeah. Nobody has cell service out here. We don't have cable TV, either. It's just one of those things you get used to. It's not so bad after a while. We find other things to do."

One of the kids came to the counter for a refill on his coffee. He gave Stone a once-over, obviously trying to be subtle about it, but his aura didn't lie: he was using the refill as an excuse to get a closer look at the newcomer.

Stone met his furtive glance with a steady gaze of his own, and the kid immediately backed down. He snatched his refilled cup and hurried back to his table.

"Don't mind the kids," the barista said. "They don't see too many strangers, so when one shows up, it's kind of an occasion. News'll be all over town by tonight."

Brilliant. That was exactly what he *didn't* want if he planned to do any investigation, but that was a problem to solve later. Maybe they didn't have cellular service out here in the sticks, but magic still worked just fine.

"Well…" He sipped his coffee, nodding approval at the rich, full-bodied flavor. "In any case, there might not be any news to report if I don't find lodging. Is there a motel around here? A bed and breakfast? Someone who's got a cabin to rent?"

She'd been shaking her head, but when he got to the part about the cabin, she stopped and raised a finger. "We don't have any motels or B&Bs in town. But you might be in luck." She nodded toward the table with the boy who'd come to the counter. He was sitting with another boy and a girl, all around seventeen. Raising her voice, she called, "Hey, Brady, can you come over here a minute?"

The other boy at the table, a short, freckle-faced kid with wild, straw-colored hair, a patchy mustache, and a plaid lumberjack jacket, stumped over. "Yeah?" Like his friend had done before, he looked Stone over. The difference was, he didn't even try to be subtle.

The barista nodded at Stone. "This is Mr.—"

"Townes," Stone supplied. "Michael Townes."

"Mr. Townes. He's lookin' for a place to get away from it all for a while. Didn't your mom say she's got that cabin out back of your house she was lookin' to rent out? She find anybody yet?"

Brady looked dubious. "Nah." He studied Stone again, this time clearly with a different focus—less curious, more critical. "But I doubt you're gonna want it."

"Why is that?"

The boy shrugged. "It's not much to look at. Nothin' fancy, you know? Just a room with a bed, a little kitchenette thing, and a bathroom you can barely turn around in. Mom was plannin' to rent it to somebody to use as an art studio, not some kind o' tourist place."

"Hmm." He was right—it didn't sound like the sort of place he'd choose. He addressed the barista again. "You're sure there's nothing else?"

"Eh, can't be certain, but I haven't heard of anything. You can look around if you want, but—"

Stone sighed. He only had a week to complete his mission, and it didn't make sense to waste any of it trying to track down lodging. "No, you're right. Brady, I'll take it if it's still available. Should I talk to your mum?" A cover story suddenly popped, fully formed, into his head, and he smiled. "Actually, the fact that it's an art studio works out nicely for me."

"You're an artist?" The barista didn't look convinced.

"I'm a writer. That's why I'm up here, looking for someplace with no distractions. I'm working on a book." He subtly shifted to magical sight, watching both her aura and Brady's.

To his delight, the faint red flashes of suspicion immediately faded, replaced by brighter ones of interest. "Really?" Brady asked. "What kind of book?"

"Anything we might have read?" the barista added.

"I doubt it." He thought of his old colleague, MacKenzie Hubbard, remembering he hadn't asked if the old grouch had finally retired from the University during his absence. "It's sort of…literary stuff. Nonfiction about obscure small towns. Probably far too dry to interest either of you. But what can I say?" He spread his hands. "It doesn't make much money, but it does feed my need to create, and it gets me out of the house."

Brady's interest vanished, but he was polite enough to mostly not show it. "You can follow me home if you want, and you can talk to Mom."

"Thank you. I'd appreciate it."

The boy waved to his friends, leaned in to kiss the girl, and headed out. Stone followed him and waited while he unlocked a mountain bike chained near several others. "It's not far. Nothing's far from anything in this town."

He wasn't kidding. Stone got back in the Jeep and drove behind Brady as he rode two blocks up and turned on a side street. Two more turns up winding lanes later, the bike veered right and plunged down a long dirt driveway toward a single-story wooden house surrounded by more trees. Brady dropped it in the front yard and waited for Stone to park.

"Come on around the back," he said. "Might as well get a look at the place before we talk to Mom. Like I said, you might not even want it."

Under normal circumstances, he probably wouldn't have. The tiny building was at the end of a dirt path well back from the house, and was barely larger than an ambitious storage shack. Brady pushed open the door, which wasn't locked, flipped on a light, and waved Stone in. "It's not much, but Mom does keep it cleaned up."

Stone said nothing. He moved past the boy and took a dubious look around. It *wasn't* much. The cramped space had a twin bed with a colorful comforter on the far side, a tiny kitchenette with a beer-sized fridge, sink, and cooktop on the left side along the wall, a table with two chairs near the door, and a pile of haphazardly stacked boxes on the right. The carpet was old and shabby, the furniture looked like it had come from a thrift shop, and the whole place smelled woody and musty. Tentatively, Stone walked forward to push open the door to the bathroom, which was barely larger than the sort one might find in an RV. It did look clean, though, which was something.

"What do you think?" Brady asked from the doorway.

"Er. You're quite sure there isn't anywhere else to stay in town?"

"Sorry. I mean, you might convince somebody to let you rent one of their bedrooms, but we don't really do tourists around here much." He grinned. "You're welcome to check around, though. I doubt anybody's gonna be beatin' down the doors to rent this place in the next day or two."

Stone reminded himself that he was on a short schedule, and fancy accommodations weren't high on his priority list. He still had to go to Tuttleton at some point soon to locate Chase Cassidy—perhaps he could find something there later. But for now, he did need a place to stay. "No, it's all right. I'll take it—for now, at least. Shall we talk to your mum?"

"Talk to me about what?" came a voice from behind Brady.

The boy stepped aside to reveal a woman who was clearly his mother: she had the same squat build, freckled face, and straw-blond hair as her son.

"Oh, hey, Mom. This is Mr. Townes. He wants to rent this place."

The woman's eyes narrowed as she shifted her gaze from her son to Stone. "You do?"

"I'd like to, yes. I'm a writer, looking for a place to get away from civilization while I work on my book. I was at the Rydell Roast today and happened to run into Brady, who recommended it."

He didn't miss the quick, sharp look she shot at her son. "If it's a problem—"

"No, no, it's not a problem. Just—surprised me a little, to be honest. Did Brady mention we don't get many visitors around here?"

"He did. That's part of what appeals to me about Rydell. My book is about small towns—the smaller and more obscure, the better. I'm from the San Francisco area, which can be quite stressful, and I'm on a deadline to get this book done or my agent will have my head."

She didn't seem impressed. "I'm not sure. This is all pretty sudden, and I don't know anything about you…"

"I promise, I'm not an axe murderer, or anything else dangerous. Just a writer on a deadline."

When she still hesitated, he pulled out his wallet. "Listen—I'll give you a thousand dollars in cash. I'm guessing that's probably more than you'd expect to get from someone local wanting the place for an art studio, right?"

She frowned, but he could see from the sudden spike in her aura that his offer was tempting. "Well…okay," she finally said. "I guess it'd be all right. Depending on how long you had in mind, anyway."

"Not long—a week at most." Stone offered what he hoped was a charming, self-deprecating smile. "I'll be honest with you—I'm planning to pop over to Tuttleton in the next day or two, so if I find something a bit more…conventional…there, I'll probably take it. But you can keep the thousand regardless. I'm getting rather desperate, to be honest, so I don't mind you taking advantage of my predicament."

She laughed. "Good luck finding anything over there. Tuttleton's no bigger than Rydell, and they don't do much tourist trade over there either." Considering, she added, "Okay. I can let you have it for a week. I won't lie, I could use the money. I warn you, though—that's got to be just for the cabin. No laundry, food service, fancy foo-foo decorations, nothing like that. Sorry—I'm not running an AirBnB here."

"That's quite all right. I didn't expect any. As long as the place is clean and everything works properly in the loo, that's all I ask." He opened his wallet, counted out a stack of crisp hundreds, and held it out to her. "Thank you, Mrs.—"

"Landis." She seemed surprised he had cash, but took it readily. "Let me go back in and get you the key, and then I'll leave you alone so you can get to your writing."

She seemed in a hurry to get back to the house, but Brady lingered. Stone wondered if it was because, in a little town like this where not much ever changed, anything or anyone new had to be interesting. "So…" he said, "what do you do around here?"

Brady grinned. "You mean, the place looks so boring that watching paint dry is exciting in comparison, and how do we all avoid sticking our heads in ovens?"

Stone mirrored his grin. "Of course not. Well…not really. Not quite so morbidly, anyway. More like—you haven't got a lot of the things most people take for granted here. What do you do instead?"

"Eh, we hang out, do a lot of mountain biking, hiking, that kind of thing. Outdoor stuff, at least when it's not raining."

Stone wondered if "that kind of thing" included getting drunk or high every weekend, or jumping each other's bones, but didn't ask. "Tell me—do you have a library in town? Or perhaps a museum?" He headed out to the Jeep to retrieve his bags, and carried them back inside.

"We have a library. It's just up Rydell Road from the coffee shop. No museum, though. We're not exactly big enough for a museum."

Stone nodded as if deep in thought. "Interesting. One of the random bits of information I found when I was researching the town was something about a history of textile arts in the area."

Brady tilted his head. "What do you mean?"

"Not sure." Stone spoke carefully, feeling like a fisherman trying to reel in a skittish catch. "My sources weren't too clear. Clothing, maybe, or…some kind of tapestry-making?"

"Uh...not really. Not that I know of, anyway. I mean, there's the Weavers..."

Stone jerked his head up. "The what, now?" Could it really be that easy?

"The Weavers. They're...you know, one of those organizations old people join, like the Oddfellows and the Lions. They don't do any real weaving, though, any more than the Masons mess around with stone. Mostly they just have breakfasts and support charities and get drunk together on weekends. So I doubt that's what you mean."

"Brady!" Mrs. Landis snapped, hurrying up the path from the house. "Leave Mr. Townes alone—he's going to want privacy to settle in." She offered a key on a fob with the Batman symbol on it. "Here's your key, Mr. Townes."

Stone shifted quickly to magical sight. The woman's tone had been far too sharp for an innocent conversation, and the bright red spikes around her aura's normal tranquil green verified that something had agitated her. Had she overheard her son telling him about the Weavers?

"Er—thank you, Mrs. Landis. I appreciate your kindness."

Her gaze lingered on him for a beat too long, and then she forced a smile. "I'm not going to lie, I appreciate the thousand dollars. I hope you enjoy working on your book."

"I'm sure I will."

She chivvied Brady back up the path. The boy looked over his shoulder a couple times before they disappeared into the house. Stone wondered if it might be useful to have another chat with him later, when his mother wasn't around. For now, though, he needed to get on with his investigation.

It didn't take long to unpack, since he hadn't brought much with him. He tossed his laptop bag on the bed, checked the windows, then headed back out. A sudden thought occurred to him as he was about to lock the door, so he went back inside and took a few moments to conjure simple wards around the door and the two windows. They wouldn't do anything but let him know if anyone had entered the place in his absence, but he wasn't entirely sure he trusted Mrs. Landis. She'd definitely reacted to Brady's comment about the Weavers. It might have been nothing—but in Stone's experience with situations like this, things that aroused his suspicions were rarely nothing.

It was mid-afternoon by now, so he spent an hour driving around the town, investigating the side streets and scoping out the local businesses. Nothing struck him as out of the ordinary—in addition to the ones he'd already found, he located a couple places catering to outdoor enthusiasts, a few more small restaurants, bars, and coffee shops, and a number of houses spread out along the various narrow streets feeding off Rydell Road. It was a pretty little town, and a couple stops to check the area with magical sight didn't turn up anything sinister.

Finally, he ended up at Rydell's small library. Amused as he pulled into the postage-stamp-sized parking lot, he recalled the days when he, Verity, and Jason had been on the trail of the Evil. How often they'd used libraries back then, poring through old newspaper archives and dusty microfiche caches. Nowadays, they all preferred internet searches when possible—they were a lot faster and provided access to a much larger pool of potential information. Especially with computer-wiz Gina on their team, they also usually turned up much more useful tidbits. Returning to a single, small-town library felt in a way like a step back, but also like returning to a simpler age.

At least if I get anything useful, Stone thought wryly. Once again, he wished he could text Verity with an update on how things were going.

The library was the size of a large suburban house, with the registration desk immediately inside the front door and two wings leading to the adults' and children's sections of the stacks. There was a workroom behind the desk, with a few more rooms at the back that looked like study spaces.

Currently, the desk wasn't occupied, so Stone paused a moment in the lobby for a look around, taking in the cheerful decorations, bulletin board full of flyers and cards advertising local services, and colorful posters displaying book covers. He got a definite feeling of home, of serenity and comfort that took him back to his childhood days visiting the library in Holmbury St. Mary during his summers off from Barrow. A quick glance revealed several groups of children, teenagers, and older adults either reading or wandering among the shelves. This was the kind of place he could see himself relaxing in for several hours, perhaps sitting next to the fireplace with a stack of good books and a drink.

For a moment, he found himself strongly tempted to do that. He quickly shook off the feeling—he had things to do, and the clock was ticking.

He started by examining the bulletin board. You could tell a lot about the character of an area by the sorts of things its residents advertised. The flyers and cards covered every inch, sometimes tacked over top of each other. Clearly, the librarians didn't cull the board very often, and the advertisers didn't come back to retrieve their offerings once they were no longer relevant. That was fine, though. Good, in fact.

Mostly, the ads were for the typical things, primarily selling various goods and services. There were ads for cars, kitchen gadgets, babysitters, housecleaning, pets, and toys. Once again, it took Stone back; most of this stuff had moved online in the rest of the world by now. The more he thought about it, the more Rydell seemed to be a little oasis time had forgotten, as if it had reached a point twenty or thirty years ago and simply...stopped. Odd, but strangely charming, too.

He'd started scanning the board from the left side, systematically examining each of the cards and flyers, but didn't find anything interesting until he'd almost reached the other side. On a faded fly-er, tacked behind three smaller cards, he caught the word *Weavers*.

After glancing around to make sure nobody was paying atten-tion to him, he quickly relocated the three cards so he could read the flyer. It was a simple one, hand-lettered with care. The top had a stylized drawing of an old-fashioned spinning wheel, followed by the words *Weavers Pancake Breakfast.* The date was a Saturday three weeks ago. Below more hand drawings of a stack of steaming pancakes and a coffee cup was an address, and *All Profits to Charity.*

Stone pulled out his phone and snapped a photo of the flyer. The whole "Weavers" thing might be a red herring, but Mrs. Landis's reaction to its mention had been odd enough to make it worth checking, especially since he was looking for a large, multi-part tapestry.

"May I help you?"

Stone turned to find himself facing a cheerful, plump, middle-aged woman. She wore glasses and a gray sweatshirt with a line drawing of a cat and *Make Friends with a Book!* As he studied her, she was studying him. "Hello. You must be the librarian."

She smiled. "The sweatshirt gave it away, I'm guessing." With a head tilt, she added, "I don't recognize you. I thought I knew every-body in town."

"Ah, no, you wouldn't. I'm just visiting."

"We don't get many visitors around here."

By now, Stone noticed several of the library's other patrons were snatching glances at the two of them. He followed her back to the registration desk, where she settled on a stool behind it. "So I've heard. I'm…an author. Visiting here for a few days to work on my book."

"Oh, a book! How cool! What's it about?"

"Obscure small towns in the western United States."

She laughed. "Well, you don't get too much more obscure than us. But wouldn't you want to look at the reference books? I can't imagine you're wanting to hire a babysitter or adopt a puppy. Besides, most of what's up there on that board is out of date anyway. I keep meaning to clear it off, but…" She made a vague gesture, as if to say, *what can you do?*

"Oh, I'll get to the reference books eventually. But I find I get more interesting information from talking to people and taking a look at the town's day-to-day activities." He waved vaguely toward the board. "For example, I'm sorry I missed the elementary school's play."

"Oh, yes, it was quite a sight." She leaned in closer and added in a conspiratorial tone, "Especially when the lead girl and the lead boy, who couldn't stand each other, started tossing scenery at each other during their big scene."

Stone chuckled. "Definitely sorry I missed it." He appeared to consider, keeping his voice casual. "Sorry I missed the pancake breakfast, too. I haven't eaten yet today, so a stack of pancakes sounds like just the thing right about now."

"Oh, yes. You're in luck—they do it once a month, so there's another one next week. Quite a few people turn out for them."

He pondered. "The Weavers. I don't think I've heard of them. Are they a family?"

"Oh, no. They're a local fraternal organization. We have bigger ones in town, too—the Lions, the Oddfellows, the Masons. In fact, I think the Masons are having a barbecue at the end of the week." She offered a conspiratorial smile. "We're small, so there's a lot of overlap in membership."

"I see." Stone didn't miss her subtle attempt to steer the conversation. He continued doing his best to look as if none of this was a big deal. "Honestly, I'm actually more interested in the Weavers, though. Local organizations are just the sort of thing I'd like to include in my book. Readers love those kinds of stories." He shifted to magical sight for a moment to watch her aura.

As he'd expected, its normal medium blue was sparking with faint red patches. Nothing too dramatic, but she was definitely more unsettled than she was letting on. She waved her hand airily. "I suppose they might. But I can point you at a lot more interesting stories, if those are what you're looking for."

"Can you? That would be brilliant. Thank you so much. But before you do that—do you mind if I ask one more question about the Weavers?"

Clearly she *did* mind, but she covered it well. Without magical sight, he might not have noticed. "Of course. I'm here to help, after all."

"Can you tell me why they're called that? Is there any actual weaving involved? Were they initially formed by a group of tailors or something?"

"Oh, no, nothing like that." Once again, her aura flashed red— brighter this time. "I'm not a member, so I can't say anything about their little secrets, but it's my understanding that it's got something to do with weaving the threads of fate, or the universe, or something like that. Sort of like how the Masons use architects as a metaphor for God." She gave a nervous giggle. "You know how those organizations are—their silly secrets are what make them fun."

"Yes, that makes sense. From what I understand, people here don't get away much, so I suppose they've got to come up with all sorts of interesting local activities."

"Exactly!" Her smile grew less nervous as a pair of ten-year-olds approached the desk with stacks of books, hanging back politely until the adults finished their conversation. "Now, if you'll excuse me a moment, I need to get these kids checked out so they can be on their way." She pointed toward the adult stacks. "If you look in the nine-seventies, you'll find some interesting histories of the local area. Just let me know if you need help."

"Thank you." Stone took the dismissal with grace, heading off toward where she'd pointed. But instead of going to the section she'd indicated, he found an unoccupied row with a good view of the desk, pulled up a disregarding spell, and feigned interest in the shelf in front of him while he watched the librarian check out books for the two children. As soon as she finished and they left, she looked left and right and then hurried to the room behind the desk.

Stone swapped his disregarding spell for invisibility and followed her. Fortunately, she'd left the door open. He slipped through and continued watching her, hoping whatever she planned to do didn't take long since he couldn't hold the spell for more than three minutes.

She'd already punched in the number by the time he arrived, so he couldn't see that. She hunched forward, her gaze shifting between the window looking out at the desk and the door. With her free hand, she fidgeted with a pen.

Someone must have answered, because her shoulders jerked. "Yes, hi," she said in a low, urgent voice. "This is Wilma over at the library. This is probably nothing, but I figured I'd let you know. I've got a guy over here asking questions about the Weavers." A pause, and then: "Yes, that's him. Tall British man, dark hair, long black coat. He says he's writing a book." Another pause. "I didn't tell him much. Like I said, it's probably nothing, but it's been a while since we've had a stranger in town."

Stone shifted position and the leather of his boot creaked softly. He froze as the librarian tensed and looked toward him, but his spell held and she turned back. "Okay," she said. "I'll try to get rid of him. I'll let you know if he asks any more questions. What?" Once again, she hunched forward, listening.

Stone craned his ears, trying to hear if she said anything else, but already he could feel the spell slipping. If he didn't get out now, he risked discovery. Damn, but he needed to do something to punch up his invisibility skills. Maybe he could ask Ian or Gabriel to help when he got back. But for now, it was time to exit, stage right.

He hurried out of the room, holding his breath, and looked around for a place to hide before he became visible again. To the right of the desk was a hallway, presumably leading to the bathrooms. At a near-run he hurried down it, hoping he didn't run into anybody coming the other way.

The door to the men's room opened to reveal a small boy. He paused, confusion wreathing his face as Stone's invisibility spell flickered. Then he shrugged and jogged out.

Stone slipped past him as the door swung shut, and let his breath out in a loud *whoosh*. He couldn't hold the spell any longer, so if anybody else was in the room they were about to get a show. As he reappeared, he shot a tentative glance around, fearing the worst.

The tiny bathroom was empty.

He leaned forward, pressing his hands against the mirror, and struggled to catch his breath. That had been close. He'd need to be more careful next time.

But on the plus side, he'd got the information he was seeking— or at least some of it. Something *was* dodgy about the Weavers, and somebody in town was already nervous that he seemed to be looking into them.

That was fine, though. Now that he knew that, he could change his tactics. Unless these people were mages themselves, they'd have a hard time keeping up with him.

But you don't know they aren't *mages,* he reminded himself. Why would Aldwyn be interested in a bunch of small-town nobodies playing dress-up? There had to be more to it than that.

He ran some cold water over his hands and rubbed his face, then dried off and headed back out. For now, it would be best to leave the library alone.

He gave a jaunty wave to the librarian as he left. "Thanks for your help!"

Her grin was wide and didn't even look too fake. "Hope you found what you were looking for!"

He wondered if she really meant that—or if she'd make any more phone calls after he left.

CHAPTER FIFTEEN

S TONE HAD NO INTENTION of trying to cook in his room's tiny kitchen, so he stopped on his way back to grab a burger at a restaurant he'd spotted during his recon trip. As he sipped coffee and picked at his fries, he pulled up the Weavers flyer image he'd snapped on his phone.

He wished again that he had internet access so he could look up the organization. Were they exclusively local to Rydell? Were there branches in other towns—like perhaps Tuttleton? Was Chase Cassidy, the guy Aldwyn wanted him to frame for the theft of the tapestry, a member too?

No point in speculating, though. He hadn't even spotted any computers in the library, which was just weird—especially when he remembered his knowledge of the world was three years out of date. Were they still stuck on dial-up out here in the sticks? Even that would let him get a message out, but he'd need to be careful. He had no idea who the librarian had called, or how many Rydell residents were connected with the Weavers.

He recognized the street name on the flyer. The town didn't have that many streets, and he'd driven around most of them today. He didn't remember the specific location, though. Was it their meeting hall, or merely some restaurant or park where they held the breakfast? That would be something to check later tonight, after it was fully dark.

Stone thought again about questioning Brady without his mother around. The boy had seemed curious about him, so perhaps he could take advantage of that if he headed back to his place. He didn't know much about fraternal organizations, but he did know they generally didn't accept children or teenagers as members, so odds were good Brady Landis wasn't associated with them.

His mother might very well be, though. He'd need to be careful.

He finished his burger, paid cash with a good tip, and drove back to the Landises' house. They hadn't told him where he could park, so he left the Jeep on the street outside and took the path to the rear, walking slowly to maximize his chances that Brady might spot him and follow.

The boy didn't, though. The house lay quiet, with only a few lights burning inside as the sun began to set. Stone wondered if there was a Mr. Landis, or if Brady and his mother lived here alone.

As soon as he approached the small building behind the house, a faint tingle told him something was wrong.

The ward he'd placed on the doors and windows had been a very simple one, so it hadn't been set up to alert him from a distance. That would have taken more time and materials, and probably aroused his hosts' suspicions. Instead, its purpose was merely to inform him if anyone other than him had entered the structure in his absence.

He was getting that feeling now.

He paused, but only for a moment. He had every right to be suspicious if someone was in the place he'd rented—there was no need to sneak around. Besides, if anyone was watching him, he didn't want to reveal his magical abilities or even the fact that he'd noticed something wrong. He settled for an invisible shield in case anyone was waiting to ambush him, then pulled out his key and opened the door with the breezy disregard of any tourist returning to his home base after a day of sightseeing.

Immediately, he knew nobody was here. The place was far too small to conceal anyone hiding, and magical sight revealed no invisible lurking ambushers. The only possible place they could be hiding was the tiny bathroom, but a quick check revealed no one behind the shower curtain.

Somebody *had* been in here, though. The ward on the door was the one that had activated, and it would only do that if the intruder had crossed the threshold. So why had they been in here? What had they been looking for?

A quick glance at the bed gave him the answer. Before he'd left, he'd tossed his laptop bag there. It was still there, but the opening was facing the pillow instead of the window. He was certain it had been pointed the other way before.

He unzipped the bag, half-expecting the laptop to be gone. But no, it was still there. He had no way to tell whether anyone had tried to access it, but even if they had, it was password-protected. Unless the residents of Rydell were hiding serious hacker skills, he doubted they'd got in.

His gaze fell on his overnight bag, which he'd left in the chair next to the bed. Had the unknown intruder snooped in there too? He checked, but couldn't tell. Whoever it had been, they'd been careful.

But they *had* been in here. The fact that they hadn't found anything didn't matter—someone had invaded his privacy and looked through his things.

What were they looking for?

And who had done it?

Was it possible Mrs. Landis had been the person the librarian had called? Had word already gotten around the tiny town that the odd newcomer was staying here and asking uncomfortable questions?

Okay, time to kick this investigation up a notch. He slung his laptop bag over his shoulder, intending to lock it in the Jeep's cargo area along with his ritual bag, and headed for the door.

Someone knocked as he reached for the knob.

Startled, he flung the door open. Brady Landis stood there, carrying a closed Tupperware container. Brady jerked, as caught off-guard as Stone was, and bobbled it.

"Brady. Sorry, you startled me. I was just leaving."

He re-established his grip on the container and flashed him a nervous grin. "Sorry I scared you. Mom felt a little guilty about taking your money and not giving you anything to eat. She made some cookies today, and thought you might like a few. They're really good—all my friends love them."

"Oh. Er. Thank you. That's very kind of you."

His gaze flicked down to the laptop bag. "Going off to do some writing?"

"Yes, maybe. I thought I'd find a coffee shop or somewhere to sit for a while and soak up the local atmosphere."

"Better hurry. Most everything except the bars and a couple of the restaurants close soon." His smile widened. "We're really not very exciting around here, Mr. Townes."

"I wouldn't say that. There are many different types of excitement."

"I guess so. Well, anyway, enjoy the cookies." He turned and started back up the path toward his house, but hesitated. "Hey, Mr. Townes?"

"Yes?"

His brow wrinkled, and he looked like he was on the verge of saying something when his mother appeared farther up the path. "Brady, stop bothering Mr. Townes and get back in here! I need you to run to the store and get some milk before dinner."

Brady glanced between Stone and his mother, looking frustrated, but it was clear who the authority was here. "Coming!" He waved to Stone and jogged up the path without another backward glance.

Stone watched him go, noting the unsettled glow in his aura—and in his mother's. *Something* was bothering the boy, and clearly it was something he didn't want his mom to know about. Maybe they could talk later.

He tossed the closed container on the table. He had a strong suspicion that if Mrs. Landis wasn't the intruder, she almost certainly knew who was. She'd probably let them in.

And what had Brady wanted to say to him?

Things were getting curiouser and curiouser around here…

Brady had been right about one thing: Rydell was definitely one of those "roll up the sidewalks" sort of towns. By the time he made it back to Rydell Road, most of the businesses were already closed and dark. The only exceptions, as she'd said, were two of the bars, a couple restaurants, and the gas station. The town didn't even have a movie theater.

To look less suspicious, especially if Mrs. Landis had alerted the town's spy network to his current plans, he chose one of the bars and spent an hour there, sipping a Guinness at a back-corner table and tapping away on his laptop. Nobody bothered him, though a few locals did cast curious glances his way. He couldn't blame them for that—even if they weren't involved in this whole Weavers thing, he was still something new, and new always attracted attention.

He waited until a little after nine p.m. before finishing his pint and closing the laptop, feigning a yawn. Most of the other customers had left by now, the exceptions being two older men at another back table who seemed to be discussing business, and an early-twenties couple seated at the bar, obviously in the beginning stages of a flirting relationship. The men looked up as Stone left, but the young couple were oblivious.

As soon as he was sure he was alone in the parking lot, he pulled a disregarding spell over the Jeep. It wouldn't stop anyone determined to spot or follow him, but it would discourage casual glances. It only took five minutes to reach the street where the Weavers held their pancake breakfast—one nice thing about small towns. He slowed as he drove by, casting a quick glance at the address and hoping it wasn't a park.

It wasn't a park. A dark, squat, two-story building sat well back from the street, surrounded by more trees and a wooden fence. The rough-hewn sign out front read *Weavers Lodge* beneath the same stylized spinning-wheel image from the flyer. Next to the sign was another one, similar to the type churches used to announce their activities. That one announced: *Next Meeting Tuesday, 7:30 p.m. Pancake Breakfast Saturday, 8 a.m.*

To Stone's surprise, he also spotted two cars parked along the side, though as far as he could tell, no lights were on in the building.

You're overthinking this, he thought, annoyed. Just because the cars were there didn't mean anybody was inside. Somebody might merely have left them there.

He kept driving past, in case anyone was watching, and continued half a mile before turning up the next tiny side street. After stashing the laptop bag in the locked cargo compartment, he paused to cast a stronger disregarding spell on the Jeep. It was easier to do the concealment when the vehicle wasn't moving, and anyone looking at it would see what they expected to see—some nondescript car parked along the side of the road.

He'd brought one of his disguise amulets, which he'd fortunately kept in his pocket instead of leaving it back in his room. Now, he slipped it over his head and calibrated it to an appearance that would fit in better with the town's aesthetic: a stocky young man with blond hair, a lumberjack jacket similar to Brady Landis's, and baggy jeans. He'd still look like a newcomer if anyone stopped him, but at least he'd fool any casual onlookers, if there were any.

The building was still dark when he reached it, and the two cars were still parked next to it. It was a little bigger than he'd expected, perhaps large enough to fit fifty people if they got very chummy. He scanned the area with magical sight, but saw only the faint green auras of the surrounding trees and the quick darting one of a cat or raccoon disappearing around the corner. No sign of human presence, not even near the cars.

Stone hurried along the opposite side and ducked around the back. Now, he'd have to make a decision. The building didn't have any windows, so peering inside wouldn't work. If he wanted to see what was in there, he'd need to break in.

If Aldwyn's tapestry is here, this is probably where they're keeping it.

He hesitated only a moment. If he broke in and someone was in there, he could deal with them. With a final unkind thought at Aldwyn for putting him up to this nonsense, he crept along the back wall until he found a door, barely visible in the darkness. He used magic to try the lock, hoping in a small town like this it might not be locked.

But no, not only was it locked, but the lock felt far stouter than he expected. Not that it would stop him, but it was another data point. Whatever was inside this building, somebody cared about protecting it.

The lock opened with a faint *click*. Stone pushed the door open with magic, slipping on a pair of thin leather gloves as he entered. He shifted to magical sight to scan the room in front of him, but no auras showed. This room was either empty or someone was hiding.

He closed the door behind him and stood still, listening. If anyone lurked nearby, some slight sound might give them away if he was quiet. But after two minutes, he heard nothing. He summoned a faint light spell around his hand and raised it to get a better look.

This was obviously the site of the famous local pancake breakfast. He stood at the edge of a large room with long tables arranged in rows. Neatly stacked folding chairs lined the walls to the left and the right, while the opposite wall had an exit on the left and a cutaway to the right that opened onto another shadowy room.

Stone hurried across, careful not to bump into any of the tables, and pointed the light through the cutaway. The room on the other side was a kitchen, with an industrial fridge, large range, and several neatly cleared work surfaces. *This is where the pancakes happen,* he thought absurdly.

Next, he checked the other exit, which led to a carpeted lobby with a few chairs spread around. A staircase stood on the other side. Out here, the walls sported a few motivational posters with the Weavers logo on them, and all the chairs were embroidered with the spinning-wheel symbol. No sign of any tapestries, though.

Stone paused, rubbing his chin. This place certainly didn't seem sinister. He hadn't visited the headquarters of too many fraternal organizations—okay, none—but this one seemed to fit the expected parameters of a small-town meeting place.

He was about to head upstairs when the back door creaked. A second later, he heard voices—two, from the sound of it. A man and a woman.

Bugger. This could be good, but not if they caught him. He darted his gaze around the lobby, but there weren't any good places to hide.

The voices were getting closer.

He dashed through the doorway leading to the kitchen and ducked low, ready to use his invisibility spell if they came in here.

They didn't. Still chattering away—it sounded like they were discussing the woman's son's recent Little League game—they swept past the opening and continued on.

Stone expected to hear the creak of the stairs as they ascended, but he didn't.

That was odd. It didn't make sense that they'd pass right through and exit and out the front door, so they must have gone *somewhere*. He rose, pulling up his invisibility spell, and crept across to the doorway.

The room was empty. The voices were gone.

Stone frowned. This wasn't making sense. *Had* they passed through? Had they gone upstairs without making a sound? It certainly didn't seem as if they were making any effort to be quiet. Their chatter had been as carefree as a couple of coworkers getting ready to start their day.

As he stood in the doorway pondering that, a door slid open to his right.

A door that hadn't been there before.

Stone barely had a chance to duck back into the kitchen before two more shadowy figures emerged into the lobby. They didn't look to the side, but instead swept past and out through the dining room. A moment later, the rear door shut behind them.

This time Stone got a better look at them, though: two men, one stocky, one tall and thin. Definitely no women.

And where had that door come from? It had been a blank wall when he'd searched the area.

Illusion? Here?

Now things are getting interesting.

He barely waited for the two men to exit the lobby before poking his head out, shifting to magical sight.

Along the same wall, where the blank surface had been before, faint blue light was fading along a door-shaped seam. A moment later, even that was gone, leaving the wall blank once more.

There was an illusionary door here. In the middle of a nondescript meeting hall in the middle of a boring, nothing Oregon town.

A slow, sly, smile spread across Stone's face. He hadn't been certain before that he was on the right track, even considering the librarian's phone call—but now he was.

He glanced first toward the back door, then the front, to make sure nobody else was coming in. Then he crept forward and put his ear against the wall where the door had been.

At first, he heard nothing. But after a couple of minutes the faint sound of a man's laugh came through.

Somebody was definitely down there—probably the man and woman he'd heard before. Maybe more people?

Only one way to find out, but he'd need to be careful. He couldn't rely on his invisibility spell to keep him hidden.

First, though, before he could do anything else, he'd need to get through that door. He stood back, reaching out with his magical senses. Illusions were tricky, even for powerful mages, since power had nothing to do with seeing through them. In this case, though, he knew the door was there, and he knew its general shape. That would help.

To his relief, this one didn't take long to see through. It wasn't a strong illusion; in fact, as Stone penetrated it in less than five minutes and examined its structure, he saw that it had been designed mostly for longevity. That made sense: there were no ley lines in Rydell, so any magical workings meant to persist for a long time would need extra effort. The concealment aspect was secondary, but it wouldn't need to be strong. Those who didn't expect a door to be here wouldn't even look for it, let alone try to see through it. It was possible some small child or animal might see through it—both were less susceptible to illusions than adults—but who would believe a toddler's story of a hidden door?

Once he cracked the illusion, the door shimmered back into visibility. He hadn't noticed it before, but the same spinning-wheel symbol adorned it, painted in strong blue. The door didn't have a knob, only a metal plate with a narrow protuberance sticking out.

Instead of swinging out or in, it clearly slid into the wall next to it, like the ship's doors on *Star Trek*.

Now came the tricky part. Was anyone watching the door on the other side? If he slid it open to reveal a room or a guard on the other side, they'd be on to him. True, he didn't look like himself with the disguise amulet, but if they knew *anyone* had figured out their little secret it could still cause problems for him down the line. Especially if this was where the tapestry was kept.

No helping it, though. If he wanted to see what was beyond that door, he'd have to get through.

He risked an invisibility spell and slid the door open a crack, leaning forward to peer through.

On the other side was a dimly-lit staircase leading down. The voices he'd heard before were louder now, but still not close. The man and woman were still chatting amiably. He heard no other voices.

He slid the door farther, using magical sight to verify he hadn't tripped any obvious alarms, then slipped through and closed it behind him. Pausing, he listened. The voices continued.

A flickering overhead lightbulb illuminated a stairway carpeted in a threadbare gold floral pattern. Faded striped paper covered the walls. The stairs descended a single story, terminating at an open doorway through which brighter light shone.

Stone knew he couldn't maintain the invisibility spell much longer. Even if he tried, he risked someone hearing his heavy breathing. Instead, he switched to something easier but not as safe: an illusion to blend in with the wall next to him. It wouldn't stand up to close scrutiny, but it might not need to if they didn't know he was here.

The illusion also allowed him enough mental bandwidth for a levitation spell, so he could descend the stairs without fear of a creaking board or footstep giving him away. Good thing nobody could hear his heart pounding, even though at this point it was more with anticipation than fear.

Silently, he floated down, keeping his back to the left-side wall. When he reached the bottom, he touched down softly in the corner and leaned forward, peering through.

Bloody hell...

He wasn't sure what he'd expected to see, aside from the man, the woman, and possibly the tapestry. Whatever it was, though, it definitely didn't include what spread out before him.

For one thing, the room was a lot bigger than he'd anticipated. He'd thought he'd find a small basement, perhaps some kind of break or recreation room. Instead, the space stretched out to nearly thirty feet long and half as wide. Three fixtures hanging from the ceiling provided illumination.

Every one of the walls was covered by large, elaborate tapestries, each one stitched to the one next to it to make a long strip that encompassed the whole room.

Stone stared at them in wonder, but only for a moment. As interesting as they were, what was going on in the room was even more interesting.

Two full-sized, old-fashioned wooden looms stood to either side in the room's center. The man sat in front of one, the woman in front of the other, facing the walls, their backs to each other. They continued to talk as their fingers flew among the warp threads, busily weaving colorful strands. Near them, a portable CD player on a table played what sounded like Fleetwood Mac.

Stone relaxed his vigilance just a little. He still maintained his illusion, but was no longer as worried about being seen. For one thing, neither the man nor the woman was even remotely facing him. For another, they seemed completely, almost unnaturally, focused on their work. He suspected he could have strolled naked through the room singing show tunes and they still might not have noticed him. He didn't intend to test that, though.

Instead, he resumed his scrutiny, taking in details and filing them away.

The woman's project was farther along than the man's, but both unfinished tapestries—along with the finished ones hanging on the walls—were, for lack of a better word, unsettling. None of them depicted any identifiable scene: human figures, landscapes, or even clearly defined abstract designs. Instead, their creation seemed to be haphazard, their colors thrown together with no apparent intent. Stone had once been impressed by a demonstration of tapestry-weaving at a museum in England, marveling at the level of complexity required to coax an intricate image out of a bunch of spools of seemingly-random thread. In this case, no such effort was happening. The man and woman were weaving away with no apparent regard for what they were creating. In fact, it almost seemed as if their hands' activity was disconnected from their banal chatter. With a shock, Stone suddenly recalled what the designs reminded him of: a series of photos he'd seen once on the internet, where spiders had been exposed to psychoactive drugs and then set free to spin webs. The resulting structures had been bizarre, but oddly compelling.

This was, in a word, *weird.*

Careful to move silently and keep the illusion running, he pulled his phone from his pocket and held it up, panning it around the room to capture video of the wall tapestries, the looms, and the two weavers. He was tempted to snap a few stills, but the camera made an audible shutter noise and, quiet as it was, he didn't want to risk rousing the pair from their trancelike focus.

Okay. Now for the good part.

He put the phone away and shifted to magical sight.

What he saw was definitely interesting, but once again not what he'd expected.

To start with, he would have bet a fair bit of money on the tapestries being magical. Probably highly magical.

They weren't. Not in the slightest. Neither were the hanging bobbins or the skeins of colorful thread they held. All of them were completely and utterly mundane.

The looms, on the other hand, were a different story.

Both of the tall wooden structures glowed with magical energy, which extended to the weavers' hands. As Stone watched in wonder, more arcane energy rose, floating in the air, forming a swirling conduit of vibrant orange that flowed to the west-side wall of the room and continued through.

What...the hell?

He focused his attention on the conduit. It was clear that whatever the weavers were doing, whatever they were creating with their efforts, it was combining with the looms' magic to form this energy. But why weren't the tapestries themselves magical? And where was the energy going? This room was underground, and the conduit seemed to be heading straight out, meaning wherever it was pointed had to be underground too.

You know, his little interior voice reminded him, *you don't have to care about this. Your job is to nick one of those tapestry sections and take it back to Aldwyn.*

Stone barely paid it any heed this time. Telling him he didn't have to care about this was akin to telling the sun not to rise. His curiosity had been well and truly piqued. Okay, so he had to do the job he'd been sent here for. But he still had six more days. And besides, he couldn't exactly march over there and cut one of the tapestries down. Not unless he knocked out the two weavers first, or waited for them to leave.

He thought about the two men who'd walked past him while he'd been hiding in the kitchen. These two, the man and the woman, had just arrived, and the men hadn't stuck around to bullshit with them before leaving. One pair in, one pair out.

Almost like they're working in shifts.

AWAKENING

He tensed as the implications of that sunk in. If his hypothesis was true, it meant several things:

Depending on the length of the shifts, potentially quite a number of Rydell residents had to be involved in this strange activity.

If they were truly working in shifts, it meant the tapestry would never be unguarded, so if he wanted to steal part of it, he'd need to do something about whichever weavers were present when he arrived to do it.

And, most worrying of all: *why* were they doing this? Why were the residents of a small town constantly weaving nonsensical designs on a pair of magic looms?

Where was that energy going, and what was it doing?

Was it powering something?

Feeding something?

A little shudder ran along Stone's neck. How long had this been going on? From the look of the tapestries on the wall and judging by the slow, deliberate rate the two current weavers were working, it had to be years. Maybe even decades. Even working nonstop, twenty-four hours a day, each of these massive tapestries would probably take months to finish.

He glanced at the wall again, this time noticing something he'd missed before: the unbroken, stitched-together strip of them wasn't a single layer. They'd been looped, hung one on top of the other. In one spot near him, Stone thought he spotted three stacked layers.

Damn. He did a little quick mental calculation: If the room was thirty by fifteen, each tapestry was six feet long, and it took an estimated six months to finish each one, that meant the Rydell weavers had been at this for a minimum of *almost twenty years.*

That was almost too improbable to contemplate.

He shifted his attention to the doorway he was standing in, noticing something else he hadn't consciously realized: to provide the opening that allowed entry, the tapestries in this section hadn't been fully stitched together. Only a single foot had been connected at the top, leaving the rest loose. Someone had pulled up the flap and attached it along the wall to provide the opening.

Good place to take your sample from, when it comes to that.

But not yet. Even if his curiosity hadn't burned with the desire to unravel (*see what I did there?* his little voice stuck in) the mystery of Rydell, there was another consideration: the other half of Aldwyn's instructions.

He couldn't just take the tapestry—he had to frame this Chase Cassidy bloke for it.

And as yet, he still had no idea who Chase Cassidy *was*, aside from a real-estate agent from Tuttleton.

Tomorrow, he'd need to take a trip over there and find out.

Something moved inside the room. He jerked his head back in time to see the woman get up from her chair.

"Be back in a minute," she called to the man. "I knew I should have stopped by the ladies' before I came down. Want anything from upstairs?"

"Nah, I'm good."

Stone went still. There was no way his blending spell was going to hide him from the woman if she walked right past him. Much as he wanted to stay and study this fascinating place more, it was time to go.

He swapped the blending spell for invisibility and floated up, pressing himself flat against the ceiling until she hurried past and exited through the upstairs door, then drifted back down. While he gave her a few moments to reach the bathroom, he glanced back at the weaving chamber. What, if anything, had changed due to the loss of one of the weavers?

Nothing, apparently. The man continued with his task, humming along with the song from the boom box. The orange energy hadn't abated in the slightest, the conduit as strong and pulsing as ever.

A flash of insight struck Stone: *Of course. That's why they have two at all times. Only one is needed, but this way one can take a break without interrupting the conduit.*

That brought up another, even more ominous question, which occurred to him as he slipped through the upstairs door and crept out through the dining room on his way out:

What happens if the conduit is interrupted?

CHAPTER SIXTEEN

STONE TRIED TO SLEEP IN the next morning before heading to Tuttleton, but his overactive mind wouldn't let him. Finally, after tossing and turning in the uncomfortable bed for more than an hour, he got up at seven a.m. He took a shower—no easy feat in the tiny cubicle—and stopped at the Rydell Roast for an extra-strength cup of coffee. While he sipped it, he reviewed the video he'd taken the previous night at the Weavers' lodge.

Obviously, none of the magical stuff he'd spotted showed up on the mundane video, but he did notice a few things he'd missed previously. Careful to ensure nobody looked over his shoulder, he leaned in to study the small screen.

The room definitely seemed to be set up for long-term occupancy. The chairs in front of the looms were high-end and expensive, surprisingly modern, like the ergonomic chairs from cash-flush tech startups. A mini-fridge similar to the one in Stone's room but newer sat on the floor next to a table, with one of those pod coffee makers on top of it. In addition to the portable CD player, an old-fashioned combo TV and DVD player was also on top of the table. Clearly, whatever force was behind the bizarre activities didn't mind if its servants caught up on the latest TV shows while they wove their crazy designs nonstop.

As he drove out of town and headed for Tuttleton, he wondered just how many of Rydell's residents were involved. Were all the members of the Weavers Lodge on the schedule, taking their shifts downstairs at regular intervals? Or was only some smaller inner circle in the know, leaving the rest of the members to their pancake breakfasts and weekly Tuesday-night meetings, oblivious to what was going on beneath their feet?

Maybe he could ask Brady Landis more about the organization when he got back. But for now, he was focused on Tuttleton.

The little town was only ten miles from Rydell, but the winding roads meant it might as well have been at least twice that. Even worse, a steady rain began to fall by the time Stone made it two miles out of Rydell, slowing him down even further. He drove with care, keeping an eye out for other vehicles, but saw none. That was good—he had no desire to be taken out by Mr. *Female Body Inspector* and his oversized truck.

Thinking about the truck made him slow the Jeep when he reached the crossroads where he'd stopped on his way in. He remembered the odd feeling of despair and futility he'd experienced, and his plan to stop and investigate the area. He could do it now, he supposed, but the rain made it an unpleasant prospect. Even with his long wool overcoat and boots, he wasn't exactly dressed for tromping around in a downpour.

He hesitated at the stop sign, considering his options, and finally decided to split the difference: he wouldn't get out and look around here right now, but he would turn right and drive up the small road heading north to see what he might spot there. If he didn't see anything interesting right away, he'd turn around and continue to Tuttleton. He still had the rest of today and five more after that to investigate, so as yet he didn't feel any overriding urgency.

The road proved a bust. The strange feeling faded quickly, leaving him on a narrow track that was barely a lane and a half wide, heavily cracked and overgrown. Clearly, nobody had been up here in quite some time. The map had mentioned an abandoned campground less than a mile up the road, though, so Stone kept going, glancing at the Jeep's odometer. With all the rain they got up here, if the place had been abandoned for a long time it might not even be visible anymore, obscured by undergrowth and trees.

But no, just as the odometer turned over a mile, he spotted a weathered sign reading *Camp Mitquni'qu.* He drove forward a bit further, but the area beyond was disappointing. There weren't any crumbling cabins or other buildings, just a cleared-out space, the remains of a few primitive lean-to structures, and what looked like a long-abandoned firepit in the center. Stone risked getting out for a few moments to scan the area with magical sight, but the feeling he'd experienced at the crossroads was nowhere in evidence here. Either whatever was causing it didn't reach this far, or the campground was just that—an old campground.

The rain had let off briefly, so before he left Stone walked around for five minutes, looking for any evidence that anyone had been here recently. Once again, he found nothing. No food wrappers, no remnants left behind by teenagers or homeless people, no leftovers from someone's campfire. That seemed odd to him—Rydell, at least, seemed like the kind of place teenagers like Brady Landis would do anything to get out of, even if it meant trekking the few miles to explore an abandoned space. But either they cleaned up after themselves very well, or they hadn't been here at all.

Okay, enough stalling.

He turned the Jeep around and retraced his route back to the crossroads, keeping an eye out for traffic coming the other way. His experience with the truck had spooked him more than he cared to admit—even if the driver *had* been distracted and hadn't seen him until the last minute, it still didn't make sense that he himself hadn't heard its approach until it was practically on top of him. He knew he was jumping to conclusions to think it was connected with the area's despairing aspect, but he'd been a mage long enough to know it wasn't a good idea to discount hunches, no matter how improbable. Perhaps there had been some kind of horrific accident or murder in the area many years ago. He made a mental note to ask someone in Rydell about it when he returned. For now, though, it was on to Tuttleton.

The rest of the drive looked very much like the one to Rydell: narrow, twisting road, overhanging trees, and no other traffic. The only difference was the rain, which had started again. Between that and the road, the five-mile trip took him nearly half an hour. By the time he reached Tuttleton, his shoulders ached with tension and the beginnings of a headache bloomed behind his eyes. He was well used to driving in the rain from living in England, but this was different.

Tuttleton had the same sort of sign Rydell did, listing its fraternal and civic organizations. Stone slowed down to read it this time, scanning for the Weavers.

To his surprise, it didn't appear. Tuttleton had Masons, Eastern Star, Moose, and the Lions Club, but Rydell's odd club was conspicuously absent. In its place were a couple of others: the Tuttleton Reading Circle, which met once a week at the library, and the Tuttleton Music Makers, which met at the theater. Those sounded fairly benign, the sorts of things small-town people would do to stave off the boredom.

Did that mean these people weren't involved with the bizarre goings-on in Rydell? How much did the people from the two towns mix? And why did Aldwyn want Chase Cassidy framed for the theft of the tapestry?

He thought back to something Jason had told him once, while they were sharing beers at some bar he couldn't even remember anymore. His friend had attended high school in Ventura, a beachside town in southern California. A rivalry had existed between his school and its cross-town counterpart. Jason's school mascot had been a cougar, while the other school's had been a bulldog. Because they were long past the time when actual live animals (especially large predatory cats) could be kept as mascots, each school enshrined a detailed stuffed version in pride of place among its sports trophies. Once, during a hotly-contested football season, a few team members from Jason's school had sneaked onto their rival's campus and "kidnapped" the stuffed bulldog. Jason wouldn't say whether he'd been involved, but Stone suspected he had. Could this situation be something similar, where Aldwyn wanted the people of Rydell to believe someone from their rival sister town had stolen something valuable to them?

It seemed farfetched. Towns didn't act like high schools—and more importantly, dragons typically didn't act like high schoolers. Sure, they weren't above encouraging their pawns to indulge in a spot of the old B and E—Stone's own theft of the game set and a scroll from Thalassa Nera proved that—but this didn't seem like the same kind of situation. And anyway, Aldwyn had given his word that no dragons were involved in this little adventure. Despite his general lack of trust for his ancestor, Stone believed him. Kolinsky had told him that dragons, even renegades like Aldwyn, didn't give their word lightly.

So it had to be something else.

A drive through Tuttleton showed him a few things. The town was about the same size as Rydell, though laid out differently. Rydell existed mostly along the central main street with a few offshoots, while Tuttleton was more spread out and less organized. Stone found a central park or square with an old-fashioned bandstand in the center, surrounded on all four sides by various businesses. From there, more streets stretched out in all directions. He drove up a few of them, finding mostly single-family homes set back from well-kept yards.

Another thing he noticed right away: even with the rain coming down hard, it was obvious that Tuttleton was as lovingly cared for as Rydell. The buildings comprising the commercial district surrounding the park were all in pristine repair, the streets were clean, the park and the bandstand were meticulously maintained, and what few people Stone spotted on the streets were well-dressed and looked happy. There were no overflowing trash cans, no flooding, no evidence of homeless or even poor people—it almost looked like something from the backlot of a movie production company.

Interesting, he thought—but was it? Maybe this area was just affluent, and maybe the people who'd settled Tuttleton and Rydell had been wealthy transplants from other parts of the country. He'd read discussions of it before, where the people from other, less-expensive states complained about rich Californians swooping in to take advantage of the lower property values and trying to change the area's culture to match what they were used to.

That didn't seem to be the case here, though. He pulled the Jeep into the rear of a parking lot a block from the central square and got out after making sure his disguise amulet was running. To be safe, in case the Rydell and Tuttleton residents ever got together to compare notes, he chose a different disguise this time: a tall, boring-looking, thirtyish man in a down coat, jeans, and a knit cap.

For the next half-hour, he strolled the square, checking out the businesses. Tuttleton had the same types as Rydell had: restaurants, bars, coffee shops, a single gas station, a small market, clothing stores, a library, and a hardware store, which he ducked inside to buy an umbrella. Unlike Rydell, though, Tuttleton seemed to be more interested in the arts: he spotted a tiny combination concert hall and single-screen movie theater, a music shop, and several flyers announcing performances by both the local schoolchildren and the Tuttleton Music Makers.

Stone got a cup of coffee to go and drank it as he walked, pausing to peer in windows like any tourist might but actually paying discreet attention to the people he passed. Magical sight revealed curiosity and slight apprehension, but no sense of malice or threat. They weren't sure why he was here, but they didn't seem to mind too much that he was.

He wasn't here to dawdle, though. He had no reason to believe the tapestry-related oddness going on in Rydell had anything to do with Tuttleton. The Weavers didn't seem to have a branch here—at least if they did, they didn't advertise it. He was here to find out what he could about Chase Cassidy.

He started, once again, at the library. This time, though, he didn't bother with the librarian, but instead looked around until he found recent copies of the town's newspapers. He'd already checked his phone and discovered Tuttleton was every bit as isolated as Rydell, with no internet access, and there were no public computers he could find at the library, so he was back to doing it old-school. He sat at a table in the back room and began leafing through the latest issue of the Tuttleton *Tattler,* which came out once a week and had eight pages.

It didn't take long to find what he was looking for: on page seven near the bottom, near an ad for the Music Makers' upcoming concert and an article about proposed improvements to the bandstand, he found another small ad: *Cassidy Real Estate Services – Don't take a chance on your home! Talk to Chase!* Below the text was a grainy black-and-white photo of the same balding, stocky man Alwyn had shown him via illusion. Below it was a phone number and the address of the agency—on the second floor of a building less than two blocks from the library, if Stone remembered properly.

Well. That was something, at least. It was mid-morning on a weekday, so in all likelihood he'd find Cassidy in his office. At least *something* was going his way.

He was about to return the papers to their place when he stopped. They were small and didn't take long to get through— perhaps he might learn a bit more about Tuttleton's recent history if he looked through a few more of them before he left. He settled back and pulled up the next one in the stack.

Mostly, he was disappointed. The usual small-town stories dominated the *Tattler*'s pages: a combination of local gossip, updates on weddings, engagements, and parties—though surprisingly few funerals—and write-ups on the various local clubs' activities, along with local government reporting and stories about what the schoolchildren were up to in their sports, academics, and extracurriculars.

Deadly dull, in other words.

Stone was about to close the fourth paper and give up on his research project when he spotted the name "Cassidy" again. He paged back.

"Hmm…" he murmured under his breath.

The headline read *Cassidy Has Big Plans for Music Makers*. Another grainy photo of a smiling Chase Cassidy, larger this time, accompanied a folksy article about how he had taken over reins of the Music Makers a few months ago, and had already set up a committee to add more music classes to the local school, all the way down to the kindergarten level.

Hmm, he thought again. It could mean nothing—there weren't that many things for people to be involved with in either of these two towns—but could it be a coincidence that Cassidy was in charge of what was apparently a popular local organization? Had Aldwyn known this? *Was* there some sort of rivalry going on between Tuttleton and Rydell?

As he picked up the newspapers and carried them back to their storage cubby, it occurred to him that, in the several he'd read through, he'd never once seen the name "Rydell." That, in and of itself, seemed odd to him. One would think, if they were the only two towns within thirty miles of each other, their residents might mingle a bit—if for no other reason than to get out of their ruts and meet some new people.

But if they did, the newspaper here didn't seem to think it was important enough to write about.

Stone paid careful attention as he exited the library. He was definitely getting noticed, but it was still in that same curious-but-not-hostile way as before. The librarian wasn't putting off the same vibes as the one from Rydell, so he didn't sneak back inside to see if she made a phone call after he left. Maybe it was because he wasn't staying here.

Or maybe he was looking for problems where none existed.

It didn't take long to reach Chase Cassidy's building. It was on the corner of two of the main streets, on the second floor of a pleasant, wood-sided structure painted periwinkle blue with white trim. The lower floor held a clothing store and a juice bar, while a stairway led up to a walkway that passed two doctor's offices, a dentist, and a hair salon. Cassidy's agency was in the back. The window had some photos of properties with write-ups, but surprisingly few.

Stone pushed open the door and entered. The office was tiny, with only a small reception area and a closed door in the back. A young woman sat behind the front desk in front of a row of old-style filing cabinets. She looked him over, obviously curious since she didn't recognize him. "Good morning. May I help you?"

"Yes. I'm visiting the area, and thinking about buying some property here. Is Mr. Cassidy available to discuss it?" He used his American accent.

She looked perplexed. "You want to buy property? In Tuttleton?"

"Er…yes, that's what I said. This *is* a real-estate agency, right? I couldn't find another one in town."

"Oh! Right. Yes, of course. Yes, we are the only one in town. Sorry—we don't get too many out-of-area folks around here, and you're the second one in a couple of days. Mostly we just help locals sell to each other, or buy land to build new places."

Hmm. Another new person? That might be worth investigating. "Interesting. It's so beautiful here, though. I'm surprised you don't get people wanting to move here all the time."

She laughed, but Stone noticed a slight nervous flare in her aura. "It *is* beautiful, but we're a long way from much of anything else. You've probably already figured out we don't have internet access here, or cable TV. Even most people who want to get away from it all don't want to unplug quite *that* much."

"That's a good point, I suppose. But I'm thinking about building a little vacation cottage, so being unplugged is a feature." He glanced pointedly past her, toward the closed door. "Is Mr. Cassidy here? Is he busy?"

The door opened, almost as if someone had been waiting for a cue, revealing the familiar, stocky figure of Chase Cassidy. He wore a dress shirt, and was adjusting his tie as if he'd donned it as an afterthought. "Hello, friend," he called with a cheery smile. "I don't think I've seen you around town. Come on back to my office and we'll chat. Can I get you a cup of coffee?"

Stone didn't miss that Cassidy almost seemed *too* cheery. "No, thank you. I actually just had one. I was walking around town, taking in the sights."

Cassidy waved him to a chair. The office was small, neat, and organized, with a desk, credenza, and another filing cabinet. No computer, Stone noticed. A series of plaques and awards hung on the wall, split about evenly between real estate and music, along with a few lovingly framed autographed baseball cards featuring Seattle Mariners players. Behind Cassidy's chair, near a window looking out on a line of tall trees, an acoustic guitar stood on a stand.

"Okay," he said when he was settled in his own chair. "How can I help you out today, Mr.—"

Stone realized he hadn't thought of a new alias. "Hubbard," he said firmly. "Jason Hubbard."

"Well, it's a pleasure to meet you. What brings you to Tuttleton? As I'm sure you've heard numerous times already, we don't get too many tourists."

"I have heard that, yes. Your receptionist seemed surprised that I'm the second stranger you've seen in a couple of days."

"Yes, it is surprising."

Stone didn't miss his evasiveness. "Was he wanting to buy property too? The new person?"

"She, actually. I'm not sure, exactly. We didn't get much chance to chat."

A woman. Even more interesting, as was Cassidy's sudden discomfort. He decided to let it go for now. "In any case, I was doing some research, and this area popped up. It appealed to me because of its beauty and isolation. I also plan to check out Rydell." He leaned forward a little, wondering if Cassidy would say anything indicating a rivalry between the two towns.

"Rydell's beautiful too." Another too-bright laugh. "You understand I'm biased, though."

Stone nodded. He made a show of looking around the office. "Are you a musician, Mr. Cassidy?"

The man's face lit up in a genuine smile. "I am! Music is pretty important here in Tuttleton. I don't know if you noticed when you entered the town, but our Music Makers organization is quite popular with the folks here. Pretty much everybody in Tuttleton plays *something*, or sings. A lot of us do both. What about you, Mr. Hubbard? Do you play?"

"I do, as it happens. I used to be in a band when I was younger." He nodded toward the guitar in the corner. "Never really picked up the acoustic, though."

Cassidy laughed. "Aha, a rocker! We've got some of that here, too, though we lean more toward classical and folk. Maybe if you do decide to buy or build here, you could join the Music Makers.

I'm the president this year, so I hope you'll forgive my little recruiting spiel."

"Of course." Stone leaned back, appearing to be in contemplation. "One thing I noticed while looking around was that the town seems very...pristine. Almost like something out of a storybook. Everything is clean and well cared for, the people all seem happy...it's a bit hard to believe. Do you not have any of the typical problems here? Drugs, crime, homelessness?"

Cassidy studied him a moment, his cheery expression slipping just a bit. "We don't, Mr. Hubbard. Our population is small, and the people who don't fit in with our...unique lifestyle here don't tend to stay long."

"Because they don't want to, or because they're...encouraged to leave?" Stone shifted to magical sight again, to watch his reaction.

The smile didn't slip any further, but the aura spiked noticeably. "Now, why would you say such a thing?" the agent asked amiably. "We would never do anything like that."

"Of course not. Forgive me." Stone offered a smile of his own. "I definitely don't want to get off on the wrong foot. This place really *is* quite beautiful."

Cassidy's aura subsided...mostly. "Don't worry about it. We understand our ways are a little unusual, but we like it here. I'm sure you will too, if you decide to join our community, even temporarily." He pulled a folder to him and shuffled through it. "I might have a couple of properties I can show you, but you'll need to give me a bit of time to gather the information. A day or so. Is that all right? As I said, we don't usually get out-of-towners."

Stone stood. "No problem. I just arrived and I'm here for a few days, so I've got time. That reminds me—are there any places to stay around here? I didn't see any hotels, B-and-Bs, or anything like that."

"Ooh. That's a good point. I'm sorry, but we don't really have anything like that. I could ask around for you, see if anyone has a room to rent—"

"Quite all right. I'll find something. Thank you, Mr. Cassidy. It was a pleasure to meet you."

Stone didn't try to stick around this time to see if Cassidy made any odd phone calls. He got out of there and didn't stop until he'd walked through the park and out the other side. He leaned against a wall under an awning and considered his options.

Cassidy was obviously hiding something—that much was clear from his aura flares. It could simply be confusion at the arrival of a new person in town, but it could also be something else. He'd seemed tense when Stone had brought up how pristine the town was, and the lack of any crime or homelessness. He hadn't asked in Rydell, but that town had seemed the same way. Did they do something with their undesirable element? And who was the woman Cassidy had mentioned? Did she have anything to do with this, or was her arrival merely a coincidence?

Most importantly, though, what did Chase Cassidy have to do with the Rydell tapestry? Why did Aldwyn want him to frame the man for the theft? Stone had thought perhaps he'd find that Cassidy was another member of the Weavers, but that organization didn't seem to exist in Tuttleton.

He hadn't noticed any signs of magic in or around Cassidy's office. Of course, that didn't mean anything, necessarily. Mages weren't easy to spot, even by other mages, unless they had magical objects or spells on them or had cast something recently.

This whole thing wasn't fitting together. Clearly, something magical was going on in the Weavers' basement—something that required at least a subset of its members to keep up the constant tapestry creation. But what did that have to do with Rydell, and Cassidy? What would happen if the weaving stopped, and what would the people of Rydell do to Cassidy if they thought he was the one who'd stolen their tapestry section?

Idly, Stone shifted to magical sight again and watched people as they walked by. He'd employed the disregarding spell, so nobody paid him any attention, allowing him to get a good look. Nothing stood out: their auras were the same composition as any other people, with the normal distribution of colors. He saw no sign of any magic around any of them, and they all looked content and happy, regardless of whether they were alone, in pairs, or in small groups.

A sudden thought occurred to him: he hadn't seen any Change-lings. Not here, and not in Rydell. Was that significant? He wasn't sure. People around here seemed fairly cut off from the rest of the world, so it was possible the magical "virus" that tripped the Change hadn't reached here. Verity had mentioned that the Change had afflicted less than one percent of the population, concentrated more highly in urban areas. But in order to be affected, one had to have latent magical blood. Maybe nobody around here did.

He was about to push off the building, reminding himself that the presence or absence of Changelings wasn't why he was here, when he noticed something from the corner of his eye.

He turned slowly, afraid if he moved too fast he'd lose whatever it was. Could it have been a person, lurking around a corner watching him?

If it was, they were gone now, ducked back out of sight. He ambled in that direction, forcing himself not to go too fast and attract attention, but when he reached the corner and peered around, nothing was there.

Just seeing things, he thought, though as usual he wasn't too sure about that.

He resumed his walk around the town, thinking about his next steps. Once again, he reminded himself that he didn't need to care about anything going on in Tuttleton. His mission was to frame

Chase Cassidy for the theft of the tapestry, which meant he needed to get hold of something of Cassidy's to leave at the scene. That shouldn't be too hard—he could either wait until the agency closed, sneak in, and take something from the office, or figure out where Cassidy lived and break in there while he was at work. He'd need to be careful, though. If he left anything too obvious, the Weavers might get suspicious.

Does that even really matter, though? He wasn't planning the perfect crime, and these people weren't exactly Sherlock Holmes. Once he finished his task, he'd be out of here and untraceable. Even if anybody suspected him, they'd be looking for "Michael Townes" or "Jason Hubbard." The worst that might happen if everything went wrong was that he'd have to burn his current fake IDs and have Kolinsky's contact build him some new ones.

Despite the lack of internet access, he couldn't find any phone books listing the Tuttleton residents' addresses. Perhaps, given how few of them there were, they didn't need one since they all knew where each other's homes were. He certainly didn't want to give anything away by asking anyone where Cassidy lived, so instead he spent the remainder of the afternoon scoping out the town, finally stopping at an attractive little diner to dawdle over an early dinner until it got dark. He sat near the front window, eating slowly and continuing his people-watching.

As he was finishing his coffee and preparing to leave, he spotted Chase Cassidy coming up the street toward the diner. There was no mistaking his rotund figure, and as he passed under the bright streetlights, Stone confirmed it. He seemed somehow furtive, moving quickly with his hands in his pockets.

He didn't look in the diner window as he passed by, appearing focused on something ahead of him. Stone rose and tossed some cash on the table. Maybe Cassidy was on his way home.

He waited until the man had passed a full block ahead of him, then left the diner and followed, disregarding spell at full strength.

Any moment, he expected Cassidy to turn off the main square and head up one of the smaller residential streets.

He didn't, though. Instead, he paused in front of the combination movie theater and concert hall. He glanced back and forth as if looking for anyone behind him, but didn't notice Stone. Then he disappeared inside.

Stone hurried after him. If it wasn't for the nervous back-and-forth check, he might not have thought anything of Cassidy's actions. Perhaps the guy was merely stopping for a movie after work. But as he drew closer, he quickly discarded that speculation. The tiny theater only showed one movie at a time, once per day. This one, a romance flick, wasn't set to start for another hour and a half. In fact, the place didn't even seem to be open yet. The marquee was dark, and inside the lights were off and nobody moved around. The door was locked.

So where had Cassidy gone?

Ah. Of course. Stone almost felt embarrassed at the crazy web of speculations he was weaving. Cassidy was the president of the Music Makers, which met in the theater building. He'd probably stopped by there to pick up something, or maybe to get the meeting room prepared. If Stone waited for Cassidy to leave, he could likely find something in the club room to plant in the Weavers' chamber. He recalled from the sign outside the town that the Music Makers met on Thursday evenings, so he didn't expect any other members to be arriving tonight.

Stone's plan to wait for Cassidy to leave was a good one, except for one thing: the theater building had to have multiple exits. If he watched the front, he could miss the man ducking out the back. Much as he didn't like it because it added an extra chance of getting caught, he'd need to go inside and wait there.

He couldn't see any indication of an alarm, which didn't surprise him too much since neither Rydell nor Tuttleton seemed to have any crime to speak of. It hadn't occurred to him until now, but when he'd been looking through the *Tattler*, he hadn't seen any mentions of crime, petty or otherwise. Either they were deliberately choosing not to report it, or there simply wasn't any. That was odd in and of itself. Even in a collection of people as small as this, *somebody* had to get up to no good occasionally. It was simply human nature.

Right now, though, it worked to Stone's advantage. He looked around for anyone paying attention, then quickly used magic to pop the lock on the theater's front door. He slipped inside, closed it behind him, and re-locked it.

After a check with magical sight to make sure nobody was lurking in the shadows to ambush him, he pulled up a weak light spell for a look around. He was standing in a small, thick-carpeted lobby. The concession stand was directly in front of him, the ticket booth off to his left, and hallways extended to the left and right. On either side of the concession stand were a pair of sweeping staircases, probably leading to the seats. Stone jogged up the one on the right side, the plush carpet muffling his footsteps.

He was right: as he reached the top, an arched opening led to a chamber with rows of banked seats, all facing an empty stage with a movie screen at the back. The whole place was quiet, clearly not in use at the moment.

Stone stopped, standing perfectly still, and craned his ears for any sound of Cassidy.

He heard nothing.

But wait…

He'd been about to find a place to hide where he could keep track of the exits when something caught his attention. He stopped, once again standing still.

Was that…music?

It was very faint, like a far-off radio playing at low volume. He couldn't make out more than a few notes, though it was enough to tell there wasn't any vocal component. Somebody in here was playing an instrument—or perhaps more than one.

That made sense too, though—perhaps some of the Music Makers members had keys to the place, so they could come here to practice.

Movement in front of him caught his attention. He ducked behind the rear row of seats and watched the stage.

Chase Cassidy exited from behind the movie screen. He paused a moment at the front of the stage, scanning the area as if picturing it full of audience members, then descended and headed up the row toward the rear exit where Stone was hiding. He didn't seem nervous now, his gait easy and his expression calm. Stone waited until he got close, then pulled up an invisibility spell. Cassidy moved past without looking left or right and disappeared through the arch toward the stairs. A few moments later, the front door closed.

Stone had a decision to make now: he could either follow Cassidy and hopefully learn where he lived, or he could remain here and try finding something he could plant in the Weavers' room. After a moment's thought, he decided on the latter. He'd need to be careful, though, since if he'd been right about the faint strains of music, somebody else was still in the building.

His eyes had become accustomed to the near-darkness now, so he didn't need the light spell. He crept down the aisle to the stage and climbed up the short stairway on the right side. The music was a little louder here, but not much. He still couldn't hear more than the occasional note. It sounded almost as if it were being muffled by soundproofing.

Backstage, behind the hanging movie screen, he found the typical items needed for a musical performance: stacked chairs, risers, instrument stands, lights, neatly coiled cords, control panels. A few soft lights illuminated the area, but only enough to keep anyone from tripping. He stopped again, facing the rear wall and listening. On a hunch, he switched to magical sight.

He didn't see anything at first, but then he happened to glance up.

Well. This *is getting interesting.*

High above him, bright-blue energy swirled. As he watched, fascinated, he quickly got the feeling it was moving almost as if in rhythm.

But *what* rhythm?

The obvious answer came quickly: the music? He couldn't be sure since he couldn't hear it clearly, but it did seem as if the dancing blue energy was responding to *something.*

He used a levitation spell to lift himself higher for a better look, though he was careful to remain below the energy's level.

What was it doing? Why was it here?

Up here, he could see something he hadn't spotted from his lower vantage point: the energy was going somewhere outside the building. It continued swirling and dancing in a bouncy pattern, but the column disappeared out through the rear wall.

Just like it did in the Weavers' room.

There were differences, sure: this energy was rhythmic and bright blue, while the Weavers' was orange and flowed more like water. But in both cases, they formed in a hidden area inside a building, and headed somewhere else *outside* the building.

Could they be related? Could Tuttleton's Music Makers and Rydell's Weavers have something in common after all?

Another thought occurred to Stone. He pulled out his phone and tapped the compass app, grateful it didn't require internet access to function. He watched as the indicator spun. When it finally settled on a direction, he tightened his hand around the phone.

The blue energy from the hidden room here pointed east—the opposite direction from the orange energy from the Weavers' chamber, which had pointed west.

Was it possible that the two were…converging somewhere in between?

He'd need a map to tell for sure. He pulled out his notebook and jotted the precise direction the blue energy was headed. It would be harder for its orange counterpart, since the Weavers' room was underground, but he thought he could make a good guess at it.

For now, though, he needed to find the room where the music was originating.

He spun slowly in place, pointing toward the main auditorium and keeping magical sight up. It didn't take long at all to trace the blue energy to a dark, windowless wall. The room, high above the backstage area, was well hidden by ropes, cords, and hanging banners, but it was obvious that was where the energy was originating. It took Stone only a moment longer to find a pull-down wooden staircase pressed up against the room's floor. When he levitated over to it and put his ear against the floor, he heard the music more clearly. It was still soft, but the strains of a classical piece he didn't know, played on what sounded like cello and violin, came through now.

Its rhythm definitely corresponded to the blue energy's movements.

This was fascinating. What was going on here—and even more importantly, what did Aldwyn know about it? Why hadn't the dragon told him anything about the strange energy and its reason for existence?

Maybe he wanted you to figure it out. Maybe this whole thing is a test.

In any case, as much as he wanted to lower that staircase and have a look inside the hidden room, it was a bad idea. There was no way, even with magic, that he could hide himself from anyone who might be inside. Did they take shifts, like the Weavers in Rydell? Did whatever the energy was converging on require a constant stream of it? If that were true, he could wait until the shift change and then try to sneak upstairs, but he had no way to know if that were even true. These musicians could remain here for hours.

No, he decided: that wouldn't be the best use of his time. He still needed to get something of Cassidy's to plant in the Weavers' tapestry room, and before he took the tapestry, he wanted to solve the mystery of where, if anywhere, the two columns of energy were converging. His magical training told him clearly that making any definitive moves before he had all the facts could be dangerous.

He waited a few more minutes to see if anybody came down from the upper room, but when no one did and the music continued to play, he sneaked back out of the theater. He glanced at his watch: only eight p.m. It had felt like he'd spent hours inside the theater, but in reality he'd only been there less than thirty minutes.

When he exited through the rear door, glancing around to make sure nobody was watching him, the first thing he noticed was more music. It was louder this time, and sounded like a small orchestra playing a cheerful classical piece. Definitely not the same one he'd heard from inside the theater, though. What was going on?

As soon as he got back to the main street, it became obvious: in the central square, a crowd was gathered around the gazebo in the middle of the park, where a group of musicians were playing.

Curious, he strolled closer for a better look. It appeared that the musicians were high-school students, and a good percentage of Tuttleton's population had gathered to hear them play. The general mood was festive, with everyone standing around enjoying the performance. A quick look with magical sight confirmed this, and also that there definitely wasn't any weird swirling blue energy shooting off in any direction.

He scanned the crowd for anyone he knew, especially Chase Cassidy, but he didn't see the man or his assistant. He was about to switch off the sight when he spotted something on the other side of the crowd.

It was hard to see among all the brightly-colored auras and the crush of bodies, but he could have sworn he'd spotted one that didn't look as calm and mellow as the others. Flashes of red sparked around it, and it appeared to be moving.

Who was it? What were they up to? Could it be Cassidy?

Stone squinted, trying to see past the other auras, but the one he'd noticed had disappeared among the swirling colors. Had it ever been there at all, or was he seeing things? He switched off magical sight, thinking perhaps he might have a better chance of spotting the person without the auric interference, and was rewarded by the sight of a figure disappearing into the crowd. By the time he'd worked his way around the edge, though, and made it to the other side, the figure was gone. The only thing he was reasonably sure about was that it had been a woman with dark hair, and possibly dark skin.

Interesting. Did the woman have something to do with what was going on, or was he seeing things where they didn't exist again? Was she the woman Cassidy had mentioned—the one who'd visited his office looking to buy property?

He'd have to worry about that later. If most of the townspeople were out here watching the performance, it meant this would be a good time to sneak into Chase Cassidy's office.

Up until now, he'd been pushing any thoughts of what he was doing to the side. He was planning to frame an innocent man for something that, depending on what the energy the Weavers were producing was doing, might have severe consequences. What would the Weavers do when they discovered their tapestry gone, and evidence that someone from their sister town had done it?

Stone hesitated when he reached Cassidy's office. So far, he hadn't seen anyone around the area—probably those who weren't watching the performance were home. But should he do this at all? If he gave it some more thought, could he perhaps figure out a way around it, so he could fulfill the letter of what Aldwyn had asked him to do, but not the spirit? Perhaps a way to leave something that might implicate Cassidy on the surface, but not stand up to strong scrutiny? He'd have to be careful, though. Aldwyn was bloody smart, and would see right through Stone's attempts to do an end run around the assignment.

You're thinking too much again. Just grab something and do it. It's not like they're going to kill the man or anything.

The sticky part was that he wasn't as sure about that as he wanted to be. But in any case, he was right: he needed to get on with it. He could consider his options once he had the item.

Sneaking into Cassidy's office was easy. Nobody was inside, and it took him only a couple of minutes to pop the lock, hurry in, and look around. He thought about examining some of the files in the cabinets, but he couldn't afford to stay that long. He doubted Cassidy kept Music Makers files in his office anyway. Finally, he settled for opening Cassidy's desk drawer. He took a moment for a cursory examination of the contents: papers, a few coins, paper clips, a stapler, a San Francisco Giants baseball cap. All of them were either too generic or too specific, though. He didn't want to count on the authorities having to use fingerprint evidence to identify Cassidy, but there was no way the man would drop his insurance papers at a crime scene. The cap seemed a reach too. If the investigators were sharp, they might figure someone was trying too hard.

He used magic to lift the papers. Beneath them lay several pink phone message slips and scraps of paper with notes scrawled on them. Better. A small phone-message slip might plausibly drop out of someone's pocket unnoticed if they were in a hurry. He selected one message with Cassidy's name on it, along with *Call Tony P. about Pine Ridge house* and a phone number.

Less than a minute later, he was outside. The concert was still going on, so he had no trouble getting back to where he'd left his car. As he drove out of Tuttleton and back toward Rydell, he was already thinking about his next steps.

CHAPTER SEVENTEEN

S TONE FOUND A PAPER MAP of the area at the Rydell gas station on his way back. He took it back to his room, checking once more to make sure no one had breached his wards before going inside. This time, it appeared no one had. Either whoever had broken in before had found what they were looking for the previous time, they'd decided there was nothing suspicious about him, or they'd figured he was too smart to leave anything incriminating lying around. He'd taken a quick look around for Brady, hoping the boy would find him again, but no luck.

He spread the map on the table and compared it with the notes he'd taken regarding the direction the Tuttleton energy had pointed. He didn't have precise information about the Rydell energy and didn't want to go back to the Weavers' room, but he could extrapolate. If the two energy trails converged someplace interesting, at least he'd have a place to start.

It didn't take long to get a potential answer. Stone leaned back in his chair and stared at the map, pondering. "Well. That *is* interesting…"

The line heading west out of Tuttleton, the one he had a precise direction for, stretched across the forested land between the two towns, passing through a point a little north of the crossroads where Stone had almost been flattened by the truck.

The place where he'd felt the strange sense of futility and melancholy.

The less precise line moving east from Rydell pointed further north, crossing nearer to the abandoned campground.

But it is less precise. Given the distance between the two towns, it was entirely possible that a slight error could aim the line in the wrong direction.

What if the two of them do converge at that spot near the crossroads?

What if they're pointing at the same place?

Energized now, Stone peered more closely at the map. He made a slight adjustment to the Rydell line, and discovered only a few degrees of difference would be necessary for both lines to either cross or meet at the same location.

Suddenly, he needed to go check that crossroads.

He glanced at his watch. It was nearly midnight. Almost everyone in Rydell would no doubt be asleep by now, so nobody would notice him leaving. He had no idea how many people in town knew about whatever was going on with the Weavers, but for now, it was probably best to keep his business to himself. He folded the map and took it with him in case anyone was still feeling nosy, reset the wards on the room, and headed out. There were no lights on in the Landis house as he drove away.

At least it wasn't raining now. He navigated the twisting road carefully, flicking his gaze to the rearview mirror often to make sure nobody was following him. It was easy to tell that was the case; he encountered no other vehicles on the road going in either direction.

When he reached the crossroads, this time he turned onto the north-facing road and drove a quarter-mile up before pulling off to the side. It was pitch-dark out here, the only illumination coming from a half-moon that kept passing behind shifting clouds. He didn't want to use a light spell, though, in case anyone might spot him. Instead, he waited near the Jeep until his eyes acclimated.

He didn't know where, exactly, he was looking. Even with his map, he couldn't be certain specifically where the two lines converged since he didn't have a precise reading from the Rydell line. The still air was cold and crisp, heavy with the scents of dampness and fresh tree sap. At first look, nothing around here seemed interesting.

But if it was visible at first look, someone would have spotted it a long time ago.

In any case, it might not be something visual he was seeking—not at first, anyway.

He closed his eyes, reaching out with his magical senses and trying to tap into the despairing feeling he'd noticed last time he was out here. He let his mind drift, recalling the way it had felt before: not just despairing, but…tired. Used up. Something that wanted to give up, but for some reason wasn't allowed to.

It didn't take long for him to notice it again. It was all around him out here, nebulous and drifting, permeating the entire area. He let it wash over him, focusing only enough to see if he could pinpoint a more precise location. He was fairly sure that, wherever it originated, it wasn't here. It wasn't far away, though.

Almost unconsciously, he opened his eyes and started walking. As he moved, he shifted his perceptions, doing something he didn't often do because it usually wasn't useful: turning off magical sight but leaving his other arcane senses running. Right now, he wasn't looking for something he could see, but trying to trace something he could *feel.*

Surprisingly, the lack of magical sight made it easier to follow the feeling. The sheer number of trees around here, each with its own pale-green aura, made it difficult to track anything else visually, but without the added distraction the feeling seemed to solidify—almost to beckon him forward.

Does it want *me to find it?*

That was exhilarating—but also potentially dangerous. Even for a mage of his power level, blindly following an unseen force trying to lure him into a dense forest wasn't necessarily the most intelligent path.

Still, as he continued his slow and careful walk through the underbrush, trying not to trip over any fallen logs or clumps of roots along the thickly-carpeted forest floor, he couldn't shake the feeling that the thing, whatever it was, didn't want to hurt him.

It wanted him to help it.

But help it do *what?* That was the question.

He'd dealt with cases like this before, even if not personally: the entity trapped in Adelaide Bonham's basement that had enticed his long-dead apprentice, and the eldritch horror buried beneath the ruined building in Massachusetts that had destroyed the lives of a whole group of teenagers when they'd strayed too close to it while on a camping trip.

You did *not* mess with disembodied forces in remote areas.

If he wanted to make the most prudent choice, he'd break free of the thing's influence and get the hell out of there, leaving the Rydell/Tuttleton area until he reached somewhere he could get internet and phone access, then consult with Eddie and Ward or even Gabriel about the situation.

But all of that would take time, and time was something he didn't have a lot of. A few days still remained of the period Aldwyn had allotted him, but he still had to get back to Rydell, somehow gain entry to the Weavers' secret chamber—which would probably require him to incapacitate the current Weavers—steal the tapestry piece, and plant the evidence implicating Chase Cassidy. And that was putting aside the big question: what would happen if he stopped the Weavers, interrupting the steady flow of energy that was feeding or powering the thing he was currently seeking?

Yes, he should make the prudent choice—but until he knew what would happen, he couldn't safely remove that tapestry piece and interfere with the energy.

This was the way to find out.

Damn, sometimes he didn't like how curious he was.

He kept walking, adjusting his mental shields to allow the strange feeling in, but to block out any direct attacks. At least if it tried to zap him, he'd have a fighting chance to hold it off long enough to fight back.

He hoped.

By now, he'd penetrated far enough into the forest so the road was no longer visible behind him. He hadn't left the Jeep's headlights on, so when he stopped and turned back, only darkness and the shadowy trunks of countless trees were visible. They seemed to close around him, blocking his path in every direction except forward. Suddenly, a strange disorientation gripped him, along with a wild thought: *Did I get turned around? Am I going the wrong way?*

But before he could dwell on that, before he could reach into his pocket and pull out his phone to call up the compass again, a reassuring blanket settled over his mind. There were no words, but the message was nonetheless clear:

Please don't stop now. You're almost there.

The feeling had an odd, pleading note, but didn't seem threatening.

Stone did continue walking, but also pulled out his phone to check the direction. He had no idea if the faint, strange compulsion originated inside his own mind or from somewhere ahead of him, but either way, he had to know.

The compass needle spun a couple times, veering wildly back and forth, and then settled.

He *was* still going the right way. He hadn't deviated from the direction he'd been heading when he entered the forest, which pointed him at approximately a forty-five-degree angle from the crossroads' intersection.

That, more than anything, calmed his mind. Nothing was trying to lure him off his path. He was going exactly where he intended to go.

He was focused so hard on trying not to trip over anything that he almost didn't notice when the trees in front of him broke, forming a clearing. He almost blundered ahead and entered it, but stopped at the last moment, remaining hidden as he peered at what lay in front of him.

It wasn't just a clearing.

It was a cemetery.

Or at least, it *used* to be a cemetery. Quite obviously, nobody had done anything to maintain or care for this space in a very long time. Only a single squat structure and the tops of a few headstones extending above the tall undergrowth revealed the place's purpose.

The feeling was strong now, permeating the air around Stone. Whatever he was looking for, it was here. He knew it.

Despair.

Exhaustion.

Pleading.

It swirled around his mind, like an insistent child tugging hard at his coat, trying to get his attention. There were still no words, but there didn't need to be any words.

It definitely wanted—*needed*—help.

But with what?

Barely realizing he was doing it, he began to walk again, breaking free of the trees and entering the cemetery's cleared space. No one was here to see him now, so he raised a hand, summoning a light spell around it, and swept it back and forth for a better view.

The area wasn't large, perhaps fifty feet on its short side and twice that on the longer side. It had no apparent organization, with weathered stone grave markers placed at haphazard intervals, as if whoever needed to bury someone here had simply chosen a spot and dug their grave with no regard for those that had come before. A few of the markers were wood, moss-coated and splintering with age. Oddly, despite the place's obvious age and state of abandonment, no new trees had grown anywhere within the clearing's boundaries.

Stone crept further in, still shining his light around. The squat structure he'd noticed before wasn't big enough to be a mausoleum. Made of cracked, weathered stone thickly crusted with moss, it stuck up two feet above the ground, barely rising above the thick carpet of vegetation. It wasn't shaped like a grave, either, but was square, three feet on a side.

It was also the source of the odd emanations. Stone was sure of it. Shifting to magical sight confirmed it: a shaft of rhythmic, bright-blue energy bathed it from the west, and another of swirling orange from the east.

He'd found what he was looking for.

Still, he moved slowly as he approached it, switching off the Sight to allow a better view of the mundane world. He paused to crouch near a few of the stone grave markers, raising his light spell close to try reading the inscriptions on them. It proved impossible, though—the markers were far too weathered and moss-covered to be legible. The only bits he managed to make out were dates on two of the markers: one read *1817,* and another read *1830.* So, some of the "residents" buried here had been interred over two hundred years ago.

Had the—*Being? Entity? Force?*—responsible for the despairing emanations been here that long too?

Stone paused again before approaching the structure, checking his mental defenses. Even now, this close, he still didn't feel any threat. There was no sense of unease, of anything unsettling, of…evil. He could be wrong, of course—if it was powerful enough, it could fool him into believing anything.

But he didn't think that was true in this case.

He turned, shining the light around to ensure nothing was sneaking up on him, and then moved forward until he was standing next to the structure, looking down upon it.

It was made of some dark-colored stone, cracked and veined. A thick blanket of needles, leaves, and moss obscured most of it, making it impossible to read any potential inscription.

The feeling probing at his mind intensified once again, its wordless pleading growing more desperate. If Stone were to put it into words, he'd have said it reminded him of the pleas of a prisoner who sees hope for the first time in years, and who fears its would-be rescuer might simply turn his back on it and depart. That would be worse than no one ever coming at all.

He considered doing just that, though—but only for a few seconds. He knew better. Whatever was going on here, he needed to see it through. He needed to know what was happening before he could decide on his next steps.

He raised the hand that didn't have the light spell, summoning a powerful, localized wind over the structure's top. The sodden needles and leaves swirled and flew off, leaving only the thick coating of moss. After a second's consideration about how to deal with that, he dismissed the wind and cast a small, even more carefully controlled ball of crackling fire in its place. It was damp enough out here, especially after the recent rain, that he didn't need to worry about starting a conflagration even if he lost control of it—and besides, he wasn't *going* to lose control of it. This was apprentice-level stuff.

It took longer than he expected to burn the layer of damp moss off the structure's top, but twenty minutes later he'd cleared it. He stood back, swiping his hand across his forehead, and studied it. Even though the air out here was chilly, he felt suddenly warm, as if he'd exerted himself a lot more than the simple spells would have required.

At first, he thought he'd done all this work in vain, that the structure's top was free of any notation. The flat surface held no hint of a seam or opening—as far as he could tell, there was no way inside. The cracks and fissures riddling the old stone made it difficult to pick out the difference between the ravages of age and specific human intent. Stone leaned in closer, raising the light.

The despairing aura changed a little, adding...anticipation? Whatever was happening here, he was on the right track.

It was like one of those puzzles where you had to pick an identifiable shape out of a series of nonsense lines. When Stone finally spotted it on the top half of the space, a thrill—half dread, half excitement—rose at the back of his neck and crept down his back.

Was he seeing things, as if picking shapes out of clouds on a sunny day, or was that a crudely-drawn version of the same spinning-wheel logo he'd seen associated with the Weavers?

But no, it *was* there. The more he stared at it, the clearer it became. It wasn't large, only a couple inches on a side, but it was definitely there, carved into the stone.

So this was a second confirmation that the Weavers, at least, *were* somehow connected with this odd graveyard, and potentially the powerful feeling of despair creeping from it.

But were the Music Makers represented here, too? A symbol to go with the energy they were feeding it?

He brightened the light a bit more and let his gaze creep down the length of the stone, scanning the corresponding area in its lower half.

It took longer this time, because there were more cracks here. In fact, even after he thought he saw it—a simple treble-clef symbol—he couldn't be sure it was truly there. He stared at it for nearly five minutes, moving the light around to get better angles on it, but still the certainty eluded him. Was he making things up, forcing something ambiguous to fit his own narrative?

There was only one way to find out, and part of him—the rational, cautious, experienced mage—wasn't sure he wanted to do it.

He turned again, suddenly certain somebody, or some*thing,* was out there watching him. He shifted to magical sight, scanning the dark trees for any sign of a color other than green. But still, no matter how hard he squinted, nothing showed up.

Nothing but the two shafts of light, anyway. They were hard to miss.

No other auras, though.

He was alone out here—unless you counted whatever was still trying to get inside his head.

He realized he was wrong: there were *two* potential ways he could learn more about this situation. He didn't like either of them, but one was definitely less destructive.

Pacing the space around the structure, he weighed them. The first was that he could open his magical senses, let the feeling in, in the hope it might provide a better sense of what it wanted. He was blocking it now—he was sure of it. His mental shields were strong, and even though they couldn't attenuate all of the energy, he could tell he was stopping a good portion of it. Enough that he'd never get the full story.

The second option was to break through the structure to see what was inside. He was sure—fairly sure, unless something arcane was protecting it—that his magic would be sufficient to crack the stone, but that would mean destroying the structure.

And if it was designed to imprison something, that might not be a good idea.

Not until he knew more about it, anyway.

And that made the decision for him.

He stopped at the foot of the structure, forcing himself to think this through. Making a rash or ill-thought decision here could be deadly—or worse. Nobody knew he was out here. He didn't even know if the people of Rydell and Tuttleton were aware of this hidden graveyard any longer. It made sense that at least the Weavers and the Music Makers might be, since they were generating the energy that somehow kept whatever was inside this odd structure fed—but was it possible even *that* wasn't true? If they'd been keeping the weaving and the music going for long enough, it might be that even *they* no longer knew the purpose of it. That seemed farfetched, but Stone had seen stranger situations, and heard about others.

The despairing feeling seemed to be growing, but he still couldn't detect any sense of menace. More like desperation, like a small, suffering child whose hopes were fading.

It could be a trap...

But it might not be. You could put an end to this.

It wasn't like Stone to waver. He usually thought decisions through and then acted on them. This time, though, he still hesitated. Whatever was going on here, it was potentially big. If he made the wrong choice—

Pleading.

Sadness.

Exhaustion.

And over all that, a stronger feeling: the sense of something that desperately wanted to die, but wasn't being allowed to.

"Okay..." Stone murmured. "This might be the biggest mistake I ever made, but I trust you. Let's see what you've got to say."

He dropped to his knees on the damp ground, pressed his palms flat against the structure's surface, and dropped his mental defenses.

Instantly, images began to flood in, as if the being had been waiting for him.

A disembodied being—very strong, but very young.

No—very old by human standards, but young by its own people's.

Two figures. Shadowy, but blazing with potency.

A large room. Old-fashioned, wooden. The walls lined with books and bottles and odd objects, all swirling together to prevent clear identification.

An elaborate circle.

Chanting.

Confusion. Where am I? How did I get here? What's happening? Not words, but only impressions.

Struggling.

Confinement.

Terror.

Darkness.

Pain.

Probing.

No sense of time—the concept doesn't exist for this being.

More probing.

Weakening.

Dying?

The blazing figures reappear. Arguing. Disagreeing.

The being doesn't understand. Why are they confining it? Why won't they release it and let it return to its home?

Misery.

Hunger.

Then, power. Not enough to allow it to break free, but enough to sustain it. To feed it.

It isn't dying anymore.

But…no. How can this be? The two blazing figures are no longer in conflict. They're cooperating. And somehow…siphoning the being's power. Harnessing its essence.

Using it.

Draining it—but never enough. Never enough to kill it. The energy they feed it sustains it, keeps it alive.

It doesn't want to be alive anymore.

Then, darkness again.

Movement.

A sense of shifting, of going to another physical place, far from the room with the circle.

It tries to protest, to tell the blazing figures it only wants to go home. But they don't listen.

They don't care.

The being is nothing but a source of power for them.

They're arguing again. They can't stand each other—but they're bound, somehow, in their shared passion. The being still doesn't fully understand, but it's been around them long enough now that even its alien thought processes are beginning to grasp some of what's happening.

It isn't going home.

It will never see its home or any others like it again.

Then, more power. The same type as before—the type that fed it and sustained it, keeping it in a peaceful, somnolent state—but stronger. Steadier. Its shadowy captors have altered the delivery method, bathing the being with energy from two sources. Why is that? Do they make it more effective, or is it simply that the captors can no longer work together? It doesn't know.

It barely cares.

It's almost forgotten how powerful it is itself. How if it could access its power, it could destroy not only its captors, but a large section of the physical world around it. The captors know this. That is why they've done what they have. The two sources are perfectly balanced, designed to keep it cowed and safe, to keep it sleeping, to blunt its rage, to siphon its energy to provide what its captors need. It doesn't know what the energy is being used for—only that it is being used.

For a while, it tries to fight. It tries to hold back the power, to interfere with the conduit. It thinks that perhaps if it can manage to interrupt the flow, its captors will return to check on it in its dark prison, and it will have a chance to break free.

The final shock comes when it discovers it can no longer touch its captors. The being is quite sensitive to energy, and it has touched the captors' energies long enough to know when they no longer exist in the world.

Have they ceased to be? Have they achieved the death it so desperately wants for itself?

How, then, does the energy still flow? How do the twin conduits persist, holding it in a state of drifting half-consciousness?

It reaches out again, desperately, trying to understand.

And it finds not two familiar bits of energy, but many unfamiliar ones.

Ones like the captors, but…not like them. Weak. Simple.

And, most shocking of all—they appear to have no knowledge of the existence of the being the captors have enslaved so long ago. Whatever the captors have set into motion still persists, but these beings know nothing about it. They go through the motions by rote, by tradition, as their fathers and their fathers' fathers have done, having no idea why they do it. And as the years go on, they add new components. Someone decides that periodically they must ritualistically destroy one of their own people, in the belief that it's necessary to maintain the bounty provided by the siphoned energy. But they don't do it out of malice or cruelty.

They are reluctant, in fact. They don't want to do it. But by now, after still more time has passed and the originator of the idea is long dead, they've convinced themselves it is necessary. They believe with all their hearts that if they do not continue the rituals, they will suffer some undefined wrath.

But the being has no wrath. Only despair. Only sadness. It doesn't hate these people, as it hated the original captors. How could it? They are no more at fault here than it is.

Perhaps it could reach them, they could help!

No matter how hard it tries, though, it doesn't succeed. The conduits hold it in a constant stasis of drifting half-sleep, draining its power, keeping it weak. It can't focus enough to reach out.

To feel, yes, but not to communicate.

All it wants to do now is die. It doesn't even care about breaking free any longer. They have drained too much of it. It's spent. It's done. Its fondest wish is to merely fade away and cease to be. Perhaps if it does that, the shreds of its consciousness will drift back to where it came from, and it will get to experience its home one final time before it passes out of existence.

It has given up on even that hope, after all the years.

Nothing will change.

No one will come.

But now, that chance has arrived. Against all possible odds, when it had given up hope that it ever would. This new creature is different. It is more like the original blazing captors, brimming with potency—but yet it isn't. It seeks knowledge, yes—but not power. No—that isn't correct. It does *seek power, but not by exploiting other beings.*

If it has power but doesn't seek harm, perhaps it *can help.*

If the being can manage to communicate with this new creature, it might be possible.

It must try harder than it has ever tried.

This might be its last chance.

Pleading.

Desperation.

Last chance.

Let me die.

Help me.

Help me.

HELP ME!

Stone screamed.

He threw himself backward, clamping his hands to his head as the thoughts rushed in stronger, pounding his brain in waves. His skull felt as if something was burning it from the inside, poking spikes through his eyes, his ears, his mouth, up through his chin.

He screamed again, or he thought he did, leaping to his feet, staggering backward. His only thought was that he had to get away from that thing.

And then he was falling backward. The white-hot, spiking pain crested, overwhelming any other thought, rational or otherwise.

He didn't feel himself hit the ground.

CHAPTER EIGHTEEN

SOMETHING WAS PATTING HIS CHEEK, gently but firmly.

An animal? Some kind of oversized insect?

He grunted, raising his hand to swat the troublesome thing away.

"You finally awake?"

He snapped his eyes open.

It was still dark. The clouds still shifted in the patches between the trees, and the half-moon still hung high above.

Someone was looming over him.

He jerked back, trying to scrabble away, but a firm hand pushed him down.

"Lie still. I don't know what the hell happened to you, but it didn't look like much fun."

Stone blinked. It was a woman's voice, low and no-nonsense. Between the dimness and his still-pounding head, he couldn't get a good look at her. "Who are you?" he rasped. "Let me up."

"Just hang on." She pressed something into his hand. "Have a little of that. It might help. Couldn't hurt. Probably."

What the hell was she on about? He lifted his hand to see what she'd given him.

It was a flask. He shook his head, amused, which was probably a mistake. "Wait. What are you doing here? How did you find this place? Were you following me?"

"Take a drink and we'll talk. Do you feel up to standing? We can go back to my car, or yours, which is probably more comfortable than soaking our asses on this damp ground."

"Little late for that, I suspect." Stone didn't know how long he'd been unconscious, but it couldn't have been long. His jeans were soaked through, but the water hadn't seeped through his overcoat yet. He regarded the flask again, and finally decided the prospect of a drink outweighed distrusting whoever this strange woman was. He flipped the top and downed a healthy swallow.

It was whiskey, and it was good stuff. He closed his eyes, relishing the sharp bite as the liquid ran down his throat. "Thanks. That hit the spot."

She took the flask back, but didn't drink herself. "Thought it might. You okay to stand? I checked you over a little, and didn't find anything too bad. Surprisingly."

He glared at her. "You *checked me over*?"

She glared right back. "Hey, when you screamed and keeled over like that, I thought you had a heart attack or something. Sue me." She stood and offered him a hand.

He considered ignoring it, but his head *was* still pounding. He wasn't a hundred percent certain he could stand under his own power. Reluctantly, he grasped her hand.

She was strong—stronger than he expected. After she hauled him up, she kept hold long enough to ensure he wasn't going to fall right back over, then regarded him. "Can you walk?"

"Of course I can walk." Now, upright and with the headache beginning to recede, he got a better look at her. She was around five-eight, with the same kind of sturdy, athletic build Amber Thayer had. She had dark skin, a steady, intelligent gaze, and hair done in short dreadlocks. He didn't recall seeing her in Rydell—but then he remembered the figure he'd briefly spotted at the Tuttleton central square earlier that night. "I'm not going anywhere until you tell me who you are. You were in Tuttleton tonight, weren't you? At the musical performance?"

She gave him an arch smile. "I think the more important question here, *Dr. Stone,* is what *you're* doing in an old graveyard in the middle of nowhere Oregon at midnight."

His head must still have been hurting more than he thought, because it took him a full two seconds to register what she'd just said. "You know who I am."

"Yeah. And I have to say I'm damned surprised to see you here."

"Why is that?"

"You said you saw me in Tuttleton. I didn't see *you.* I'm guessing you were using some kind of disguise, right?"

Stone didn't answer, and refused to move forward. "Who the hell *are* you?"

"My name's Renata Huxley. You can call me Ren."

"Okay. You realize that means nothing to me, right?" He looked her over again. She wore jeans, hiking boots, a buttoned shirt, and a dark-colored down jacket. He was certain he'd never seen her before.

"Again, not surprised. We do a pretty good job of keeping ourselves under the radar. Safer that way."

"We?" He looked around, expecting to see more people converging on them. "Who's 'we'?"

This time, it was her turn not to answer. "Where have you been, Dr. Stone? You've dropped out of sight for over three years. I'm having a hard time believing you settled down at your house in England to spend more time with your research and your cat."

A little knot of tension began forming at the base of his skull. It joined the fading remains of the headache, which brought him back to what he'd just experienced at the strange structure. "Listen," he said, pulling his notebook from his inner pocket. "I need to write some things down before I forget them. Very important. If you want to talk to me—and I *definitely* want to get some answers from *you*—you're going to have to wait for me to finish."

She looked as if she might protest, then nodded once. "My car's not far from here, if you want someplace to sit down."

"It's all right. I'll do it here." He looked around until he spotted a sturdy-looking headstone, then leaned against it and opened the notebook.

"I'd ask you if you need a light—but I'm guessing you can make your own."

He didn't miss the sly, amused tone in her voice, and jerked his chin up. "You know about me, don't you, Ms. Huxley?"

"Agent Huxley, actually. And yeah. I know quite a bit about you, Dr. Stone."

Another chill temporarily drove off his desire to get his notes down. "Are you here because of me? Did you follow me to this area?" How could she—or her agency, whatever it was—possibly have known? It was inconceivable that Aldwyn would have told them.

"Nothing to do with you. That's why I'm so surprised to see you here. And a little worried, to be honest."

"Worried?"

She nodded grimly. "Yeah. Because my partner's missing. And because if you're here, it means something pretty big is probably going on in this area."

He wanted to ponder further on that, but the notebook called. The impressions he got from communing with the strange being didn't seem to be fading, but there was no way he'd take chances. He didn't want to have to contact it again. He wasn't sure his head—or his sanity—could survive the experience.

He scribbled fast as the impressions tumbled over each other, and his mind moved in the background trying to process what he'd experienced. It was farfetched and fascinating: an entity that was decades, probably centuries old, its very life energy siphoned and harnessed by the residents of two small towns to keep them prosperous. A being fed by magical energy generated by constant activity: music from Tuttleton, weaving tapestries on the magical looms from Rydell.

Two powerful beings—almost certainly mages—who'd been bitter rivals but forced to work together to take advantage of the power they'd discovered. Where had they come from originally? Where had the wooden room with the books and the circle been? Why had they moved the entity here? He doubted he'd ever know the answer to those questions.

It was another, more immediate one that disturbed him more, though. The being had given him a nebulous image of something of immense power deep beneath the ground here. Perhaps *that* was why the two mages had chosen this place. And worse, the entity had implied something else: that the two sources of energy holding it in its stasis, the blue from Tuttleton and the orange from Rydell, maintained a delicate balance, holding back a power that could destroy the entire area if it were disrupted.

Did that mean he *couldn't* disrupt it? That if he stole the tapestry as Aldwyn had bidden, it would break the flow of energy and bring on the destruction? Kill all the people in the area? Possibly even make the area uninhabitable?

Had Aldwyn *known* this?

That didn't make sense, though. Such a thing would destroy Stone, too. If Aldwyn wanted to destroy his scion, there would have been far easier ways to do it. He'd *had* him for three years, helpless, held in his own kind of stasis, with obvious access to him. If he wanted to blow up the area to unearth some massively powerful *something,* and all it took was interrupting the flow of power, he could have sent in some expendable human agents.

So there had to be more going on here than appeared at the surface. Some hidden motive of Aldwyn's.

Stone growled, slamming the notebook shut. Whatever it was, was eluding him at the moment. His head hurt, his thoughts were sluggish, and he couldn't afford that right now. Not with this woman here—this agent of gods-knew-what organization—who knew far more about him than he was comfortable with.

He still had a few days left. There was no way Agent Huxley had any idea of what he'd learned from the entity. He could give it some more thought later, when he was alone.

Forcing himself to remain nonchalant, he put his notebook back in his pocket. "So," he said. "If you're not following me, Agent Huxley, would you care to tell me what led you here?"

"Here as in this area, or here as in this graveyard?"

"Both, actually. What were you doing in Tuttleton tonight, slinking around through the crowd at the musical performance?"

"I told you. I was looking for my partner. He disappeared."

"When?"

"Two days ago."

"And you expected to find him here?" He looked around. "How did you even *find* this place? It's fairly remote."

"How did *you* find it?"

"If you know anything about me, Agent, I'm sure you can work that out on your own."

She narrowed her eyes. "You used magic, obviously. But why? What's here that *you* were looking for? And you might as well call me Ren."

"It's…a long story. I can't tell you all of it, so don't ask."

"How about you tell me *some* of it."

He considered. "What agency are you part of, anyway? What's your purpose?"

"Ah, so that's the way we're going to play it, are we? Trading questions and avoiding answers?"

"It's up to you. You haven't told me much of anything yet, have you?"

She sighed in obvious frustration. "Your file says you can be a real pain in the ass, Stone. I see they got that part right."

"My file." He gave a satisfied nod. "I suspected somebody might have one on me. Is it nice and thick?"

"You don't know the half of it. Where *have* you been for the past three years?"

"On holiday."

"Yeah, right."

"Am I wanted for anything, Agent? Are you planning to put the cuffs on me and bring me in? Because unless there's a lot more to you than meets the eye—or you've got a lot of help—I promise that won't be as easy as you might hope."

She waved him off. "You're not wanted, even though you probably should be. There've been some fairly sketchy activities associated with your history."

"So, why not, then?" He looked around again, shifting to magical sight to ensure nobody was approaching them. The blue and orange energy was still there, and he could still feel the overwhelming sense of melancholy and desperation. It seemed less intense now, though. Perhaps sharing its story with him had rekindled the being's hope that he might help.

I'll help you, he thought, wondering if it could hear him. *But you've got to give me some time. I don't want to botch this.*

"Why not? Because despite your often unorthodox way of doing things, our organization is pretty convinced we're all on the same side."

"And which side is that?"

Now she looked frustrated. "We're all trying to take down the bad guys. Or at least I hope that's what you're doing."

He shrugged. "Sometimes. Usually, I'm just trying to satisfy my outsized curiosity."

"Yeah, we know that about you too. You make cats look bad by comparison." She looked at her feet. "Anyway, right now, my number-one concern is finding Rick."

Stone studied her briefly with magical sight. The same flashes of red he'd spotted earlier that evening were still there, but now he had a context for them. She was concerned about her partner. He didn't think she was lying. "Tell me about him. You said he disappeared two days ago. Were the two of you here together, investigating something?"

"Yeah. We got a tip that something weird was going on in this area."

"That's not very specific."

She gave him a look. "You, of all people, should know that in cases like this, we don't usually *get* anything specific."

He had to allow that. "Okay, fair enough. So you both showed up in Tuttleton and started poking around. Did you go to Rydell?"

"Why would we go to Rydell? Tuttleton was where it was supposed to be happening."

"Whatever *it* is. Okay. So did you find anything?"

Her gaze sharpened. "Are you saying something's going on in Rydell, too?"

"Did you find anything?"

"No. Not a damn thing. This place is like fucking Mayberry. Everybody's happy, the whole town seems to be into playing music, the streets are clean, no crime, no drugs…"

"And you didn't think *that* was odd?"

"Of course we did. But that didn't mean we knew why."

"Okay. So did you separate? Is that how he disappeared?"

"We had to stay in two different places. Tuttleton doesn't have any hotels, or B-and-Bs. We found a couple locals close to each other to rent rooms from."

A sudden thought occurred to Stone. "Agent Huxley—Ren—do you have a way to communicate with the outside world? Some special government cellular frequency or something?"

Again, her eyes narrowed. "They do have phones here, Dr. Stone. Cellular doesn't work, but they have land lines."

"Yes. They do. Did you call to report your partner missing?"

A brief look of confusion crossed her face. "Well…no. Not yet. I thought I could find him on my own."

"Isn't it protocol when something goes wrong to call in backup?"

The confusion turned to a glare. "Don't tell me how to do my job, Dr. Stone."

Something was odd here, but he couldn't put his finger on it. He let it go for now, but held it in the back of his mind for later examination. "Okay. So how did he disappear?"

"Like I told you we were staying at two different places. Neither of us liked it, but we didn't have a choice. And besides, we thought something supernaturally weird was going on around here, not necessarily something dangerous. And we certainly didn't think so many people might be involved." She began pacing around in a small area in front of Stone. "We stayed at one of the bars going over our notes until they closed, then I dropped Rick at his place and drove on to mine. When I went to pick him up the next morning, he wasn't there."

"He wasn't there?"

"Yeah. The people he was living with said he'd gone out for an early-morning walk in the woods. His stuff was still there, but he hadn't left a note for me or anything."

"And this was odd."

She rolled her eyes. "*Hell* yeah. Rick isn't much of an outdoorsman, and he's a straight arrow on the job. There's no way he'd wander off on his own."

"I see." He rubbed his chin, thinking. "Was he supernaturally talented?"

"No."

"Are you?"

"No. What are you getting at, Dr. Stone?"

He shrugged. "Just seems a bit odd to me that an agency that investigates the supernatural would send a couple of mundanes on a job like this."

"We're not just garden-variety *mundanes*. We're well trained. We've got…supernaturals in our organization too, and they provide us with a lot of information."

Stone wondered why the agency hadn't sent them, but didn't say it. Perhaps they didn't have many, and they were elsewhere engaged. That wasn't the issue, though. "Okay, so your partner just wandered off without taking any of his gear with him, and hasn't turned up since?"

"Yeah."

"I assume you thoroughly questioned the people he was staying with."

"Of course I did. I also checked Rick's room. Didn't find anything suspicious. Everything I saw points to exactly what they claim happened."

"What led you out here, then?" He gestured, encompassing the graveyard.

"I looked at the maps of the area, and noticed the abandoned campground north of here. I was going to investigate it when I saw a Jeep parked by the side of the road. I assume that's yours?"

"Yes."

"Figured I'd check it out. Surprised the hell out of me when I got close and heard you screaming. And I was even *more* surprised when I ran over to help and saw who you were. Believe me, out of all the people in the world I thought I might find here, you weren't even on the long list." Her gaze hardened. "What *are* you doing here, Dr. Stone?"

"Same as you. Investigating a tip about something odd."

She indicated the structure he'd been examining. "And it led you to that?"

"It led me to a lot of things. This is just the most recent." The cold water soaking his jeans legs was beginning to get annoying. "Excuse me a moment," he said, and summoned a warm wind to dry his clothes.

"Nice trick."

"Yes, I've got quite a number of them. Which I'm sure you know if you've read my file." He considered. "Are you going to get in my way, Agent Huxley?"

"That depends. Are you going to get in *mine*?"

"I've got some things I need to do. I haven't sorted them all out yet, but I've got to do them."

"What things?"

"I can't tell you that. But I'm starting to wonder if your missing partner and what I'm involved in might not be related."

"What makes you think that? You don't know anything about him, do you?" Her voice grew suspicious.

"Not a bloody thing. I was as surprised to see you—or *anyone* else who was looking for odd goings-on around here—as you were to see me. But perhaps we can help each other."

"How?" She was looking suspicious again, but also interested.

Stone didn't want to take the time, but on the other hand, having someone—even a mundane with supernatural training who didn't freak out at the first sight of something unusual—on his side might be useful. Especially if, as he was beginning to suspect based on the impressions he'd gotten from the being, he was going to have to shut down both energy sources simultaneously to free the being and prevent catastrophe. "I could help you look for your partner, to start with."

She almost waved him off, then looked thoughtful again. "You're talking about a tracking ritual."

"Ah. You *do* know your stuff. Or at least some of it. Mage 101, anyway. But yes, I could do a ritual and help you find him, assuming he's still in the area."

The suspicion was back. "And what do you want in return? There's no way I can turn a blind eye if you want to do anything illegal."

"Honestly, I doubt you could stop me. But that's beside the point, since that isn't my intent." It was a lie, of course—stealing the tapestry was by definition illegal. But she didn't have to know that, and it wasn't as if he planned to kill anyone. "No, I might need your help with something else, though. There may be something I've got to do that requires two simultaneous actions some distance apart. I've got a lot of clever tricks up my sleeve, but being in two places at once regrettably isn't one of them."

Her eyes narrowed. "What are you talking about?"

"Let's get to that when the time comes. Are you willing to help me, as long as it's not anything illegal?"

She considered, turning away from him for a few seconds. "Yeah," she finally said with reluctance. "At least I'll consider it. That's the best I can do until I have more information." She looked around. "So, when can we do this ritual?"

"Now, if you like." He glanced up at the sky. It appeared relatively clear, which meant they were unlikely to get a deluge in the next half-hour or so.

"Where? Here?"

"Why not? I don't want to do it in Tuttleton—it would arouse too much suspicion." Privately, he wondered if Huxley's partner might have found his way to Rydell, but both towns were easily within his range from here.

"You just carry ritual materials around when you travel?"

"I do when I'm investigating. All I'll need is a tether object—have you got one?"

"Yeah. Rick left a couple of things in the car. You want me to go back and get them?"

"I'll go with you."

"Don't trust me?"

"It's not that," Stone said grimly. "I don't want to let you out of my sight. Something very strange is definitely going on around here, and I don't want you ending up like your partner."

Her hard gaze lingered on him, but finally she nodded. "Okay. I don't really want to let *you* out of my sight, either."

They walked in silence for a while. Finally, she asked, "What was happening back there? What made you scream and pass out? Was it something about that weird little monument you were in front of?"

"No," he lied. "I was using that as a dry place to kneel. It was something about the cemetery as a whole."

"So you think something bad is there?"

"Not sure yet. *Something* is there, but I'm not sure it's malevolent, or merely powerful."

"What do you plan to do about it? Do you think it's behind the oddness Rick and I were investigating?"

He wondered how much he should tell her. The last thing he wanted was a bunch of mundanes, or even one mundane, blundering around causing trouble. But on the other hand, if she was smart, telling her what she was up against might give her more caution.

"I'm...not sure yet. I think it might be. But what I *do* know is that whatever it is, it's got to be handled carefully. Please believe me, Agent Huxley, when I tell you that if you act rashly, without knowing what you're doing, you could cause something catastrophic."

"Your file says you've got a flair for the dramatic, too," she said dryly.

"I won't deny it, but I hope it also says I know my stuff. I wouldn't say that if I didn't mean it."

"Let's get Rick back first. Then we'll talk about the rest."

They reached the edge of the forest. Stone's Jeep was still there, and now a dark four-door sedan was parked behind it. Stone waited while Huxley opened the trunk and returned with a denim jacket.

"I don't have anything great," she told him, handing it over. "I left his wallet and other things in his room. We're here undercover as a couple of friends visiting the area thinking about moving here, so there's nothing that identifies him as an agent. He likes this jacket, though."

Stone pulled his leather bag from the Jeep, gathering a few ritual materials and shoving them in his pockets. He wouldn't need many for this. He stowed the bag headed up the road to the north. "We don't need to go back to the cemetery. There isn't anywhere to make the circle there anyway. I'll go up this little spur road a bit. I doubt anyone will come by to see us."

She watched with interest while he built the circle, using mostly small rocks and twigs since chalk wouldn't work on the wet road. "You aren't going to tell me where you've been for the last three years, are you? We've usually got you under observation, at least from a distance. But after you attended your caretaker's wedding, you might as well have disappeared off the face of the earth. Your son did a good job pretending you still existed, but that kind of thing doesn't fool us."

Stone wasn't sure he was happy about being "under observation." He grunted a noncommittal reply and continued with his circle.

"I guess it's none of my business. Believe it or not, Dr. Stone, we're not spying on you."

"Bloody well *sounds* like you are."

"We like to know where you are. You and others like you."

He wondered who those "others" were, but didn't ask. "There. That's the circle. Simple, but we shouldn't need much. Toss me the jacket—and have you got a photo of your partner? I always like to be able to visualize the person I'm looking for."

"Yeah. Hang on." She pulled her phone from her pocket, swiped through a few screens, and held it out.

Stone stepped out of the circle for a closer look. The photo showed Huxley and a white man standing next to each other in what looked like a park. The man was a few years younger, a few inches taller, and athletically built, with short brown hair and a cheeky smile. He wore a T-shirt, jeans, and a San Francisco Giants baseball cap.

"That was taken a year or so ago," Huxley said.

Stone was about to turn away when something poked at his brain. Something about the photo that caught his attention—something he'd seen before, recently. But what was it?

When it came to him, a thrill of dread accompanied it. "Agent…that cap he's wearing. Does he wear it often?"

"Oh, yeah, all the time. He's a huge Giants fan. I'm a football fan, but—"

"Did he wear it on your assignment up here?"

Her eyes narrowed. "Yeah. It fit with his cover persona. Why?"

He didn't answer right away; in fact, he barely saw her. He was watching a scene in his mind's eye: looking down into Chase Cassidy's desk drawer, where an identical hat lay among the papers and office supplies.

He hadn't thought anything of it at the time, but now another memory came back: the framed baseball cards on the wall.

Seattle Mariners cards.

A chill settled deeper into the back of his neck.

"Stone? What's going on? Do you see something?"

He snapped back to the present. "Er. Maybe. Let me do the ritual."

She grabbed his arm. "If you know something—"

"Let me do this, Agent Huxley. Let go of my arm."

She looked as if she might argue, but finally released him. "Okay. Fine. What do you want me to do?"

"Just keep an eye out for anyone approaching. This shouldn't take long."

I hope I'm wrong, or it won't take long at all.

He wasn't wrong. It took barely five minutes to get his answer. He wondered how he was going to tell her.

"Stone?"

There was an odd edge in her voice. Did she already suspect? He said nothing, but merely turned back to face her.

"What is it?"

He bowed his head. "I'm sorry."

"You're sorry?" Her voice rose to a sharp crack. "Sorry about what?" Then she got a better look at him, and her eyes widened. "Oh...God. Are you saying he's—"

"Dead," he said softly. "Yes. I truly am sorry. I wish I could give you better news."

"Rick's...dead?" She looked as if she couldn't believe it, and refused to let it in. Only for a moment, though. Then she let out a long, slow exhalation and her expression firmed—the agent, now, instead of the grieving colleague. "Are you sure?" All the sharpness was gone now, replaced by dull resignation.

"I'm sure. The answer was definitive."

She swallowed. "So...what's it mean?"

"I don't know. If you know anything about tracking rituals, they don't reveal location, or who was responsible. Only that the energy no longer exists, and he's probably still somewhere nearby. The answer came back too fast for anything else."

"Nearby?" She looked around. "You mean in this area, or literally close to where we are now?"

"I don't know. I'm good at this, but even for me, the information I get isn't that precise."

She nodded without looking at him. "Yeah. Yeah. I know that." She clenched her fists. "I want to tear this damn town apart, make these people tell me what they know. But I can't do that. I still have a job to do."

"Agent…"

"Ren."

"Ren." He spoke carefully. "You…you're going to have to call in others now, right?"

"I don't know." She sighed and shook her head. "There *aren't* that many others. Our agency is small and specialized, and we don't have that many field agents. The ones we *do* have are all on assignment. Even if I called, it would take them days to wrap up what they're doing and get here."

It almost sounded like an excuse. Stone remembered what she'd said before, about not calling to consult with anyone else on the landline, and a vague suspicion began to form in the back of his mind. For now, though, he merely nodded. "All right. I'll help you—I said I would, and I will. I've got some thoughts on who might know about this."

Her chin snapped up. "You do? Who?"

"Someone in Tuttleton. Someone I was investigating. But I can't think of *why* he might have—" He froze as another bit of the strange impressions he got from the being popped into his mind.

They ritualistically destroy their own people, in the belief that it's necessary to maintain the bounty provided by the siphoned energy.

Oh, bloody hell…

"What? You know something, don't you?"

"I'm…not sure. But I think I need to go back to that graveyard."

"Why? Do you think Rick's there?"

"I don't know. But I might have a way to find out more." Without waiting for an answer, he used magic to gather the spent ritual materials, then jogged back toward his car.

"Stone, wait!" She caught up with him. "What are you hiding from me? If you know where Rick is—"

He stowed the materials in his bag and slammed the door. "I don't. That's the truth. Please—just let me do this. I don't want to, so don't make it harder."

"You don't want to do what?" She continued following him as he plunged into the forest, back toward the cemetery.

He didn't answer. This time he held the light spell high, since he didn't need to hide it from anyone. He broke through the tree line and hurried back to the squat structure, and only then did he pause.

Huxley caught up. "There *is* something about this thing, isn't there?"

"Yes."

"What? Is there something in there?"

"I don't know, and it would be very dangerous to find out without more study. But there *is* something in this graveyard. A powerful entity. I didn't tell you the truth before. When you discovered me, I was…communicating with it."

"What the *hell?*" She glared down at the structure, curious in spite of her grief. "You were *talking* to some supernatural being?"

"Not talking, per se. There weren't any words. But communicating. I think I've got to do it again, and I don't want to."

"Why not?"

"You saw what it did to me before. I honestly don't think there's anything malevolent about it. I think it's in distress. But it doesn't know its own strength."

"So you're afraid if you try talking to it again, it might fry your brain."

"The thought had crossed my mind, yes." He took a deep breath. "But it doesn't matter—I've got to do it. Not just to try finding your partner, but because I didn't get everything I needed from it before."

"What else do you need?"

He shook his head. "Agent Huxley, you've got to promise you won't interfere when I do this. If you distract me, it could make things even more dangerous than they already are."

She glared at him, but finally nodded. "Yeah, okay. I don't like it, but I know what kind of power you're slinging. I'll stay out of your way."

"If you want to do something to help, keep watch and make sure no one comes around here."

"Do you expect them to?" She looked around in suspicion, as if anticipating a whole platoon of enemies would come crashing through the trees.

"No. But I don't have all the answers yet. Things are starting to come together, but they're not there yet. If I'm right, this is a lot bigger than I suspected, and potentially a lot more dangerous. So look sharp. I'm trusting you."

"You *can* trust me," she said, pulling a pistol from inside her jacket. "You do what you need to do. Just find out what happened to Rick."

Stone studied the structure again, switching to magical sight. The energy was still there; whatever they'd been doing hadn't disturbed it. Now, though, there was a new feeling to go with the despair and exhaustion.

Grief.

That's odd...

But was it? Was the creature picking up on Renata Huxley's grief over her lost partner? Was it trying to tell him it didn't have anything to do with it?

Stone hoped so. He took a few centering breaths, dropped to his knees at the structure's foot, and reached out again.

The same feelings flooded through him, but this time he was ready for them. Instead of merely letting them come, though, he made an effort to direct his own thoughts, to form questions without words. He pictured Rick and sent a nebulous question along with the thought.

At first, he didn't think he was going to get anything. The creature's mental processes were so alien, so unlike anything he'd ever experienced before, that he wasn't sure it could even comprehend what he was sending. His head began to throb again, but not as badly as before.

Then, gradually, the impressions began to solidify. There was a strange urgency to them now, as if the creature was desperate to tell him something. He did his best to open his mind, to be receptive to what it was trying to communicate.

Despondency.

Exhaustion.

Pleading.

But then: *confusion.*

Beings. Here.

Here before.

Digging.

See me! I'm here!

Please! Help!

But no help came. The beings departed.

They returned.

They departed.

There was no clear sense of time, but Stone got the impression this occurred many times over a long period. Years. Decades.

The sacrifices?

And then, all at once, he had the answer—the thing the being was trying to tell him. Shocked, he slumped forward, gripping the edge of the structure.

But it wasn't done yet.

Fear.

Image of the two swirling flows of energy.

Image of one disappearing.

Rage.

Uncontrollable power.

Massive destruction.

Regret.

Sorrow.

Pleading.

Image of both energy flows.

Rage recedes.

Stone thought he got it now, and tried to send a message: *if we stop only one flow, you're afraid you'll lose control of yourself? You'll...blow up? Take out the whole area?*

Strong sense of affirmative, laced with even stronger regret.

It doesn't want to do that. It's afraid.

Image of both energy flows, then none.

Peace.

Fading.

Nothingness.

Stone's heart beat faster. *I was right, wasn't I? We need to shut down both sides simultaneously to avoid destruction. If we do that, you'll just...fade away? Cease to be? And that's what you want?*

Affirmative.

Peace.

Hope.

Approval.

Pleading.

He let his breath out in a *whoosh. That's it, then. That's what we've got to do.*

He was preparing to disengage when another fleeting thought struck him—one he was sure hadn't originated in his own mind.

Power.

Enormous power, deep under the ground. Buried. Old. So old.

Older than you? Stone sent.

Affirmative.

What is it? Why is it there?

Exhaustion.

Regret.

Pleading.

Stone's head pounded harder as he felt the leading edge of what had occurred last time: a growing frustration, almost like a fretful child who needed a nap. It was getting stronger, swelling with power. If he stayed in contact, he might get more—but he might also get hit harder.

Reluctantly, he broke the communication, staggering back. Before it severed, he felt the creature's approval again.

It doesn't want to hurt me.

Strong hands gripped his shoulders, keeping him from falling over. "Stone?"

Panting, he got his feet back under him and swiped his hair off his forehead. He was sweating. "Give me...a moment."

"Are you okay? You're not gonna pass out again, are you?"

"No. No..." He stumbled over to one of the headstones and leaned on it. "I'll be all right in a moment."

She offered him the flask again, and he gratefully took another swallow.

"Did you find what happened to Rick?"

He'd almost forgotten about that, amid the enormity of what else he'd learned. He bowed his head. "I think so."

"Where is he?" Her eyes were wide, her expression intense as she crouched to focus on him.

"Here."

"Here? In this cemetery? What the hell?"

"Just...a moment." He pushed off the headstone, allowed a moment to get his bearings, then summoned the images the creature had sent him, of where the humans had been on the far side of the space. He began walking slowly, half-watching the view in front of him and half the images in his mind's eye. When he arrived at the cemetery's edge, a few feet from the tree line on the other side, he stopped.

Huxley followed him, clearly confused. "Are you sure you didn't get your brain scrambled again, Stone?"

In answer, he bent and used magic to clear pine needles and dirt from the ground in front of him. It was easier than it should have been, because the damp dirt under the carpet of needles was loose and fresh.

Behind him, Huxley gasped.

A heavy, black body bag lay in a shallow grave in front of them, crusted with mud.

"How…did you know that?" she whispered. She raised her gun, pointing it at him, but there was no fire behind the gesture. "How…"

Stone didn't react to the gun. He knew she wasn't going to shoot him. "The being told me. It didn't do this. It showed me an image of other beings—humans—bringing him out here to bury him in the night. And I don't think he's the only one. Only the most recent."

She only seemed to be half-listening. She knelt next to the grave, heedless of the muddy ground. Extending a shaking hand, she took hold of the bag's zipper and slowly pulled it down. When she revealed the body's face, her shoulders slumped and her breath caught.

"Oh, God…Rick…"

Stone stood grim guard behind her. "I'm so sorry, Ren."

She swallowed hard, but seemed to steel herself. When she spoke again, her voice was cold and steady. "Who did this?"

"We've…got to talk."

"The only think we've got to talk about is who *did* this, so I can haul their ass in." Her expression was fierce, the kind of glare that would make most normal people wet themselves.

Stone stood strong because he had to. "Agent Huxley, please. There's a lot going on here that you don't know about. I know more now, and I'll tell you—but you've got to listen to me. As much as I hate to say it, there's a lot more at stake here than the loss of your partner, horrific as that is. If we don't play this right, this whole area and everyone in it could be in danger."

He hoped she was dedicated enough to her job to allow her to put aside her personal feelings for the moment; if she wasn't, he wasn't sure what he'd have to do next. He watched her silently, waiting for her to reach her conclusion.

She didn't want to—that much was obvious. Stone understood all too well what she was struggling with, how strong the temptation was to simply give in to her rage and grief and never mind the consequences. He'd experienced it himself, more than once.

But thankfully, she *was* the professional she appeared to be. After a long time she rose, squared her shoulders, and took several deep breaths, then fixed a hard stare on Stone. "Talk to me."

"Yes. We...should go, though. I'm sorry, but for now we need to cover him back up, so no one will know we were here. But first, I need to get a look at him."

"What are you talking about, cover him up? You want to just...*leave* him here?"

"I don't want to, but for now, yes. It's necessary." He indicated the area around the body. "As I said, I'm certain he's not the only one. When you bring your people out here, after we've dealt with the main problem, I expect they'll find a lot more, buried in unmarked graves among the headstones."

Again, she paused, but finally nodded. "I don't like it. I don't like it a damned bit. But I'm starting to suspect I'm in over my head here."

"You would be—if you were alone. But you're not. We'll get this sorted out, I promise, and then you can take Rick home."

She held his gaze a moment longer. "You said you needed to look at him. Why?"

He was already bending to unzip the body bag further. "I need to check something. Give me a moment, and I'll tell you."

But he didn't need to tell her. As soon as he had the zipper down to reveal the upper half of Rick's body, it was obvious.

The knife cuts on the torso were precise and careful, forming several symbols on his pale chest.

"That's a ritual killing," Huxley said in a dull tone. "That's what you were looking for, wasn't it?"

"Yes." He wanted to get a look at the whole body, including any contents of the pockets, and examine it with magical sight, but it wasn't necessary. He had the information he needed. He zipped the bag closed and used magic to cover it back up with the muddy dirt and needles until it appeared as undisturbed as it had before. Huxley stood back and watched with her hands at her sides and her head bowed.

"What...*are* these people?" she asked. "Why would they do this to him? Why *him?* Because he didn't live here? Do they kill every newcomer who shows up?"

"I don't think so." He indicated for her to follow him. "Let's go back to the cars. We need to go someplace where we can talk without being seen."

CHAPTER NINETEEN

THEY DROVE NORTH, to the abandoned campground. After Stone checked the area with magical sight to make sure no one was around, he invited Ren into the Jeep and told her what he'd found in Rydell and Tuttleton. The only parts he left out were his arrangement with Aldwyn, including the bit about framing Chase Cassidy, and his suspicion about Cassidy's involvement in Rick's death.

She listened with growing shock. At one point, she pulled out her flask and had a long swallow. She offered it to Stone, but this time he declined.

"Damn," she said when he finished. "You know, if it was anybody but you telling me this story, I'd have them packed off to a room with soft walls." She stared out the window, obviously not seeing anything in the real world. "So this is all just... These people have been playing music and weaving tapestries for God knows how long without ever stopping, just to keep this...thing, whatever it is, fed?"

"Fed, appeased...I'm not honestly sure exactly what it is. But I doubt they even know *why* they're doing it anymore. Evidence suggests this has been going on for decades—maybe even longer than that. By this point, they've lost the meaning, and just continue on because they've *always* continued on."

She shook her head. "That's…hard to believe. But then again, I've seen some pretty weird shit in my career. So there's no actual magic involved, except for these…energy streams?"

"The looms are magical. The tapestries aren't, as far as I can tell. I think the looms' purpose is to focus the intent of the weavers and form it into energy. I didn't get a look in the Music Makers' loft at the back of the theater, but I'd wager quite a lot of money that there's something similar in there. Maybe special instruments or something."

"And…if this energy is stopped, it might disrupt this thing and blow up this whole area? That's even harder to believe. Is this thing you talked to really *that* powerful? That angry with these people? I mean, yeah, I don't blame it for being pissed, if they've been harnessing its power for decades to keep their pristine little towns going, but…still."

"It really is that powerful." Stone wished he'd taken her up on the flask; his head was starting to hurt again. "But it's not vengeful. That's the interesting part. It's hard to tell because it's so alien and our minds don't really connect very well…but I think it might be a child, or at least a young adult, by its people's standards. Even after all this, it doesn't want to hurt anybody—except perhaps the mages who did this to it in the first place. But they've been dead for a long time, and it knows that. They're probably dust by now."

"So it just wants to…die?" Her eyes glittered in the darkness as she turned to look at him. "This…child wants to die? And you're going to help it do that?"

"I don't see another choice. I don't think there's any other way to help it at this point. That came through fairly clearly. It just wants this to end."

She bowed her head.

"Do you have a problem with that? Because we don't—"

"No," she said quickly.

A thought occurred to him. "You have children, don't you, Agent Huxley?"

She glared, but then nodded. "Yeah. Two. Fourteen and ten. I'm divorced, so they spend most of their time with their dad because I'm usually running all over hell chasing supernatural crazy, but…yeah."

"This isn't like that," he said gently. "I probably shouldn't have worded it that way. It's young, yes, but it's immensely powerful. It's got to be dealt with one way or the other, because inevitably at some point the flow of energy from one side or the other will be disrupted for some reason, and the results will be catastrophic."

"So you want to—let me make sure I get this right—shut it down from both sides at the same time."

"Yes. That's why I need your help. I can't do this alone. It's going to be tricky because we don't have any way to communicate with each other, with cell phones buggered up. You *don't* have phones that work here, do you? Or portable radios?"

"No." She sounded frustrated. "Nothing works around here, except the land-line phones. Rick and I suspected something's interfering with everything else."

Stone wasn't surprised, now that he knew what was going on. He wasn't sure it was because the magic that held this whole crazy patchwork together didn't want anyone communicating too much with the outside world, or whether it was just a side effect. But either way, it was the reality they had to deal with. "Okay, then. We'll do it the hard way." He glanced at his watch. "We've got to go to Tuttleton and Rydell, and shut both sides down at the same time. We'll have to synchronize our watches like they do in the old spy films, and give ourselves enough time to get into position. Do you think you can do that, Agent Huxley?"

"I'm serious—after everything we've already been through, call me Ren. And yeah, I can do it." She patted the gun on her hip. "If they give me any trouble, I can deal with them."

"I don't think they're violent, or armed."

"What about Rick?" she snapped. "They were sure as hell violent with *him.*"

"But that was a ritual. It's different."

"It's still murder. And does that mean they've got mages here? That'll make things a lot more difficult."

"No. I don't think they do."

"But the ritual—"

"The ritual was pointless. There was no magic involved in it."

She stared at him. "What?"

"It's true. The symbols…carved into his body weren't anything magical. I didn't detect any magic around his body." He sighed. "Ren…the being didn't have anything to do with the ritual. It's something the people around here cooked up on their own, likely quite some time ago—long before this current crop of them were active. Someone probably convinced them it would help bolster their weaving and music and whatnot. Humans can come up with all sorts of rubbish, believe me."

She looked at her lap. "So Rick wasn't just murdered—he was killed for nothing." Then she glared. "And you know who did it, don't you?"

"I know someone who was probably involved," he said carefully.

"Who? Because if you want me to help you, you've got to help me. I need to know who did this to Rick, so he doesn't get away."

Damn. He was hoping she'd forget about that. "Ren…"

Her glare intensified. "Is there some reason you're not telling me? You're not protecting him, are you?"

"No. I'm not. And yes, there's a reason. It's just…hard to explain."

"Start trying. Like I said, I'm not helping you unless you tell me."

"I will tell you. But not until after we've done what we need to do."

"Why? What difference does it make?'

He shifted uncomfortably in his seat, trying to come up with the right words. She had every reason to be angry, to want to ensure the man who killed her partner—or at least was complicit in it—was brought to justice. But he couldn't fulfill Aldwyn's job and frame Chase Cassidy for the tapestry theft if the man was in custody, or dead.

"Listen," he finally said, deciding the truth—or part of it—was the best approach. "There *is* a reason I'm here in town, and it has to do with the man you're looking for. I can't tell you what it is, but there's something I've got to do before I let you have him."

Her eyes narrowed. "Are you going to hurt him?"

"No."

"Look. Stone. I'm not sure how much I trust you. Like I said, I've read your file and I think you're on the right side, but you're also known for doing some fairly out-there things, including some that aren't just borderline illegal, but well over the line. If this guy killed my partner, I want to bring him in. And you're not going to stop me."

Stone felt the time ticking. If anyone figured out they were in that graveyard, or even realized they were missing, somebody might be looking for them. He couldn't do this without Huxley, and he couldn't force her to help him. "Okay," he finally said. "I'll tell you who it is—if you give me your word you won't do anything against him until after this is settled. That's the best I'll do."

"Why is this so *important* to you? Is this guy a mage?"

"No."

"Does he have any way to slip out of town?"

"Not that I'm aware of. As far as I know, he's nothing more than a normal, unremarkable human." *Except that he's in charge of half of a bizarre cult that's forgotten the purpose of its existence is holding a supernatural being in slavery.*

The seconds passed, and only the sound of Huxley's harsh breathing split the silence. "Okay," she finally said, grudgingly. "You tell me his name, and I'll leave him alone until we shut this thing down. Best I can do. Who is he?"

Stone hoped he wasn't making a mistake. "His name is Chase Cassidy. He's—"

"The real-estate guy?" She sounded astonished. "The dumpy little guy in the office?"

"Yes. He's the head of the Music Makers, who keep half the flow going from their little room at the theater."

"Holy hell." She shook her head. "I went to see him, with our cover story about wanting to move to town. How do you know it's him?"

"I broke into his office earlier tonight, looking for evidence, and saw Rick's baseball cap in his drawer. I didn't think anything of it at the time, until you showed me the photo."

Her shoulders slumped. "Damn…"

"Hold it together, Ren. You gave your word."

"So, what do you want to do with him? Why can't I bring him in?"

"I can't tell you that. All I can say is that I won't physically injure him. I can't, since I'll be going back to Rydell. You'll need to take the Tuttleton part, so I've got to trust you."

Several more seconds of silence passed, followed by a sigh. "You can trust me. My word's good. But as soon as that thing's powered down, I'm going after him."

It wasn't an ideal solution. If anyone coordinated stories, they'd soon realize that Chase Cassidy couldn't have stolen the tapestry if he was in Tuttleton. *But maybe an illusion can help muddy the waters a bit.*

"Okay," he said. "Let's do this while it's still dark and we won't have half the townspeople to contend with."

"What's the play?" Her tone was all business now.

He explained the location of the hidden room above the theater's backstage area. "You'll need to get inside the theater without being seen, then pull down the ladder at the right time and stop the musicians from playing. There should only be a couple of them. Do whatever you need to do, but stop that music. Got it?"

"Got it. And meanwhile, you'll be stopping the weavers in Rydell?"

"Exactly. If we do this right, we'll stop both energy flows at the same time."

"And that...thing...that being...will just disappear? Float away?" Now, she sounded wistful.

"It's got to be done," he said gently. "It's what it wants. Let's not apply our human morality to something we have no way to comprehend."

She gave a reluctant nod. "How will I know we did it?"

"Don't know. I guess because we don't get blown to kingdom come?"

"You've got a great reassuring manner, Stone."

"So I've been told. Are you ready?"

"No. I'm not sure it's *possible* to be ready for something like this. But I've got a job to do, so I'll do it. I want to talk to you later, though. After all this is over."

"Count on it. I've got a lot of questions for you, too." He pointed at his watch. "Let's do this."

He was sure the distant feeling of agreement and encouragement he got was only in his mind.

At least mostly sure.

CHAPTER TWENTY

STONE HAD GIVEN THEM BOTH AN HOUR to get back to their respective towns and do the job. That should be plenty of time to make the slow, twisty drive, get into position, and wait for the proper moment. He'd even built in a little extra time in case anything went wrong, though he couldn't see what could at this point. It was well after midnight by now, which meant the citizens of the two little towns should be snug in their beds.

Except for the pair of weavers and their musician counterparts, anyway.

He didn't like having to trust Ren. It wasn't that he thought she wouldn't fulfill her part of the mission—or at least try to. She seemed like a competent agent who wouldn't let her personal feelings get in the way of duty, she definitely had extensive knowledge about the supernatural, and most importantly, she seemed to have believed his admittedly wild story. Aside from the loss of her partner, which would have upset anyone, she'd taken what he'd told her remarkably in stride. But she was still an X-factor. He'd only known her for less than an hour, and he didn't know her capabilities.

He wasn't proud of it, but he didn't like relying on mundanes when something this big was on the line. He wished Verity were here, or Ian. But he had what he had, and he had to admit he could do worse than no-nonsense Agent Renata Huxley. He only hoped she'd keep her word and not try confronting Cassidy.

Twenty-five minutes later, he reached Rydell. The town was quiet, the streetlights along Rydell Road illuminating closed businesses. No other vehicles were on the road. Even the bars were dark. If his and Huxley's actions had aroused any suspicions, the people here were doing a good job of hiding it.

He glanced at his watch, confirming he still had thirty-five minutes before he had to be at the Weavers' hall. He didn't want to get there at the last minute, but the place was literally two blocks up and one over. If he showed up this early, he'd have to wait either inside or outside the building until the appointed time, risking discovery.

The Landises', where he was staying, was less than five minutes from his current location. He didn't expect to be coming back here after he and Ren finished, so he decided to stop at his room and pick up the items he'd left there. That way, he could stash them in the back and be ready to head out before anybody caught on that he was missing.

The Landises' house was as dark as all the others along the winding, unlit road, but Stone didn't take chances. He parked the Jeep a quarter-mile away, shut off the lights, and walked silently up the path past the house to the cabin.

He hadn't left much inside—only his overnight bag with his clothes in it—so it took him only two minutes to gather them, sling the bag over his shoulder, and head back out. Another glance at his watch told him he still had twenty-five minutes to get back to the Weaver building. Plenty of time. He'd sneak inside and hide with a disregarding spell, then head downstairs disguised as Chase Cassidy, incapacitate the two weavers with stunning spells after making sure they'd got a good look at him, drop the phone message, and grab the section of tapestry. If the whole process took five minutes, he'd be dawdling.

"Mr. Townes?"

The whispered words nearly startled him into dropping his key as he locked the door behind him. He whirled around, barely managing not to summon a defensive spell.

A shadowy, hunched figure stood a few feet behind him. It raised its hands, still whispering. "Please—I'm sorry I scared you. It's me. Brady Landis."

Oh, bloody hell, not now. He'd wanted to chat with Brady before, convinced the boy had been trying to tell him something before his mother showed up to interrupt them, but this wasn't the time. He glanced at his watch again. The minutes were ticking.

"Brady, I'm sorry, but this isn't—"

Brady quickly glanced back at the house. "Please, Mr. Townes, keep your voice down." His whisper was full of urgency.

Stone followed his gaze. The house remained dark. "What is it?" he whispered back. "What do you want? I'm tired, and—"

Brady was clearly nervous, scared, or both. He swallowed hard. "You have to help me. I don't know who else to ask."

"Help you with what?"

Deep breath. Swallow. "Something's...weird in this town. I think you know it. I don't know what it is, but...my girlfriend's missing. And I think something terrible's going to happen to her!"

Stone winced. This was getting nothing but better. Another look at the house. "Are you worried about your mum hearing you?" He realized too late that he'd completely forgotten to use his American accent.

It was a testament to how freaked out Brady was that he didn't even appear to notice. "No. Not Mom. She's not here. But...somebody, maybe. Can we go somewhere? Away from here?"

"I don't have a lot of time, Brady. I—need to be somewhere very soon, and it's important."

The kid looked like he was about to fall apart. Red patches bloomed on his cheeks, and his forehead was dotted with sweat. "Please—just give me a few minutes so I can explain." He looked like he was using all his willpower to restrain himself from grabbing Stone's arm and dragging him away.

A brief thought struck Stone: what if the townspeople *had* figured out something was up, and sent Brady to stop him? Two things convinced him otherwise, though: first, a quick look at the boy's aura revealed it to be in full-blown turmoil, and second, how could they possibly know of his and Ren's plans? The only two beings who knew were Ren herself and the entity in the graveyard, and he didn't think either of them had spilled the beans.

He made a quick decision he hoped didn't doom them all. "Okay. Come back with me to my car. We can talk there. But I can't stay long."

"Thank you," Brady panted, and took off at a jog back toward the street. He stopped to wait for Stone to indicate the direction, then followed him to the Jeep.

"Okay," Stone said when they were inside under a powerful disregarding spell. "What's going on? What do you mean, strange? And what's this about your girlfriend?"

Brady took several deep, gulping breaths, to the point where Stone was tempted to slap him to get him back on track. But then he sputtered out, "I haven't lived in Rydell very long. My parents are divorced, and I was living with Dad in California. But then he got reassigned overseas for his job, so I had to move in with Mom. That was six months ago." His gaze darted around as if he expected someone to be sneaking up on them. "This place is weird, Mr. Townes. I can't explain it, but it's…like…too perfect. Everybody's too happy. Nothing ever goes wrong. And nobody ever leaves."

"What do you mean, nobody ever leaves? You must have tourists, don't you?"

"People come here sometimes. But they either leave the same day or…they end up staying. And I feel like whatever's got hold of the town, it's starting to get hold of me. I *should* want to leave, to get out of here and run as far away as I can, but…I don't."

A chill ran up the back of Stone's neck as he remembered the couple of times he'd thought about driving out of Rydell, going somewhere with cell service so he could update Verity, but had decided not to. Also, how Ren Huxley had told him something similar. Was the area's insidious magic already working on *them*, too? Even through his shields?

"Brady, this is fascinating—I'm not joking. But I don't have time for this now. Perhaps we can talk later?"

"I don't think there *is* a later." His voice shook. "My girlfriend's been acting weird for the past couple of days. She was giving away stuff I know she cared about, and she seemed happy to do it. Not...you know, like she was suicidal or anything. I almost felt like maybe she was going away, and didn't want to tell me."

The chill intensified. "Did she say anything to you? Anything strange?"

He nodded miserably. "She...broke up with me. Earlier tonight. We went out for coffee, and she told me it would be best if we didn't see each other anymore."

"But there hadn't been any trouble between you?" Stone hoped he wasn't wasting time going on about some failed high-school relationship, but his growing fear suggested he wasn't.

"No. Nothing. She'd seemed...preoccupied for a while. A couple weeks. But I thought she was just busy with school." The boy's pleading gaze rose to meet his. "Mr. Townes, I'm really sorry to bother you with this, but you're the only new person I've seen in a long time. I need somebody who isn't...involved." He leaned in closer. "This is gonna sound crazy, I know, but...I think maybe something's going to happen to her tonight."

"Something? What kind of something?" He thought of Rick, back in Tuttleton, and the townspeople's bizarre, pointless sacrifices. He hoped Brady's girlfriend wasn't already dead, but even if she was, with only twenty minutes remaining he didn't have time to do a ritual to find out.

"Something…bad. I don't know what, but…I think it's true."

"Brady," he said reluctantly, "I'm sorry. I don't know where she is, and I haven't got time to run around looking for her. I've got something very important I need to do very soon. Maybe I can help you when I finish, but I've got to go."

Brady took a breath. "I…think I might know where she is. Where they…took her."

"Where?"

"To the church, over on Water Street."

Stone remembered the place. It was the opposite direction from the Weavers' Hall, but only a few blocks away. "What makes you think she's there?"

Long pause. His eyes glittered in the darkness. Was he trying to hold back tears? "I…thought Mom might be involved. Remember how she tried to stop us from talking before? So when I heard her on the phone, I hid and listened. She said something about 'the ceremony' and the church. I didn't know what to do."

"Bloody hell…When was this? Is she still at your house?"

"No. She left about a half-hour ago." He gripped Stone's arm. "Please, Mr. Townes—help me. I can't get Hannah back on my own. I don't have a gun or anything, and it won't do me any good to call the police. They're probably in on it too."

Damn. Nothing was ever easy. If he did this, he risked revealing himself, and possibly missing the deadline for reaching the Weavers if anything went wrong. But if he *didn't* do it, he'd have a teenage girl's death on his conscience.

Twenty minutes. It was enough time—but he'd have to go in hard and fast. "Okay," he said, starting the ignition. "But we've got to go *now,* and I can't stay long. Show me where it is, and then stay out of the way. Got it?"

"Yeah. Thank you."

Stone was already driving. He didn't answer. He hoped he hadn't just made a big mistake.

CHAPTER TWENTY-ONE

THE RYDELL COMMUNITY CHURCH on Water Street looked dark from the outside. No cars were in the parking lot. Stone pulled up next to the front door and glared at Brady. "You stay here. Do *not* follow me in, no matter what you hear."

"I won't. Please help Hannah."

He wasn't so sure he could trust the boy to keep his word, but he didn't have time to waste. Fifteen minutes left. He swung out of the Jeep, slammed the door, slipped his disguise amulet around his neck, and ran up to the doors.

They were locked, but that didn't stop him. A simple spell unlocked them, and another flung them open. Stone raised his shield and ran inside.

He was standing in an empty, darkened lobby, with another pair of doors on the other side. These weren't locked, though. He shoved through them and stopped, shocked.

There had to be thirty people in the church's sanctuary, arranged in a rough circle around a central, cleared area. Tapestries, similar to the ones in the Weavers' room, hung along both side walls, blocking the windows. The pews had all been pushed back and stacked, revealing an elaborate circle drawn in the empty space, surrounded by flickering candles on stands. In the middle of the circle was an altar, and on the altar lay the robed body of a blond girl around Brady's age. Stone recognized her as the same one he'd seen at the coffee shop with him when he first arrived in town.

Even though this was a church, there was nothing Christian about the altar, nor the symbols covering the drape beneath the girl's body.

He took in the scene fast, shifting to magical sight, processing the incoming information fast: the girl was still alive. They hadn't carved her up yet. The crowd was in some kind of light trance.

But most important of all—there was no trace of magic in this room. Whatever these people were doing, it wasn't an actual arcane ritual. He'd have guessed it was all an elaborate, theatrical show if it hadn't been so obvious every person in this room believed in what they were doing.

No time for subtlety. "*Stop!*" he boomed, using magic to amplify his voice until it echoed from the rafters. "Everyone back off. Now!"

The group's trance broke, and they all spun to face him—including Brady's mother.

"You don't belong here," a man said, taking a step toward him. "Get out of here. Now."

"That's not happening." He raised a hand, using a wall of concussive energy to shove the man back. "Everybody step back away from the girl. I'm not telling you again."

"Stop him!" Brady's mother yelled. "He'll interrupt the ceremony!" She didn't sound so much angry as terrified.

"There isn't going to *be* any ceremony." Stone strode forward, using his spell to continue pushing the crowd back, staggering several of them into almost falling. "This is all rubbish. I know what you're trying to do here, but it isn't really doing anything. It's all fake. You're killing your own people for *nothing.*"

"He's an outsider!" somebody else yelled. "Get him!"

"Hannah!" screamed a voice from behind Stone.

Oh, damn it...

Stone didn't spin around—there was no way he was going to turn his back on this crowd—but he did shoot a fast glare over his shoulder. "Brady, you idiot, I told you to stay in the car!"

But Brady wasn't listening to him. He surged forward, his eyes only for his girlfriend on the altar—but Stone's force wall stopped him.

"What's going on?" he cried, scrabbling at the invisible barrier. "Why can't I get through? Hannah!"

"Finish the sacrifice!" someone else screamed. "Before it's too late!"

A flash of metal rose. From the corner of his eye, Stone he saw Brady's mother raising a knife over the girl's prone body.

Okay. Enough subtlety. I haven't got time for it.

Stone raised his hands and sent a concussive wave radiating out from him in an arc, above Hannah's level. One by one, the crowd members shrieked, gasped, and tumbled over. In less than ten seconds, the entire crowd lay draped across each other on the floor.

"What did you *do?*" Brady yelled, nearly hysterical in his terror. Now that Stone's barrier was no longer active, he pushed forward toward Hannah. "Did you kill them?"

"No. I knocked them out. They'll come to in a while."

Brady's gaze darted between him and Hannah. He reached her, gathering her limp body into his arms. "Is *she* dead?"

"No. She'll be fine. I'd keep her away from anyone else in town for a while, though. At least until tomorrow morning. Take her someplace and hide. And don't let her run away from you, even if she wants to." He looked at his watch again. Ten minutes. He'd be cutting things short, but it wouldn't take that long to drive to the Weavers' hall from here. If he made it and his plan succeeded, he suspected the strange energy that had gripped the townspeople would dissipate—and if he didn't, none of it would matter anyway. "I've got to go now, Brady. Will you be all right here?"

Brady looked thoroughly overwhelmed. His arms were shaking as he picked Hannah up. "I—They were gonna kill her..." he muttered. "My own mom..."

"Don't blame them too much. Something had control of them. The same thing that kept you from leaving town." He was already striding toward the doors.

"But...what *is* it?"

Stone didn't answer. Maybe he could explain later, but probably not. He didn't see himself staying around here any longer than necessary. But for now, he had places to be.

He pushed through the doors and headed out through the lobby, shield still up in case anybody else had shown up outside. All he had to do was get to the Jeep, and—

He stopped in the act of shoving open the outer doors, a cold, hard knot forming in the pit of his stomach.

The Jeep was gone.

CHAPTER TWENTY-TWO

*N*o, *no, no!*

Stone stopped at the top of the steps and jerked his head around, trying to spot any sign of his vehicle.

Had he left the keys in it? He didn't remember, but he *had* been in a hurry.

Who had taken it, though? They didn't have crime in this town. Unless…

Had someone in the crowd spotted him and figured out what he was up to? Had they slipped out after Brady had come in, and taken the Jeep? Possibly to warn the Weavers?

He looked at his watch again. Barely eight minutes remained. There were no other cars in the area; the people inside must have walked to the church tonight. He could try to find another one, but by the time he did and got it started, too many of his precious minutes could have ticked away.

No. He'd have to run.

He was fast, and in good shape. He could still make it if he started now. He'd have to push hard, but he could do it.

With one final glance toward the church to make sure nobody else was coming out, he took off toward the Weavers' Hall.

The streets were dark, making running along the uneven dirt shoulder treacherous. Stone chose to run in the road, hoping it would remain as deserted as before. In his jeans and the dark down jacket of his illusionary disguise, he wouldn't show up well to traffic.

Another look at his watch: six minutes. Was Ren already in place? Had she broken into the theater and was even now hiding in the wings, checking her own watch and preparing to pull down the ladder to the hidden room at the appointed time? Had anyone seen her? Caught her? Was she in trouble?

He wished once again that his cell phone worked, so he could send her a text that he was running late. So she could assure him things were fine on her end. What if he *did* arrive late, and she set her side into motion before he arrived?

He couldn't think about that.

He'd have to get there in time.

His breath huffed hard as he forced himself to pump his legs harder. He was a distance runner, not a sprinter. He could be fairly fast in a short sprint, but a mile wasn't a short sprint. Already his chest was starting to burn, his legs to hurt. Reluctantly, he slowed his breakneck speed a little; if he tripped or lost his wind trying to go too fast, he'd never make it.

I've got time. I can do this.

Sudden lights appeared in front of him, dazzling his eyes.

A car? Where did that come from? Maybe I can commandeer it, and—

It sped up, tires squealing, and veered sharply to its left.

Straight toward him.

Heart pounding, Stone acted on instinct, without conscious thought. Using a combination of muscle power and magic, he flung himself to the side.

He hit hard, taking the brunt of the impact with his right arm and shoulder. Pain flared as he rolled over and over, finally slamming into the thick trunk of a pine tree. Adrenaline surging, he leaped back to his feet, trying to spot the vehicle that had nearly run him down.

It was already fading into the distance, its lights off now.

What the hell was that?

No time to speculate, though. He raised his arm to check how much time he had left.

No! How much *more* could go wrong tonight?

His watch, which he wore on his right wrist, was dead, its face shattered. He must have landed on it when he fell. Terrified, he yanked his phone from his pocket—but its screen was blank. Either the battery had run down or something about the energy in the area was interfering with it.

He had no idea how much time remained before Ren acted to stop the music in Tuttleton.

He stood there a moment, his heart still thumping hard, and wanted to scream.

Why was the Universe fighting him so hard on this? Did it *want* these two little towns in Oregon and everyone in them to be destroyed?

Bugger that, Universe. Not if I can help it.

He threw himself forward again and kept running.

The first thing he saw when he reached the Weavers' Hall, pulling up short and bending over, panting, with his hands on his knees, was his own Jeep. It was parked in the alley around the corner from the rear door, where he'd sneaked in last time he'd been here.

So someone did *steal it. Someone knows I'm coming.*

Let's not disappoint them, then.

His chest still burning with exertion, he pulled up his shield and jogged to the door, using magic to fling it open.

He half expected someone—perhaps several someones—to be waiting for him, standing in the dining room with guns pointed toward him. But the room was empty, magical sight confirming no hidden auras.

What are they doing?

But that thought quickly left his mind as his gaze fell on something that made him stop, shoulders slumping, dread rising in his core and radiating outward.

The big clock on the wall on the other side of the dining room, still ticking away as if the world around it wasn't about to end.

The hands showed *12:36.*

He'd missed his time.

He was too late.

CHAPTER TWENTY-THREE

N o, he told himself. *Stop it. Don't panic. That clock might be wrong.*

It was possible. Probable, in fact. What were the odds that some small-town meeting hall's clock was as accurate as a precisely calibrated watch?

Maybe he was rationalizing—but they *were* still alive. Nothing had blown up yet. If Ren had handled her end of the mission and shut down the Music Makers, something should have happened, right?

Maybe he *did* still have time.

Gathering the last of his energy, he vaulted across the room to the lobby, pausing only long enough to use magical sight to find the illusionary door. It was a lot easier this time, since he'd found it before and knew where it was. He almost flung himself downstairs, but remembered at the last second that he hadn't altered his disguise amulet to make him look like Chase Cassidy. He quickly did that, then took the stairs down two at a time.

The two Weavers, a man and a woman, looked up, startled, when he appeared in the doorway.

"Chase?" the man demanded. "What are you doing here? Is something wrong?"

Stone knew he was flying blind now. There was no clock in this room, so he had no idea what time it was. He'd have no choice but to take a dangerous chance.

The Weavers hadn't moved from their seats. They both looked scared, but their fingers flew among the threads as their gazes remained fixed on him.

"What do you want?" the woman asked. Her voice shook. "Is the ceremony complete? Did someone find the body?"

Stone thought of Ren, grieving for her lost partner, and didn't hesitate. *Here goes. I hope I'm not wrong.*

He raised a hand and sent a powerful stunning wave at the pair. It hit them, knocking them over backward in their expensive ergonomic chairs. They barely had time to make a sound, their eyes big and wide and terrified, before they were sprawled on their backs, unconscious.

There it is, Stone thought. *Now, we wait.*

He shifted to magical sight to take a look at the looms, and what he saw brought the hard, cold knot back to his stomach.

Now, instead of the swirling orange energy forming around the pair of looms and streaking out of the room, the energy had turned a muddy red—the color of dried blood. It no longer exited the room, but seemed to be growing, filling the area. And worse, something else was growing too—a feeling of pressure, as if something powerful was being held back, and might not be much longer.

This couldn't be good.

Had their plan failed? Had they mistimed their actions, or had the plan not been a sound one at all?

Something was happening—that was all he could be sure about.

Breathing hard, heart still pounding, he spun to face the long, stitched-together tapestry. They *were* still alive. Nothing had blown up yet. He hurried to it, ripping a section free with magic and hastily rolling it into a messy cylinder so he could tuck it under his arm. Then, with one last look at the two unconscious Weavers and the growing miasma of red-brown energy, he dashed up the stairs and out through the back door.

Still, no one stopped him. The Jeep was still there, but no sign remained of whoever had taken it. Stone flung open the door, which was unlocked, and thrust the tapestry piece into the rear compartment. He had no idea what his next step was, except that he needed to get out of Rydell.

He'd barely had time to panic that the key wasn't in the vehicle when he happened to glance toward the passenger seat. There it was! Perhaps the Universe was at least slightly on his side tonight.

As he started the vehicle, he realized the feeling of pressure he'd discovered in the Weavers' room was still present. Even up here, it still pushed at him—and it was getting stronger.

What did it mean?

Reluctantly, he shifted to his magical senses again, reaching out, trying to touch the alien mind of the being at the cemetery. Was it still there? Had it already blown up, and the explosion had only taken out the cemetery itself?

As soon as he opened his mind to it, the feelings rushed in like a raging, uncontrollable river. Still no words, but the meaning was clear nonetheless:

Helpmehelpmehelpme

Can'tholditmuchlonger

Pleasehelpnonono

HELPME!

Stone gripped the steering wheel. *Oh, gods—it's still going to blow, but it doesn't want to. It's trying to hold it off!*

Maybe he'd still have a chance to avert devastation—but only if he hurried.

He tried sending reassuring thoughts to the being, but had no idea if they were getting anywhere.

CHAPTER TWENTY-FOUR

S TONE WOULDN'T HAVE THOUGHT IT POSSIBLE for him to cover the twisty and treacherous five miles from Rydell to the crossroads in ten minutes. Apparently, however, complete lack of regard for personal safety coupled with adrenaline-charged reflexes did the job. He didn't want to contemplate how many times the Jeep almost went off the road, though.

Time for that later. Maybe in his nightmares.

If he survived the experience.

He slammed on the brakes, skidding to a screeching stop in the middle of the intersection. If anybody else came by now they'd hit the Jeep, but that thought didn't even enter his mind. He continued projecting encouraging thoughts, a sort of supernatural pep talk, to the creature, even though he still had no idea if they were getting through. The strange psychic swelling was growing stronger the closer he got to the graveyard, like a balloon straining against too much water. It could go at any moment. Magical sight revealed the air was almost fully red-brown now, the nauseating color glowing bright against the darkness.

Stone barely watched where he was going as he pushed through the trees. He tripped twice, but both times leaped back up and kept going. By the time he finally broke through the trees and into the hidden cemetery, his heart hammered with dread. He had no idea what he might see, but feared the worst.

Most of the cemetery still looked as it had before—peaceful, overgrown, untended for years. Only the squat structure that housed the creature was any different. There, the red-brown energy hovered in a bright ball visible to normal sight, so intense it hurt Stone's eyes to look at it. Two black, scorched spots at the top and the bottom showed where the Weavers and Music Makers emblems had once been etched. The blue and orange energy conduits were both gone.

So Ren *had* completed her part of the mission.

Stone didn't stop. He couldn't allow himself to, or his terror would get the worst of him and paralyze him before he could act. Instead, he threw himself to his knees at the structure's foot, pressing both palms against the cracked surface. Heedless of what it might do to his mind, he opened himself fully to the creature.

Helpmehelpmecan'tstopcan'tmakeitstop

Stone sent it formless, encouraging thoughts. His head was already throbbing from the booming, wordless voice slamming around inside it, but he ignored the pain. *It's over. You can go now. You're free.*

Can'tstoppleasehelp

It was the oddest feeling—almost as if the power was growing and waning at the same time. It *wanted* to go, but something wasn't allowing it. The sensation of water against a balloon swelled stronger.

Pleasehelpcan'tstopplease

Stone's hands hummed with the energy, and his head pounded so hard he feared it would explode before the creature did. Was there no way to stop it? Had all their efforts been in vain?

please...

It didn't have a "voice," *per se*, but the formless thoughts did have a sort of "flavor." Stone was more certain than ever that this being was young—perhaps even an infant of its species. Its countless years of captivity had stunted it, prevented it from growing and experiencing the universe as its kind were meant to do. And now, without the energy that had been keeping it in slavery, both sustaining and draining it, it didn't know what to do. It didn't know how to control its own energy. It was like a two-year-old in the body of an adult. For all intents and purposes, it had been sleeping for all these years, barely aware of what was being done to it. His contact with it had awakened it, and now it had no idea what to do with these confusing new sensations.

I did this—I've got to stop it.

pleasehelpme

The most tragic part of the whole thing was how little ill will it bore them—any of them—with the exception of the two long-dead mages who'd captured and imprisoned it so many years ago. It didn't want to hurt the townspeople for unwittingly sucking it dry to power their idyllic lifestyle. It didn't want to hurt Stone for opening its consciousness to the monstrous things that had been inflicted on it.

All it wanted to do was go away. Dissipate into the cosmos.

Die.

cantgetouthelphelphelp

He didn't know what to do. What did it mean, "can't get out"? *Nothing's holding you now. You're free. You can go.*

The energy wasn't holding it in place anymore. Why didn't it escape?

But then, all at once, the answer came to him.

It didn't go because it *couldn't* go. It was like a tiny animal who'd been held in a cage for its entire life. It had no idea what existed beyond that cage. Even when the cage was removed, the animal was so used to the confinement that it made no move to leave it.

And in this case, the confinement was literal.

Hold on, he sent, lurching back to his feet and taking a few steps back. *I'll help you. I know what I need to do now.*

He hoped he was right, because the energy was swelling harder now. The red-brown glow around the structure was becoming, if possible, even more intense. The balloon couldn't hold much longer, and he knew instinctively that if it blew, it would mean the end of not just him and the creature, but everyone in the two tiny towns.

Hands shaking, still projecting encouraging thoughts, he gathered magical energy to him, holding it in place, letting it grow like the creatures energy was growing, dancing and swirling, pouring in from Calanar until his nerves screamed with the intensity of it all.

Here you go, my friend. Be free.

He pointed his palms at the structure and released the energy in two bright beams.

For a moment, the structure resisted. Whatever it was made of, it was stronger stuff than mere stone or concrete. But then, gradually, it began to glow—first orange, then yellow, then white-hot—and then it was gone.

Stone raised his shield and stepped back, but he need not have done so. With the top of the structure gone, he could now see into the space it revealed. It was black—so black it hurt his eyes to look at it. The black of pure Void.

But in the center of that velvety void, a small ball of energy hovered.

Stone had never seen anything so beautiful. Even as tiny and weak as it was, it was made of colors it was possible no one else on Earth had ever seen. The pain in Stone's head dissipated, replaced by other feelings: purest relief, gratitude…even…joy?

He bent his neck to stare at the little thing as it darted back and forth, dancing in the void, hitting the walls of the vessel that contained it like a bird caught in a windowed room.

Up here, he sent to it, raising his hand to form a light spell as a beacon.

It jumped once, almost as if to say, "Oh!" Then it leaped upward toward the light. For a second, it hovered in front of Stone's face.

You can go, he sent it. *You're free.*

The Universe seemed to hold its breath. The little thing hovered, still uncertain, obviously weak and diminished but still somehow joyful. Then, with a final flash of gratitude, it winked out.

Just like that.

No explosion, no dissipation, no pain.

Just…gone.

The red-brown light vanished too, and so did the strange void inside the vessel. All that was left behind was the dark cemetery, the whispering trees, and the faint overhead light of the half-moon behind the clouds.

And then the sky opened up and the rain began to fall again.

Stone almost laughed—such a fitting end to this evening, to be soaked to the skin while standing in a muddy old cemetery.

He didn't laugh, though. And he didn't stay. There was no need to anymore. As he trudged back to the Jeep, his thoughts were as muddled as the creature's had been: relief that it was over, happiness that it had finally been released from its ages-old prison…but also sadness that its only choices had been captivity or death. It had deserved so much more.

Ren would get her man, for sure. Chase Cassidy—and probably a lot of other upstanding citizens of both towns—would probably spend a lot of years in jail, for crimes they didn't even understand why they committed. The authorities would probably find many more bodies in the cemetery, and maybe other places around the area—countless victims of a ritual sacrifice that had never been necessary. He wondered how the townspeople would feel now that whatever strange compulsion had held them in their places almost as much as the creature's had. Would they leave now, since they could? Would they feel guilty? Would they adapt to their small towns' re-entry into the real world, complete with crime and addiction and decay?

Would they even remember there had ever been another way?

And what about Brady Landis, whose mother had certainly been involved with at least one of the sacrifices? What would become of him?

He climbed into the Jeep, fired it up, and drove toward Tuttleton.

He didn't know the answers to those questions—and he wasn't sure he wanted to. He had the tapestry. He'd fulfilled Aldwyn's task, though maybe not quite in the way the dragon had intended. Ren might want to stay behind and mop this up, but he didn't.

From now on, as far as he was concerned, the people of Rydell and Tuttleton were on their own.

CHAPTER TWENTY-FIVE

S TONE SENT A MESSAGE TO VERITY as soon as he got cell service. He pulled off the road and texted: *I'm back in communication. All is well.*

He didn't expect her to answer, since it was nearly four a.m., but the dots started cycling almost instantly.

Hey! What's been going on? I was starting to worry when you disappeared.

Long story. I'll tell you all when I get back. At least as much as I can, anyway.

Looking forward to hearing it. But you're really okay?

He thought about it. His head still hurt from his contact with the being, his whole body was stiff after his involuntary spill on the road, and he was dead tired. He glanced into the Jeep's rear compartment, where the tapestry piece was safely stowed. *I'm fine. Slightly the worse for wear, but nothing to concern yourself with.*

Good to hear. Looking forward to seeing you again, and so is everybody else. Including Raider.

It's nice to be missed. I'll be in touch sometime tomorrow.

He tucked the phone away and resumed driving, on the way to where he could turn the Jeep in and take the ley line home. There wasn't much traffic on the road this early, so he let his mind wander over the events of the last couple hours.

After he was sure the being was safely gone—either dead or returned to wherever it came from, he'd never be sure—he'd driven to Tuttleton at a much more sedate pace and pulled up in front of the theater. The lights were on and the front door was open, which was odd.

Odd, at least, until he got inside. Ren Huxley was in the lobby, pacing around, keeping an eye on three handcuffed people seated along a bench. Stone didn't recognize two of them, but the other was Chase Cassidy. All three looked confused and miserable.

"Agent Huxley," he called. "I see you've got things under control."

She looked frazzled, but determined. "I haven't got a damned idea what's going on here. Did it work? Did everything go the way you expected?"

"Not…quite. I had to do a little fancy footwork at the end, but all's well that ends well."

"So the whole place isn't going to—" She turned away from her three prisoners, and made an "explosion" gesture shielded with her body so only he could see it.

"No. Everything is fine." He thought about Rick, and all the other people whose lives had been sacrificed for someone's crazy idea of what needed to be done. "Well…as fine as it *can* be, anyway. I see you've caught Mr. Cassidy. Who are these two? The musicians from the loft?"

"Yeah. It went down just like you said." She continued to speak under her breath, so the three others couldn't hear her. "I waited until the right time, then pulled down that ladder and climbed up. I found these two—" She gestured at the other two prisoners. "—up there, calm as anything. The guy was playing the cello, and the woman was playing the violin. They seemed really agitated when I made them stop. They freaked out, almost."

The male prisoner chose that moment to jerk against his cuffs. He stared at the two of them imploringly, with wide, scared eyes. "You people don't know what you've done!" he yelled. "You've got to let us back there! You're going to kill us all!"

Stone strolled over and stood in front of them. He wasn't in disguise now, so even Chase wouldn't recognize him. "Calm down, all of you. Everything's fine. Nothing terrible is going to happen."

"We're not crazy!" the woman pleaded. "You don't know what's going on!"

"I know exactly what's going on. And it's over. We've stopped it. Here, and at the Weavers' Hall in Rydell. You don't have to do it anymore. You're free. Well, some of you are, anyway. It will be up to Agent Huxley and her people to sort out which of you participated in the sacrifices. Things might not go as well for you."

"Those sacrifices were necessary!" Chase Cassidy yelled. He, too, seemed scared rather than angry.

Stone moved over until he stood directly in front of him. "You're wrong, Mr. Cassidy. That's the sad part. I don't know who started the delusion, who decided to add a little extra narrative to what was already a fairly strange story, but they were no friend of any of your people's." He crouched, locking his gaze with the man's. "The truth is, there *was* something to all the weaving and music-playing. That part actually *did* do something effective, which isn't necessary anymore. But the sacrifices? Purely fiction, no doubt cooked up by some delusional mind. And you lot all just went *along* with it." He rose, and shrugged. "I don't know what will happen to you, but I'm guessing they'll dig up a lot of bodies in that little hidden cemetery. Am I right, Mr. Cassidy?"

Cassidy's only response was to bow his head.

Stone returned to the other side of the room, where Huxley was using the land line behind the concession stand to talk softly to somebody. She hung up when he approached. "I've already made contact with my organization, and some local authorities. They'll be here soon."

"That's good. Are you all right?"

"Yeah." Her tone was rough, and she didn't quite meet his eyes. "It's the job, Dr. Stone. It can be dangerous sometimes, and we all know something like this might happen. Right now, it's up to me to handle this, coordinate the people who show up, and confer with my agency to figure out how to spin this so we don't all come off looking like kooks."

"I imagine you've got quite a lot of practice with that."

"You don't know the half of it." She regarded him speculatively. "What are you going to do?"

"Now? I don't want to be involved in any of this, officially at least. Is that going to be a problem?"

"Nah. If it hadn't been for you, I might have ended up like Rick. So thank you for that. It *will* go into your file, though."

"I suppose I can't do much about that. And from what you say, that file is already fairly sizeable."

She gave him an arch half-smile. "We don't use real file cabinets anymore, but if we did, you'd have your own drawer. Maybe your own cabinet."

"Fame in my own time."

She looking away, obviously with something on her mind.

"Something else? I'll hang about until your reinforcements show up so you're not alone with this lot, but I've got to go soon."

"I… This isn't the first time you've interacted with somebody from my organization, is it?"

"I doubt it, though I never met them officially. I presume your people were the ones at the auction in San Francisco?"

"Yeah, that was us. File says they spoke to you, but didn't reveal who they were."

"They said they were part of some agency. I think there was another one, too—a man who went by Glenn Turman?"

She smiled. "Yeah, he's one of ours too."

"What are you getting at?"

"Well…this is all unofficial, you understand, since I don't have the authority to bring it up. But now that you know about us, and we *know* you know about us, there are…opportunities. Assuming you're open to them."

"What kind of opportunities? If you're trying to recruit me for your organization, I'm afraid the answer is no. If you know anything about me, you know I don't play well with authority."

"Oh, hell no. I'd pity anybody who had to supervise you. But we do deal with a lot of very interesting cases. Not *this* interesting, usually, but we both know I was in over my head here. Would you be open to a potential consulting relationship—nothing official—if we should happen to encounter another case we could use some help with?"

Stone couldn't help being intrigued. But he was tired, and this wasn't the best time to make these kinds of decisions. "I don't know, Agent. Possibly, if it *were* unofficial. But I thought you said you had people like me among your ranks."

"We do…but not people like *you*." She dropped her voice even lower. "Don't let this feed your ego, Stone—that's another thing I know from your file, that it's about the size of the Goodyear blimp already—but you're off the charts compared to our people. Plus, you're a lot better at…shall we say…the kind of out-of-the-box thinking that we need to deal with the stuff we deal with."

"I'll think about it. You know how to get in touch with me."

"Yeah. We do. I still want to know where you've been for the past three years, though."

"We all want to know something, Agent Huxley." Stone glanced toward the door, where three pairs of headlights had appeared. "I think the cavalry has arrived, so right now I'm going to take my leave. You'll be all right here?"

"Yeah. I'll be fine." She paused, then gripped his arm. "Thank you, Dr. Stone. I don't think I even have my mind around everything that happened tonight, but I feel like you did something big."

He shrugged. "Eh. I did what I came here to do. Glad I could help with the rest. Take care, Agent. And…" He jerked his chin toward Chase Cassidy. "Don't rough him up too much. I honestly don't think he completely knew what he was doing—and if he did, he thought he was saving the lives of everybody in two towns. Keep that in mind when you deal with him."

"Yeah." Her tone suggested she wasn't sure she'd go along with that. "You better go, though, if you don't want to answer a lot of questions."

He'd slipped out through the back door then, and waited until the newcomers were inside the building before sneaking back into the Jeep and driving off at a sedate pace. Nobody had followed him, so he supposed Renata Huxley had headed them off.

Now, an hour later as he pulled into the parking lot of the rental-car agency, he thought again about her offer. It still intrigued him. On the one hand, he didn't fancy getting involved with some buttoned-down government Men in Black crew—but on the other, they had the kinds of resources even he didn't have access too. What kinds of interesting cases were they keeping under their hats?

It was something to think about, definitely—but not now.

Now, he wanted to get back home, settle up with Aldwyn, and get back to his friends. Oh, and get Raider back—assuming his lovesick tabby could tear himself away from Luna.

CHAPTER TWENTY-SIX

S TONE'S PHONE RANG the morning he arrived home. He'd barely unpacked his overnight bag and was preparing to text Verity about picking up Raider when the landline buzzed.

When he picked it up, a voice spoke before he could even say hello. Two words: "Return home."

He hung up with a sigh, without responding. Whoever Aldwyn had arranged to spy on him, they were apparently earning what he was paying them.

There was no point in dragging it out. He gathered the tapestry into a neat roll and formed the pattern for the Surrey house. If the old dragon wanted him to go somewhere else, he'd need to drive the portal.

To no one's surprise, he reappeared inside the same room he'd been pulled to before. "Well," he said, annoyed, "you don't waste any time, do you?"

It was hard to discern Aldwyn's expression. His face was stern, but it was always stern. He certainly didn't look happy. His gaze flicked to the tapestry, then away. "Sit down, Alastair."

Stone didn't sit. He held out the rolled tapestry section. "Here it is, all tied up and ready to go. I frankly haven't got a clue why you wanted it—it's quite ugly, if you ask me. Certainly doesn't go with your décor here. Perhaps you've got someplace tackier that I haven't seen yet?"

Aldwyn didn't take the bait. "And the other part of my assignment?"

"That was a bit trickier. I did the best I could to convince them Mr. Cassidy did the deed, but there were...extenuating circumstances." He watched the dragon carefully for a reaction.

"I am aware." Now, there was no mistaking it: he definitely didn't look happy.

"I did the best I could, and that's the truth. And what do you mean, you were aware?" Stone suspected, of course, that Aldwyn knew exactly what had happened, but he didn't plan to give him the satisfaction of revealing that.

Aldwyn made a noncommittal grunt. He still made no move to take the tapestry.

Stone waggled it. "Don't you want this? I went to a lot of trouble to get it, you know." When the dragon still didn't answer, he grinned. "Let's get it all out on the table, shall we? You never wanted the tapestry at all. And you underestimated me, Aldwyn. That's never a good idea."

"Indeed?" The single word was ominous.

"Indeed." Stone pretended like he hadn't noticed the shift in tone. "The truth is, my dear dragon, that you didn't trust me enough to tell me what you *really* wanted—which is a good thing, because I'd have figured out a way to get around it."

"And what do you believe I really wanted?" Aldwyn's posture was relaxed, but his eyes weren't.

Stone wondered how close he was to getting zapped, but didn't care. He'd had his fill of being jerked around by an overgrown magic lizard, even if the two of them *were* related. "You were after whatever powerful...*something*...was buried deep under the crossroads between those two towns. There was a reason you didn't tell me about Tuttleton. You sent me after the Weavers because you knew I'd figure out they were up to something that needed to be stopped—but you neglected to mention that there was another town doing the same thing. You *wanted* me to disrupt the Weavers so the thing they were sucking dry would lose its mind and take out the area. Then you could simply waltz in afterward, after everybody was dead, and take possession of the land. Not to mention having a giant crater in the ground would make it easier for you to get hold of whatever's buried down there." He wheeled on Aldwyn. "How am I doing so far? Have I got it right?"

Aldwyn's gaze grew, if possible, even colder.

"I think I do," Stone said brightly. "And even further, I think it's not just that you'll have a harder time getting your scaly little paws on whatever's buried there...but that you *can't* get it without the explosion to take out most of the earth above it. Not to mention it would look fairly suspicious if you swooped in to scare all those people off their land. I think the other dragons might take an interest in what you were up to if you did that. What *is* buried under there, anyway? Care to share?"

"You do not know how close you are to death at this moment, scion."

Stone flung himself into the other chair and faced Aldwyn. "Why? You dragons take adhering to your agreements fairly seriously, don't you? You gave me an assignment: get the tapestry, and frame Chase Cassidy for the theft. Frankly, I still don't know why you added that second part. Maybe you *did* want me to find out about what was going on in Tuttleton. I don't know, and I don't care. But the point is, I did *exactly* what you told me to do. I couldn't do otherwise, right? The oath made it so I didn't have a choice."

He leaped from the chair and indicated the tapestry. "You told me to steal a section of tapestry from Ripley, Oregon. I did that. You told me to frame Chase Cassidy. I used an illusion to disguise myself as Cassidy, and I left behind something I stole from his office. As far as the people of Ripley are concerned, Cassidy did the deed. So, I've upheld the agreement. It's not *my* fault there was a lot more going on that you chose not to tell me about. If you want to punish me for that, go right ahead. But just be honest about it: you're angry because I outplayed you in your little chess game, and without breaking my original agreement." He stopped, arms crossed, and regarded the dragon challengingly.

For a moment, he thought he'd taken it too far, and he was about to find out what happened when his theoretical immortality met a full-strength magic blast from a full-grown dragon. Several interminable seconds passed while he stood, his gaze locked with Aldwyn's, and all but dared his ancestor to do it.

But finally, Aldwyn relaxed. He gave a wry, chilly smile.

"You are correct, scion."

That was a surprise. "Correct...about what?"

"Everything. Your assessment of the matter is accurate."

"I didn't expect you to admit it."

Aldwyn shrugged one shoulder. "Am I displeased about the ultimate resolution? Yes. Your actions have set my plans back to a considerable degree. But on the other hand—you have proven yourself a worthy ally. You are intelligent, quick-thinking, and you look beyond the obvious. Those are valuable traits."

Stone held up a hand. "Hold on a moment. Let's get one thing straight right now: I am *not* your 'ally.' Don't ever think that. You outmaneuvered me before, so that means I've got two more tasks I've got to fulfill for you. I don't like it, but I can't see a way around it. Don't think for an instant, though, that I don't plan to pay you back for what you did to me. You took three years of my life, Aldwyn. And worse, you put my son in danger."

"Your son was never in any danger. And three years is insignificant."

Stone had to remind himself that Aldwyn didn't know he was probably immortal—and it that it was best if he never found out. "Maybe for *you*. Not for me. I owe you for that, and I *will* pay that debt. Not right away, but some day."

Aldwyn didn't seem concerned. "I invite you to try, if you wish. Like all of your kind, you are short-sighted, and fail to see the advantages I could offer you. But no matter. As you said, you owe me two more tasks. Despite the inconvenience you have caused me, I must agree that you performed as directed. We will call this one satisfactorily completed." He stood, and turned away—an obvious dismissal. "I will be in touch when I am ready for you to perform the second task."

"No rush. Take your time."

When the dragon didn't respond, Stone turned to look behind him. As he suspected, the swirling portal had once again reappeared there. He thought about making some flippant remark before he left to see if he could get a rise out of the old lizard, but didn't.

Aldwyn, he decided, wasn't worth the mental effort.

CHAPTER TWENTY-SEVEN

JASON AND AMBER had put quite a lot of work into their Santa Cruz home in the last three years. Stone, remembering the ramshackle one-bedroom structure they'd scraped together all their money to purchase, barely recognized the place. Even from the outside, he could see they'd added at least two rooms, replaced the roof, painted the whole thing, and built out the living room to add more space and a handsome bay window. Currently, a seven-foot-tall Christmas tree sparkling with multicolored blinking lights and dozens of ornaments held pride of place in the window, blocking everything past it except for a warm, cozy glow.

Jason answered the door before he knocked, a big grin on his face. "Hey, Al. I'm really glad you could come."

"So am I." He hadn't seen much of his friends in the last week, and was embarrassed to admit that with everything else he'd had on his mind, he'd completely forgotten that Christmas was coming up. When Jason and Amber had invited him for Christmas dinner, he'd accepted happily. With Aubrey and Susan spending the holidays with Susan's adult children in the Cotswolds, his friends' offer had saved him from a lonely holiday dinner of Chinese takeaway shared with Raider.

"Hey," Verity called, coming out of the kitchen. She wore a festive apron and held a spoon in an oven-mitted hand. "You made it. I thought you'd get lost."

"If you'd seen where I've been driving recently, this is easy by comparison." He held up the two bottles of wine he'd brought. "Let me put these somewhere—I've got quite a lot of other things out in the car, including what I hope aren't totally inappropriate gifts for the little ones." He hadn't met Jason and Amber's children yet, and thus had sought Verity's and Susan's advice for what might be proper gifts. And then, because he was him, proceeded to ignore it.

"Why does that not surprise me?" came a dry voice. A moment later, Amber appeared in the doorway. She held the small hand of a little brown-haired girl, barely visible behind her left leg. The child peeked around her mother, eyes big and half-scared, half-curious. She wore a sweatshirt with a smiling, toothy T-Rex on the front, green footie leggings, and a reindeer-antler headband with jingle bells, and clutched a worn teddy bear in her free hand. When she caught sight of Stone, she shrank further back, almost dragging her hand from her mother's.

Amber gently pulled her forward while Jason looked on, smiling. "Alice...this is your Uncle Alastair. Remember we told you about him?"

The little girl's eyes got even bigger. She studied Stone, whipcord-tense like a kitten ready to bolt at the slightest threatening move, but still curious about this new addition to her familiar environment. She said nothing, though.

"Remember, pumpkin?" Jason crouched next to her, his big hand nearly engulfing her shoulder. "He helped Mama back before you were born. You were named after him."

She took a tentative step forward, her wide-eyed gaze never leaving Stone. "Unca...Alicer?"

Stone chuckled. "Close enough. It's a pleasure to meet you." He didn't crouch; he was afraid if he did, a non-zero chance existed that she might lunge forward and fling her arms around him, and he wasn't ready for that. Instead, he extended his hand.

Jason laughed. "You don't shake hands with three-year-olds, Al."

"I'm...a bit out of my depth here, in case you hadn't noticed. But I am genuinely glad to meet you, Alice. I've heard a lot about you."

Alice looked like she didn't know exactly what she was supposed to make of this tall stranger, but she obviously didn't intend to run away. It was almost possible to watch her thought processes by reading her facial expressions: *this is somebody new, so he might be scary—but Mommy and Daddy don't think he's scary so maybe he isn't.* Finally, she let go of her mother's hand and continued forward until she stood in front of Stone, craning her neck so she could hold eye contact with him. "How come you never come here?"

"I've... been away," he said softly. Despite his trepidation, he decided it was rude to tower over her, so he crouched. "I'm back now, though, so you'll likely be seeing more of me."

She tilted her head, processing that. She looked at him, then back over her shoulder at her parents. Then she tentatively held out her teddy bear.

Stone, now in completely uncharted waters, shook the bear's paw. "It's a pleasure to make your acquaintance as well, Mr. Bear."

Alice giggled. "You're funny."

"You wouldn't be the first to tell me that—though the others probably meant it in a different way."

She eyed him a moment longer, then pulled the bear back and retreated next to Jason. Despite offering the toy, she seemed relieved he hadn't taken her up on it.

Amber, out of their line of sight, had disappeared while they were talking. She returned now carrying a squirmy, tow-headed toddler. "And this is Jaden." She grinned. "Don't worry, Alastair. I'm not going to hand him to you. Baby steps."

Stone, with no idea what to do—you couldn't even make a pretense at shaking a baby's hand, and in any case he had no idea where it had been—smiled. "It's a pleasure to meet you too, Jaden." He didn't know what else to say, so instead he shifted to magical sight.

Immediately, the boy's appearance changed. Instead of a chubby, pink-skinned blond baby, Amber held what looked like a shaggy, humanoid wolf puppy.

"Well," he said, intrigued. "I'd say he looks just like his parents, but…"

Jaden, whose gaze had been wandering around the room as a baby, taking in all the twinkling lights and people, suddenly focused on Stone, staring at him like he was the most interesting thing he'd ever seen.

"Fascinating…" Stone murmured. "Do you think he can tell I can see his true form, even at that age?"

"Hard to say," Jason said. "It's possible, though. He can be a lot more intense than a typical kid his age when he wants to be. It can be a little off-putting when we introduce him to folks who don't know what's going on. He freaked out an old lady in the store the other day because he just fixated on her." He took the boy from Amber, gripping his ankles and hanging him upside-down. Jaden giggled and shrieked.

Alice immediately joined in. "Me too! Me too!"

Stone shifted from foot to foot, suddenly uncomfortable with all the chaos.

Amber caught on. "Come on, you two monkeys," she called, taking Alice's hand. "Go play with your toys with your dad, and let the other grown-ups have some peace for a while. Dinner's ready soon."

Jason shot an apologetic grin over his shoulder at Stone, then took Alice's hand, slung a still-giggling Jaden over his shoulder, and headed out the door.

"Sorry," Amber said, also grinning. She seemed amused by Stone's discomfiture. "Life with kids. What can I say?"

"No apology necessary. I'm a guest in your home. And in any case, I know next to nothing about children, but even I can see how happy they are. And you two as well," he added softly.

Amber's amusement turned to fondness as she watched Jason and the kids through the doorway. "Yeah. Life's good."

"Come on in the kitchen," Verity said, waving her oven mitt. "Dinner's almost ready, so you can open the wine."

He followed her and Amber through another doorway, noticing instantly that they'd upgraded the kitchen as well. Mouthwatering smells of roasting turkey, vegetables, and stuffing filled the house.

"I'm glad you got through whatever it is you had to do," Amber said. "V told us you had to go do something, but that you couldn't say what it was."

"I'm glad, too. I wish I could tell you more about it, but…"

"It's all good."

He'd told Verity as much as he could about what had happened, leaving out only that Aldwyn had been behind it. She'd listened, intrigued, and asked a lot of questions, some of which he could even answer.

"Nice that you finally got to verify there *is* some kind of agency out there, though," Amber continued, arranging the vegetables on a serving platter. "Though after meeting Redhead and Dad Bod at the auction, it didn't surprise me."

"Nothing surprises me anymore, to be honest." Stone levitated the serving platter and the two bottles of wine he'd brought, and followed her out while she carried a huge roasted turkey like it weighed nothing at all. "It should be interesting to see where the relationship goes, though. It does open some new possibilities." He still hadn't decided how he felt about that, but had come to the conclusion that he was willing to see it through, for a little while at least.

He also tried hard not to think about Aldwyn and the two remaining tasks hanging over his head. That wasn't so easy.

"Well," Verity said, "tonight let's not think about any of that. I'm just happy to be here, sharing the holidays with family." She shot Stone a pointed look as she said that, and a warm feeling rose deep inside him. He'd never had much luck with most of his *real* family except for Ian, but his found one—Verity, Jason, Amber, Aubrey, Eddie, and Ward, not to mention these two youngsters who promised to grow up into some very interesting people— suited him just fine. He hadn't told Jason and Amber yet, but he'd already set up handsome trust funds for both Alice and Jaden, so neither of them would ever have to worry about their educations no matter where they decided to pursue them. Until then, he'd have to stretch his comfort zone to relate to them while they were small— but he'd stretched his comfort zone in a lot of directions lately.

Compared to those, this one didn't seem nearly as hard as he might once have thought it would be.

Alastair Stone Will Return in
BLOOD TIES
Alastair Stone Chronicles
Book Twenty-Nine

Look for it in early 2022

WE LOVE REVIEWS!

If you enjoyed this book, please consider leaving a review at Amazon, Goodreads, or your favorite book retailer. Reviews mean a lot to independent authors, and help us stay visible so we can keep bringing you more stories. Thanks!

If you'd like to get more information about upcoming Stone Chronicles books, contests, and other goodies, you can join the Alastair Stone mailing list at **alastairstonechronicles.com**. You'll get two free e-novellas, *Turn to Stone* and *Shadows and Stone!*

WHO IS THIS R. L. KING, ANYWAY?

R. L. King lives the kind of exotic, jet-set life most authors only dream of. Splitting her time between rescuing orphaned ocelots, tracking down the world's most baffling cheese-related paranormal mysteries, and playing high-stakes pinochle with albino squirrels, it's a wonder she finds any time to write at all.

Or, you know, she lives in San Jose with her inordinately patient spouse, three demanding cats, and a crested gecko. Which, as far as she's concerned, is way better.

Except for the ocelots. That part would have been cool.

You can find her at *rlkingwriting.com*, and on Facebook at www.facebook.com/AlastairStoneChronicles.

Printed in Great Britain
by Amazon

75583200R00208